The Sea Sisters

Lucy Clarke studied English Literature at Cardiff University. She has worked as an advertising executive and a presenter of enterprise events for students. She is now a full-time novelist. She spends her winters travelling and her summers at her home near Bournemouth, where she lives with her husband, James.

Find out more at *www.lucy-clarke.com*

LUCY CLARKE

The Sea Sisters

HARPER

Harper
An imprint of HarperCollins*Publishers*
77–85 Fulham Palace Road,
Hammersmith, London W6 8JB

www.harpercollins.co.uk

A Paperback Original 2013
3

ISBN: 978 0 00 748134 7

Set in Birka by Palimpsest Book Production Limited,
Falkirk, Stirlingshire

Printed and bound in Great Britain by
Clays Ltd, St Ives plc

FSC™ is a non-profit international organisation established to promote
the responsible management of the world's forests. Products carrying the
FSC label are independently certified to assure consumers that they come
from forests that are managed to meet the social, economic and
ecological needs of present and future generations,
and other controlled sources.

Find out more about HarperCollins and the environment at
www.harpercollins.co.uk/green

For James

I would like to thank the following people for making this book possible: my agent, Judith Murray, for her advice and wisdom; my friends and early readers whose feedback and enthusiasm has been so incredibly helpful; my parents, Jane and Tony, for their unwavering encouragement and support, and finally, I would like to thank my husband, James, for always believing in me.

1

KATIE

London, March

Katie had been dreaming of the sea. Dark, restless water and sinuous currents drained away as she pushed herself upright on the heels of her hands. Somewhere in the flat her phone was ringing. She blinked, then rubbed her eyes. The bedside clock read 2.14 a.m.

Mia, she thought immediately, stiffening. Her sister would get the time difference wrong.

She pushed back the covers and slipped out of bed, her nightdress twisted around her waist. The air was frigid and the floorboards were like ice against the soles of her feet. She shivered as she moved through the room, her fingers spread in front of her like sensors. Reaching the door, she groped for the handle. The hinges whined as she pulled it open.

The ringing grew louder as she picked her way along the darkened hall. There was something troubling about the sound in the quiet, sleep-coated hours of the night. *What time would it be in Australia? Midday, perhaps?*

Her stomach stirred uneasily remembering yesterday's terrible fight. Words had been sharpened to injure and their mother's name had been flung down the phone line like a grenade. Afterwards, Katie was so knotted with guilt that she left work an hour early, unable to concentrate. At least now they'd have a chance to talk again and she could tell Mia how sorry she was.

She was only two steps from the phone when she realized it was no longer ringing. She hovered for a moment, a hand pressed to her forehead. Had Mia rung off? Had she dreamt it?

Then the noise came again. Not the phone after all, but the insistent buzz of the flat intercom.

She sighed, knowing it would be late-night visitors for the traders who lived upstairs. She leant towards the intercom, holding a finger to the Talk button. 'Hello?'

'This is the police.'

She froze, sleep burning off like sea mist on a sunny day.

'We'd like to speak to Miss Katie Greene.'

Her pulse ticked in her throat. 'That's me.'

'May we come up?'

She released the front door, thinking, *What? What's happened?* She switched on the light, blinking as the hall was suddenly illuminated. Looking away from the glare she saw her bare feet, toenails polished pink, and the creased trim of her silk nightdress against her pale thighs. She wanted to fetch a dressing gown, but already the heavy tread of feet sounded up the stairway.

She opened the door and two uniformed police officers stepped into her hall.

'Miss Katie Greene?' asked a female officer. She had greying blonde hair and high colour in her cheeks. She stood beside a male officer young enough to be her son, who kept his gaze on the ground.

'Yes.'

'Are you alone?'

She nodded.

'Are you the sister of Mia Greene?'

Her hands flew to her mouth. 'Yes . . .'

'We are very sorry to tell you that the police in Bali have informed us –'

Oh God, she began to say to herself. *Oh God* . . .

'– that Mia Greene has been found dead. She was discovered at the bottom of a cliff in Umanuk. The police believe she fell—'

'No! NO!' She spun away from them, bile stinging the back of her throat. This couldn't be real. It couldn't be.

'Miss Greene?'

She wouldn't turn. Her gaze found the noticeboard in the hallway where invites, a calendar, and the business card of a caterer were neatly pinned. At the top was a map of the world. The week before Mia left to go travelling, Katie had asked her to plot her route on it. Mia's mouth had curled into a smile at that, yet she indulged Katie's need for schedules and itineraries by marking a loose route that began on the west coast of America and took in Australia, New Zealand, Fiji, Samoa, Vietnam and Cambodia – an endless summer of trailing coastlines. Katie had been tracking the route from Mia's infrequent bursts of communication, and now the silver drawing pin was stuck in Western Australia.

Staring at the map, she knew something wasn't right. She turned back to the police. 'Where was she found?'

'In Umanuk,' the female officer repeated. 'It's in the southern tip of Bali.'

Bali. Bali wasn't on Mia's route. This was a mistake! She wanted to laugh – let the relief explode from her chest. 'Mia isn't in Bali. She's in Australia!'

She caught the exchange of glances between the officers. The woman stepped forwards; she had light blue eyes and wore no make-up. 'I'm afraid Mia's passport was stamped in Bali four weeks ago.' Her voice was gentle, but contained a certainty that chilled Katie. 'Miss Greene, would you like to sit down?'

Mia couldn't be dead. She was twenty-four. Her little sister. It was inconceivable. Her thoughts swam. She could hear the cistern downstairs humming. A television was playing somewhere. Outside, a late-night reveller was singing. *Singing!*

'What about Finn?' she asked suddenly.

'Finn?'

'Finn Tyler. They were travelling together.'

The female officer opened up her notebook and spent a moment glancing through it. She shook her head. 'I'm afraid I don't have any information about him currently. I'm sure the Balinese police will have been in contact with him though.'

'I don't understand any of this,' Katie whispered. 'Can you . . . I . . . I need to know everything. Tell me everything.'

The police officer described the exact time and location at which Mia had been found. She told her that medical assistance had arrived swiftly on the scene, but that Mia was pronounced dead on their arrival. She explained that her body was being held at the Sanglah morgue in Bali. She confirmed that there would be further investigations, but that so far the Balinese police believed it was a tragic accident.

All the while Katie stood completely still.

'Is there someone you would like us to contact on your behalf?'

She thought instantly of their mother. She allowed herself a moment to imagine the comfort of being held in her arms, the soft cashmere of her mother's jumper against her cheek. 'No,' she told the officer eventually. 'I'd like you to leave now. Please.'

'Of course. Someone from the Foreign Office will be in touch tomorrow with an update from the Balinese police. I'd also like to visit you again. I've been assigned as your Family Liaison Officer and will be here to answer any questions you have.' The woman took a card from her pocket and placed it beside the phone.

Both officers told Katie how sorry they were, and then left.

As the door clicked shut, the strength in Katie's legs dissipated and she sank onto the cold wooden floor. She didn't cry. She hugged her knees to her chest to contain the trembling that had seized her. Why had Mia been in Bali? Katie didn't know anything about the place. There was a bombing outside a night-club some years ago, but what else? Clearly there were cliffs, but the only ones she could picture were the grass-covered cliffs of Cornwall that Mia had bounded along as a child, dark hair flying behind her.

She tried to imagine how Mia could have fallen. Was she standing on an overhang and the earth crumbled? Did a sudden gust of wind unbalance her? Was she sitting on the edge and became distracted? It seemed absurdly careless to fall from a cliff. The facts Katie had been given were so few that she couldn't arrange them into any sort of sense. She knew she should call someone. Ed. She would speak to Ed.

It was her third attempt before she managed to dial correctly. She heard the rustle of a duvet, a mumbled, 'Hello?' and then silence as he listened. When he spoke again, his voice was level, telling her only, 'I'm on my way.'

It must have taken no less than ten minutes for him to drive from his apartment in Fulham to hers in Putney, but looking back she wouldn't remember any of that time. She was still sitting on the hallway floor, her skin like goose flesh, when the intercom buzzed. She stood groggily. The floorboards had marked the backs of her thighs with red slash-like indentations. She pressed the button to let him in.

Katie heard the thundering of his feet as he took the steps two at a time, and then Ed was at her door. She opened it and he stepped forward, folding her into his arms. 'My darling!' he said. 'My poor darling!'

She pressed her face into the stiff wool of his jacket, which scratched against her cold cheek. She smelt deodorant. Had he sprayed himself with deodorant before coming over?

'You're freezing. We can't stand here.' He led her into the lounge and she perched on the edge of the cream leather sofa. *It's like sitting on vanilla ice cream,* Mia had said the morning it was delivered.

Ed removed his jacket and draped it over her shoulders,

rubbing her back with smooth circular strokes. Then he went into the kitchen and she heard him open the boiler cupboard and flick on the central heating, which rumbled and strained into life. There was the gush of a tap as he filled the kettle, followed by the opening and closing of drawers, cupboards and the fridge.

He returned with a cup of tea, but her hands didn't move to take it. 'Katie,' he said, crouching down so they were eye level. 'You are in shock. Try and drink a little. It will help.'

He lifted the tea to her lips and she sipped it obediently. She could taste the sweet milky flavour on her tongue and the urge to retch was immediate. She lurched past him to the bathroom with a hand clamped to her mouth. The jacket slipped from her shoulders and fell to the floor with a soft thump.

Bending over the sink, she gagged. Saliva hit the white ceramic basin.

Ed was behind her. 'Sorry . . .'

Katie rinsed her hands and splashed water over her face.

'Darling,' he said, passing her a blue hand towel. 'What happened?'

She buried her face in it and shook her head. He gently peeled the towel away, then unhooked her dressing gown from the back of the bathroom door and guided her arms into the soft cotton. He took her hands in his and rubbed them. 'Talk to me.'

She repeated the details learnt from the police. Her voice sounded jagged and she imagined that if she were to glance up at the bathroom mirror, her skin would be leached of colour, her eyes glassy.

As they moved back to the lounge, Ed asked the same question to which she wanted the answer: 'Why was your sister in Bali?'

'I have no idea.'

'Have you spoken to Finn?'

'Not yet. I should call him.'

Her hands shook as she dialled Finn's mobile. She pressed the phone to her ear and listened as it rang and rang. 'He's not answering.'

'What about his family? Do you know their number?'

Katie searched in her address book and found it, the Cornish dialling code stirring a faint memory that she wasn't ready to grasp.

Finn was the youngest of four brothers. His mother, Sue, a curt woman who was often harassed, answered, sounding half asleep. 'Who is this?'

'Katie Greene.'

'Who?'

'Katie Greene.' She cleared her throat. 'Mia's sister.'

'Mia?' Sue repeated. Then immediately: 'Finn?'

'There's been an accident—'

'Finn—'

'No. It's Mia.' Katie paused and looked at Ed. He nodded for her to go on. 'The police have been here. They told me that Mia was in Bali . . . on a cliff somewhere. She fell. They're saying she's dead.'

'No . . .'

In the background she could hear Finn's father, a placid man in his sixties who worked for the Forestry Commission. There was a brief volley of exclamations muffled by a hand over the receiver, and then Sue returned to the line. 'Does Finn know?'

'I'd imagine so. But he's not answering his mobile.'

'He lost it a few weeks ago. Hasn't replaced it yet. We've been using email. I've got his address if you want—'

'Why were they in Bali?' Katie interrupted.

'Bali? Finn wasn't.'

'But that's where they said Mia was found. Her passport was stamped—'

'Mia went to Bali. Not Finn.'

'What?' Katie said, her grip tightening.

'There was an argument. Sorry, I thought you knew.'

'When was this?'

'Good month ago, now. Finn spoke to Jack about it. From what I heard they had a falling-out – God knows what about – and Mia changed her ticket.'

Katie's thoughts whirled. Mia and Finn's friendship was unshakable. She pictured them as children, Finn with a wig of glistening seaweed draped over his head, Mia bent double with laughter. Theirs was a friendship that was so rare, so solid, that she couldn't imagine what would be terrible enough to cause them to separate.

*

Ten days later, winter sun flooded Katie's bedroom. She lay perfectly still, her arms at her sides, eyes shut, bracing herself against a distant threat she couldn't quite recall. She blinked and, before she had a chance to recall why her eyelids felt stiff and salted, grief bowled into her.

Mia.

She curled into herself, tucking her knees to her chest and pressing tight fists to her mouth. She screwed her eyes shut, but disturbing images bled into her thoughts: Mia dropping silently through the air like a stone, the rush of wind lifting her dark hair away from her face, a rasped scream, the crack of her skull against granite.

She reached for Ed but her fingers met only with the empty curve of where he'd slept. She listened for him and, after a moment, was relieved to tune into the light tapping of a keyboard coming from the lounge: he would be emailing his office. She envied him that – the ability for his world to continue, when hers had stopped.

She knew she must get to the shower. It would be too easy to remain cocooned in the duvet as she had done yesterday, not rising until after lunch by which time she was drowsy and disorientated. Taking a deep breath, she forced herself from beneath the covers.

Drifting towards the bathroom, she passed Mia's room and found herself pausing vaguely outside the door. They had bought this flat using the small inheritance they received after their mother's death. Everyone was surprised that they were moving in together, not least Katie, who had vowed she'd never live with Mia again after their acrimonious teenage years, yet she'd worried that if Mia didn't put her share of the inheritance into something solid, it would slip through her fingers as easily as water. Katie had been the one to organize viewings, deal with estate agents and solicitors, and run through the rain with a broken umbrella to sign the mortgage papers on time.

Wrapping her fingers lightly around the brass door handle, she turned it. A faint trace of jasmine lingered in the cold, stale air. Mia had positioned her bed beneath the tall sash window so she could wake and see sky. A sheepskin coat, which once belonged to their mother, was draped over the foot of the bed. It was an original from the Seventies with a wide, unstructured collar, and she remembered Mia wrapping herself in it all winter like a lost flower-child.

Beside the bed a pine desk was heaving with junk: an old stereo, unplugged and dusty; three cardboard boxes bulging with CDs; a pair of hiking boots with their laces missing; a mound of paperbacks, well thumbed, beside two pots of pens. The bedroom walls were bare of the photos and paintings that had adorned Mia's previous rooms and she'd made no attempt to decorate; in fact, it was as if she had never intended the move to be permanent.

Katie was the one who'd persuaded her sister to move to London, using words like 'opportunity' and 'career', when those words had never belonged to Mia. Mia spent her days wandering the parks, or drifting in one of the rent-a-rowing-boats in Battersea Park, as if dreaming she were somewhere else. She'd had five jobs in as many months because she would suddenly decide to get out of the city to go hiking or camping, and take off, just leaving a note pushed under Katie's door and a message on her employer's answerphone. Katie tried searching out job opportunities using her recruitment contacts, but fixing Mia to something was like pinning a ribbon to the wind.

Noticing a pair of mud-flecked running shoes, she remembered the evening Mia announced she was going travelling. Katie had been in the kitchen preparing a risotto, slicing onions with deft, clean strokes. She tossed them into a pan as Mia wandered in, a pair of white earphones dangling over the neckline of her T-shirt, to fill her water bottle at the tap.

'Going running?' Katie had asked, blotting her streaming eyes with the sleeve of her cardigan.

'Yeah.'

'How's the hangover?' When she'd gone to shower before work, Katie had found Mia asleep on the bathroom floor wearing a dress of hers borrowed without asking.

'Fine,' she replied, keeping her back to Katie. She turned off the tap and wiped her wet hands on her T-shirt, leaving silver beads of moisture.

'What happened to your ankle?'

Mia glanced down at the angry red cut that stretched an inch above her sock line. 'Smashed a glass at work.'

'Does it need a plaster? I've got some in my room.'

'It's fine.'

Katie nodded, tossing the onions with a wooden spoon, watching their sharp whiteness soften and become translucent. She turned up the heat.

Mia lingered by the sink for a moment. Eventually she said, 'I spoke to Finn earlier.'

Katie glanced up; his name was so rarely spoken between them.

'We've decided to go travelling.'

The onions started to sizzle, but Katie was no longer stirring. 'You're going travelling?'

'Yeah.'

'For how long?'

Mia shrugged. 'A while. A year, maybe.'

'A year!'

'Our tickets are open.'

'You've already booked?'

Mia nodded.

'When did you decide this?'

'Today.'

'Today?' Katie repeated, incredulous. 'You haven't thought it through!'

Mia raised an eyebrow: 'Haven't I?'

'I didn't think you had any money.'

'I'll manage.'

The oil began to crackle and spit. 'And what, Finn's just taking a sabbatical? I'm sure the radio station will be thrilled.'

'He's handed in his notice.'

'But he loved that job . . .'

'Is that right?' Mia said, looking directly at her. The air in the kitchen seemed to contract.

Then Mia picked up her water bottle, pushed her earphones in, and left. The pan started to smoke so Katie snapped off the hob. She felt a hot flash of anger and took three strides across the kitchen to follow but then, as she heard the tread of Mia's trainers along the hallway, the turning of the latch, and finally the slam of the door, Katie realized that what she felt most acutely was not anger or even hurt, it was relief. Mia was no longer her responsibility: she was Finn's.

*

It was mid-afternoon when the phone rang. Ed glanced up from his laptop; Katie shook her head. She had refused to speak to anyone, allowing the answerphone to record friends' messages of condolence that were punctuated with awkward apologies and strained pauses.

The machine clicked on. 'Hello. It's Mr Spire here from the Foreign Office in London.'

A nerve in her eyelid flickered. It was Ed who reached for the phone just before the message ended. 'This is Katie's fiancé.' He looked across to her and said, 'Yes, she's with me now.' He nodded at her to take the phone.

She held it at arm's length, as if it were a gun she was being asked to put to her head. Mr Spire had called twice since Mia's death, first to request permission for an autopsy to go ahead, and later to discuss the repatriation of Mia's body. After a moment, Katie pressed her lips together and cleared her throat. Bringing the phone towards her mouth, she said slowly, 'This is Katie.'

'I hope this is a convenient time to talk?'

'Yes, fine.' The dry, musty warmth of the central heating caught at the back of her throat.

'The British Consulate in Bali have been in touch. They have some further news concerning Mia's death.'

She closed her eyes. 'Go on.'

'In cases such as Mia's, a toxicology report is sometimes requested as part of the autopsy procedure. I have a copy of it in front of me, which I wanted to talk to you about.'

'Right.'

'The results indicate that at the time of death, Mia was intoxicated. Her blood alcohol content was 0.13, which means she may have had impaired reflexes and reaction times.' He paused. 'And there's something else.'

She moved into the lounge doorway and gripped the wooden frame, anchoring herself.

'The Balinese police have interviewed two witnesses who claim to have seen Mia on the evening of her death.' He hesitated and she sensed he was struggling with something. 'Katie, I'm very sorry, but in their statement, they have said that Mia jumped.'

The ground pitched, her stomach dropped away. She hinged forward from the waist. Footsteps crossed the lounge and she felt Ed's hand on her back. She pushed him away, straightening. 'You think she . . .' Her voice was strained like elastic set to snap. 'You think it was suicide?'

'I am afraid that based on witness statements and the autopsy, the cause of death has been established as suicide.'

Katie reached a hand to her forehead.

'I understand this must be incredibly hard—'

'The witnesses, who are they?'

'I have copies of their statements.' She heard the creak of a chair and pictured him leaning across a wide desk to reach them. 'Yes, here. The witnesses are a 30-year-old couple who were honeymooning in Bali. In their statement, they say that they had taken an evening walk along the lower cliff path in Umanuk and paused at a lookout point – this was close to midnight. A young woman, matching Mia's description, ran past them looking extremely anxious. The male witness asked if she needed help and Mia is said to have responded, "No." She then disappeared along what used to be the upper cliff path, which has apparently been disused for several years. Between five and eight minutes later, the witnesses looked up and saw Mia standing very near the cliff's edge. The report says that they were concerned for her safety, but before they were able to act, she jumped.'

'My God.' Katie began to tremble.

Mr Spire waited a moment before continuing. 'The autopsy suggested that, from the injuries sustained, it is likely that Mia went over the cliff edge facing forwards, which collaborates with the witnesses' reports.' He continued to expand on further details, but Katie was no longer listening. Her mind had already drifted to the cliff top.

He's wrong, Mia, isn't he? You didn't jump. I won't believe it. What I said when you called – oh, God, please don't let what I said . . .

'Katie,' he was saying. 'The arrangements are in place to have Mia's body repatriated to the UK a week on Wednesday.' He required details of the funeral parlour she had selected, and then the call ended.

She felt shooting pains behind her eyes and pressed the arched bones beneath her eyebrows with her thumb and index finger. In the flat below the baby was wailing.

Ed turned her slowly to face him.

'They are saying it was suicide,' she said in a small, strained voice. 'But it wasn't.'

He placed his hands on her shoulders. 'You will get through this, Katie.'

But how could he know? She hadn't told him about the terrible argument she'd had with Mia. She hadn't told him of the hateful, shameful things she'd said. She hadn't told him about the anger and hurt that had been festering between them for months. She hadn't told Ed any of this because there are some currents in a relationship between sisters that are so dark and run so deep, it's better for the people swimming on the surface never to know what's beneath.

She turned from Ed and stole to her room where she lay on the bed with her eyes closed, trying to fix on something good between her and Mia. Her thoughts led her back to the last time she had seen her, as they hugged goodbye at the airport. She recalled the willowy feel of Mia's body, the muscular ridges of her forearms and the press of her collarbone.

Katie would have held on for longer, treasured every detail, had she known it would be the last time she'd feel her sister in her arms.

2

MIA

London, October Last Year

M ia felt the soft cushion of her sister's cheek pressed against hers as they held each other. She absorbed the curve of her chest, the slightness of her shoulders, the way Katie had to stand on the balls of her feet to reach.

Mia and Katie rarely hugged. There had been a time, as children, when they were entirely uninhibited with each other's bodies – squeezing onto the same armchair with their hips pressed tight, plaiting thin sections of each other's hair and securing bright beads at the ends, practising flying angels on the sun-warmed sand with their fingers interlaced. She couldn't say at what point that physical closeness was lost to her. Katie remained warmly tactile; she welcomed people with a hug or kiss, and had an inclusive way of reaching out mid-story to place her hand on someone's arm.

The last time they had embraced like this must have been on the morning of their mother's funeral, a year ago. Dressed in black, they had exchanged forthright words on the narrow landing of their childhood home. Eventually it was Katie who had extended her arms when, in truth, the gesture should have been Mia's. They had clasped each other and, in whispers broken with relief, a truce was made. But not maintained.

Now, as they held one another in the check-in area at Heathrow, Mia felt a tightening in her throat and the prick of tears beginning beneath her eyelids. She stiffened and let go. She wouldn't look at Katie as she picked up her backpack and hoisted it over her shoulders, tugging her hair free from beneath it.

'So this is it,' Katie said.

'I suppose so.'

'Got everything?'

'Yes.'

'Passport? Tickets? Currency?'

'Everything.'

'And Finn's meeting you shortly?'

'Yes.' Mia had arranged it so his and Katie's paths wouldn't have to cross. 'Thanks for bringing me,' she added, touched that Katie had taken the day off work to do so. 'You didn't have to.'

'I wanted to say goodbye properly.' Katie was dressed in a well-cut grey dress beneath a light caramel jacket. She slipped her hands into the wide pockets. 'I feel like I've barely seen you recently.'

Her gaze slid to the floor; she'd been finding reasons to stay away.

'Mia,' she said, taking a small step forward. 'I know it's

probably seemed like I'm not happy for you – about you travelling. It's just hard. You leaving. That's all.'

'I know.'

Katie reached out and took her hands. Her sister's fingers were warm and dry from her pockets and her own felt clammy within them. 'I'm sorry if London hasn't been right for you. I feel like I pushed you into it.' Katie twisted Mia's silver thumb ring between her fingers as she said, 'I just thought, after Mum, it would be good for us to stay together. I know you've been having a tough time lately – and I'm sorry if you haven't felt like you could come to me.'

An oily slick of guilt slid down the back of Mia's throat: *How could I come to you?*

She thought back to the day she'd booked this trip. She had woken on their bathroom floor, her cheek pressed into the cool, tiled floor, which smelt of bleach. Her dress – a jade one of Katie's – had twisted around her waist and her shoes had been abandoned, one beneath the sink, the other caught on the pedal of the bin.

Katie, wrapped in a soft blue towel, had been standing in the doorway. 'Oh, Mia . . .'

Mia's head had throbbed and the sour taste of spirits furred the back of her throat. She had pushed herself upright and a bolt of pain clenched at her temples. Snapshots of her evening flashed in her mind: the low-lit red booth, the empty whisky glasses, the grungy beat of an R&B track, the musky tang of sweat in the air, another round, a cheer of male voices, a familiar face, the irrepressible desire for risk. She remembered slinging her bag over her shoulder, tipping the final whisky down her throat, and then weaving along a darkened corridor. The memory of what happened next was so fresh and laced with so much shame, that she knew she had to leave. Leave London. Leave her sister.

A passenger announcement boomed over the tannoy bringing her back to the present.

Katie said, 'I worry about you.'

Mia withdrew her hand, pretending to adjust her backpack straps. 'I'll be fine.'

They both turned as a middle-aged couple hurtled past, the man muttering, 'Christ!' as he pushed a luggage trolley behind his wife, who was struggling to run in heels, her painted finger-nails gripping a bundle of documents. The man glanced across at Katie. Even when rushing for planes, even when their wives were at their sides, men couldn't help but look. They were drawn to her like bees to a honey pot, or like flies to shit as Mia had once said in anger. It wasn't just Katie's petite figure or honey-blonde hair, it was a warm confidence that breathed through her pores, saying, *I know who I am.*

Katie didn't notice the admiring glance as her attention had been caught by someone else. Finn came loping towards them wearing his daily uniform of T-shirt, jeans and Converse trainers. A tattered army-green backpack hung easily off one shoulder.

Katie took a slight step backwards, aligning herself with Mia, and fed her hands deep into her pockets.

Finn's gaze moved slowly over them both. Then the corners of his mouth turned up in an easy, wide smile. 'The Greene sisters!' If there was any awkwardness on his part, he didn't show it. 'Coming with us, Katie?'

'I'll be living the trip vicariously from all the emails Mia will be sending.'

Mia smiled. 'Hint duly noted.'

An airport vehicle towing a row of luggage trolleys beeped as it rolled towards them, causing the three of them to bunch together.

'So how are things?' Finn asked Katie. 'It's been a while.'

'Yes, it has. Everything is fine, thank you. Work's busy. But good. And you? How are you?'

'Feeling pretty pleased about having a year off.'

'You both must be. It's California first?'

'Yes, for a few weeks of coast-side cruising, and then on to Australia.'

'Sounds wonderful. I'm incredibly jealous.'

Is she? Mia wondered. *Would she want this: wearing her life on her back and moving from place to place with no plans?*

'Right,' Katie said, taking the car keys from her handbag. 'I best get going.' She glanced at Finn, her face turning serious. 'You will look after her, won't you?'

'You know that's like asking a goldfish to babysit a piranha.'

Her features softened a little. 'Just bring her back safely.'

'I promise.' He leant forward and kissed her on the cheek. 'Take care.'

She nodded quickly, pressing her lips together. 'You'll call?' she said to Mia. 'You've got your mobile?'

'I'm not taking it.' Then, seeing Katie's expression, she added,

'It's too expensive abroad.' But cost wasn't the real reason: Mia didn't want to be contactable.

'I've got mine if you need us,' Finn said. 'You've got my number still?'

'Yes. Yes, I think so.'

There was a brief silence between them all. Mia wondered what Katie would do with the rest of her day. Catch up with a friend over coffee? Go to the gym? Meet Ed for lunch? She realized she had no idea how her sister spent her time.

'Can you let me know when you've arrived?'

'Sure,' Mia replied, with a shrug she hadn't intended. She wanted to tell Katie that she loved her, or say how much she'd miss her, but somehow she couldn't find the words. It had always been that way for her. Instead, she lifted a hand in wave, then turned and left with Finn.

*

Pressing her nose against the window, she watched London disappearing beneath the white wings of the plane. They rose through a layer of cloud and suddenly the view was swallowed. She sank back in her seat, her heart rate gradually slowing. She had left.

On her lap rested her travel journal. She'd bought it at Camden Market from a stall that sold weathervanes, maps and antique pocket watches. She'd been drawn to the sea-blue fabric that bound the cover and the thick cream pages that smelt like promises.

She opened it, clicked her pen against her collarbone, and wrote her first two lines.

People go travelling for two reasons: because they are searching for something, or because they are running from something. For me, it's both.

She tucked the journal into the seat pocket alongside the laminated flight-safety procedures, and then closed her eyes.

*

As the plane descended over the Sierra Nevada range, Mia gazed at the clouds drifting below. They looked soft and inviting, and she imagined diving into them, being caught in their fleecy hold and floating with the air currents.

'Not as comfy as they look,' Finn said, as if reading her mind.

Finn Adam Tyler was her best friend and had been since they'd met aged 11 on the school bus. Four weeks ago she'd called him at work to tell him she was going travelling. She was sitting on the kitchen worktop, her heels dangling against the fridge door. When he answered, she said only, 'I've got a plan.'

'What do I need?' he'd replied, a throwback to their teenage years when a plan, if conceived by one of them, had to be adhered to by the other.

She grinned. 'Your passport, a resignation letter, a backpack and a typhoid jab.'

There was a pause. Then, 'Mia, what have you done?'

'Reserved two round-the-world tickets: America, Australia, New Zealand, Fiji, Samoa, Vietnam and Cambodia. The flights leave in four weeks. You coming?'

There was silence. It had hung between them long enough for her to wonder whether her impulsiveness had been a mistake, whether he'd say of course he couldn't just up and leave his job.

'So this typhoid jab,' he'd said eventually, 'is it in the arm or the arse?'

She looked at Finn now: his knees were pushed against the seat in front, a newspaper spread on his lap. The mousey curls of the schoolboy she'd known had now been cut short and rough stubble shadowed his chin.

At the end of their row a voluptuous woman with dangling gold earrings unclipped her seat belt and stepped into the aisle. She moved towards the toilets, gripping the backs of headrests for balance. Mia turned to Finn. 'I need to talk to you.'

'If it's about that last meal, I swear, I thought you wouldn't want to be disturbed.'

She smiled. 'It's something important.'

Finn folded the newspaper over and gave her his full attention.

A few rows in front the faint grizzling of a toddler started up.

Mia tucked her hands beneath her thighs. 'This may sound odd,' she began uncertainly, 'but after I booked our tickets, I realized that there was another place I needed to visit on this trip.' She should have talked to Finn about it sooner, only she was afraid to voice the idea in case she set in motion something she wasn't ready for. Sometimes she wasn't aware that an idea was brewing until it suddenly popped into her mind and she acted upon it. 'I've booked us an extra stop.'

'What?'

'After San Francisco, we've got a flight to Maui.'

'Maui?' He looked blank. 'Why?'

'It's where Mick lives.'

She waited a beat for him to place the name. It had been a long time since he'd heard it.

'Your dad?'

She nodded.

The grizzling child had found its stride and a captive audience; the crying grew louder and something was tossed into the aisle.

Finn was staring at her. 'You haven't talked about him in years. You want to see him?'

'I think so. Yes.'

'Has he . . . have you been in contact?'

She shook her head. 'No. Neither of us.' Mick had left when she and Katie were young children, leaving their mother to bring up her two daughters alone.

'I don't understand. Why now?'

It was a fair question, but one she wasn't sure how to answer just yet. She shrugged. Ahead, she heard a taut whisper from the toddler's parent: 'That. Is. Enough.'

Finn ran the knuckle of his thumb under his chin, a habitual gesture when something was worrying him. 'What does Katie think?'

'I haven't told her.'

She could see Finn's surprise and sensed he wanted to say more, but Mia turned to the window, ending the conversation.

She willed her thoughts to drift away with the clouds, knowing it wasn't the only thing she was keeping from her sister.

3

KATIE

Cornwall/London, March

Katie sat pin straight on the church pew, her feet pressed together. Biting sea air crept through the cracks in the stained-glass windows and twisted beneath the heavy oak door. Her fingers were curled around a damp tissue, Ed's hand resting on top. Eighteen months earlier had seen her seated in this same pew when they buried her mother, only then it had been Mia's fingers linked through her own.

Her gaze was fixed on the coffin. Everything about it – the polished shine to the elm wood, the brass clasps keeping it sealed, the white lilies arranged on top – suddenly looked wrong. Why had she chosen to bury Mia beside their mother, when her sister had never once visited the grave? Wouldn't cremation have been more suitable, her ashes dispersing on a breeze over a wild sea? *Why don't I know what you'd have wanted?*

It would have been almost impossible to conceive that Mia was inside the coffin had Katie not decided, two days ago, that she needed to see the body. Ed had been cautious on her behalf.

'Are you sure? We don't know how she may look after the fall.' That's what people were referring to it as: *the fall*, as if Mia had no more than slipped in the shower, or toppled off a stool.

She wouldn't be dissuaded. Seeing Mia's body would be agony, but to not see it would leave her with the smallest fraction of doubt – and if she allowed that doubt to grow over time to hope, she'd be in danger of deluding herself.

When Katie had stepped behind the heavy purple drape in the funeral parlour, she could have fooled herself that Mia was merely sleeping. Her willowy figure, the sweep of dark hair, the curve of her lips, looked as they always had. Yet the proof of death lay in Mia's skin. After months of travelling she would have been deeply tanned, but death had left behind its ghostly pallor so that her skin appeared a strange insipid shade, like milk spilt over a dark floor.

The funeral director had asked if Katie wished to choose an outfit for Mia to be buried in, but she had said no. It had seemed presumptuous to dress Mia, for whom fashion was something indefinable. She fell in love with clothes for their story, choosing a loose shift dress in a deep blue that reminded her of the sea, or picking a second-hand pair of heels because she liked to imagine the places they'd already walked.

On the night Mia died she had been wearing a pair of teal shorts. They had been arranged too high up her waist, not slung low over her hips as she would have worn them. Her feet were bare, a silver toe ring on each foot, her nails unpainted. On her top half she was wearing a cream vest over a turquoise string bikini. A delicate necklace strung with tiny white shells rested at her throat, a single pearl at its centre. She looked too casual for death.

Katie had reached out and placed her hand on Mia's forearm. It felt cold and leaden beneath her fingertips. Slowly, she traced her fingers towards Mia's inner elbow where thin blue veins criss-crossed, no longer carrying blood around her body. She drew her hand over the ridge of Mia's bicep, across her shoulder and along the smooth skin at the nape of her neck. She brushed the faint scar on her temple, a silver crescent, and then her palm rested finally against Mia's cheek. She knew the back of Mia's skull had been cracked open on impact, but there were no other marks on her body. Katie was disappointed: she had been hoping for a clue, something the authorities had missed that would prove Mia had died for a reason more bearable than suicide.

Carefully, she untucked Mia's vest and rearranged her shorts so they rested on her hip bones. Then she leant close to her ear. Her sister's skin smelt unfamiliar: antiseptic and embalming lotion. She closed her eyes as she whispered, 'I am so sorry.'

'Katie?' Ed was squeezing her hand, pulling her thoughts back to the funeral. 'It's you, now.'

He moved his hand to her elbow and helped her stand. Her legs felt light and insubstantial as she left the pew and drifted towards the lectern like a spectre. She tucked her tissue into her coat pocket and pulled from the other a square piece of card on which she'd noted a few sentences.

She glanced up. The church was full. People were standing three deep at the back. She saw old neighbours, friends of Mia's from her schooldays, a group of Katie's girlfriends who'd made the long journey from London. There were many people she didn't recognize, too. A girl in a black woollen hat sobbed quietly, her shoulders shaking. Two rows back, a thin young man blew his nose into a yellow handkerchief and then tucked it beneath his order of service. She knew that the circumstances of Mia's death would be lingering in everyone's thoughts, but she didn't have the answers to address their questions. How could she when she didn't know what to believe herself?

Katie gripped the lectern, cleared her throat twice, and then began. 'While the authorities have made a grey area of Mia's death, her life was a rainbow of colour. As a sister, Mia was dazzling indigo, challenging me to look at the world from new perspectives and see its different shades. She was also the deep violet that drove all her actions straight from her heart, which made her passionate, spontaneous and brave. As a friend she was vibrant orange, spirited, plucky and on the lookout for adventure. As a daughter, I think our mum—' she struggled on that last word. Closing her eyes, she focused on swallowing the rising lump of emotion.

When she opened them, she could see Ed nodding at her, encouraging her on. She took a deep breath and began the sentence again. 'As a daughter, I think our mum would have said Mia was love red, as she filled her with happiness, warmth and laughter. She was also the sea green of the ocean, in which she spent her childhood splashing and tumbling through waves. Her laughter – infectious, giddy and frequent – was brilliant yellow, a beam of sunlight falling on whoever she laughed with.

And now that Mia has gone, for me only cool, empty blue remains in the space where her rainbow once danced.'

Katie left the card on the lectern and somehow her legs carried her back to Ed's side.

*

The coffin had been lowered into the ground and the funeral party were returning to their cars when Katie saw him.

Finn looked different from the man she'd said goodbye to at the airport. His usually fair skin was bronzed, his hair lightened by the sun to a golden brown, and he looked older, too, having lost the boyish softness in his cheeks. Finn's family had been unable to get in contact with him until three days ago. He had boarded the first flight back to London and arrived yesterday. Flanked by two of his brothers, he glanced up and saw her. His eyes were bloodshot and the skin around his nose was red raw. He moved towards her warily.

'Katie—' he said, but faltered when he saw her expression.

Her voice came out as cold and flat as the sky. 'You left her, Finn.'

He closed his eyes and swallowed. She saw that his lashes were damp. Beyond them a car door slammed and an engine started.

Katie was standing with her back to the stone archway at the rear of the church. She thrust her hands deep into her coat pockets. 'You were supposed to be travelling *together*. What happened?'

The question seemed painful for him and he looked beyond her as he answered. 'We had an argument. It should never have happened. Mia didn't want to be in Australia—'

'So she went to Bali,' Katie finished. 'Why?'

Finn's left foot, in an unpolished black shoe, jigged up and down. She remembered the gesture; she'd once thought it was a mark of impatience but later understood it to be a sign of nervousness. 'We'd met people who were going out there.'

'I just don't understand any of it.' Katie's hands were beginning to tremble in her pockets. She balled them into fists and lifted her chin. 'Why was she on that cliff top?'

'I don't know. We didn't speak after Australia. She emailed once—'

'You didn't think to tell anyone?' Her voice was growing louder and she was aware of glances being exchanged between Finn's brothers who were hanging back.

He turned his palms towards the heavy grey sky, helpless under the fire of her questions. 'I thought Mia would have said—'

'You should have stopped her!' A sharp gust whipped Katie's hair in front of her face. She swiped it aside.

'She is headstrong,' he said. 'You know that.'

'*Was* headstrong. *Was*. She's dead!' The last word was the cold truth between them and the power of it pushed Katie on, anger rising like venom in her throat. 'You promised me you'd look after her.'

'I know—'

'She trusted you, Finn. I trusted you!' She stepped forward, extended her arm and slapped him, once, hard, on the left cheek.

Above, two seagulls screamed.

No one moved. Finn, shocked, held his face. Katie felt a smarting in her fingertips. After a moment it looked as if he was going to say something, but all that came out was a sob. She had never seen him cry before and was shocked at the way his face collapsed, as if the tears dragged all of his features downwards.

She watched, motionless, until she felt the firm pressure of Ed's hand on her shoulder. He steered her away, moving towards an area near Mia's grave where tributes had been laid. He didn't mention what had just happened, but simply buttoned up his dark overcoat, and then began carefully picking up the tributes. One at a time, he read each message aloud.

Katie wasn't listening. She was still thinking of the red hand-print she'd left on Finn's cheek, as if he'd been branded. She had never hit anyone before. Ed would later tell her that Finn was grieving, too, and she should have allowed him the chance to explain – but what was there to say? Mia was dead. If she didn't blame Finn, she was only left with herself.

'This is unusual,' Ed commented. He was holding a single flower; from its blood-red centre three white petals swept outwards like fans. He passed it to Katie, who lightly fingered the velvet petals. It looked like a type of orchid and she brought it close to her face to smell it. The scent conjured up another place – somewhere sweet and warm, filled with fragrance and light.

When she looked up, Ed was holding the small card that came with the flower. 'What is it?' she asked, noticing the change in his expression.

He said nothing, just handed the card to her.

Turning it over, she saw that the sender hadn't included his or her name. There was only a single word on the card: *Sorry*.

*

After the funeral there had been drinks at the village pub, where people huddled by the fire, stamping their feet to get the blood moving again. Katie stayed for an hour at most, making sure she thanked everyone who'd journeyed a long way, before quietly slipping out.

As she and Ed crossed the car park, someone called out, 'You're leaving?'

They both turned. It was Jess, her best friend, a girl who used to take Katie dancing to a bump-'n'-grind club in a dingy corner of their university town, but who now had a high-flying job as the sales director of a pharmaceutical company.

'Sorry, I know we've hardly talked, but . . . I . . .'

'Katie,' Jess said, flicking her cigarette to the ground. 'It's okay.'

'Thanks for coming today. It means a lot. And thanks for your messages, too.' Jess had called every day since Mia's death, leaving voicemails telling Katie how loved she was and passing on news and condolences from mutual friends. 'Sorry I haven't been in touch. I keep meaning to ring . . . but, well . . .' Katie stalled, not knowing how to explain. She was grateful to Jess – to all her friends – but she hadn't felt ready to talk about Mia. Not yet.

'You've lost your sister. I understand.' Jess stepped forward and wrapped Katie in her arms. 'No more apologies, okay? Just take your time. We're all here for you when you're ready.'

'Thanks,' she sighed, breathing in the cigarette smoke that clung to Jess's hair.

Jess squeezed Katie's hands and then turned to Ed, wagging her finger. 'You make sure you look after her, you hear?'

He smiled, putting an arm around Katie's waist. 'I intend to.'

It was Jess who'd introduced Katie to Ed at a riverboat party on the Thames. Katie had just come out of a relationship and wasn't interested in rejoining the dating scene so soon. Yet, Ed, with his handsome face, quick-witted banter and devastating smile, managed to persuade her otherwise. They had slipped free of the party the moment the boat moored and went on to a bar where they shared a bottle of Merlot and talked and laughed until the place closed. Eighteen months later, Ed got down on one knee to offer her a diamond ring and a lifetime together. She found herself grinning and saying yes.

It was a long drive back to London, but Katie couldn't stay in Cornwall with the sharp sea air and the waves that whispered with memories. In the flat, she unzipped her black dress, which fell to the floor with a swoosh. She stepped from the dark puddle into a fleecy jumper and pair of jogging bottoms belonging to Mia. The hems trailed around her feet as she padded along the hall. She hesitated only a moment before entering Mia's room.

Her sister's backpack was propped against the bed. It had been flown back from Bali several days ago, but Katie hadn't wanted to look through it before. Airport tags curled around its straps and strands of Indian leather were attached to each zip. There was a badge on the front of a woman in a hula skirt, and a picture of a daisy had been doodled on a side pocket in thick black marker. She unbuckled it, loosened the drawstring and reached inside.

Pushing her hand into the belly of the bag she felt her way through various items, pulling out one at a time like a game of lucky dip. She tugged free a burnt-orange beach dress that smelt of jasmine laced with the holiday tang of suncream and salt. She smoothed out the creases and then set it on the bed. Carefully, Katie removed more items: a pair of Havaiana flip-flops with worn-down soles; a travel towel stuffed into a net bag; an iPod in a clear case; two novels by authors Katie hadn't heard of; a slim torch gritted with sand; and a man's jumper, with thumb holes in the sleeves. Finn's?

She continued searching until her hand met something hard. Katie had been told that Mia's travel journal had been located by the police, who had examined it, but found nothing that could be considered as evidence.

Mia had always kept journals. Katie found it disconcerting that her sister preferred to share her feelings on paper rather than in person. As a teenager the temptation to read one had been irresistible. She had twice searched Mia's room hoping to uncover information that only her journal would reveal but, for all Mia's clutter and disorganization, she was fastidious about hiding them.

Carefully, Katie slid the journal free. Glimmering sea-blue fabric was stretched across the cover and it felt heavy in her hands. She traced a finger down the spine and then opened it carefully, as if Mia's words were butterflies that might flutter free into the air.

She turned the pages slowly, admiring her sister's elegant handwriting. In some things, Mia was lackadaisical and careless – her wallet was a brick of receipts, and her books were dog-eared with doodles filling the margins – yet the handwriting in her journal was graceful and refined. The entries were crafted around pencil sketches, handwritten notes, corners of maps and fragments of memorabilia from places she'd visited. Each page was a work of art brimming with its own tale.

'Everything okay?' Ed was standing in the doorway to Mia's room.

She nodded.

He glanced at the backpack. 'You're going through her things?'

'I've found her travel journal.'

He straightened, surprised. 'I didn't realize she kept one.' He pushed his hands into his pockets. 'Are you going to read it?'

'I think so. Yes. There's so much I don't know about her trip.' *And about her*, she thought. They'd barely spoken while Mia was away. She wondered when this distance had grown between them. They used to be close once, but not lately. She sighed. 'Why did she go, Ed?'

'Travelling?'

'Yes. She booked the trip so suddenly. Something must have happened to make her leave.'

'She was just impulsive. Young. Bored. That's all.'

'I shouldn't have let her go.'

'Katie,' he said gently, 'you've had a long day. Perhaps you shouldn't be looking at her journal tonight. Wait till morning, at least. I was just about to make us a snack. Why don't you come into the kitchen? Keep me company?'

'Maybe in a minute.'

When the door closed, she flicked through the pages and picked an entry at random. As she began to read, her gaze jumped from phrase to phrase – '*cinder desert*', '*Finn and me*', '*deep violet sky*', '*lunar landscape*' – as if each word was too hot for her mind to settle on. She squeezed her eyes shut and then reopened them, trying to focus on a single sentence. But it was hopeless; her gaze roamed over the words, but her mind refused to digest them.

Frustrated, she flicked on. She passed an entry where a sketched bird took flight from the bottom of a page, and another where Mia's writing spiralled around an invisible coil as if being sucked downwards. Her heartbeat quickened when she realized she was travelling towards the back of the journal, her fingertips skimming the edges of each page as they drew her to Mia's final entry.

Reaching it, Katie paused. There would be things, she knew already, which she'd rather not learn, but like a passer-by being drawn to the sight of a crash, she was unable to look away.

Staring at the final entry she saw that just one side of the double spread was filled. The adjoining page was missing; it had been ripped out leaving behind a jagged edge near the spine of the journal. Her eyes fixed on the remaining page, which was filled with an intricate pencil drawing of the profile of a female face. Within the face a series of detailed doodles had been drawn:

a roaring dark wave, a screaming mouth, falling stars, a hangman with six blank dashes, an empty phone dangling from a wire.

Katie snapped the journal shut and stood.

She shouldn't have looked; it was too soon. Already new questions were swimming to the surface of her thoughts. *What did the illustrations mean? Why had a page been torn out? What had been on it?* She pushed the journal back towards the bag as if returning it to the backpack would stop the stream of doubts rushing forwards, but in her hurry the journal fell free of her hands, and as it spilt to the floor, something glided from its pages.

Bending to retrieve it she saw it was the stub of Mia's first boarding pass: London Heathrow to San Francisco. Her fingers moved across the smooth white card as she thought about Mia arriving in San Francisco full of the anticipation of travelling. She tried picturing the places Mia visited, wondering about the people she had met, imagining what she might have experienced – but Mia's travels were a mystery, six lost months Katie was desperate to understand. Six months that the journal held the key to.

As she held Mia's plane ticket between her fingers, an idea began to form.

*

Katie barely slept that night as the idea shaped itself into a purpose. The next morning she rose early and strode into Putney High Street searching for a travel agency. She placed Mia's itinerary on the desk of a woman who wore coral-pink lipstick on cracked lips. 'I would like to book the same route.'

She could have done it online, but felt the decision was too important to be made on the click of a button. Perhaps she had anticipated hesitation from the saleswoman, as if someone would tell her this was a foolish, impulsive idea, but instead the lady had taken a sip from her steaming mug of coffee, then simply asked, 'When would you like to go?'

Now, five days later, she sat on the wooden floorboards in her bedroom trying to pack. The contents of Mia's backpack fanned around her feet, and her own clothes waited tentatively in half-built piles within a purple suitcase. She was usually a decisive and methodical packer, but she had no clue what to pack for this trip. In a few hours she was due to board a flight to San Francisco, exactly as Mia had done six months earlier.

Her bedroom door opened and Ed entered, carrying two mugs of tea. He passed her one and then lowered himself onto the floor beside her, his suit trousers pulling tight across his knees and revealing half an inch of skin above his socks.

She took a sip of tea. He made it exactly how she liked it: not too strong, a generous splash of milk and half a spoonful of sugar.

He eyed the piles of belongings sceptically. 'There's still time to change your mind. Work would have you back, you know.'

She had quit her job as a senior recruitment consultant as she'd walked back from the travel agency. After dedicating herself to the same company since graduation, she had only needed a five-minute phone call to leave. 'I can't go back.' The idea of returning to the office, taking a seat at her corner desk beneath the air-conditioning vent that aggravated her eyes, and pretending that placing candidates was still important to her, seemed utterly ludicrous.

'Why not wait a few weeks? I am almost certain I'll be able to juggle holiday. We could go together . . . not everywhere, but Bali. You can see where—'

'I need to start this from the beginning.' Katie's coping mechanism was structure. After her mother's death, she had ruthlessly filled her diary with social engagements, taking command of every free hour that might otherwise have been idled away in the folds of self-pity. She attacked her job with equal vigour, working around the clock with such steely focus that, three months later, she got a promotion.

Losing Mia felt different. Work and social distractions were no match for her grief, which was thick and black. Finding Mia's travel journal seemed like a small glimmer of light in the gloom, so she had made a decision to follow it, entry by entry, country by country, in the hope that retracing Mia's steps would help her to understand her death. For the first time since the police arrived on her doorstep, Katie felt as if she had a sense of purpose.

'I know we've talked about this,' Ed said, 'but I am still struggling to understand your logic.'

'You know how difficult things were between me and Mia before she left,' she said, setting aside her tea. 'And I let her go . . . I was *relieved* to see her go.'

'Mia's death is not your fault.'

Wasn't it? She had seen Mia was unhappy when they were living together, but she had let her loose anyway. Mia was her little sister, her responsibility. And Katie had failed her. 'The journal is all I have left. It's a link to six months of her life that I missed.'

'So read it. I've already told you I'm happy to do it with you.'

She'd discovered Ed thumbing through the journal the morning after she'd found it, checking that there was nothing that would upset her. She knew he was being kind, but she didn't want his protection; she wanted his support. Now she'd taken to keeping the journal with her at all times.

'But once I've finished reading it,' she explained, 'there'll be no more new memories of Mia. That'll be it – she's gone.' She imagined flicking through the pages time and time again until the words had become dull and meaningless, like a set of old photographs that have faded with the years. But Katie knew that by reading each entry in the countries where Mia wrote them, and experiencing some of the things she had experienced, then it would feel as if she was with her – that those six months hadn't been lost. 'I need to do this, Ed.'

He stood and crossed her bedroom to the window and opened it. Katie caught the heavy bass booming from a car stereo below. He spread his hands on the low windowsill and, for several moments, just stared at the street below.

'Ed?'

'I love you,' he began slowly, turning to face her, 'but I believe you are making a mistake. What about everything you're leaving behind? What about our wedding?'

They were due to get married in August. They had booked an intimate country house in Surrey, which they'd planned to take over for the weekend with their closest friends and family. Katie's evenings had been occupied with searching for a band that would play beyond midnight, deliberating over the choice of cheesecake or profiteroles for dessert, and collecting vintage photo frames to create a display on the cake table. The excitement and anticipation that had only recently consumed her now seemed as if it had been part of a life that was no longer hers.

'I won't be away for long. A few months at most.'

'I know you're going through hell right now,' he said, pushing aside a cream lantern to make space to sit. 'I wish, I really wish, there was something I could do to make this easier for you. But all I can say to you, darling, is that I truly believe it will help if you can begin looking towards the future, rather than the past.'

She nodded. There was some sense in that.

He indicated the spot beside him and she moved across the room and sat. She could smell the residue of his shaving foam, mixed with the fresh tones of aftershave. He looked handsome in his suit; the slate-grey tie had been a present from Katie and she liked to imagine his hand brushing the raw silk in a meeting, his thoughts trailing from the boardroom to her.

'This isn't the answer,' he said, looking at Mia's journal which she still held. She heard the smile in his voice as he said, 'Come on, you hate flying! You've never been outside of Europe. It is just not safe for you to go backpacking on your own.' He placed his hand on her thigh, rubbing gently. 'Let's work through this together. Here.'

Ed always had a practical way of assessing situations; it was one of the many things she admired about him. Perhaps this was a mistake. Flying to the other side of the world and giving no indication of when she would be back was unfair on Ed, she knew that much. 'I don't know what the right decision is any more.'

'Katie,' he said quietly, 'eventually you are going to have to let her go.'

She ran her fingers over the sea-blue cover of the journal, imagining all the times Mia had written in it. She pictured her swinging lazily in a hammock, her tanned legs stretched in front of her, a pen moving lightly over the cream leaves. The journal contained the most intimate details of Mia's thoughts, and Katie held it in her hands.

'I can't,' she said. 'Not until I know what happened.'

Ed sighed.

She wondered whether he had already decided what had happened. In the time he'd known Mia, he had seen her at her worst – impetuous, wayward and volatile – but he didn't know the real Mia; the one who swam like a fish in the sea, who kicked off her shoes to dance, who loved catching hailstones in her palms. 'It wasn't suicide,' she said firmly.

'Perhaps it wasn't.'

And there it was. The '*perhaps*'.

She stood, picked up Mia's empty backpack and began care-fully replacing items she had taken from it. From her own suitcase she grabbed a pile of clothes, her washbag and her passport, and squeezed them into the backpack, then buckled it shut. She shoved her suitcase in the wardrobe, closing the door with a satisfying smack: what good was a suitcase where she was going?

Ed was on his feet. 'You're actually doing this?'

'I am.'

She could see he was hurt and that he wanted to say something more. There were a thousand reasons why she shouldn't go: she had never travelled alone before; her career would suffer; she was grieving and would do better with company. They had been through all of these reservations, Ed giving pragmatic advice, just as she would have offered someone else. Only now she felt differently. Now it wasn't about practicalities, risk assessment or smart decision making. It was about her sister.

4

MIA

California, October Last Year

Mia's legs rested on the dash of the battered Chevy they'd rented. She pressed her bare toes against the windscreen and then withdrew them, watching the toe-prints of condensation slowly disappear. Beside her, Finn was drumming his thumbs against the steering wheel in time to a blues number playing on the radio.

They were driving south along the famous Highway One, leaving San Francisco in their wake. They'd spent far more time there than intended, having been captivated by the city's offbeat charm. On their first night they took a room in a cheap motel, dumped their backpacks and went for dinner at a busy Thai restaurant that served incredible sweet chilli prawns. The owner tipped them off about a basement club a couple of blocks away and, in spite of their jet lag, they found themselves drinking and dancing until their feet throbbed. They surfaced, hours later, to find dawn breaking over the city, and stumbled across an early-morning coffee house where they bought cinnamon bagels with fresh coffee and sat on the edge of the bay watching a pale pink sun climb over Alcatraz.

Low-lying fog stalked them down the coast and clung to the sea like a damp cloak obscuring any view of the horizon. Mia wound down the window and stuck her head out, squinting towards the sky. 'Sun's coming out.'

'I'll stop at the next lay-by.'

A few miles on was a gravel viewpoint on the cliff top. Sure enough, the sun was burning through the fog to unveil a rugged, grassy coastline. Wildflower-strewn cliffs, which she imagined would be spectacular in spring, staggered down to an untamed bay frothing with white-water.

She stepped from the car barefoot, interlocked her fingers above her head and stretched, her stomach pulling taut. The air fizzed with salt and she inhaled, closing her eyes.

Finn leant against the car with his arms folded loosely over his chest. 'Look at this place.'

'You want to go down?'

'Sure.'

They found a narrow footpath that wound down the impressive cliff face, cutting back and forth to steal the incline from the steepest parts. Reaching the bottom, Mia was the first to jog towards the shore and plunge her feet in the sea. 'Hello, Pacific!' she bellowed. Then she turned to Finn. 'Swim?'

'Here? It looks pretty rough.'

'You can look after my clothes, then,' she said, pulling off her top and wriggling free from her shorts, leaving her in mismatched underwear. Her body was lean and muscular; she thought herself too angular to be considered beautiful, although she'd grown used to the jut of her hip bones and her small breasts, and wasn't abashed in front of Finn. They'd seen each other's bodies hundreds of times – she knew the broadness of his shoulders, the way his belly button protruded slightly, seen the coarse hairs spread from around his nipples across his chest.

'Good London tan,' she said, referencing the lily-white shade of his chest as he stripped from his T-shirt.

'Good slacker's tan.'

She laughed, and Finn took the opportunity to race past her, splashing through the white-water and hurdling small waves before the sea finally took his legs from under him. He tumbled forwards, flattening his body and spreading his arms so he hit the water with a slap, sending silver droplets skyward.

Mia was still laughing as she waded in to join him. The cold water was like a vice at her ankles, which reached its grip to her knees and caused a shaving nick to sting. A gull cawed overhead and she glanced up, watching it glide on the breeze. The seabed dropped away suddenly and water rose over her cotton pants and towards her stomach, which she sucked in away from the sea's bite. She took a quick breath and then dived under.

When she surfaced her dark hair was slicked to her head like oil. She kicked her legs and swam with clear, smooth strokes.

'Don't go too far,' Finn called. 'I only do *Baywatch* rescues on red-pants days.'

The waves rose and fell beneath her. One took her by surprise and white-water slipped over her head like a blanket. She rubbed the water from her eyes and then took off in front crawl, feeling the tightening of her muscles as they worked to propel her forward. On every second stroke she turned her head for air, and felt the weak sun brush her face.

Eventually, when her legs began to stiffen from the exertion and the cold, she slowed and swam parallel to the shore, looking at the cliffs from a new angle. It was an impressive coastline – dramatic, weather-beaten and empty. The space was intoxicating, a physical relief after London where she had felt as if she could never quite catch her breath. Away from the city, away from the memory of who she'd become, it was the first time in months that Mia felt at ease.

*

That evening, they sat on a picnic bench clutching tin mugs filled with hot chocolate. She could hear waves breaking in the distance, a soft rumble, almost like a far-off lorry passing by. She slipped a silver hip flask from her back pocket and unscrewed the cap. 'Whisky?'

Finn pushed his mug towards her. 'Good job on dinner.'

Having camped often in their youth, they had mastered one-pot dishes to a level of wizardry. Tonight, Mia had offered to cook, serving noodles with thick slices of salami, simmering with peas, chunks of mushroom, a few cherry tomatoes and a shake of seasoning. 'Always tastes better outdoors,' she said, splashing whisky into both mugs. 'It's been so long since we've camped together.'

'London parks don't have quite the same appeal.'

'True.' She smiled. 'But – really – are you enjoying London?' Finn had moved there after graduation, renting a flat above a butcher's shop. It backed onto a railway line, and water shook from the kitchen tap whenever a train passed.

'I do. I did. It was a change after Cornwall.'

'What, Friday nights at SJ's didn't do it for you?'

'No, I love leopard print and Lycra on fifty-year-olds.' He grinned. 'London wasn't for you, though?'

'I guess not.' She had missed the sea with a deep ache and found her dreams were filled with beaches and empty horizons.

'Is that why you wanted to go travelling?'

She stretched the sleeves of her jumper over her hands and then wrapped them round the mug to keep warm. 'I was ready for a change.'

'It's been a tough year. You deserve a break.'

Do I? she thought. It had been Katie, not her, who stayed stoically at their mother's side throughout her illness. Mia had closed her eyes to the beakers of pills, the clumps of hair in the shower tray, the new gauntness in her mother's cheeks – because it was easier. Anything was easier than watching her strong, capable mother wilt. She felt the hard little pebble of guilt that lived in her stomach and she reached for the hip flask, putting her lips around the cool metal mouth.

Finn slung his arm around her shoulder. 'You okay?'

She nodded.

'Listen, Mia.' His voice was serious and she glanced up. 'When your mum was ill, I know we weren't hanging out so much – but you did know I was there for you, didn't you?'

'Course,' she said, embarrassed by his earnestness. They had never broached the subject of the four strained months when a wall had reared up between them, stacked with hard bricks of resentment and cemented by Mia's silence. She wasn't sure she was ready to now.

Sensing that, Finn pulled his arm back and said, 'So tell me about Mick. When did you decide you wanted to see him?'

'I found a photo of him when I was clearing out Mum's wardrobe.' In the picture he was standing onstage with a band in front of a banner that read BLACK EWE. The band looked as if they'd just finished a set, their faces red and glistening with sweat. A man with long black hair that had turned damp at the temples stood in the centre, holding a guitar loosely at its neck and staring intently at the camera. Beside him, Mick looked exuberant and fresh in a fitted suit and pointed brown shoes that turned up at the toe. He had no instrument to hold like the others, so he had shot a double-handed finger-gun at the camera and cocked his head to one side with a wink. It was a gesture that Mia would never have made, far too assured for it to look natural on her, yet she liked the picture as she saw a similarity between her and her father in the strong shape of their noses and possibly the curve of their lips, too. 'I suppose seeing the picture made me curious.'

'You haven't been curious before?'

'Not really. Well, maybe a little,' she conceded, thinking of a comment her grandmother made years ago that had always stuck with her. Mia had been in the bath, the water turning brackish from the mud caked to her knees. She wriggled and protested at having her hair washed, her grandmother eventually snapping, 'Such an awkward, independent thing, aren't you?' And then adding under her breath, 'Just like your father.' The illicitness of that name had lingered in the steamy room for a long moment. Long enough for the comparison to settle deep into Mia's thoughts.

Finn tilted his mug to his lips, finishing his drink. 'How come you haven't talked to Katie about your visiting him?'

Mia thought for a minute. 'Sometimes when people give you their opinions, they can end up becoming your own. I didn't want that.'

A car pulled into the campsite, the headlights briefly illuminating them before the engine was cut. A couple got out and began staking out their tent by torchlight.

The few sentences they'd just shared were the most Mia had admitted to anyone, even herself. For now, that was enough. She reached across for Finn's mug. 'I'll wash up.' Then she hopped from the picnic bench and disappeared to the water tap.

Later, after she'd cleaned her teeth, spitting the paste into a bush, she climbed into the tent with Finn. It was pitched with the shadow of a scrub-covered hillside in the background and the salty breath of the sea to the fore. They lay with their heads on a folded beach towel, poking out of the tent so they could gaze up at the stars. They'd spent countless nights sharing a tent or lying like sardines in the single beds in each other's rooms. Their friendship was close and easy even now, a gift that Mia would always be grateful for.

'Shooting star,' she said, pointing.

'Didn't see it.'

'It's hard to when you have your eyes closed. You should sleep.'

They pulled their heads inside, zipped up the tent, and lay next to one another, just as they had done a thousand nights before.

*

The ground was unforgiving beneath Finn and he moved his weight onto his side, avoiding a ridge that was digging into his shoulder blade.

Mia was already asleep. He lay listening to the faint murmur of her breath and the crickets singing in the undergrowth beyond the tent. What Finn loved about camping was that life moved at a slower pace. A simple meal took longer to prepare; a bed for the night had to be erected and then dismantled; a shower and change of clothes became a luxury rather than a daily routine. He took more time to absorb the sounds, smells and rhythm of a place, and to pay attention to what he was thinking.

Mia shifted, her hand slipping from her stomach and coming to rest on his forearm. He felt the heat from her skin against his. He could have moved his arm from beneath hers, yet he remained still. Unchecked in the darkness, he found his thoughts straying to a summer's evening when he and Mia were 16 years old.

They were at a gig watching an American punk band called Thaw, who they'd been lobbying to see for months. Mia had worn a pair of pale jeans ripped across her thighs that she'd bought from a second-hand shop called Hobos. She'd painted silver eyeliner in sharp flicks at the edges of her eyes and brushed something on her cheekbones that made them shimmer. She looked older than the bare-faced girl he'd helped to reel in a mackerel earlier in the day, and the transformation both unsettled and appealed to him.

The band met all their expectations: the arena was pulsing with energy, the mosh pit was frenetic and with each song the crowd grew wilder. Mia was effervescent, dancing wildly with her hands thrown skyward. She turned and shouted something to a burly man with a thick neck who had been standing behind them. The man cupped his hands together and, before Finn realized what was happening, he watched Mia place her foot in the sweaty palms and be tossed into the air. Her body arched backwards, her arms outstretched at her sides like open wings, and she was caught by a sea of hands, crowd surfing over the tops of people's heads.

The black Beastie Boys T-shirt she wore – one she and Finn shared as they could only afford one between them – rode up her waist exposing her smooth, slender stomach. The lighting crew picked out this ethereal girl with her wave of dark hair and spotlighted her journey to the front. A group of men, sweating heavily and thumping their fists in the air, whistled and catcalled at her. Every inch of Finn's body tensed at their remarks, and he imagined beating a path through the audience and shutting them up.

The crowd continued to buck and writhe, illuminated by brilliant blue and white laser lights, and he strained to keep Mia in sight. Ducking to the side of a lanky man, he was able to spot the bouncers pulling her over the safety barrier. He didn't know how she'd find her way back to him and four more songs were belted out before he saw her.

Squeezing through an impossibly tight gap, she stood before him, her cheeks flushed, her forehead glistening with sweat.

'Mia!'

As the band launched into their final track, the audience surged forward, pinning her against him. Instinctively, he gripped her waist fearing she could slip beneath their feet. Thrust together he felt the heat of her midriff through her damp T-shirt. Unfazed by the crowd, which roared beneath a thick haze of smoke, Mia placed her hands around Finn's face and kissed him briefly on the lips.

The crowd heaved backwards; Mia slipped free from his hands. She turned towards the band and carried on swaying and rocking. Finn remained rooted to the spot, while a thousand other people danced on.

There are key incidents in everyone's history – pivotal points on which the axis of life can swivel, and a seemingly innocuous action can flip the entire direction of one's fate. For Finn, that kiss changed everything. Mia, the girl he'd always knocked around with, became an enigma to him overnight. At school the next day, every ordinary interaction – holding a test tube while Mia added magnesium ribbon, eating ham sandwiches together on the bench beneath a sycamore tree, sharing a pair of earphones on the bus ride home – became fused with his new desire. It was as if he'd stepped out of his body and into someone else's. He was so unnerved by this shift that he bunked off the final two days of term to give himself space to think.

When school broke up for the summer, Mia cycled to his house with her tent, sleeping bag and a bottle of vodka she'd bribed Katie into buying, and told him they were going camping in the forest that backed onto the cliffs. He could think of no excuse good enough to refuse, so he grabbed his sleeping bag and followed.

That evening, an unforecast downpour drove them into the tent before dusk. They played cards and drank vodka, and Finn stole furtive glances at Mia and wondered how he'd never before noticed that her eyes were the lush green of emeralds. Once the rain stopped, they unzipped the tent onto the dark forest steeped in a rich, earthy smell. They stood in the damp heather, the hems of their jeans turning sodden, and felt drunk and exuberant. The moon that night, a perfect silver disc, looked so spectacular that for no reason at all, Finn howled like a wolf. Mia giggled and then howled, too.

In the seventy-two hours since Mia had kissed Finn, he'd thought constantly of how it would feel to kiss her back. Properly. 'Mia,' he said, moving in front of her unsteadily. She looked at him, still grinning. She wore no make-up, and in the moonlight her skin looked luminous. 'God, you're so beautiful!' he said suddenly. Then he reached a hand to her cheek and leant forward to kiss her.

Moments before his lips reached hers, Mia pulled back.

'Finn!' She laughed, thumping his chest. 'I thought you were being serious for a second! Don't weird me out!'

Finn had bent forward, pretending to laugh too, when actually it felt as though he'd taken a punch in the gut.

He didn't see her for three weeks after that as he joined his family on holiday in northern France. On that trip, Finn lost his virginity to a seventeen-year-old girl named Ambré, who was working as a cleaner in the park where they stayed. She wore a pink bra and no pants beneath her uniform, and invited Finn to her caravan each afternoon on her three-o'clock break. While he was genuinely thrilled by the arrangement, it gradually exposed the depth of his feelings for Mia. He not only yearned to touch or kiss her in the way he was doing with Ambré, he also missed other things, like the sound of her laughter, or the way she'd bite the tip of her thumbnail when she was concentrating, or the determination in her voice when she'd tell him, 'I can do this.' He missed Mia's friendship – and wasn't prepared to risk that again.

When he returned home, he and Mia slipped back into their old routine, the night in the forest never mentioned again. A chorus of other girls, and later women, quietened his infatuation and he was grateful that their friendship returned to its usual tune. Yet today, when Mia had stripped to her underwear at the beach, revealing her exquisite slender body, a low note of desire had been struck and had resonated in his thoughts in the hours since.

He knew the great risk of allowing that forbidden note to sound louder, so Finn carefully eased his arm from beneath her hand and, reluctantly, rolled away.

5

KATIE

California, March

Katie pulled down the beige plastic blind of the aeroplane window, closing out the view. She didn't need to see that they were flying above the clouds, that the ocean was thirty thousand feet below them, or that the white wings of a Boeing 747 were the only thing keeping them from spiralling down to earth.

The first time Katie flew, she had clutched the armrests so hard that her knuckles turned white. Beside her, Mia's eyes had been wide, her pupils dilated, with what Katie had first imagined to be fear but then, as she'd watched the smile break over her face, recognized to be awe. She couldn't understand how Mia could be so mesmerized, when her own insides churned with panic. Katie's fear hadn't been passed down from an anxious adult, or grown out of horror stories from friends or television: it was something that lived inside her. She was 9 years old then. Flying should have been an adventure.

After that flight, Katie had taken two further plane journeys

– and with each her fear grew into something living that would begin hissing at her weeks before takeoff. She'd discovered that the only way to silence the fear was to avoid it: when there was a university ski trip, she signed up after learning they would be travelling by coach; when their mother received a small windfall and offered to take the girls away, Katie said what she'd like to do most was a cruise; when Ed talked of visiting Barcelona, she persuaded him to go to Paris via the Channel Tunnel.

Now, as she twisted the sleeve of her cardigan, turning it tightly between her fingers and then unwinding it and starting again, it wasn't the fear of the plane's engine failing, or the capability of the pilot, that concerned her. What made her throat tighten and her heart clamber against her chest was the boxed-in enclosure of the plane, the small seat with its fixed armrests, the two passengers – one asleep, one reading – blocking her exit to the aisle, the seat belt pinned across her lap, the eleven-hour journey that couldn't be paused. She would be quietly trapped here, hour after hour, with nothing to distract her, so that for the first time since the news broke, she was sitting entirely still. Her mind seized the opportunity to focus on the one word she had been trying to avoid: 'suicide'.

Suicide was something she associated with the mentally ill, or people suffering from a dreadful, incurable illness – not able-bodied, able-minded 24-year-olds halfway through a world adventure with their best friend. There was no logic to it. But it had happened. There were witness statements, an autopsy report and a police account that said it had.

She had obsessively looked up the word 'suicide' on the

Internet and was shocked to learn that it was the tenth leading cause of death – above murder, liver disease and Parkinson's. She had read that one million people committed suicide each year and, staggeringly, that one in seven people would seriously consider committing suicide at some point in their lives. She discovered that drugs and alcohol misuse played a role in 70 per cent of adolescent suicides.

But what the Internet, the witnesses and the Balinese police didn't know was her sister. Mia would never have jumped. Yes, she could be unpredictable, swinging from energetic reckless highs to crushingly troubled lows, and sometimes it did seem that she felt things so deeply it was as if her heart lay too close to her skin, but she was also fiercely brave. She was a fighter – and fighters don't jump.

Katie believed this wholeheartedly. She had to, otherwise she was left with the agonizing knowledge that her sister had chosen to leave her.

*

San Francisco International Airport seemed the size of a town. Katie lost herself in the crowd, letting them lead her up escalators, along advert-lined corridors, and down brightly lit stairways, before eventually arriving at the baggage-claim area. She picked a spot at carousel 3, standing several paces back to allow eager travellers space to reach their belongings and disappear on new journeys.

As she waited for Mia's backpack to pass beneath the heavy

plastic teeth of the carousel, she played a game with herself, trying to match pieces of luggage to their owners. The first couple were easy; she knew that the padded black ice-hockey bag belonged to the broad teenager with a lightning bolt shaved into the back of his sandy hair, and that the pair of ladybird-print cases would be passed to twin girls in identical blue coats. It was a small surprise, however, when the gentleman in a tired panama hat reached not for the tan leather suitcase she had predicted, but a sleek silver case with the sheen of a bullet. But then, neither would she have matched the smartly dressed blonde woman in charcoal ankle boots and a fitted blazer to the tattered backpack that she reached for.

Grabbing a worn strap, Katie hauled it from the carousel using both hands. She struggled to put it on, bending her arms in awkward contortions to force them through the straps, and then jumping a little to shift it into position. She felt compressed by the weight of it, and bent forward at the waist to balance out the load.

She trudged through the arrivals gate where a crowd watched eagerly for their loved ones, their eyes moving quickly beyond her to see who followed. A heavyset man in a Giants sweater ducked beneath the barrier and ran forward, throwing thick arms around the boy with the hockey stick. Katie didn't rush to leave the airport, excited to see San Francisco, as Mia and Finn might have; instead, she joined the crowd on the other side of the arrivals barrier, set down her backpack, perched on top of it and watched.

Time ran away as Katie sat perfectly still, hands placed

together in her lap. She began to understand the rhythm of arrivals, anticipating the empty space alongside the barriers between flights, which filled in correlation to the overhead screen announcing the next set of arrivals. If a flight was delayed or there had been a hold-up, then two groups of passengers could arrive at the same time, and the barrier would be pressed taut.

There were fathers collecting daughters, girlfriends being met by boyfriends, husbands waiting for wives, grandparents beaming at grandchildren – but the reunions she searched out were always those between sisters. Sometimes it was difficult to tell which women were friends and which were siblings, but more often Katie knew instinctively. It was in the casualness of how they embraced, the way their smiles were completed when they saw each other, or how a joke quickly passed from one pair of lips to a smile on the other. It was in the same angle of their noses, a gesture they both displayed, or how they walked arm in arm, as they left together.

A woman with fox-red hair spilling over the shoulders of her kaftan placed a hand to her mouth when she saw her sister. A purple silk scarf partly concealed the sister's bald head, but the strain of illness showed in her sallow skin and gaunt cheeks. The redhead reached out and squeezed her sister's fingers, then lightly touched her empty hairline and then, finally letting go of whatever composure she'd privately been battling to maintain, embraced her in a long clasp, sobbing over her shoulder.

If someone had watched Katie and Mia, she wondered whether they'd have guessed they were sisters. Katie's fair features were distinct from Mia's strikingly dark looks, but someone paying attention might have noticed that their lips shared an equal fullness, or that their eyebrows followed the exact same arch. If they had listened closely they would catch crisply articulated word endings from years of good schooling, but might have noticed that they still mispronounced the word 'irritable', both placing the emphasis on the second syllable, not the first.

Vivid memories of Mia flew into her thoughts, details from their childhood she hadn't thought of in years: lying together in the sun-warmed rock pools that smelt like cooked seaweed; doing handstands in the sea with salt water filling their noses; their first bike, cherry red, which Katie would pedal while Mia perched on the white handlebars; fighting like pirates on winter-emptied beaches with seagull feathers tucked behind their ears.

Katie had loved being an older sister, wearing the role like a badge of honour. *At what point*, she wondered, *did our closeness begin to fade? Was it triggered by our feud when Mum was dying? Or maybe it had begun long before. Perhaps it wasn't one incident, rather a series of smaller incidents, an unravelling, like a favourite dress that over time becomes worn: first a thinning at the neckline, then a loss of shape around the waist, and finally a loose thread opens into a tear.*

'Ma'am?' A porter in a navy uniform, with dreadlocks tucked beneath his cap, stood beside her. 'You've been here since I came on shift.'

She glanced at the time displayed on the bottom of the arrivals board. Two hours had slipped away from her.

'Somethin' I can help you with?'

She stood suddenly, her knees stiff from holding the same position. 'I'm fine, thank you.'

'You hopin' to find someone?'

She glanced to where two young women were embracing. The taller one stepped back and took the other's hand, raising it to her lips and kissing it.

'Yes,' she answered. 'My sister.'

*

Later that day she heaved the backpack onto the bed and looked around the motel room, hands on hips. The walls, glossed beige, were decorated by two framed prints of tulips, and the windows wouldn't open so the warm fug of other people hung in the air. She noted the television remote bolted to the Formica desk, and the Bible and phone directory stacked on the bedside table. It wasn't the sort of room that encouraged a lengthy visit, but this was where Mia had stayed, so Katie would stay here, too.

Her first impulse was to unpack, but she was a backpacker now following Mia's route, moving on again tomorrow, and the next night, and the night after that. As a compromise she fetched out her washbag and placed it in the windowless bathroom next to the thin bar of soap provided by the motel. Exhausted from travelling, she wanted to lie down and rest, but it was only five o'clock in the evening. If she allowed herself to sleep now, she would wake in the night, battling to keep the dark memories at bay. Deciding she would get something to eat instead, she splashed cool water over her face, reapplied her mascara and changed into a fresh top. She grabbed her handbag and Mia's journal, and left.

The receptionist gave her directions to the Thai restaurant where, according to the journal, Mia and Finn had their first meal. Katie wound her way through San Francisco's wharf area as the sun went down, stopping only to call Ed to let him know she'd arrived safely.

Evening fog hung like smoke over the water and she pulled her jacket tight around her shoulders, wishing she'd worn another layer. In the journal, Mia had noted that San Francisco was a '*melting pot of artists, musicians, bankers and free spirits*', and that she had loved '*the electric pulse of the downtown*'. In another time, Katie might have agreed and found herself smitten with the quirky architecture, the winding streets, and the eclectic shop fronts – but tonight she hurried on.

She arrived at the restaurant, a lively place where circular tables were packed with people talking, laughing, eating and drinking. A waiter led her towards a window seat; a group of men looked up appreciatively as she passed, conversation only resuming when she was well beyond them.

She straightened her jacket on the chair back while the waiter removed the second place setting. Jazz played through sleek speakers in the corners of ochre walls and above the music she tuned into a wash of American accents. The smell of warm spices and fragrant rice reached her and it struck Katie how hungry she was, having not managed to eat anything on the plane. She ordered a glass of dry white wine and by the time the waiter returned with it, she had chosen Penang king prawns.

Without the prop of a menu there was nothing to occupy her attention and she felt faintly conspicuous dining alone. It would be one of many small hurdles she'd need to face each and every day of this trip and suddenly the scale of the undertaking daunted her. She locked her legs at her ankles and tucked them beneath her chair, then flattened her hands on her thighs, consciously trying to relax. She congratulated herself: she had boarded a plane for the first time in years, and was now sitting alone in a restaurant, in a country she'd never visited. *I'm doing just fine*. Reaching for her wine, she drained half of it, then set Mia's journal in front of her.

On the plane she'd only read the first entry, enough to learn where Mia and Finn stayed and ate. She had promised herself that she would savour each sentence, breathing life into the entries by experiencing them in the places Mia had been. Opening the journal, she felt oddly reassured by the company of Mia's words, as if it were her sister sitting in front of her. She smiled as she read, *'Even Finn blushed when the waiter swapped his chopsticks for a spoon. Not even a fork – a spoon!'* She pictured the remnants of Finn's dinner spread across the starched white tablecloth, Mia laughing the infectious giggle Katie had always loved.

She thought of the times she'd heard Finn and Mia's explosions of laughter through her bedroom wall, great whooping sounds that would go on for minutes, each of them spurring on the other. If she went next door, she might find Finn with a pair of trousers belted at his ribs taking off one of their teachers with uncanny accuracy, or see that they'd drawn handlebar moustaches and wire spectacles on each other's faces in black felt-tip. She wished she could step into the room and laugh with them but often she found herself frozen in the doorway, her arms folded over her chest.

It wasn't that Katie resented their friendship – she had a tight group of friends herself who she could call on in any crisis. What she did resent, and it took her some years to pin down the essence of this, was the way Mia responded to Finn. She laughed harder and more frequently in his company; they talked for hours covering all sorts of topics, when Mia was often a silent presence at home; and he had a knack of diffusing her dark moods, which Katie seemed only able to ignite.

'Excuse me? Is this chair free?'

Startled, she glanced up from the journal. A man in a pastel-yellow polo shirt indicated the chair opposite her.

'Yes.' Imagining he intended to remove the chair, she was taken aback to find him lowering himself onto it, placing a tall glass of beer at her table and stretching a hand towards her. 'Mark.'

His fingers were short and clammy. She didn't return her name.

'I'm here with my squash buddies,' he said, nodding to the table of men she'd passed on her way into the restaurant. 'But having lost, *again*, I couldn't sit through the point-by-point debrief. You don't mind me joining you, I hope?'

She did mind. Enormously. In other circumstances, Katie would have explained that she was unavailable, softening the blow with a flattering remark, and then the man could have been on his way, dignity intact. However, with the weariness of the day leaning on her shoulders, her usual social graces eluded her entirely.

'So,' Mark said, taking her silence as encouragement, 'where are you from?'

She placed her left hand, engagement ring facing towards him, on the stem of her wineglass. 'London.'

'Big Ben. Madame Tussauds. Covent Garden.' He laughed. 'I visited a couple of years back. Damn cold. Pretty, though. Very pretty.'

She picked up her wine and took a drink.

The man's gaze moved to the journal. 'Notebook?'

'Journal.'

'You're a writer?'

'This isn't mine.'

He angled his head to see it more clearly. She noticed his eyes were positioned unusually close together; it made him look reptilian. 'Whose is it?'

'My sister's.'

'Getting the dirt on her, are you?' She smelt alcohol on his breath and realized from the glassy sheen in his eyes that he was drunk. She glanced around, hoping the waiter might be nearby with her dinner.

'So tell me . . .' He made a waving motion with his hand.

'Katie.'

'So tell me, *Katie*. What are you doing with your sister's journal?'

She flinched at this stranger's casual reference to Mia's journal.

She wanted to snap it shut and be rid of this overconfident, drunken clown. 'It's private.'

'Bet that's what she thought when she was writing it!' He laughed, then picked up his beer and took a gulp; she could see his inner lip squashed against the rim of the glass.

'I'm sorry. I think you should leave.'

He looked affronted as if he'd thought the conversation had been moving along successfully. 'Seriously?'

'Yes. Seriously.'

His knee bashed the table as he stood, causing it to rock. Katie's wineglass teetered, but she caught it by the stem just before it fell. She wasn't quick enough to save the beer. Golden liquid, light with bubbles, spilt over the open journal. Horrified, she grabbed her napkin and blotted it, but the beer was already seeping into the pages, turning the smooth cream sheets dark and ridged. She watched with dismay as the precise, neat writing on the page began to blur.

'You idiot!'

Two women at the next table turned to look.

The man raised his hands in the air. 'Easy, lady. I just came over to be nice.' He pushed back his chair with force. 'Guess the game's up,' he said maliciously, motioning to the soiled journal.

'Fuck you.' The swear word felt sharp and delicious on her tongue.

The man strode back to his friends, shaking his head.

She bit down on her lip, desperate to maintain control, but tears were already threatening. Clutching the damaged journal, she scooped up her handbag and coat.

By the time the waiter had set down a dinner for one, Katie was already at the door. She had left behind her home, her job, her fiancé and her friends because of a desperate need to understand what happened to Mia. But as she burst onto the pavement, damp air closing in on her like cold breath, she wondered if she had made a terrible mistake. *I'm sorry, Mia. I don't think I can do this.*

6

MIA

Maui, October Last Year

Finn laced up his hiking boots in the dark, with a foot on the wheel arch of the hire car. He'd set his alarm for 4 a.m. and driven Mia along winding roads and hairpin bends to the highest point in Maui, atop the Haleakalā volcano, to watch the sunrise. At an elevation of ten thousand feet it was bitterly cold, although they had been warned that by midday it would become scorching with almost no shade for hikers to rest.

'How much water have you got?' Mia asked, her voice still husky from her doze in the car.

'Enough for us both.' He zipped up his coat, locked the car, and tightened the straps of his pack.

They struck out by the light from their head torches. He led, wanting to pick out a route with firm footing. Night hiking could be dangerous as changes in the terrain were difficult to judge, but the path proved smooth and descended steadily into the crater basin. Neither of them spoke, the only sound being the loose cinder ash crunching underfoot like snow.

It was still before dawn and the air was dry and chilled; Finn's cheeks felt as if they'd been stretched taut. He glanced back to check that Mia was close behind and the beam of his torch illuminated her face. She'd fastened her hair into a loose knot and wore a black fleece zipped to the chin. Her expression was set and determined.

'Okay?'

'Okay.'

They continued on as the sky bled from black to a deep violet and silhouettes of looming volcanoes and cinder cones began to emerge. Fit and strong, Mia kept a good pace; she'd once told Finn she loved hiking for the simplicity of travelling from one point to another under an open sky. Since arriving on Maui, she had spent many hours walking the beaches alone, and Finn guessed that she used the time to think about her father. They had been on the island a week, but she hadn't visited him and Finn hadn't asked why. Mia would go when the time was right.

Over the years he'd become good at deciphering how Mia felt from the small clues she gave him. For instance, if they were in conversation and she looked up at him from the corners of her eyes, chewing slightly on her bottom lip, it was often an indication that she wanted to talk about something important, and he'd need to slow and soften his voice to give her space to do so. He'd become attuned to such signals after thirteen years of friendship – longer than many marriages – yet the signs he couldn't confidently translate were what she felt for him.

He stopped. 'Let's watch from there,' he said, pointing to a raised area just off the trail where they could view the sunrise. The sky had lightened to a soft indigo and he removed his head torch, threw down his pack and leant against it. Mia sat beside him, drawing her knees towards her chest. She yawned and he saw the slight arch of her back.

From her pack she pulled a thin blanket borrowed from the hostel and draped it around them both. He could smell her shampoo: peach and avocado. Heat spread through his body. He swallowed, closing his eyes. It was dangerous to be feeling like this.

'Finn,' she said, her lips close to his ear.

'Yes?'

'Thank you – for coming to Maui.'

'It would've been a different story if your dad lived in Kazakhstan,' he quipped, forcing a smile.

'I mean it.' She was studying him closely. Too closely. 'I really appreciate you being here.' She leant into him, lifted her chin, and placed a kiss on his cheek.

He was 16 again and standing in the crowded concert hall, sweat trickling down his lower back, the taste of Mia's lips fresh on his.

He saw the truth of it now as he had back then: he was in love with Mia.

In the Hawaiian language, 'Haleakalā' meant 'House of the Sun'. The first light broke on the horizon, sending pink slithers into the sky and painting the underbellies of clouds silver.

'My God!' Mia said, sitting forward.

A brilliant red sun began to appear from behind the crater,

a majestic god in all its awesome glory. As it rose, light flooded the lunar landscape, turning everything a deep earthy red. Now he could make out the towering cinder cones and crater basin, which emitted an ethereal quality that he could only compare to pictures of the moon. Within minutes, the full sun bloomed from behind the volcano like a smile, and they felt the first blush of warmth on their faces.

It was an otherworldly sight; one of many incredible things they would experience together on this trip. He looked ahead to the weeks and months to come – spending hour after hour in Mia's company – and glimpsed a type of exquisite torture unfolding. He would be able to lie beside Mia, listening to her breath slowing into sleep, but wouldn't be able to hold her. He would eat dinner with her as the sun went down, but would never reach across to touch her hand. He would listen to all the things that busied her mind, but would not share the one thing on his.

Travelling together for months in such intimate proximity would be impossible, deceitful even. He felt he was being driven towards making a decision with only one choice: *Tell her*.

*

Mia kicked off her hiking boots and then peeled away the damp socks, revealing pink and swollen feet. Dust caked her shins, stopping at the exact line at which her socks had begun. She'd caught the sun on her shoulders, nose and cheekbones, and stepped gratefully into a cool shower, feeling the water slide over her skin.

They were staying in the Pineapple Hostel on Maui's north shore. Mia liked the rainbow colours of the dorms and the vegetable patch in the garden and, on another evening, she might have taken advantage of the hammocks, or sat in the shade of a palm tree to read. Right now, however, her mind was elsewhere because on the hike she had decided that tonight she would visit Mick.

She rolled deodorant along the hollows of her armpits and then combed her wet hair into a single smooth rope that glistened like liquorice. She pulled a fresh T-shirt from her backpack and slipped it on with a pair of shorts, then grabbed her bag.

Finn was in the communal kitchen cooking pasta and chatting with a group of windsurfers who'd just arrived at the hostel.

'Sorry to interrupt,' she said, placing a hand lightly on his arm. 'I'm going to see Mick.'

'Now?'

'Yes.'

'Excuse me a second,' she heard Finn say. He followed her out of the kitchen. 'Wait, Mia. Are you sure? I could go with you.'

'I'd like to do this on my own.'

He nodded. 'You know where you're going?'

'The hostel owner said it's a ten-minute walk.'

'It's getting dark.'

'I'll take a taxi back.'

Finn rubbed a knuckle beneath his chin. 'Well, I hope it goes all right.'

She left at once, so she didn't have time to change her mind. She walked through the small town of Paia, an offbeat place dotted with health-food stores, vegetarian cafés, surf shops and beachwear boutiques. Sugar-cane fields backed onto the town, lending a sweet smell to the air, and everywhere looked lush and green, as if she'd stepped outside after a burst of heavy rain.

Two young boys emerged from the neck of a footpath with wet hair and bare feet, surfboards thrust underarm. Rather than turning right into the street that would deliver her to Mick's house, Mia found herself taking the footpath, which led her through palm and papaya trees, to a wide stretch of beach.

The air smelt fragrant, a crush of petals infused on the humid air. She slipped off her flip-flops and padded through the warm sand, which had taken on the pinkish hue of the evening sun. Her calf muscles and the backs of her thighs ached from hiking so she found a stretch of deep sand and sank down into it.

Clean sets of waves rolled in from the ocean in neat lines, like a watery army. She watched as each wave rose gracefully to a fluid peak and then broke in a powerful cacophony of spray and froth, sending white-water roaring towards the shore.

Beyond the breaking waves a lone surfer caught her attention. He paddled hard as a great mound of swell grew beneath him, and he was suddenly propelled onto it. He rose to his feet and dropped down the glassy face of the wave. He cut two smooth and fluid turns, carving white spray with a flick of the board's tail, and then popped over the back of the wave moments before it closed out in a boom and a crush of foam. Mia realized she had been holding her breath watching him.

From her bag she took out her journal and placed it on her knees. The four lines of her father's address were written on a scrap of paper that she'd stuck in the centre of a double page, around which she'd begun to write brief notes and questions.

Writing was Mia's way of organizing her thoughts; when she could see words physically taking shape on a page she would then recognize threads of feelings or emotions that she'd allow to simmer, unidentified. Talking had never come as easily. She admired the way Katie would flop onto a chair, cup her hands lightly around her face, and air whatever grievance was troubling her. Regardless of the advice Mia or their mother gave, it was obvious that it was the act of talking that helped clear Katie's mind, in the way a brisk walk on a frosty morning clears the sinuses, and she would always leave brighter for it.

Looking at the double page now, Mia noticed that two questions stood out more prominently than the other notes, and she circled them both. The first was simply: '*Who is Mick?*'

She knew the basic facts: Mick had been 28 when he met their mother, seven years her senior. They married four months later and bought a small house in North London where Katie and Mia were born. Mick worked in the music industry and set up three independent labels during his career; the first two went bust and the third he sold before retiring to Maui. Few of these facts had been elaborated on by their mother, always reluctant to talk about a man who had so little input into her daughters' lives. When pushed, she had described him as charismatic with a shrewd head for business, but added that he was deeply selfish and never committed to the responsibilities of fatherhood.

The second question Mia had circled was more complicated. Even as a child she had sensed how different she and Katie were. Teachers praised Katie's positive work ethic and her popularity amongst classmates, but complained about Mia's disruptive behaviour and the lack of care applied to her studies. Katie became the benchmark against which Mia was measured, never the other way round.

The comparisons other people made, however, were nothing against those Mia and Katie drew between themselves. Mia had sometimes wondered if their differences were more pronounced since, oddly, their birthdays fell on the same day – 11 June – but with three years between them. The year Mia turned 12 and Katie 15, Mia asked to celebrate with a beach barbeque, and Katie, who was nearing the end of senior school, wanted a party. Their mother offered a solution: they would have a party at the beach.

Katie invited a dozen school friends; the boys headed straight for the water and the girls basked in the early-evening sun. Mia left to explore the next bay along with Finn, who was the only person she'd thought to invite. They spent their time digging for lugworms or chasing each other, swinging thick ropes of seaweed above their heads. They rejoined the party only when they could smell the burgers cooking, and then took their loaded plates to the rocks where they sat together eating and throwing the occasional scraps to the cocky gulls that gathered nearby.

Mia watched Katie moving seamlessly from friend to friend, checking that they had enough food, that their drinks were full and that they were enjoying themselves. She noticed how the girls brightened as soon as Katie joined them, and the boys' gazes would linger on her. One of the party, a diminutive girl who'd earlier been caught unawares by a wave that soaked the bottoms of her jeans, sat alone, deflated after the incident, her paper plate sagging on her knees. Noticing her, Katie slipped apart from the group she was with and sat beside the girl. She touched the damp line of the girl's jeans, and then whispered something that made her laugh hard enough to forget the cool denim at her shins. When Katie stood and reached out her hand, the girl took it and then followed Katie as they moved to rejoin the larger crowd.

Mia was impressed. At 15, when most teenagers were awkward and temperamental, Katie had an intuitive ability to put people at their ease. From her vantage point on the rocks, she saw Katie join their mother beside the barbeque as she heaped the last of the blackened sausages onto a spare plate. As they stood close, their blonde heads leaning towards one another, their gazes levelled at the sea, it suddenly struck Mia how similar her mother and sister were. It was more than their physical likeness, it was a likeness etched into their personalities. They shared a gregarious manner and a gift for understanding people, both able to read gestures and expressions in a way that was entirely alien to Mia.

The realization of their similarities unsettled Mia, but it wasn't until years later, when her mother's cancer was moving into its final stages, that she understood precisely why. Mia was visiting home and had swung into the drive – three hours late according to the schedule Katie had emailed her. A headache thumped at her temples and alcohol fumes emanated from her pores.

When she let herself in, Katie was coming down the stairs holding a leather weekend bag at her side. 'Mum's sleeping.'

'Right.'

Katie reached the bottom step and stopped. Up close, Mia could see her eyelids were pink and swollen. 'You're three hours late,' Katie said.

Mia shrugged.

'An apology would be nice.'

'For what?'

Katie's eyes widened. 'You've delayed me by *three hours*. I had plans.'

'I'm sure your boyfriend will understand,' Mia said with an arched eyebrow.

'Don't make this about us, Mia. It's about Mum.' Katie lowered her voice. 'She's dying. I don't want you to look back and regret anything.'

'What, like the way I regret having you as a sister?' It was a childish, dirty remark, which Mia didn't feel proud of.

As Katie moved past her, she said to Mia, 'I have no idea who you are.'

In that comment she had hit upon the very thing that had

always troubled Mia: if she didn't take after her mother the way Katie did, then it could only lead Mia in one direction – Mick. And since all she knew of him was that he had abandoned his family, the second question she had circled in her journal was: 'Who am I?'

Glancing up, she saw that the shadows of palm trees had clawed their way across the beach. She stood, dusting the sand from the backs of her thighs, knowing it was time to answer those questions.

As she moved along the beach, her gaze was caught again by the lone surfer paddling for a wave. He rode the liquid mountain as gracefully as a dancer, arching his body and turning his hips to catch the right motion. Mia watched him, rapt, and still didn't move off as he paddled back in to shore, letting a small ridge of white-water carry him almost to the beach. Then he slipped from his board and stood, hooking it beneath his arm as he waded in.

The man, who looked to be just a few years older than her, had a closely shaven head and a dark tattoo that stretched across the underside of his forearm. He squeezed a thumb and forefinger against the corners of his eyes, flicking away the salt water and blinking. He set his board down, removed his ankle leash, and then turned back to the ocean where a final blaze of red sky fringed the horizon. He stood with his arms loosely folded over his chest, his chin raised. The posture was stoic, resolute, yet somehow contemplative, too. Mia was intrigued by the way he watched intensely as if he were in communion with the ocean.

Minutes passed and the red sky faded to a warm orange glow, and still he did not move. Mia knew she should go but, as she stepped forwards, the man turned sharply.

He looked directly at her and his expression was one of affront, as if she had intruded on a moment intended for him alone. There was no hint of his mouth softening into a smile, or his eyebrows rising in acknowledgement. Thick lashes shadowed dark eyes and the intensity of his gaze bore into her. His eyes held her fixed and she felt heat rising in her cheeks. For a moment, she thought he was about to say something but then he dipped his head and turned back to the horizon.

She moved on, leaving the beach in his watch. She followed a narrow footpath, which eventually brought her out in front of a row of beach-front properties. Sprinkler systems kept trimmed lawns fresh and green, and large cars with tinted windows were parked on tarmac driveways. Mick's house, number 11, was two storeys with a terracotta roof, stonewashed walls and blue shutters framing the windows. Bright tropical plants grew in curved flower beds that bordered the path to the front door, and she caught the sweet smell of frangipani in the air.

She hovered awkwardly at the edge of the driveway. Her heart was beginning to pound and she shoved her hands in her pockets to stop the trembling of her fingers. For every minute she waited, her anxiety doubled. The visit wasn't simply an exercise in curiosity; it was far more crucial to her than that. Mia had always felt like an outsider in her family, and had taken a strange comfort in the idea that somewhere in the world was her father, a man she was *just like*. She had come to Maui to hold up a mirror to him, wondering if she would see herself in its reflection.

She drew in a long, steady breath, and then placed one foot in front of the other. When she reached the front door she steeled herself and pressed the bell.

7

KATIE

California/Maui, April

Katie glanced up at the floodlit sign for San Francisco International. A rush of passengers with luggage trolleys weaved around her, and a busy procession of taxis, mini-buses and coaches ducked in and out of drop-off bays. A car horn hooted twice. Headlights were flashed. A door slammed. Then overhead, the roar of a plane taking off filled the sky.

She slipped her phone from her pocket, dialled, and walked into the airport.

Ed answered. She could hear a tap running in the background and imagined him standing in a towel, smoothing shaving foam over his face.

'It's me.' She hadn't spoken to anyone in two days and the weakness in her voice startled her. She cleared her throat. 'I'm at the airport.'

'Where?'

'San Francisco.' She hesitated. 'I'm flying home.'

She heard him turn off the tap. 'What's happened? Are you okay?'

When she had set out on this journey, she knew Ed had questioned the wisdom of her decision. It was one thing for Mia to travel to far-flung corners of the world, but Katie was cut from a different cloth and he'd doubted she'd be able to cope so soon after losing her sister. 'I can't do this,' she admitted.

'Katie—'

'I really wanted to. I can't bear to think that . . .' She broke off as tears slipped onto her cheeks.

'It's okay, darling.'

She swiped at the tears with the back of her hand. It wasn't okay. She had only been in America for twelve days. Leaving England she'd felt certain that retracing Mia's route would bring her closer to understanding what happened, yet the further she travelled, the more distance she felt from Mia. She hadn't danced till dawn in San Francisco's downtown, or swum in her underwear in the Pacific; she hadn't the energy to hike into Yosemite to look down from the tops of waterfalls, or gaze up at age-old redwoods; neither did she have the courage to stay in the colourful hostels Mia and Finn had visited, or put up a tent beneath a sky of stars. She could no more travel like her sister than she could understand her.

Instead, she had found herself drifting from hotel to hotel, ordering fast food or room service to avoid eating out, and watching films long into the night simply to put off sleeping.

She spent her days driving along empty coast roads, then parking up and sitting on the bonnet of the car with a rug around her shoulders, listening to foam-crested waves smashing against rock.

Memories of Mia lined Katie's days. Some she invited in to provide comfort, as if she wouldn't feel the cold space of Mia's absence if she could wrap herself in enough of them. Other memories arrived unannounced, carried on the smell of the breeze, or freed by a song playing on the radio, or emanating from a stranger's gesture.

Ed, gently and without reproach, said, 'It was too soon.'

He was right – had been right all along.

'Have you bought your ticket yet?' he asked.

'No.'

'I want you to put yourself on the next flight home. Don't worry about the cost. I'll take care of it. I just want you back here, safely.'

'Thank you.'

'God, I've missed you. Why don't I arrange to take some time off? We can lock down in my apartment for a few days. I'll cook for you. We'll watch old DVDs. We can go for long walks – it's feeling more like spring now.'

'Is it?' she said distractedly.

'Your friends will be pleased. Everyone's been worrying about you. My inbox has never been so full! Once you're home, you will start to feel better. I promise.'

Returning to England, to his apartment, to his arms, was what she needed. She should be in a place where her friends were only a Tube stop away, where she could find a super-market without the need of a map, where she knew the cinema and gym schedules so that every free hour could be filled. This new world that she had stepped into was too big, too remote from what she knew.

'Ring me as soon as you've booked. I'll pick you up.' He paused. 'Katie, I can't wait to see you.'

'Me too,' she said, but even as she ended the call, an uneasy disappointment settled in her chest.

She hoisted on Mia's backpack, familiar now with the technique of throwing it over her shoulders, and found the queue for the ticket desk. It snaked around a maze of barriers and she joined behind a family whose toddler lay asleep on top of a stack of black cases on their trolley.

The queue shuffled forwards and Katie moved with them. When it paused, she unzipped the side pocket of the backpack and pulled Mia's journal free. She trailed a finger over its scuffed corners and down the bent and worn spine. The cream leaves had thickened and browned from the spilt beer and she thumbed through the wrinkled pages.

Finding the journal had been a gift so precious that Katie had wanted to treasure every word of it. She had been reading an entry a day, but now that she was leaving Mia's path there was no reason not to read on. She turned to the page she'd left off at – Mia and Finn driving through the furnace of Death Valley – and began to read.

She learnt about the man-made beauty of the Hoover Dam and a little roadside stall that sold the best beef tacos Mia had ever tried. She read that Mia and Finn shared a warm beer as they watched a turkey vulture circle above the Grand Canyon. She discovered that they'd hiked in Joshua Tree National Park, scaling huge red boulders to secure the best views.

Mia, you seemed so happy: what changed? You were experiencing all these incredible things with Finn, yet ended up in Bali alone. Why were you on that cliff top in the dead of night? Were you thinking about what I'd said? Did you do it, Mia? Did you jump? God, Mia, what happened to you?

Her gaze burnt into the journal as she snapped through page after page. It was like cracking open Mia's chest, pulling back the bones and flesh, and looking straight into her heart. Everything Mia had felt or experienced was laid bare. Katie ignored the weight of the backpack pressing down on her shoulders and rushed through sentence after sentence, swallowing entries whole in her impatience to understand. Then she came across a name in the journal so astonishing that she placed a hand to her mouth to contain her gasp.

Mick.

Mia wrote that she planned to visit their father, who neither of them had seen in more than twenty years. Mick's name was weighted so heavily with disappointment for their mother that Mia and Katie had never felt any desire to contact him. Until now. She flicked on, hoping Mia's idea of visiting had been concocted on a whim.

But more details followed. Mia had stuck a scrap of lined paper in the centre of a double page with what must be his address written on it. Surrounding it was a splattering of words, facts, musings. She noticed that two questions had been circled in black pen: '*Who is Mick?*' and '*Who am I?*' The questions pricked at her thoughts and a memory burst into her mind.

Two months before Mia went travelling, she'd woken Katie at three in the morning. 'Lost my keys,' she had slurred, a finger to her lips. Kohl eyeliner was smudged beneath her eyes and a pair of scuffed heels dangled from her hand.

'Oh, Mia,' Katie sighed, helping her through the doorway. 'Why do you do this to yourself?'

'Because,' she answered, staggering past her and into their lounge, 'I am a fuck-up.'

Katie had left her for a moment and gone into the kitchen. She gripped the cool edges of the sink and closed her eyes. Several times a week she would find evidence of similar nights out – the front door slamming at an ungodly hour, her medicine box raided and the headache tablets missing, the aftermath of late-night snacks littering the kitchen worktop. The drinking and the dark moods that followed were a reaction to losing their mother, so Katie never mentioned her disrupted sleep or the mess she cleared up in the mornings.

As the older sister, making sacrifices for Mia came naturally to her. When Mia was 6 and refused to speak in the school nativity play, it was Katie who'd gone onstage, holding her sister's clammy hand and saying the words for her. When Mia, at 17, thought she might be pregnant, it was Katie who'd raced back from university and missed her summer ball. When Mia spent her student loan on a trip to Mexico and couldn't cover her rent, it was Katie who'd lent her the money – never minding that she was short herself. It was as if their personalities were balanced on a seesaw: Mia had claimed the wild, high ride and Katie was left on the ground. She loved her sister fiercely, but lately she'd found herself resenting her, too.

Music suddenly blasted from the lounge and Katie thought immediately of their neighbours below, a serious couple with a baby.

'Mia—' she began, marching into the room – and then stopped.

Mia was dancing in the space between the sofa and coffee table, her hair swaying down her back. She closed her eyes as she swirled to the music; it was a soul track from one of their mother's old albums. Mia's fingers stroked the air as if feeling her way through a stream of notes. She spun round, the skirt of her dress filling with air. When she opened her eyes and saw Katie, she grinned and extended her hand.

For a moment, Katie glimpsed the eight-year-old Mia, mud streaked and soaked, dancing in their garden in a summer downpour. Katie found herself being pulled forwards, drawn into the music, drawn into her sister. Her shoulders began to loosen and her hips swung beneath the silken touch of her nightdress. She smiled as Mia took her other hand, spinning her beneath a raised arm.

They made each other laugh with silly moves and outrageous gestures. Mia jumped onto the sofa using it as a podium, her bare feet sinking into the leather cushions, her fingertips stretched towards the ceiling. Katie remembered a sequence from a childhood dance routine they'd learnt in front of her bedroom mirror and executed it now with such serious precision that she could have been ten years old again. They collapsed on the sofa, laughing. Mia wrapped her arms around Katie who accepted the gesture for what it was – a rare burst of affection made accessible by alcohol.

When the track ended, the room sank back into silence. They stayed in each other's arms, their hearts thumping from the exertion. In the darkness, Mia said, 'You remind me so much of Mum.'

'Do I?' Katie said softly, cautious of chasing away the intimacy that had fallen on them like a beam of sunshine.

'You two could have been sisters.'

A long silence stretched between them, and was broken by a question pitched by Mia. 'Do you ever wonder why Mick left us?'

Surprised, Katie sat up. 'He left because he was selfish.'

'Maybe there's more to it than that.'

'Yes,' she said. 'He was flawed.' Through the window, the flashing blue lights from a police car passed. 'Why are we even talking about him? He never cared about anyone but himself.'

'How do we know?'

'He abandoned us. That's how.' Katie stood.

Mia tucked her feet to her side and Katie saw that her soles were filthy.

'Have a glass of water before you sleep.'

As she left the room, she heard Mia say, 'What if I'm like him?'

Katie paused, not sure if she'd heard right. When Mia didn't speak again, she continued to bed.

At the time, she had dismissed the remark as a drunken rambling, rather than considering that Mia could have been voicing a real fear. Now, eager to find out where Mia's journal entry about Mick led, she flipped overleaf.

Stuck on an otherwise clean page was the stub of a boarding card from a flight to Maui. Mia and Finn had gone there the day after the entry was written.

'How may I help you?' A woman with a buttercup-yellow scarf knotted over her blouse smiled at Katie from behind the ticket desk. Katie had reached the front of the queue.

'I'd like to book a flight, please.'

'Certainly. And where will you be flying to?'

Glancing down at the journal, she wondered if Mia's decision to see Mick was somehow tied to what happened in Bali. If she flew home now, she would have no choice but to accept the authorities' account of Mia's death. She'd never know the truth.

She closed the journal carefully. 'I'd like a ticket to Maui.'

*

It was dawn when Katie stepped from the plane into the sweet, humid air of Maui. Tour operators draped leis of fresh hibiscus flowers around their guests' necks, and Katie slipped quietly through the perfumed crowd and into a taxi.

She rolled down the window and felt the warmth in the air loosening the tension in her neck and shoulders. She was dropped off at the Pineapple Hostel on the north shore of the island. The owner, who wore three silver rings in his bottom lip, told her, 'Dorm 4 is empty. Go along the hall, up the stairs and it's on your right. The bathroom is opposite. Enjoy. *Mahalo*.'

Katie thanked him and followed the brightly painted corridor. She passed cheaply framed photos of towering waves ridden by windsurfers, and beneath each the location was printed in white letters: MAUI. She thought how surreal it was to be here, knowing almost nothing about the island, when a different decision just hours ago would have seen her alighting back into freezing temperatures in London.

It was her first experience at a hostel and she was relieved to find the dorm clean and airy. There were four bunk beds with bright green sheets and yellow pillows, and she set her backpack against the nearest one, claiming the bottom from habit.

When Katie was 9, Mia 6, they had asked for canary-yellow bunk beds for Christmas. They didn't need to share a room – there were two other empty ones in the house – but Katie liked the idea of having someone nearby as she fell asleep, and Mia liked having something wooden in her room she could climb. There was no argument as to who slept where: Katie wanted the bottom bunk so she could tuck a sheet into the corners of the mattress above, making it drape down like the canopy in a princess's room, and Mia was delighted by the top so she could pretend she was on the highest deck of a ship. She stuck stars on the ceiling for the sky and dragged in the blue bath mat, which became the sea. She'd call Katie up, who was less confident negotiating the flimsy wooden ladder, and they'd sit with their legs crossed, describing the things they saw in the water.

Now, Katie took her mobile from the backpack and switched it on. It beeped immediately, with three new messages from Ed. She sat on the edge of the bunk bed, her neck craned forward, and called him.

'Katie! Where are you? I've been worried about you.'

'My flight left almost immediately. There wasn't time—'

'You're at Heathrow? Already?'

'No. Listen, Ed,' she said, placing a hand to her forehead. 'I had chance to think. I've decided to carry on with the trip.'

'Where are you?'

'Maui.'

'Maui! What the hell is going on?'

'It felt wrong giving up.'

'You can't just fly off to God knows where without telling anyone! It's not safe. You're acting like Mia.'

She knew the comparison was meant to chastise her, but privately she felt pleased by it. She pulled off her ankle boots and socks with one hand, and placed her bare feet on the wooden floor of the dorm. It felt wonderfully cool.

'We should be making these kinds of decisions together,' he continued. 'You need to talk to me.'

'I'm sorry. You're right. I hate being apart, I really do. It's just I've realized exactly how much I need to do this.'

'A few hours ago you called to say you're coming home. And now you're in Maui and it's all back on. I'm honestly not sure if you're in the right state of mind to be doing this.'

'What does that mean?'

'The Katie I know is decisive and level-headed.'

'Yes, she is. But she's also just lost her sister and deserves a little leeway.'

'I'm not arguing with you, Katie.'

'So show me that you support me.'

'I support everything you do. I'm just finding it difficult to believe that travelling alone is the best thing for you right now. I'm worried you're chasing ghosts.'

'And I'm worried,' she said levelly, 'that if I come home now, I will have let Mia down.'

There was a strained silence. She turned her engagement ring with her fingers, the diamond glittering in the light.

'Our invites went out today,' Ed said.

She had ordered them through a design company that were laser cutting the edges with flowers. She hadn't realized they'd be sent so soon.

He added, 'The wedding is in four months.'

'Yes.'

'You'll be home in time?'

'Of course.'

'Because,' he said, his voice softening, 'I've no idea what I'd do with a hundred Cath Kidston tea-light holders if you're not.'

She smiled. 'I'll be home.'

She put the phone away and lay down on the crisp green sheet with Mia's journal. Despite Ed's concern, for the first time since she'd left England, she felt as if she was thinking more clearly.

She opened the journal at the page with Mick's address and trailed a fingertip over the unfamiliar words. It was strange to think of her father living nearby; she imagined a large modern house, a man with silver hair, a wardrobe of smart suits.

When they were girls, Katie and Mia would sometimes talk about their father in low voices after dark. Mia would lean over the edge of the bunk, poking her head under the princess canopy to ask, 'What is Daddy like?' Katie thought she was being clever by making up abstract comparisons that kept Mia confused for days. 'He is like Moby Dick,' or, 'He reminds me of the songs in Mum's David Bowie album.' When Mia asked what she meant, Katie would just shrug and tell her to read the book or listen to the record.

The real reason she avoided giving a proper answer was because she didn't know what their father was like. Her memories were pieces of two different puzzles that wouldn't slot together. She held a few crisp, wonderful recollections – like the one that played out in their old kitchen in North London where the red-tiled floor was freezing underfoot, even in summer. Katie was meant to be asleep, but had come downstairs to ask for a glass of milk. Not finding either of her parents in the lounge, she had wandered towards the kitchen where she heard music playing. Her mother was being swirled in her father's arms, laughing wildly. She watched for a moment; she saw the glint of her father's gold watch where his shirtsleeve ended, caught the smell of his aftershave mixed with a sweet tang of whisky, saw her mother's hair coming loose from a tortoiseshell clip. Spotting Katie, her father stopped dancing.

Fearing she might be told off for being out of bed, she began to yawn, but he took her by the hand and spun her, too. She laughed as she'd seen her mother do with her head thrown back and her mouth open.

There were other memories, though, that she had been careful not to share, like the time when Mia was 2 and she needed seven stitches across her right temple. Katie and her mother had been at a ballet performance and, during the interval, when Katie was pirouetting in the drinks lounge, her mother's name was called over the tannoy. At the front desk, the theatre manager said, 'Grace Greene? Your husband is on the phone.' Katie watched the colour drain from her mother's face and her eyes grow frighteningly wide as she held the phone close to her ear.

After that she remembered the evening in frames, like the illustrations in a comic book. She recalled a taxi ride in the dark. A hospital desk she couldn't see over, even on tiptoe. Her sister lying in a bed with polished metal sides. Her mother's pale hands clasped around her bag as she spoke to their father.

He said that Mia had tripped on the landing and fallen down the stairs, but over time other clues surfaced that suggested something entirely different. A nurse mentioned a motorbike; a neighbour had said her father's name and used the word 'irresponsible'.

They returned from the hospital the following day to find that their father and his belongings were gone. It wasn't the only change. As time went on their mother seemed listless and vacant and, when she took her evening bath, Katie would hear her crying above the gush of the water.

Even as a child she could see the link between Mia's accident and their father's leaving. She remembered standing in the doorway of their mother's bedroom, watching as Grace dabbed concealer on the dark circles beneath her eyes, and asking, 'Did Daddy leave because of Mia?' Her mother had dropped the gold make-up pot, taken three paces across the carpet, grabbed the top of Katie's arm with one hand and slapped the back of her thighs with the other. Three months later, their belongings were in boxes and they took a coach to Cornwall.

Now, turning the pages of the journal, she had an uncomfortable feeling that this meeting with Mick would somehow be entangled with the rest of Mia's trip. Stretched on her bunk she read swiftly but closely. She didn't notice two other travellers coming in and out of the room, or hear the tropical rain begin to beat against the window. She simply continued to read, utterly absorbed in the pages of the journal as Mia recounted what happened the evening she arrived at their father's house.

8

MIA

Maui, October Last Year

Mia waited on the doorstep. Even at dusk the air still held its warmth and she could feel a thin slick of sweat under the waistband of her shorts. She hooked a finger into the back of them and waggled it a little, encouraging air to reach her skin. Sweat prickled underarm and beads of moisture formed between her breasts as she waited.

She listened, barely breathing, for the sound of footsteps and eventually heard them, fast strides to reach the door. She took a step back, folding her arms and then refolding them less tightly.

Mick was exactly her height. He wore a loose white shirt with black shorts, to which a mobile was clipped. His face was rounder than she'd recalled from his photo, a definite fullness about the jowls, and his hair was steel grey, thinning at the sides, but cut short. He had Katie's eyes, she could see: hazel with pale lashes.

They studied one another closely. Mia wondered what he

made of the young, silent woman on his doorstep. Should she have dressed so casually in shorts and flip-flops, when perhaps a dress and sandals might have been more appropriate, more like something her mother or Katie would have worn?

Then, Mick chose his first word. It had the force of a slap: 'Yes?'

He didn't know who she was.

Her gaze fell away from his and came to rest on the doormat between them where a fly, caught in the weave, struggled to turn itself upright. When Mia had imagined this meeting – and she had imagined it many, many times – she had pictured an embrace of sorts, Mick instinctively reaching for her, and that first hug between father and daughter sealing an unspoken connection. She had prepared for rejection, too: Mick explaining that too much time had elapsed, or shielding her from the view of a second wife who didn't know of her existence. Yet, in all the imagined scenarios, she had never once considered that he wouldn't recognize her.

When she looked up, Mick was still waiting, his eyebrows raised and his head tilted slightly to the side. His lips were turned up in one corner, a half-smile. She couldn't tell if it was encouragement to speak or bemusement at her silence.

'I am—' she began, her eyes searching his face, hoping to catch the moment when it might click and she'd be spared this humiliation. 'I'm Mia.'

His expression didn't change.

Would she have to say it? Did she need to tell him that he was her father? It was a relief that Finn hadn't accompanied her; for someone to witness this would have been too much.

Finally she said, 'I'm your daughter.'

The half-smile vanished. He blinked rapidly and his gaze mapped her features, perhaps searching for clues he'd missed before. 'Sorry, I . . . I didn't realize who . . .'

She remained facing him. After a moment he stepped aside and said, 'You'd better come in.'

She walked through a cool white hallway, following it until she reached a tastefully designed kitchen. An L-shape of granite-work surfaces framed the large room and glass-fronted cabinets housed elegant wineglasses. Many of the appliances had been chosen in stainless steel: a cordless kettle, a double oven with a digital clock, a sleek fridge. The walls, white again, were bare save for an electric guitar sculpted into a clock, and four discreet Bose speakers pumping out a Neil Young track.

Mick picked up a slim remote from a glass dining table piled with magazines, song sheets and post, and stopped the music. He looked shaken. 'This is a surprise.'

Mia still couldn't find her voice and was aware of heat rising in her cheeks.

'Take a seat on the deck,' he said, indicating a set of French doors thrown open onto a garden. 'Drinks. I'll make us drinks.'

She moved outside and was drawn to the edge of the garden where a low stone wall was all that separated Mick's property from the beach. The air was salt tinged and fresh, and she breathed in deeply. In the low light of evening she could just make out the faint line of the horizon, a washed-out blue fading into deeper shades of mauve and dusky navy. Somewhere far off, waves were breaking and she centred her thoughts on the sound.

'Magnificent, isn't it?' Mick said, joining her. He handed her a large glass of something clear. He watched as she took a sip. It was sweet, alcoholic and ice cold, fulfilling all her requirements.

They moved back to the deck and Mia took a seat at a teak table with a parasol positioned at its centre. Mick unhooked his mobile from its clip and placed it in front of him before sitting. A tiny blue light on the phone flashed every few seconds. He took a packet of cigarettes and a lighter from his pocket. 'Do you smoke?' he asked, offering her one. There was a tremble to his fingers.

'No.'

He lit a cigarette and inhaled deeply, closing his eyes. It afforded Mia a moment to look at him. Mick had changed dramatically from the trim, suited man in her photo. The muscles in his arms had turned slack and a neat paunch strained against his shirt. Thin red skin stretched over the bridge of his nose and his eyelids looked heavy.

He exhaled a drift of smoke into the air, the cigarette returning much of his composure. 'So,' he said, stretching forward to tap ash into a wooden bowl, 'are you here in Maui alone, or is Katie with you?'

Her sister's name so soon was a small surprise. 'I'm with a friend.'

He nodded and she wondered whether he was disappointed or relieved.

'Where are you staying?'

'The Pineapple Hostel.'

'I know it. It's only a few minutes from here.' Mick rested his left arm over the back of his chair. 'Will you stay long or are you travelling elsewhere?'

She understood that he was gauging her intentions. Who was she with? How long would she be here? What did she want from him? 'I'm travelling for a few months,' she told him. 'We started in California. Thought we'd make Maui our next stop. From here we're flying to Western Australia.' It was the most she'd said since she'd arrived and her throat felt dry and tight. She picked up her drink and let an ice cube knock against her tongue.

'We?'

'Me and Finn – my best friend.'

A long silence stretched between them. Mia focused on the contents of her glass. She had imagined that the words would come easily – there would be a flow of conversation to start filling in the years – yet now that she was here, she felt as if there was so much to say that she couldn't decide which words should come first.

They finished their drinks in silence. Mick stubbed out his cigarette and went to the kitchen, returning with fresh drinks and two citronella candles that he lit, their sharp lemon scent filling the air. He drank quickly, the alcohol barely touching the sides of the glass. In that she recognized their first similarity.

'I heard about your mother passing away,' he said finally.

She wondered how.

'It must have been hard for you and Katie.'

'Yes.' She couldn't think about her mother now. This, being here, was already too much.

'How is Katie?'

'Good. We have a flat together in London.'

'Yes?'

'She's working in recruitment.'

He smiled, and she took that as encouragement. 'And yourself?' he asked. 'What do you do?'

She shrugged. 'I've been doing some casual work – bar jobs, waitressing, that kind of thing. I'm not sure what I want to do yet.'

'I trained as a chef before I found the music industry.'

It was the first new fact she'd learnt about him. Her father had been a chef. Had he ever cooked for them? She considered whether she had any inherent culinary know-how, but couldn't think of any.

Mick explained how his career began at a French restaurant in West London. One of the young waiters there had an incredible singing voice but lacked the confidence to do any gigs. Mick put him in touch with a fantastic guitarist he knew from university and later began taking bookings for them – for a cut. Within six months, Mick had brought on a drummer and bass guitarist, and the new band were doing so well that he found the money for an album to be recorded. That was the start of his first record label.

Mick talked quickly, one sentence rolling into the next, one story unfolding into another, either to avoid the quiet awkwardness or else to delay the more serious discussion of why Mia was there. The more he spoke, the more she felt herself withdrawing, silence closing around her throat like a pair of hands. She knew she was being odd, but it was as if the subject of his desertion was too big to even broach.

'Mia?'

She glanced up, unsure how far away she'd drifted.

Mick was staring at her, looking directly into her eyes. 'Are you interested in music?'

'I love it,' she said, twisting a broken strand of hair around her fingertip. 'Listening, not playing.' She loved going to gigs and feeling the rhythm of the music beating deep within her chest. London had been good for that, a saving grace in the city.

'You said you've come from California. What did you make of it?'

Mia unwound the strand of hair from her finger and tucked her hands beneath her thighs. 'The beaches were wilder than I expected. And quieter. It was beautiful.'

'Did you fly into LA?'

'San Francisco.'

'I lived in LA for seven years,' he said. 'Fantastic place – so much buzz.'

So much buzz. Would she ever choose that phrase? No. Katie would have. She could see flashes of her sister in Mick – a shared confidence, an ease with words.

'I had an office overlooking the beach,' he continued. 'Not a bad spot to be in after London.'

After London. After he left them. She needed to steer the

conversation towards their lives there. She concentrated on recalling the details she'd written in her journal, but all the words seemed to be swimming in her head and she couldn't grasp any of them.

Mick's mobile rang. He answered immediately. 'James! Yes, yes . . . That's right . . . Absolutely.' He checked his watch. 'We're still on.'

Mia drained her drink. She should have eaten before coming out here. Already she could feel the muscles in her face beginning to loosen. She set down the empty glass, suddenly noticing that dusk had been swallowed by night.

'Give me twenty?' Mick was saying. 'Looking forward to it.'

He placed the phone back on the table. 'I'm sorry, but I've got to meet a colleague for dinner. I'd lost track of time.'

'Oh.' He was cutting her visit short when there was still everything to say.

'It's been nice to see you,' he told her, rising. He moved away from the table, triggering a floodlight that illuminated the deck. She blinked in the sudden brightness, disorientated for a moment.

When she looked up, Mick was already moving through the kitchen, towards the hallway. She followed, deciding there would be another chance to talk. Perhaps it was right to ease into their reunion, hold off discussing the bigger issues until next time.

On reaching the front door, Mick said, 'Thank you for visiting.'

She nodded. 'I'm here for a fortnight.'

'You'll love the island.'

There was no reference to seeing her again. Surely this couldn't be his intention? 'I'm free tomorrow.'

Mick didn't look at her as he said, 'Tomorrow isn't so good. My lawyer's here all day.'

She waited a beat, sure he would offer an alternative, but he said nothing. A click of air freshener was released on a timer somewhere. The smell of artificial pine filled the hall, catching at the back of Mia's throat. 'The day after?'

Mick rubbed his hand on the back of his neck, his composure beginning to wane. He rolled onto the balls of his feet and cast his gaze at the ceiling. 'I can't do this, Mia.'

'Do what?' she said, her fingers beginning to work the edges of her pockets.

'See you again. Be who you want me to be. It wouldn't be fair to either of us.' He shook his head sharply. 'There's a lot you don't understand.'

'So tell me,' she said, hearing her voice rise.

'It's all in the past. Let's leave it be.' He placed his hand on the door handle. 'Sorry, but I need to get going.'

She stared at him for a moment, unable to believe they'd reached this point so soon. She suddenly felt light headed, insubstantial, as if the crush of disappointment had dissolved her.

'I'm sorry that this wasn't what you'd hoped for,' he said with feeling, and then he opened the door onto the night.

*

Stunned, Mia drifted away as her father closed the door gently behind her. She shook her head, thinking, *Was that it?* Where were the similarities between them, or the connection she'd been sure she'd feel? Humiliation burnt across her cheeks: she had flown to Maui, visited her father's house, accepted his drinks and conversation, yet all the while he had been biding his time until the moment he could ask her to leave.

She wished Katie had been with her. Katie wouldn't have accepted Mick's dismissal. Mia pictured her sister grilling him for answers, her fierce eloquence tying his excuses in knots. The image emboldened her momentarily and she considered turning round, going back. But deep down, she knew she didn't have the heart for it.

Eventually the path delivered her to the beach where she'd earlier watched the lone surfer. The air smelt briny and sharp. She glimpsed the dark curves of distant waves, their arching backs licked silver by moonlight.

She threw down her bag, kicked off her flip-flops and plunged her feet into the sea. The water felt powerful and alive at her ankles, sucking the sand from beneath her toes. She drew in a deep lungful of air and let the whoosh of waves fill her ears. Thoughts of Mick began gradually washing away, like words drawn on the shoreline.

She waded forwards and a small wave broke over her thighs, soaking the hem of her shorts. A second bowled into her but she didn't recoil. Cool water soaked through her shorts and into her knickers. She tasted something thrilling about being alone at the edge of the ocean and she let the moon draw her towards it.

Water rose over her waist, causing her stomach to shrink away from the cold.

In a fluid motion, she bent her knees and pushed forwards, letting the sea catch her and bear her weight. She kicked away from the shore, making deep smooth strokes, her T-shirt clinging to her skin.

The sea was a balm. She dived under, dark water slipping over her head. She glided with her arms outstretched, her fingers meeting in a neat point. She broke the surface to snatch a breath, and then dived down again, deeper this time, water gushing down the neck of her T-shirt.

She stopped kicking and let her body go still. Gradually she began floating up with her back to the sky, her limbs spread like a starfish. As children, she and Katie used to do this, letting their hair fan around their faces while they listened for the songs of mermaids. She heard the fizzes and clicks of the sea, and imagined angelfish swimming beneath her, silent and curious. Heat began building in her lungs as the desire for air grew. She forced herself to remain still, feeling the dark slopes of waves lift and drop her body as if she were a piece of driftwood.

The underwater rhythm shifted and she was aware of a new sound overlaying the gentle melody. It wasn't the draw of a wave, more like fast sloshes of water hitting a wall. She tried to concentrate on where it was coming from, when suddenly she felt pain at the back of her head. There was a rush of noise and she was yanked upwards, her head snapping back. She gasped as she broke the surface, gulping in air.

She heard a shout, and then she felt herself plunging under

again, salt water filling her mouth and shooting up her nostrils. Her clothes bulged, dragging her downwards, and she flailed underwater, disorientated.

Finally she surfaced again, gasping. There was more shouting and she kicked out, thrashing her way towards the shore. As soon as her feet found the seabed, she staggered through the shallows.

A man waded after her. 'You okay?'

'Get the fuck away!' she shouted, her heart racing.

He stopped. 'I thought . . . shit, I thought you were drowning.'

'I was swimming!'

'You were in your clothes. Not moving. It looked like, like you were . . .' He didn't finish.

'You were watching me swim?'

'No,' he said, shaking his head. His eyes were wide, startled. 'No. I was paddling back in. I saw a shape in the water. You were just floating there, face down.'

Now she noticed the surfboard under his arm.

'I'm so sorry,' he said again, and she could tell by his voice that he meant it. 'I didn't mean to scare you.'

She pushed her wet hair from her face and hugged her arms around her middle. 'So what, you surf in the dark?'

'Sometimes.'

She was absorbed by the image of him alone in the black, hollow waves. 'It must be dangerous.'

'The moon's a good floodlight.'

She wondered what drew him into the ocean, risking his life for the thrill of a wave.

As he lifted a hand to wipe water from his eyes, she noticed the dark tattoo snaking across the underside of his forearm. 'You were here earlier,' she said suddenly, remembering seeing him on the shoreline, staring out to sea with a meditative focus. 'I saw you when you paddled in.'

He looked at her with his head tilted to one side. 'Yes,' he said, eventually. 'I remember.'

His voice was deep, gravelly. Did she hear an accent?

'You're cold,' he said.

She hadn't realized she was shivering.

'I've got a towel.' He moved past her and she found herself following. He had a bag stowed further up the beach from which he passed her a towel. She used it to tussle her hair dry and then wrapped it around her shoulders.

The man took out a box of matches and knelt down in the sand beside a pyramid of branches and twigs.

'You built this earlier?'

He nodded. He struck a match and she caught its gunpowder scent. Cupping a hand round the flame, he lit the kindling in several places. He blew gently on the flames, which flickered and grew in response. The firelight illuminated his face; she saw the glistening water in his eyebrows and his dark, serious gaze beneath.

Once the fire took he moved back to his bag and pulled out a jumper. 'Here, wear this if you like.'

She could have declined, walked away then and returned to the hostel. She knew Finn would be waiting for her, wondering how the reunion with Mick had gone. But she wasn't ready to leave. Not yet. 'Thanks,' she said, taking the jumper. With her back to him, she peeled off her sodden T-shirt and bra and pulled it on. She tugged the sleeves down over her hands and her thumbs nestled into the holes that had been worn into them.

She sat beside the fire while he changed into dry clothes. When he returned, he handed her a bottle of beer.

'Cheers,' she said, twisting the cap free. 'I'm Mia.'

He said her name aloud, once, as if that was the only way he would remember. 'Noah,' he offered, hooking an elbow around his knees. He looked at her sideways. 'So, you often go swimming in your clothes?'

She shrugged.

'There are strong currents around here. Someone should be watching out for you.'

'Who watches out for you?'

He smiled.

'I thought I was alone,' she told him eventually. 'Me and my sister used to do it when we were younger – just float and listen to the sea.' But that had been years ago, before Katie had become afraid of the sea, before they had drifted apart. Mia missed the summer afternoons they used to spend at the beach dive-bombing from the rocks or searching the shoreline for shells. The *Sea Sisters*, they had been nicknamed as children. 'I just had the urge to do it again.'

He looked at her for a moment, fixing his dark eyes square on hers. She wondered if he thought her foolish, but he said nothing.

They drank in silence, watching the hypnotic flit and quiver of the flames. The thick smell of woodsmoke filled the air. Occasionally, Mia glanced at him, absorbing small details: the dark hair on his legs that thinned at his ankles; a tear in the seam of his T-shirt that ran an inch along his side; the casual grip of his fingers holding the beer loosely at its neck.

'So when did you start surfing?' she asked later.

'When I was a kid. We lived near Melbourne, a couple of kilometres from the beach. I used to cycle down after school and watch all the old guys styling it up on long boards.'

'Did you teach yourself?'

'No, there was this guy, Reuben. He was ancient, but whenever the swell pushed through, he'd be out. He wasn't looking for the big waves or big moves, but he just had this poise on the water no one could match. I hung around on the beach whenever I could, just watching.' He took a swig of his beer. 'Eventually I plucked up the nerve to ask him for a lesson – said I'd wash his ute in return. We had a deal. He'd take me surfing whenever the swell was right, and I made sure he drove the cleanest ute in Melbourne. He spread the word about my car-washing talents. Five months later, I owned my first board.'

'I like that,' she said, smiling. 'You earned it.' She ran her fingers through her damp hair, loosening some of the tangles. 'So what brings you to Maui? Are you travelling?'

He nodded.

'With friends?'

'My brother.'

'Really? You must get on well.'

He shrugged.

'Where's he tonight?'

'At a bar in town.'

'Why aren't you there?'

He thought for a moment. 'I like my own space sometimes.'

She smiled, knowing exactly what he meant. She uncrossed her legs and stretched them towards the flames, warming her toes. The firelight caught the line of her shins and she could feel Noah's gaze on them. 'Where's next on your route?' she asked.

'We're heading back to Australia for a couple of months. After that, I don't know. We'll follow the swell.' He threw a stick on the fire and then asked, 'How about you? Where are you from?'

'Cornwall. It's in the south-west of England.'

'You get good Atlantic swells there. Cold, though.'

'You get used to it.'

He finished his beer and took out two more, passing one to Mia. 'Where do you live now?'

'I moved to London almost a year ago. My sister and I bought a place there.' She traced the back of the beer bottle with her thumb, thinking about the flat with its tall sash windows that only opened three inches, so she never felt as though she could get enough air.

'You didn't enjoy it?' he asked, perhaps reading something in her expression.

'I guess I'm not a city person.'

He nodded, but kept looking at her, as if there was more to say.

She drew a breath. 'It was a mistake moving there. Our

mother died a few months earlier and I think we both needed to prove something to ourselves by living together.'

'To show you were still a family.'

'Yes, that was exactly it,' she said, surprised by the acuteness of his observation. He intrigued her, this man who surfed at night and preferred a beach fire to a bar. There was a sense of autonomy about him that she recognized in herself, too.

'Is your sister still in London?'

'Katie. Yes, she is. She's happy there.'

'Where are you happy?'

She heard the lull of the waves, like soft murmurs from a lover. 'By the sea.'

They continued to talk, swapping stories of their seas. She discovered that his was the clear blue water of the Tasman Sea with its peeling waves and roaming bull sharks, and she explained hers was the Atlantic, fringed by granite and slate cliffs and stalked by herring gulls.

When she spoke he listened intently, his eyes never leaving her face. His focus gave her confidence and she felt something within her releasing, as though a small door in her throat had been nudged ajar. She talked about her mother's cancer and how Katie played nurse and she played truant. She told him how the weekend she moved to London, she'd lain in Hyde Park staring at the clouds, trying to pretend she was elsewhere. She confided that she'd come to Maui to meet her father, who'd humoured her for an hour and then asked her to leave. As she talked, the fire burnt low and her hair dried in stiff waves from the salt.

Suddenly she looked up. 'Sorry, I've talked too much.'

'No you haven't,' he said studying her closely. His eyes were dark, serious. What was it about them? They seemed somehow older than the rest of his face. She could feel herself drawn to him.

Noah picked up a thin branch and prodded at the glowing embers. Her gaze travelled from the grip of his fingers, over his wrist and to the black tattoo spreading towards his inner elbow. 'Your tattoo,' she began, 'when did you have it done?'

'Ten months ago.' He threw the branch on the fire. Orange sparks flickered into the sky. He angled his arm towards the firelight and she could see that the wave had been skilfully tattooed so its power was captured in a rush of water crumbling from the crest. At the bottom there were six discreet numbers.

The tattoo intrigued her. It wasn't an adolescent attempt at rebellion like the Arabic words branded on the pale backs of the boys she went to college with. It had been done recently and was inked on the tender skin on the underside of his forearm. 'It's beautiful,' she said, reaching out and tracing the curve of the wave with a fingertip.

Instantly the atmosphere became charged and she was aware of heat emanating from where their skin touched.

Noah looked at her. She was surprised by how much she wanted to kiss him. They were strangers, yet somehow she felt as if they already knew each other. An overwhelming rush of desire filled her and she reached a hand to his cheek, feeling his stubble against her palm.

He blinked as if startled by the touch. For a moment she

thought he was going to pull away, but then he leant forward and pressed his mouth gently against hers. His lips were soft and warm, and she closed her eyes as he drew her closer, kissing her deeply. His tongue explored her mouth and she could taste the sea on his lips.

Her hands eased beneath the cotton of his T-shirt, feeling the muscular ridges below his shoulder blades.

He rose up onto one knee and, cupping a hand behind her head, he tilted her backwards, so that she was lying beneath him, her hair spilling over the sand. He ran his tongue from her collarbone to her throat. Her head swam.

A sky of stars hung above her and the heat of the fire spread along her side. Her thoughts melted free of her mind, so that the disappointment of earlier was lost to the press of his body, to the warmth of his skin, to the feel of his lips on her neck. She let herself dissolve fully, exquisitely, into this stranger.

9

KATIE

Maui, April

Katie closed the journal and pushed it aside. She pressed her hands to her forehead where a tension headache threatened. Once she might have been shocked by the risk Mia had taken with a stranger, but shock fell away beneath her anger at Mick.

Mia had been sheltered from many of the details of their father; this had left a blank canvas on which she could project any number of fantasies. Her disappointment at the reunion ran deep: eight neatly written pages attested to that. Katie snatched up the journal again and located the single sentence that had pulled her up short and made her heart crack: '*I wish Katie had been with me.*'

She wished that too! She wished she'd listened when Mia tried talking about Mick, rather than dismissing the conversation. The dull aching in her forehead spread, taking a firm grip of her temples. Moving to the backpack, she fished in the front pocket for headache pills. Her fingers brushed over a tube of

120

suncream, a pack of tissues, and then they reached an inner zip. She slipped her fingers in and they met with something slim and glossy that she couldn't place. She tugged it free and found it was a photo.

Her eyes widened in surprise, and then she felt the oily rise of nausea at the back of her throat.

The picture was taken years ago when Mia was 8, Katie 11. Their mother had driven them to the local town for a day out and, carrying beach towels and costumes, they'd strolled along the promenade snacking on cola cubes from a paper bag. Mia had been the first to spot the merry-go-round glinting in the sunlight, the singsong tinkle of its music carried on a light sea breeze.

It arrived every spring and stayed for three weeks before slipping away in the night, leaving only a faint ring of dead leaves and dust behind. Rather than painted ponies, what rose and fell on each twirl of the merry-go-round were seahorses. Each looked as if it had been dipped in a different ocean and dripped with the shade of the sea – cobalt blue, cerulean, navy, azure – and they always begged their mother to let them ride on it.

The cheerful lady who ran the merry-go-round beamed when she saw them. 'Ah, it's the Sea Sisters!' They had earned this title because each year, after riding the merry-go-round, they'd play for hours in the sea while their mother sat on the shore with her book, drinking coffee from a polystyrene cup.

'What in heaven is this?' the lady said, pulling a small shell from behind Mia's ear with a flourish. 'And what have you got there?' she said to Katie, who glanced down at her red sundress to find a long white feather poking out of her pocket.

They chose two seahorses next to one another. Katie tucked her feet into the imaginary stirrups of the sapphire seahorse she'd picked, and shot up and down in a rising trot. Mia rode a sky-blue seahorse on the outside so she could feel the wind against her face as they spun.

'Girls,' their mother called, pointing her camera at them.

They stretched out their arms and linked hands, grinning, the glitter of sea caught in the background. The photo used to be pinned to Mia's bedroom wall in Cornwall, but Katie hadn't seen it in years. Written on the back, in Mia's faded childish hand, were the words '*Sea Sisters*'.

Now, with a trembling finger, she traced the rough edge of the picture. It had been torn in two: Katie's image ripped from the photo and discarded.

How could you, Mia? Did you give up on us? Had we grown that far apart? Or did you rip me out after our last fight, hating me for what I'd said? Questions circled like vultures, swooping down to claw through her grief. She shoved the torn photo into the journal and clapped it shut. Locating the headache tablets, she swallowed two, then changed into a cotton dress, and left the hostel.

*

The anger was coiled tight and muscular in her stomach as she strode to Mick's front door, the whitewashed walls dazzling her in the midday sunlight. She rang the bell and waited, exactly as Mia had done six months earlier.

When the door opened, she was prepared for Mick not to recognize her or to dismiss her with a weak apology. What she wasn't prepared for was the way his whole face broke into a wide smile. 'Katie!'

She remembered his voice. It was rich and deep and he let the second syllable of 'Katie' float away from his lips, which made her name sound special. She searched his face for features she could recall from her childhood and found another memory in the roundness of his chin and the hazel of his eyes. He looked older than she would have imagined, the years etched in the heavy lines across his forehead and the loss of shape to his lips, now just thin lines.

'You are so beautiful.' He smiled, shaking his head. 'So like her.' For a moment she imagined he meant Mia and her anger softened as she wondered what he saw between them. Katie had given up wearing make-up since being abroad, and her hair was unstyled and hung loosely around her face. He reached a hand towards it: 'Your mother's colour exactly.'

She flinched.

His hand dropped to his side.

Eventually she said, 'Can I come in?'

'Yes, of course.' He stepped back, allowing her space as she passed, but his gaze followed her closely as she moved along the hallway, her sandals making hard clicks on the flagstoned floor.

In the kitchen a fresh bacon sandwich, half eaten, was cooling on a plate, the sweet meaty aroma filling the room. Katie positioned herself by the sink, with her arms folded over her chest. She felt the cool stainless steel through her dress.

Mick stood opposite. He was wearing a pair of beige summer trousers and a casual cotton shirt that had creased around his middle. It was hard to place him as the young man who had spun their mother across the red-tiled floor of their kitchen. 'I was so sorry to hear about Mia's death. It was tragic, desperately tragic,' he said emphatically. 'I understand how difficult it must be for you—'

'You can't possibly.'

'I just meant that having—'

'You didn't come to her funeral.' She had been undecided about letting Mick know about Mia's death. Their mother hadn't wanted him to be told when she passed away, but Ed argued that this was different: Mia was his daughter. Katie eventually agreed and got in contact with the last company Mick had owned, who were able to provide a current number for him. She had called and left a brief message on an answering machine explaining what had happened. She didn't know whether he'd get the message and wasn't sure she cared.

'I am sorry, but it didn't feel appropriate,' he said. 'The flowers reached you?'

'Yes.' The morning of the funeral, an extravagant bunch of calla lilies arrived with a card. It was the first written word she had received from Mick in two decades. The card had said, '*Losing the two people you love most in the world is almost unbearable. My heart goes out to you.*' She had got rid of the flowers, snapping the thick stems in half so they'd fit in the plastic cylinder of her bin.

Her thoughts snagged on another flower sent in tribute: the single orchid that came with a card reading, '*Sorry.*' She still had no idea who it was from and found it an odd message, more apology than condolence. Ed had photographed the flower on his phone, saying he'd show it to his mother – a keen gardener – who might be able to identify it. Katie pulled her thoughts back to Mick. There were many things she needed to say and, walking here, she'd ordered them into key questions as she did when interviewing a candidate, beginning by making the interviewee comfortable and then building up to the pertinent, revealing questions.

As she opened her mouth to begin, Mick said, 'Let me make us both a drink. What would you like? Something cold?'

She wanted to say no but her throat felt dry and papery. 'Water.'

He fetched two glasses and a jug from the fridge and poured their drinks, sunlight catching in the stream of water. He handed her a glass, suggesting they take them onto the deck. She refused. The gesture was too similar to the one he'd made to Mia; instead, she took a quick drink and then set the glass behind her on the draining board.

'I did wonder if I might hear from you sooner . . . after Mia's visit.'

She wouldn't admit that she had only learnt about it yesterday, so she said nothing.

'I'm sorry if it was a shock.'

'I was shocked at how you treated her.' Katie's anger was beginning to uncoil, hot and swift. She grasped it. 'Mia travelled thousands of miles to see you. She deserved more of a welcome.'

'She took me completely by surprise.' His palms opened to the ceiling, 'I didn't even recognize her—'

'I heard.'

'I would have liked things to have been different—'

'I'm sure Mia would have, too.'

Mick nodded, his head lowered. She saw tiny beads of sweat clustered at his hairline.

She was rushing, tripping him up before he'd had a chance to speak. She must slow down and focus on what Mia had come to Maui to find out: who their father was. In order to do that, Katie needed a question answered for herself. 'Mick,' she said, her voice softening a note to draw him into her question. 'What happened to Mia the night you left us?'

His head tilted to one side, an eyebrow raised. 'Your mother never told you?'

'No.'

'But you remember the evening?'

'I remember Mia had an accident. I remember you were looking after her.'

He patted his hands against the pockets of his trousers, looking for something – a cigarette, she guessed – and seemed agitated when he couldn't find it. He moved to the glass dining table at the edge of the kitchen and pulled out a chair and sat heavily. He interlocked his hands and rested them on the table. When he spoke, he focused on the space between his arms, which made his head hang – a man already defeated. 'You need to know what happened that night? How I could have left? How I could have stayed away all these years? I'll tell you – it's right that you should know. But first, you need to understand that it's never as simple as one event, one person, one decision.'

She waited.

'I never wanted to be a father.' He looked up to gauge her reaction, but she gave none, so he continued. 'I enjoyed my life too much to give it all up. When Grace fell pregnant with you, I think she believed she could change me. Maybe I hoped she could, too.' He glanced beyond the French doors at the sound of a lawnmower firing up.

'The night of the accident, your mother and I had argued over Mia. I'd been away a lot – you know I was in music?'

'Yes.'

'Sometimes I used my work as an excuse to get away. I didn't spend enough time with you or Mia.' He scratched the back of his neck. 'Particularly, Mia.'

It seemed an odd remark, but Katie linked her hands together and let him continue.

'Your mother had arranged for me to look after Mia – the two of you were off on a trip somewhere.'

'Ballet,' she said. 'We went to the ballet.'

'That's right. Your mother and I fought before she left, and Mia – God, she always seemed so sensitive to anything like that – screamed from the moment the front door closed. Maybe you'll think me ridiculous, but it was as if she knew, just knew, that I didn't want to be there.' He picked up his glass and took a drink.

'What happened?'

'I couldn't stop her crying. I tried holding her, giving her a bottle, reading to her. Nothing worked. I thought I'd leave her for a few minutes, see if she'd settle herself. So I got a whisky and took it down to the bottom of the garden. It was the only place I could hear myself think.'

She watched as he found a forgotten cigarette in his shirt pocket and lit it hastily, a tremor noticeable in his fingers. He drew in a breath and then moved to the French doors, opening them and exhaling outside.

'I will never know how she managed it – God, she was only two! – but Mia somehow got herself out of that cot. I hadn't closed the back door and she found her way into the garden. I'm ashamed to admit, one glass of whisky had turned into more. I didn't even notice her.' He shook his head. 'At the old house, you might remember, you could walk alongside it out onto the street.'

Katie nodded.

'That's what Mia did. I've no idea why. Maybe she was trying to follow the direction of your mother's car. Who knows?'

Katie hadn't heard any of this before. Her palms felt damp. She couldn't shake her sisterly concern for Mia's safety – even though the worst had already happened. She unlocked her hands and pressed them against her thighs.

'There was a motorcyclist, a guy who turned out to be the husband of your mother's dentist – something like that. The police said he was going fast. He wouldn't have seen her until the last moment. He swerved. Came off his bike. As the bike spun free it glanced off Mia.'

She squeezed her eyes shut, remembering her sister in the hospital bed, white gauze taped across the gash in her temple, which would later scar into a silver crescent.

'The police came to the house.' He put out the cigarette on the door frame and flicked the stub onto the deck, pushing it between a gap in two boards with his heel. 'It was very sobering. I felt . . . well, it's difficult to describe how you feel when you know that you've put a child's life at risk. The guilt is immense.'

The smell of the cooked bacon had lost the fullness of flavour and gone sour, greasy. Katie's stomach turned.

'The police took me to the hospital, but I couldn't face going into Mia's room. I watched from the corridor when you and your mother arrived.' He closed his eyes, as if drifting back to the memory. 'You both pinned yourselves to Mia's side, squeezing onto her bed. You held her hand the whole time.'

Katie remembered that now. There was a tiny needle going into the fine skin on the back of Mia's hand. She'd had to hold her fingers very carefully so as not to knock it.

'When your mother came into the corridor to speak to me – even before she'd said a word – I knew it was over.' He shoved his hands in his pockets. 'She had been a generous wife to me; she'd forgiven so much in the past. I think, in time, she might even have forgiven the accident. What she couldn't forgive, though, was that I didn't go to Mia's bedside. She said, and I will always remember this, "If it had been Katie in that hospital bed, you would have been with her."'

From the doorway, Mick looked directly at her. 'She was right.'

Katie brought a hand to her mouth, astonished. He had voiced a suspicion of favouritism that she'd harboured even as a child, sensing a lack of love in the blurred memories of how he had treated Mia. She remembered that he would let Katie sit with him to watch cricket, while Mia was always kept at a distance. He would occasionally laugh with Katie if she judged his mood right, but Mia's gurgles and smiles couldn't draw any warmth. She recalled her mother, so protective of Mia, threading her arms around her and telling her how loved she was, as if there was some doubt.

'That's a terrible thing to say.'

He ran the back of his hand along his forehead, wiping away the moisture. 'Perhaps a better man would have overcome his jealousies. I was desperate to love you both equally, I truly was,' he implored. 'But I could never get past the fact that Mia wasn't mine.'

Her world slowed down to contain only his last words: *Mia wasn't mine.*

*

The blood drained from Katie's face and her legs felt weak. She gripped the edges of the sink behind her. 'I don't under—' but she did understand. She saw it all clearly now. 'You are not Mia's father.'

The surprise was his, too. 'I thought you knew?'

She shook her head.

'But you . . . you said Mia had told you about her visit?'

'I read it. Her journal. She wrote that she came here – you sent her away.'

His eyes widened. 'She came back – it was a few days later.' He put both hands behind his neck. 'Jesus! I can't believe you didn't know.' He paced onto the deck, then turned back towards the doorway as if unsure where to anchor himself. 'When Mia came here the second time she was angry. She wanted answers. I either had to shut the door on her again, or give them to her.'

A wave of nausea swirled in Katie's stomach. She spun to face the sink and took slow breaths through her nose. Somewhere within the house the shrill ringing of a phone began. Neither of them moved. When the phone stopped she turned to face him. 'Am I your daughter?'

'Yes,' he answered. 'You are.'

The truth tasted bitter. She imagined Mia learning this, the discovery shattering the foundations of her family. Katie despised Mick suddenly – couldn't bear to be near him. Her chest felt tight. She needed space to think.

'I am sorry for all of this,' he offered, and she could see that he was.

She left the kitchen and moved along the hallway, eager to leave.

'Katie—'

She paused, but didn't turn.

His voice was tentative as he asked, 'Will I see you again?'

131

She turned then and looked at him. He was no longer the exuberant but aloof presence from her childhood memories; he was a man approaching sixty who had been absent for most of her life. Katie had done her growing up with a mother and sister she adored. He was too late. She shook her head.

Mick sucked in his lips, nodding.

All that mattered to her now was understanding how Mia had felt. She pushed through the front door and, by the time she reached the driveway, she was running.

She ran as swiftly as she could in the direction of the hostel. She passed a woman walking two grey dogs on bright red leads, a surf shop where boards stood in a rack waiting to be hired, a tourist speaking into a payphone in a language she didn't recognize. The heat engulfed her as she ran, turning her feet damp in her sandals and making her dress cling against her thighs. Eventually she reached the hostel and burst into her dorm, ignoring a young man talking into a headset on his laptop.

She yanked Mia's journal from the backpack and set it on her bunk. She flicked to the page she'd read up to this morning and pushed aside the ripped photo – Mia, with Katie no longer in the same frame. She kept turning the pages, skimming over a dinner Mia had with Finn, and past a visit to the airport when they couldn't afford to change their tickets, and then onto a small sentence that had been circled: '*I need to see him again.*'

Katie turned the page slowly, her heart in her mouth. This could change everything. This truth Mia was about to learn would rock even the strongest person. But if that person was already vulnerable, had already lost her mother, and felt things so deeply you could read her heart on her face, would this be enough to trigger a downwards spiral that took her so low, it seemed there was no way out?

10

MIA

Maui, October Last Year

M ia felt as if the room were filled with water and she was sinking, breathless. Her vision darkened. She tried to suck in air but all she swallowed were Mick's words: *You are not my daughter.*

Half an hour earlier she had been eating French toast at a breakfast bar with Finn and talking about their plans for Australia. Mid-sentence, Mia stopped short. Across the street she had seen Mick. He was carrying a box of groceries and had paused to talk to a man with a thinning ponytail. Mick said something, the other man laughed, and then they walked on separately. She watched him cross the road and return in the direction of his house.

Finn, who had followed her gaze, asked, 'Is that him?'

'Yes.'

'You should speak to him.' She was surprised by the firmness in his tone and when she turned, she saw his jaw was set.

'I can't.'

'I will, then,' he said, standing.

'What are you doing?'

'The guy is an arsehole, Mia. You've travelled all this way.'

'Finn, don't,' she said, her hand on his arm.

He looked at her for a long moment. Then his face softened. 'Sorry, it's not my place. I just hate seeing you upset.'

After visiting Mick four days ago, Mia kept catching herself in imagined conversations, airing all the things she wished she'd said. She owed it to herself to stop imagining and act. 'You're right. I do need to talk to him.'

Leaving her knife and fork splayed on her plate, she said, 'I'll meet you back at the hostel.'

She jogged lightly to Mick's house with the sun prickling at the back of her neck. When she arrived, she ignored the bell and rapped three times on the front door. A moment later, Mick answered, holding a punnet of tomatoes.

'Mia.' He didn't look surprised to see her, more resigned as if he was about to undertake a task he'd hoped to avoid. 'I think we need to talk.'

They had moved through to the kitchen where the box of groceries waited on the counter beside a packet of pasta and two courgettes. Mick put down the tomatoes and faced her.

This time, Mia did not lose her voice. It was strong and level as she said, 'I want you to know that I haven't come to Maui to ask you to be a father to me – I've come here to understand why you left. I deserve that, at least.'

'You do.' He looked at her closely. 'I'm only afraid you won't like the answer.'

She waited.

'Perhaps we should sit down.'

'What is it?' she said, not moving an inch.

Mick squeezed the bridge of his nose. 'I am sorry, Mia, but you are not my daughter.'

And that was how it came out.

'Here,' Mick said, taking her by the elbow, 'you need air.' He led her onto the decking and helped her into a chair. She bent forwards, putting her head between her knees. Mick opened the parasol in the centre of the table, casting her into shade.

He fetched a glass of water and placed it in front of her. She sat up slowly and lifted it to her lips.

Mick pulled out a chair opposite.

'Katie?' Her voice was small. She had lost the thunder and conviction of earlier.

He nodded. 'She's mine.'

Katie was his. She wasn't. Mick stood between them like an impossible divide.

'I had always thought your mother would have told you.'

Of course her mother had known. How could she have kept this from her?

'When you came here a few days ago,' Mick said, shaking his head, 'I was staggered you thought I was your father.'

She remembered his shock when she announced, 'I'm Mia. Your daughter.'

'I feel terrible for asking you to leave. I'd convinced myself that it wasn't my place to tell you the truth when Grace hadn't. Pathetic, I know.'

She wished she hadn't come here, wished she hadn't flown to Maui. But it was too late to rewind now. She had no choice but to go forward. 'Who is he?'

Mick crossed his legs and set his hands in his lap. 'His name was Harley.'

'But you and Mum were married . . .'

'Yes.'

'She had an affair?'

'Yes.'

Mia would never have expected that. 'Did you know?'

'Not until later,' he answered. Then he added, 'Although perhaps I always suspected.'

She looked beyond Mick, out to sea. A light breeze made ripples across the water that glittered in the sunlight.

'Your father was a musician,' he offered. 'The front man of a band I managed, the Black Ewe.'

She straightened, remembering the photo she found in her mother's belongings – Mick alongside a band called the Black Ewe. On the reverse, her mother had written the names of the men: '*Harley*' had been written in the centre, beside '*Mick*'. She pictured the man with the black hair who stared intently at the camera. Or, as she now realized, at the person holding it.

'You knew him, then. You were . . . friends?'

'He was my brother.'

Her skin grew hot.

'We both met your mother on the same night, after a gig. We were at the bar when she was introduced to us. I happened to offer her a drink first – and it was me, six months later, who married her.' He shrugged. 'But as it turned out, Harley was in love with her too.'

'How did the affair start?'

'Distraction and disillusion, I imagine. I was distracted by my career and Grace was disillusioned by her husband.' He lit a cigarette and took a long draw, the ember glowing red. 'Mia, back then I was a different person. When the Black Ewe took off, I was so fired up about the music and about success, family life took a back seat. I booked tour after tour and was out of the country more often than I was in it. Grace got left at home with a young baby. I think she knew my lifestyle on the road wasn't entirely savoury – there were drugs and plenty of booze, and other women too.'

'So she turned to Harley?'

'Yes. I didn't blame them for the affair. I hadn't been a good husband. Or brother.'

'Did he love her?'

'Very much,' he answered without hesitating. 'But his love was too intense, obsessive almost. Grace's feelings could never match his and I think the ferocity of his love scared her.'

Mick lifted the cigarette to his lips again and Mia shifted to avoid the drift of smoke. She levelled her gaze at the water, noticing white caps forming on the tips of waves. 'When Mum was pregnant with me . . . did you know that the baby wasn't yours?'

'Yes, but Harley didn't.' He tapped the ash from his cigarette. 'Grace said she'd end the affair and come back to me if I could accept Harley's baby as my own. I thought of the alternative:

her leaving me for him. Jealousy and pride are powerful emotions. I dropped the Black Ewe from my label, cut Harley out of our lives, and stayed.'

She wondered how her life might have been altered by that one decision.

'It was so much harder than I expected. You were a constant reminder of what had happened between Grace and Harley. You were just a tiny baby – none of this was your fault – but every time I looked at you, I saw him.' He stared at her closely. 'You're so much like him. God, your eyes! I should have seen it the instant you arrived. His were the same emerald green. Your mother always said how unusual Harley's eyes were. You have his hair, too, but your mother's smile.'

'You left because of me?'

'I realized that I would never be a good father to you. So, yes, I left.' He held the memory of what that end point was in his gaze, but chose not to share it and Mia did not ask.

He stubbed out his cigarette.

Mick had left Katie and her mother because he didn't love her enough. She felt as if she'd been tossed around in the ocean, buffeted by waves until she was exhausted and weak. She was desperate to leave but there was still one more thing she needed to know.

'Harley,' she said, the name feeling alien on her tongue. 'Do you know where he is now?'

'Sorry, Mia, but he died a long time ago.'

It was just another fact in a sea of things she'd discovered today. There was too much to feel – she knew there'd be plenty of time when she would feel all of this acutely. For now, she let it wash through her and asked, 'When?'

'Years back – he was twenty-four.'

Her eyebrows rose at that. 'So young. What happened?'

'It was such a long time ago,' he said, as if that would be enough.

'What happened to him?' she repeated.

'I'm sorry, Mia.'

A needling of anxiety began at her brow. 'I need to know.'

He sighed. 'My brother was complex. He had so much talent. He was a phenomenal songwriter – a poet, really. I've never heard lyrics that touch his. His fans saw this wild, irrepressible man on stage launching himself into the crowd or dancing like he was possessed – but none of them knew how much he had to drink before he came on.' The breeze toyed with the edge of the parasol and blew a dusting of ash across the table. Mick brushed it away, smudging grey streaks into the wood.

'Harley wasn't always an easy person to get on with. He was very up and down. Things that washed off other people's backs, ate Harley up. He thought deeply about everything. It made him insular sometimes, and he could go for days without speaking to anyone. Other times he was wild, completely out of control.' Mick paused; thought for a moment. 'If I'm honest, I'm not sure he ever truly liked himself.'

Mia felt a shiver travel along the nape of her neck: in a handful of sentences Mick had described her.

'After Grace, he lost sight of everything, even his music. The band split up, I was gone, and he drained his money on booze and drugs. In a matter of months, he'd lost it all. He was a wreck.' He sighed. 'We were close, once. He was an astounding musician, but fronting a band never suited him. It was me that pushed him to do it. I had the business brain but not the talent. And I resented him for that.'

Mick wiped at a streak of ash he'd missed. 'I knew him better than anyone, so I understood exactly how hard it would have been for him after Grace. I heard he was feeling low, but I never called him.' Mick looked past Mia as if she were no longer there and he was alone with his memories. 'I was his brother. I knew how deeply he felt things.' His eyes were glassy. 'It was my responsibility to look after him, but my pride got in the way. I'll always be sorry for that.'

'What happened?' she asked, nervous now.

He looked at her and she saw the sadness in his face. 'Harley was found dead in a hotel room.' His voice didn't hold as he said, 'He hanged himself.'

*

Dazed, Mia returned the way she had come, but everything had changed.

She wasn't Mick's daughter.

Her father had committed suicide.

Her mother had kept it a secret.

Katie was her half-sister.

The sun blazed down against the crown of her head as she hurried along the pavement with her eyes to the ground. Her breathing was ragged and she could hear the blood pounding in her ears. Everything she believed had been a lie.

She had to call Katie. She needed to hear her voice. There was a payphone near the edge of town and she began to jog to it. Her legs felt disconnected from her brain. She ducked around two teenagers slurping milkshakes, then crossed the road, barely glancing to check the traffic.

The front edge of her flip-flop caught on a crack in the concrete and she stumbled forward, stubbing her toes. She bent and snatched off both flip-flops and, clutching them in one hand, she ran, the pavement rough and hot beneath her feet.

When she reached the payphone, she pulled her credit card from her wallet. *Speak to Katie. Tell her everything.* She lifted the receiver and slid the credit card into the slot.

She heard the dialling tone and screwed her eyes tightly shut, trying to remember the international code for the UK. When it came to her, she stabbed in the numbers with trembling hands.

A few seconds later, Katie answered. 'Hello?' The line crackled and fizzed, and Katie's voice sounded distant, as though the two of them were already separated.

Half-sisters.

Half.

She hated the term being applied to her and Katie, as it nailed a divide between her and all that remained of her family.

She wanted to let the tears that were damming her throat flood free. She wanted to hear her sister, who would be both pragmatic and loving, tell her she would be okay, that she loved her. But spiky doubts crept into her thoughts. Might Katie love her just a fraction less? Hadn't she always noticed how different Mia was from her? Wasn't Mia the reason why Mick had left?

'Hello?' Katie repeated.

Mia clamped her teeth over the words she couldn't say and placed the phone lightly back in the receiver. She couldn't tell her.

Mia had needed to come to Maui to find out if she was a reflection of her father. And now she would have to live with what she'd discovered.

11

KATIE

Western Australia, May

The heat was inescapable and the flies ferocious, yet there was a rugged beauty in the vast, barren landscape of Western Australia. Katie had spent a month riding the backpacker bus south, following the entries in Mia's journal. The endless stretches of flat, scrub-lined road became a kind of comfort as she rested her head against the bus's sun-warmed window and was lulled and rocked into mindless oblivion.

Now she had reached Lancelin, a small coastal town north of Perth where crayfish boats docked at the jetty each afternoon to unload their catch. She lay beside a concrete pool in the shade of a sun umbrella, the journal open in front of her. It was before ten but already the heat was fierce, the wind having not yet arrived.

She glanced up as a plane cut a sharp line through the cloudless blue sky. It left behind a trail of white vapour, which she watched until it gently feathered away. Mia had once told her that jet trails were clouds that had been inhaled by a plane, then expired in a long white whoosh. Katie hadn't corrected her. She was intrigued by the magical places Mia's imagination wandered to and thought if she followed closely enough, she might glimpse those places, too.

Half-sisters, she mused. Could you only be *half* when your *whole* lives were inextricably linked?

She pushed a loose strand of hair away from her face, thinking how she minded the term. She and Mia had always been very different – but now those differences had been given a label: half-sisters. She wished Mia was here to talk to. She wanted to be back in their flat, curled into opposite corners of the sofa, talking with mugs of tea in their hands. Together they'd have been able to make sense of it, perhaps eventually have laughed about it. But Mia was gone and learning this now only stretched them further apart.

Tracing a finger over a sentence in the journal, Katie tried to feel the indentations of Mia's words. Her entries no longer sparkled with descriptions of places she'd travelled to, the way they once had in California; now they simmered with a quiet fury. Her anger was initially directed at their mother for concealing the truth about Harley. The moral code she'd taught her daughters had been grounded in truth and honesty, so her transgression from these rules cheated Mia of her beliefs.

More concerning, though, were Mia's later entries, which showed a growing fixation with Harley. The page in front of Katie now was a transcription of song lyrics Mia had found on an obscure internet site, and she'd circled words and verses to find a connection to a father she'd never known. The adjoining page was dotted with questions: *'What was he like?' 'Who did he care about?'* '*Where did he think of as home?'* It seemed to Katie that the unwritten question around which the others orbited, was: *Am I like him?* Harley had committed suicide at the age of twenty-four: Mia's age. That cold fact must have torn at Mia's thoughts, just as it tore at Katie's. She tried not to pay attention to the voice in her head that whispered of history repeating itself, but she couldn't deny the disturbing symmetry.

There was a sudden rushing of feet over concrete and then she felt cold fingers gripping her waist. She cried out as she was lifted up, the journal slipping through her fingers and landing with its pages splayed on the poolside, like a hastily erected tent.

She heard Ed's laughter, loud and close to her ear, as he held her against his wet body and began jogging away from the pool towards the beach. Sand flicked up as he ran, stinging her dangling legs. His grip was too tight, his wrist bone pressing painfully against her thighs. Her bikini top had become twisted and she could see the dark pink edge of her nipple exposed in the harsh light.

The shore was only feet away and she kicked and swivelled in his grasp, which made Ed laugh harder, delighted by her resistance. He waded into the sea and the smell of salt stole her breath. Water splashed and slapped at her skin. Suddenly she was flipped backwards and the world swivelled. Glaring sunlight seared off the water and she blinked, disorientated. The ends of her hair brushed the sea.

'Please, Ed!' she whispered, choked by fear.

Ahead, a hurdle of white-water rushed towards them, water popping and spraying, salt fizzing in her nostrils. She screwed her eyes shut, waiting for the smack of water against her face and the briny taste of the sea to fill her mouth. Then, in a swift movement, Ed flung her upright. He delivered her back to shore, placing her gently on the sand.

She gulped in air with a hand pressed to her chest.

'Katie?' he said, turning to her. 'Are you okay? You knew I was joking, didn't you?'

She nodded without looking at him so he couldn't see the tears in her eyes. She'd never told him she was afraid of the sea.

He placed a wet hand on her shoulder, squeezing it lightly. 'Sorry. I couldn't resist. You looked so gorgeous and serene lying by the pool. I wanted to steal you.'

'It's fine,' she said. 'You took me by surprise, that's all.'

Ed had arrived in Australia five days ago, having managed to take a fortnight off work. She had met him at Perth Airport where he hugged her so enthusiastically he'd lifted her off her feet.

'Shall we go for a stroll to dry off?' he asked.

She glanced at him: water dripped down his face and his eyes were bright and hopeful. He would be pleased if she walked with him; they needed occasional moments of lightness in order to sustain them. But she knew Mia's journal was still lying care-lessly on the poolside. She imagined grit sinking into the folds of each page, the sun bleaching the colour from the jacket.

'I might go for a shower,' she said with a light smile. Then she walked back to the pool and carefully gathered up the journal, dipping her mouth low to it and blowing the grit from its pages.

*

Katie wrapped herself in a soft cream towel and then wiped her palm in a circle over the steamed mirror. She peered at her damp face. The bridge of her nose was dotted with sun freckles but there was a gauntness to her cheeks and beneath her eyes that the sun couldn't brighten. Since Ed had arrived she'd taken to applying make-up again, but found the routine had lost some of its reward.

'Darling?' He was stretched out on the bed, a newspaper discarded at his side, one bare ankle crossing the other.

They were staying in a hotel, not the modest backpacker lodge Mia had written about. Katie had taken Ed there on his first night but, exhausted from jet lag, he hadn't appreciated the strumming of a guitar drifting from the adjacent dorm until two in the morning.

'Come over here.'

She crossed the room and perched beside him. There was a pair of foam earplugs on the bedside table. 'Did you hear the other guests?'

'I'm not certain there are other guests,' he said with a raised eyebrow. 'Those are for the sea. The waves are incessant.'

The sea? 'In London you fall asleep to a cacophony of traffic.'

'Ah, the melodic sounds of the city.' He smiled at her. 'Talking of London, you know your friends want me to bring you home with me? Everyone's worried about you.'

'They don't need to be.'

'Don't they?'

'No,' she said, running her fingers through her wet hair. 'I'm fine.' She could imagine them saying how out of character she was behaving – but Katie didn't care. She needed to be here.

'I've been meaning to ask: you remember at Mia's funeral someone sent that orchid? Did you show the photo you took to your mother?'

The bed creaked as he sat up. 'Yes. She looked it up. She thinks it's a moon orchid.'

'Moon orchid,' Katie repeated slowly. 'Does she know anything about them?'

'They originated in the tropics,' he said, then looked away.

'What is it? Did she say something else?'

'I don't see this as important,' he said with a sigh, 'but the moon orchid is the national flower of Bali.'

She blinked, surprised. 'Bali?'

'Yes.'

She rubbed a finger over her lower lip. 'Don't you think it's strange that someone would choose that particular flower?'

'Not really. They probably just liked the look of it, didn't know its history.'

'But why send it anonymously? Why write, "*Sorry*"?'

He opened his palms. 'I don't know. Perhaps they did it through a florist and only part of the message was transcribed.'

'Maybe,' Katie said, although she couldn't help wondering if there was some relevance to it, or what it was they were apologizing for.

'Why don't you lie down?' Ed said, making room for her on the bed.

She lay back, her wet hair dampening the pillow.

Ed propped himself up on an elbow and studied her. 'I can't believe that in three months we'll be married.'

She smiled, but the remark produced an anxiety in Katie that she wouldn't allow herself to dwell on.

He traced the line of her collarbone with a forefinger. 'Mrs Katie Louth,' he said to himself as if trying it out for size. 'Very sexy.'

'I haven't decided if I'll take your name.'

He arched one eyebrow. 'Is that right?'

'I just want to give it some thought. Not everyone takes their husband's name.'

'Don't tell me you want one of those awful double-barrelled surnames? Greene-Louth sounds like an STD.'

She laughed. 'No, not double-barrelled, then!'

He looked at her closely. 'You're the last Greene, aren't you?'

She nodded, feeling a rise of emotion in her throat.

'Then you should keep your name. I don't need you to take mine. Knowing I get to take you to bed every night for the rest of my life is all I'm interested in.' He untucked the corner of the damp towel and unwrapped her as though she was a gift. He placed his mouth on her neck and kissed her slowly. His lips were warm and she wanted him to put his arms round her and stay close, holding her to him.

His mouth travelled downwards, moving over her collarbone, kissing a pathway to her breasts, his tongue reaching her nipples. Katie held herself still as his tongue trailed over her ribcage and the softness of her stomach, skirting her navel and flicking over her hips. She closed her eyes and tried to relax, focusing on the sensation of Ed's touch. Before Mia's death their lovemaking had been frequent and passionate, but now she felt no desire.

His mouth grazed the top of her pubic bone.

'Ed.'

He murmured from beneath the sheet as his lips moved lower.

'I should get dressed,' she said, squirming out of reach. 'We need to leave soon.'

He snapped back the covers and got out of bed. He moved to the desk, pulled out a chair and opened his laptop.

She dressed with her back to him. They were visiting the Slade Plains where Mia and Finn had gone skydiving six months before. Although Katie had no intention of jumping herself, she wanted to see the place where her sister felt brave enough to plummet through the sky with only a parachute as her lifeline.

She was back in the routine of trying to limit herself to reading only one of Mia's entries a day, which gave her trip a structure and a sense of purpose. With each page, her under-standing of Mia's travels deepened. The journal had become her companion, unfalteringly honest and faithfully at her side.

Once dressed, Katie turned to Ed, who was still absorbed in his laptop. 'We need to leave now if we want to make the bus.'

'I'll pass,' he said without looking up.

'You said you'd come with me.'

'I just don't feel inclined to traipse out to the desert to watch a bunch of adrenalin junkies throw themselves from a plane.' He pushed his chair back. 'I'd much rather spend the afternoon drinking wine at a nice restaurant with my fiancée.'

'I have to do this. It's in the journal.'

'Don't you hear how ridiculous that sounds? It's a fucking journal! Not a rule book.'

'I know it's not a rule book. I *want* to go there,' she said, her tone rising to the challenge of his. 'Don't belittle what I'm doing, Ed. It's important to me.' She grabbed her bag from the bedside table and, as she did, she found her fingers closing round his earplugs. She slipped them into her pocket. *He can damn well listen to the sea!*

As she reached the door, he said, 'I just don't see why anyone would pay to fling themselves from a plane. It's unnatural and goes against every human instinct.'

'That's what I want to understand.'

*

Katie had watched the safety video, signed the disclaimer and been fitted into a blue jumpsuit that was faded and fraying at the knees. She now sat at the back of a six-seater plane with a complicated harness fastened around her middle. Anger or adrenalin had propelled her this far, but now she regretted it. Her entire body trembled and her breathing felt too shallow. She was terrified simply sitting in this plane: jumping from it was unthinkable.

The pilot shouted something and then an instructor moved over to the doorway, unhooked a latch and yanked the door open.

Katie gasped. The noise was incredible, as thunderous as if they'd dived into a breaking wave. The rush of cool air set every nerve ending on edge. She fought to tie her hair back, which was whipping across her face.

In front of her a thin man with acne scars stood while his instructor attached himself to the man's harness, checking and rechecking buckles and straps. The pair moved towards the open door, shuffling like prisoners in their jumpsuits. She glanced away for a second, and when she looked back they'd vanished.

She felt a firm tap on her shoulder. 'Your turn,' shouted her jumpmaster, a young man with tight blond curls and crooked front teeth.

'I'm not jumping.'

He began manoeuvring her, strapping himself to the back of her, pulling hard on each buckle to check it was completely secure.

He'd not heard her above the noise. 'I'm not jumping!' she shouted.

'You don't like dumplings?' he shouted back with a grin, then pulled her goggles down over her eyes. He was teasing her, of course. But then he started moving towards the plane door.

'No!' she said, spreading her arms. 'I'm! Not! Jumping!'

'Your choice. But I want you to see the view before deciding.'

She could feel her pulse racing. She took a deep breath and told herself she could do this. She nodded to the jumpmaster. 'I'll look.'

'We're going to sit,' he said and she obeyed, sitting between his legs, and then together they shimmied along the plane floor towards the doorway. The wind became fiercer, blowing away words, thoughts, breath.

'Put your arm on the handle,' he shouted. 'It's safer.'

She reached for the handle and braced herself. The noise! Her heart drilled at her chest. Below lay a grid of scorched fields, the sea shimmering in the distance.

'See that step on the wheel strut? I'm going to put my right foot on it, and then I want you to do the same.'

She shook her head. 'I can't.'

Very close to her ear, as if his voice was coming from inside her, he said, 'Yes, you can.'

Could she? This wasn't her, jumping from planes. But there was a thrill in stepping so far outside of herself. *What would Ed think if he saw me now?* She felt a heady sense of defiance and, very slowly, she stretched her foot to reach the wing strut. The trouser leg of her jumpsuit flapped furiously in the wind and goose bumps spread across her body.

'You want to do this?' he shouted.

'I don't know! I don't know!'

'Cross your arms over your chest.'

She did as he said, feeling as if she were making a prayer of her body. Then she felt him leaning forward to grab an upper handle. Her hairband was snatched by the wind and her hair whipped in front of her goggles.

'No! No!' Panic was thick and acidic in her stomach. Every muscle in her body was clenched tight, arching away from the open exit.

Then she was aware of him leaning further forward so her whole body was suspended beneath him.

He let go.

Her mouth opened with the utter shock of the freefall, and the insides of her lips turned as dry as the earth below. She hurtled through cold air currents and wisps of clouds. Blood pounded in her ears.

A long, soundless scream burnt in her throat. She was petrified of the parachute failing, the lines getting tangled, an injury on landing – but mostly, Katie screamed because as she plummeted through the sky, she could imagine with horrifying clarity her sister's terror the moment her feet left that cliff top.

12

MIA

Western Australia, November Last Year

The soles of Mia's feet peeled away from the edge and she fell. Her ears were awash with the roar of the wind, the flap of her clothes, the pounding of her heart. Cold air rushed into her mouth, which had opened into a perfect 'O'. The sharp pump of adrenalin was so fierce that it seemed as if only getting this close to death had made life start to pulse deep in her veins.

There was a sudden, rough yank and she felt as if she were being hauled upwards. She heard the canopy of her yellow parachute fill with air as it opened like a buttercup blooming.

She took a short, hard gasp of air.

'Okay?' shouted her jumpmaster, who was harnessed to her back.

Her cheekbones hurt from the press of the goggles, and the feeling of weightlessness had vanished as the nylon straps of her harness dug into her upper thighs and waist. 'Yes,' she answered finally. 'I'm okay.' And then she started to laugh. The sound bubbled from her mouth and was grasped by the wind. Her smile stretched so wide that wind slipped beneath her goggles, making her eyes water. Her whole body shook with delight as they glided towards the ground.

Below, a crimson chute carried Finn. He had jumped first, snapping on his goggles, saluting, and then setting his feet squarely on the wing strut, ready. She had seen him leap from the plane with a grin and, after that, there was no hesitation: if Finn jumped, she would follow.

She made a quick prayer that he would land safely, and watched as his chute collapsed in a soft sweep of red, like a lung exhaling. She imagined him stepping free of his harness and shading the sun from his eyes as he searched the sky for her.

As they neared the ground, the jumpmaster reminded her of the landing instructions. She drew her knees towards her chest while he steered them into the final descent. The ground came up faster than she was expecting and they landed hard, a cloud of dust rising to greet them. The moment she was released from the harness, she raced over to Finn, pulling off her goggles.

His face was flushed and sweat dampened his hairline. He was grinning. 'How was it?'

'Incredible! I thought my stomach would drop away – like on fairground rides – but it felt like I was flying, not falling.' She threw her arms around him, feeling the heat of his body through the coarse jumpsuit. 'Thank you!' Skydiving had been a surprise that Finn had organized, only revealing it on the sweltering bus ride to the dive centre.

'You're welcome.'

'It was exactly what I needed.' And Finn knew that. A month ago he'd found her leaning against a payphone in Maui with her head in her hands. He had hooked his arm around her waist and led her back to the hostel, where he made her sweet tea and listened as she told him about Harley.

Travelling through Western Australia she'd felt like no more than a shadow at Finn's side, or a silent presence lying awake in their tent at night. He'd spent hours helping her trawl Internet sites searching for snippets of information about her father or giving her the space she needed to think – as if he knew what she needed before she knew herself. 'I've been crap to travel with, haven't I?'

'If you hadn't jumped, I'd have pushed you.'

She began to laugh, but suddenly there were tears running down her cheeks. 'Oh, God,' she said, turning away embarrassed.

'Mia?'

She wiped the back of her hand across her face, saying, 'I'm fine.' But the adrenalin rush had released something and the tears wouldn't stop.

'You know I'd never have pushed you. I'd have cut your lines instead – no witnesses that way.'

She was half laughing, half crying now. 'Sorry. Ignore me. My head's a mess.'

'You've had a lot going on.'

She shrugged.

'Come on, talk to me.'

She looked towards the sky, blinking to stem the tears. Her

fingers clenched into fists at her sides. 'It's so fucked up. Everything about it is fucked up.'

'Are we talking about Harley?'

She nodded, then pulled the sleeves of the jumpsuit over her hands. 'The whole reason I went to Maui was to find out what Mick's like. Understand who he is.' She paused. 'Maybe even see if I'm like him.'

'But instead you found out that he's not your dad. Harley is.'

She nodded again. 'Mum lied to us our whole lives. She didn't even tell us the truth when she knew she was dying. And I just keep thinking, *Why?*' She sniffed, dried her eyes with her sleeve. 'Maybe she didn't want us to know she'd had an affair, or that Katie and I are half-sisters. Or maybe,' she said, slower now, 'it was because she didn't want me to know that Harley was my dad.'

He waited.

'When Mick was describing him, I remember thinking, *It's like he's describing me*. It was surreal. There were so many similarities between us.'

Finn was listening intently, his head tilted towards her.

'But he hanged himself.' She swallowed. 'My dad hanged himself when he was my age.'

Another light aircraft took off in a cloud of red dust.

'Mia?'

Her voice was small, the anger dissipated. 'I'm so scared I'm like him.'

Finn stepped closer, forcing her to meet his eye. 'I'm going to tell you this once, so I want you to remember it.'

She held his gaze.

'You are not Harley. Or your mum. Or Katie. You, Mia Greene, are *you*.'

'But I'm not sure I know who that is.'

He slung his arm around her shoulder, smiling. 'I do.'

*

They returned to the hostel only to shower and change, and then left for the tavern. Finn struck out across the sand dunes, Mia following. 'It's a steak night for me,' he said, picturing a thick slab of meat with a blue-cheese sauce.

'I'm going cheeseburger with extra bacon.'

'Don't try and intimidate me.'

As the dunes ascended, Mia ran ahead, calling, 'Last one to the top buys the drinks!'

He bolted after her, sending thick sweeps of sand cascading behind him. He managed to hook his hand into the back pocket of her shorts and yank her back. She laughed, swatting at his arm, and finally broke free, taking the last few strides to the top.

As Finn drew level with her, he saw that the beach below was awash with people. Music blared from speakers planted on the back of a pickup truck, in front of which a crowd danced with their hands thrown in the air. A roaring beach fire glowed orange and people sat cross-legged in the sand playing bongos and didgeridoos. The air smelt of woodsmoke and marijuana.

'Want to take a look?' he asked.

They bounded down the dunes together, his trainers filling

with sand. At the bottom they threaded through a throng of people standing around a smoking barbeque. An old Bedford van was parked on the tideline, its full beam illuminating a handful of men bodysurfing the white-water rumbling into shore. They wandered deeper into the crowd, Mia rocking her hips to the rhythm of the music.

They paused by a flare-lit circle where a girl, painted silver, was spinning a hoop around her waist. She gracefully raised one arm and the hoop seemed to coil up, reaching the tips of her fingers. With a flick of her wrist she sent the hoop to the ground and skipped through it, then continued to twirl it round her waist like an orbit.

'She's incredible,' Mia said.

'This is porn for hippies,' Finn replied.

She laughed and linked her arm through his. Instantly, the heat from her grip surged through his body and his heart rate increased. 'Mia,' he said, leading her away from the densest section of crowd. 'I need to talk to you about something.' From the outset of this trip he'd wanted to tell her how he felt, but the right opportunity hadn't arisen. Since their talk this afternoon she'd seemed buoyant, light hearted again, and he sensed it was time.

'What is it?' she said, nudging him.

He took a deep breath. 'Do you remember when we were 16, we went to that Thaw gig at the Guildhall? You crowd surfed.'

Her eyes brightened. 'That was an amazing night! Whatever happened to that band?'

'When you came back through the crowd, you kissed me.'

'Did I?'

She stopped. He felt her arm slip free of his.

His heart was pounding. Had she anticipated what was coming? Had it been that obvious all along? He waited, his heart in his mouth.

When she said nothing, he glanced at her. Her eyes were wide, unblinking, and he followed the direction of her gaze. It was fixed on the man moving towards them. He was barefoot, wearing shorts and a dark T-shirt through which Finn could see the square set of his shoulders. The man stopped in front of them. 'Mia?'

She pressed a hand to her chest. 'Noah? My God! What are you doing here?'

'A big swell's moving in. A group of us are heading south for it.'

'I can't believe it's you,' she said, a smile spreading over her face.

'You're staying here?'

'We've been at the hostel for a few nights.'

Finn, having not been introduced, stretched out his hand. 'I'm Finn.' It was the first time Noah's gaze left Mia. They shook hands and Finn felt the powerful but easy grip of Noah's fingers. 'So how do you know each other?'

'We met in Maui,' Mia said, looking at her feet.

Maui? She had never mentioned him. Finn felt the excited apprehension of only moments ago ebb away and be replaced by a different kind of anxiety.

'You travelling north or south?' Noah asked him.

'South. We came down from Broome.'

'Hot up there. It'll get cooler as you drop.'

'You're from Australia?' Finn asked, noting the accent.

'South coast. Near Melbourne.'

'Right.'

When no one said anything more, Finn suggested, 'I guess we should be heading on to the tavern. Maybe see you later, Noah.'

'Do you mind if I catch you up?' Mia said suddenly.

What could he say? That he did mind? That the way her face lit up when she looked at Noah made him feel as though he'd been punched in the gut? He thought of the conversation he and Mia should be having, the one in which he would tell her that she was the most incredible woman he'd ever met; the one that would end with a kiss. 'Sure. I'll order your cheeseburger. Extra bacon, right?'

'Right.'

He watched as she and Noah moved off together, maintaining a couple of inches between them. Two bare-chested men burst from the crowd, hooting and spraying up sand with their feet. Instinctively, Noah put his arm around Mia, drawing her away from their path, exactly as Finn would have done – only then Noah's arm remained there.

*

Mia had not allowed her thoughts to wander too near the memory of the night they'd met, when she'd experienced an opening of something deep in her chest. But now, feeling Noah's arm around her waist, she allowed herself to remember: the gaze that held hers, the brush of his lips along her collarbone, the taste of salt on his skin.

Leaving the party in their wake, they moved wordlessly along the beach, listening to the fading base line of music. Moonlight illuminated the wind-ridged sand and she imagined that if she glanced over her shoulder, their two sets of footprints would be marked out like a pathway.

'I suppose you'll be wanting your jumper back?' she said with a small smile. She remembered how it had brushed the tops of her thighs as she'd padded back to the Pineapple Hostel at dawn, the scent of smoke and salt lingering in the fibres of the fabric. She had worn it only once since, on a cool night in Geraldton when she couldn't sleep. She'd slipped from her tent and sat on the ground wrapped in the faded jumper, her thumbs hooked through the small tears in the sleeve.

'Keep it. It looked better on you.'

Ahead on the dunes she noticed the red glow of a cigarette and made out the faint silhouette of a man – a partygoer, perhaps, who'd strayed too far from the herd. Apart from him, the beach was deserted and the emptiness was alluring. 'How long will you be staying on the west coast?' she asked.

'A few weeks. A low pressure's riding in to Margaret River.'

'The wine region?'

'Yes. It's unusual for swell to hit at this time of year, so we want to see what's going to happen.'

'Finn and I are heading that way.'

'Are you?' he said, and she found herself hoping he was pleased.

As they continued along the beach she caught sight of something glimmering in the sand. She bent down and collected a shell from the tideline. It was oval shaped, the size of her hand, and the outside felt rough and calloused. Angling it towards the moonlight she saw that the inner layer was an iridescent bed of mother-of-pearl. She ran her finger across it and felt the whorls beneath her fingertip. 'What would've lived in this?'

'Abalone – it's a type of sea snail. Muttonfish, we call them. Tough as a rag to eat. A delicacy in Asia, though.'

'Really?'

'It's been overfished, like anything with a price tag. Abalone divers can make a fortune on a good day.'

'The shell is beautiful.'

'You're lucky to find one that size here.'

She glanced up and saw that the guy who'd been standing on the dunes was moving towards the shoreline and into their path. His dark clothing blended into the night and he stopped at the water's edge and turned to face them. The steady hold of his gaze made her uneasy. He drew a joint to his mouth and inhaled deeply, the heady smell of marijuana drifting downwind.

'Beautiful night, isn't it?' he said.

They stopped.

'Going anywhere nice?'

'Just walking,' Noah answered, and she could hear the tension in his voice. 'I thought you'd still be at the party.'

'Wasn't in the party spirit.'

The man stepped towards Mia, close enough for her to smell the smoke on his breath. His face was unshaven and his clothes looked dishevelled. 'And who are you?'

Her fingers tightened around the shell at her side. 'Mia.'

'Where are you from, Mia?'

'England.'

'How very nice.' He scratched at his upper arm suddenly, as if bothered by a mosquito. 'As Noah's forgotten his manners, I better introduce myself. I'm Jez, his brother.'

Brother?

He put the joint to his lips and extended his hand. His fingers felt bony and callused.

She searched for a similarity she must have missed. His hair was thinning, small blond tufts sprouting from his head, and his mouth was narrower than Noah's, but there was something shared in the prominence of their brows.

'So you're a *friend* of Noah's?'

She hesitated, unsure. 'Yes.'

'What brings you to Australia?'

'I'm just travelling.'

'You smoke, Mia? Fancy getting stoned?'

'She doesn't,' Noah cut in. 'We've got to get going. See you later,' he said, moving off.

They walked in silence. Mia turned the shell through her

fingers, waiting for Noah to say something. When several minutes passed without a word, she asked, 'So that's the brother you're travelling with?'

'Yes.'

'He's older than you?'

'By three years.'

'Same gap between me and Katie. What's he like?'

'He smokes too much weed.'

She glanced at Noah sideways. There was something troubled in his expression. She was going to ask more, when he said, 'I'll walk you back to the tavern now.'

She didn't want their night to end like this. In Maui, she had left Noah beside the cooling embers of the beach fire, not talking of phone numbers or email addresses, because that had never been her way. It was only when she had woken the following day and drew his jumper to her face that she had found herself wanting to know more about him. There had been other men, other one-night stands, but with Noah it had felt different. When he looked at her, it was as if he saw exactly who she was. She had taken to jogging along the beach in the hope of seeing him. But she hadn't. And then she and Finn had flown on.

Now she realized that she didn't want to let him go again.

She stopped walking.

He turned to face her and she felt her heart beginning to race. 'That night in Maui,' she began. 'I felt like . . . there was a connection between us, or something.'

He lowered his gaze. 'Mia—'

A cool feeling crept over her skin, as if he was about to say something she didn't want to hear. Before he had a chance, she stepped forward and kissed him.

'No,' he whispered against her lips. 'You don't want this.'

But as her fingertips met his skin, every cell in her body was telling her that she did.

13

KATIE

Western Australia, June

E d drove with his elbow resting on the sill, his forearm turning a reddish brown in the afternoon sun. Katie watched the vineyards of Margaret River flashing by in rich strips of green, an earthy breeze filling the car and stirring her hair.

'There is a winery,' he was saying, reaching for a booklet by the gearstick, 'that runs a vine-to-bottle tour. It's in here somewhere.' He handed her the booklet. 'Seeing as we drink so much of the stuff, it might be interesting to understand how it's produced. What do you think? There's wine tasting at the end,' he added hopefully. 'Shall I book?'

What Katie thought was that a winery tour was not the purpose of visiting Margaret River: Mia was. But what Katie said was, 'Yes, do.' Only three days of Ed's visit remained and she was determined that they'd enjoy them.

'I've been thinking about the wines for the wedding. The sommelier from Highdown Manor suggested a Pinot Grigio for

169

the white. Californian, I think. I ordered a bottle while you were away and, I have to say, it was better than I expected. No hangover either.'

'Perfect,' she said, glancing at the roadside where a dead kangaroo was slumped with an engorged stomach; a swarm of flies buzzed around its lifeless black eyes.

'I meant to tell you, Jess said the bridesmaid's dress arrived. No alterations needed. She offered to look for shoes if you think you'll run out of time.'

'She was meant to be one of two bridesmaids.'

Ed glanced at her. She hadn't realized she'd made the remark aloud.

'You do still want to go ahead with the wedding?'

Her thoughts were stalled by the sudden shift in conversational gear. 'Of course.'

'But?'

She rolled the wine booklet into a tube and then smoothed it flat again. 'It's just hard imagining Mia not there.' She had pictured them getting ready together, Mia teasing her for the meticulous schedule with allocated time slots for breakfast, manicures, hairstyling and make-up. Old tensions would have been put aside for the day and they'd have drunk champagne in glass flutes, raising a toast to their mother. Mia would have helped her step into her wedding dress and told her it was beautiful, and then cursed the thirty ivory buttons she had to do up by hand.

'I know it is, darling. I've given a great deal of thought as to whether we should postpone the wedding. If we did postpone it – say for a year – what difference does it make? Mia still wouldn't be there. I came to the conclusion that we should go ahead as planned because it gives us both something positive to focus on. Life has to move on, doesn't it? Our wedding can be the first stage of that.'

That was the whole problem: she wasn't ready for her life to move on. Not without Mia in it.

Ed swung the car into a petrol station. 'I'll fill up.' He cut the engine, then leant over and kissed her on the cheek, the conversation closed.

Without the air conditioning, heat engulfed the car. She tugged down her dress; the lining was clinging uncomfortably around her middle. She was eager to reach their hotel and drench herself beneath a cold, powerful shower. Car journeys always left her restless and sticky, something about leather seats against the backs of her thighs or the sugar-rich car snacks that coated her teeth. She wound down the windows and breathed in the deep petrol fumes.

A rusted pickup pulled in on the other side of the pump, music blaring from rolled-down windows. Surfboards were slung in the back and in the passenger seat a girl of about Mia's age sat with her feet propped on the dash. Her toenails were painted electric blue. A man stepped out in scuffed flip-flops, his heels cracked and dirty. He flicked open the fuel cap and clunked the nozzle in. As she watched, she wondered if he was anything like Noah, the enigma in Mia's journal who her entries were weaved around.

Katie felt intrusive reading some of the intimate descriptions of their romance, yet was also glued to the pages as she discovered her sister's growing feelings. She'd read that the day after Mia had been reunited with Noah, she had climbed into the passenger seat of his van, which smelt of neoprene and warmed surf wax, and they'd bounced along unsealed roads, dust flying in their wake, till they reached an empty beach. They swam out to a tiny island where they stripped off their swimsuits and lay drying on the sun-baked rocks. Noah talked to her about spear fishing and a shoal of Spanish mackerel that had coiled above his head like a silver whirlwind, far too beautiful to spear. She talked about travelling and the ocean, and of books by Hemingway that had given her a thirst for both.

Mia wrote pages and pages about him, decorating the entries with swirling doodles that blossomed from the margins. She detailed every interaction and transcribed verbatim a conversation about music. Other entries were overshadowed by doubt as she questioned why Noah preferred to sleep alone each night, or interpreted his quietness as a cooling off. Finn featured only as a passing comment, and Katie found that she missed the descriptions of him.

Ed bent his head to the window. 'Would you like anything?'

'No, thanks.'

She watched him walk into the kiosk, swinging the car keys around a finger. She turned in her seat and reached for Mia's journal. Pulling it onto her lap, she opened it at the latest entry. The date caught her eye: '*Christmas Day*'.

She remembered that they had spoken that day. The phone had rung just as she was leaving the flat, and she'd run across the hall with her handbag bouncing against her hip. She was thrilled to hear Mia's voice, but what should have been a festive chat turned sour. The journal entry would contain Mia's frank opinion on the conversation and the thought of reading it filled Katie with dread. She bit down on her lip, knowing that this phone call was only a prelude to their final devastating argument weeks later.

When Ed returned, he placed a handful of mints between them. 'The chap said we're only a couple of kilometres from the hotel.'

She nodded.

He started the engine and then glanced at the open journal. 'What is it?'

'Nothing,' she said, closing it and putting it away.

'Katie?'

She swallowed. 'I think Mia's next entry is going to be about an argument we had. I remember her phoning me from Margaret River.'

He pulled out of the garage, accelerating sharply to slip between two cars in the fast-moving traffic. When he was back in his lane, he said, 'And you think it'll be difficult reading about it?'

'Perhaps.'

'What was the argument about?'

She hesitated. 'Sister stuff.'

'When was this?'

'Christmas.'

His eyebrows rose. 'Just after I proposed.'

'Was it?' she said, hoping to keep her tone light.

They drove the rest of the way in silence.

Ed stopped the car alongside a tall manor house with a regal green front door and brass knocker. There would be no dorm beds or guitar playing here. 'I'll check in and take the bags up. Why don't you stroll into town to clear your head?'

'I think I'll just take a shower. Cool off.'

'A walk might do you good. You could have a look at the restaurants, too. See where you fancy going for dinner.'

'Okay,' she agreed, unclipping her seat belt.

'If it will help, why don't we read that entry together when you're back?'

Katie smiled, but she had no intention of reading the journal with Ed. How could she when the argument had been about him?

*

Katie wandered through the small town of Margaret River, glancing into shop windows. Heat radiated from the sun-baked pavements and the metallic bodies of parked cars, and she felt the prickle of perspiration at the backs of her knees.

She passed an art gallery with a smart navy frontage and framed paintings of white sailboats in the window. She paused, admiring the soft curves of their sails, full and proud with wind, and the skill with which the artist had captured the shimmer of evening light reflecting off the water.

A bell announced her entrance into the gallery, causing a

redheaded man to look up from his book. He smiled, said, 'Afternoon,' and then returned to reading.

Paintings filled the crisp white walls and she chose to look at one positioned beneath an air-conditioning vent, grateful for the chilled air against the nape of her neck. The painting was an abstract of a woman's hand. From the fine lines running over her knuckles and the ridges in her short nails, Katie guessed it belonged to a woman in her fifties or sixties. The hand clasped a cheap biro, the plastic end chewed and splintered, incongruous against the refined poise in which it held the pen above quality writing paper. The painter had obscured most of the words so that the eye was drawn to only one phrase: '*When we were young.*'

Mia used to be a great letter writer; Katie had forgotten that. When Katie was away at university she had been the recipient of many of them. While they fought face to face, and phone calls proved disastrous, in letters they shared an easy dialogue. Mia's style was conversational, darting from one thought to the next, her digressions amusing Katie who would read them greedily. Katie would write back, sharing secrets of men she was in love with or nightclubs she'd visited, painting a colourful picture of university that she hoped Mia would admire. Yet when they saw each other, even if the visit fell on the heels of a warm and intimate letter, they somehow reverted to form and would find themselves bickering within hours.

Katie moved on, gliding from picture to picture, enjoying the range of paintings displayed in the small gallery. At the back of the room three shelves were filled with art supplies and she found herself picking up a tube of acrylic paint. She had the sudden urge to dab a new brush deep into the paint and slide it across a clean canvas. At school she'd shown a flare for art, able to be bold on the page in a way that seemed out of reach in person. She loved the quiet of the art room with its square desks and the sharp smell of white spirit. Mia was furious when Katie gave it up, deciding that it wouldn't be as well received by the university admissions system as A-level History. She'd rolled her talent away, along with her paintings, and hadn't thought about it since.

She picked up a set of twelve acrylic paints housed in a silver tin, along with a pad and two brushes, and went to the till. The man placed his book face down and ran the items through the till. She returned to the hotel with the supplies tucked underarm like a secret.

At the reception desk she was handed her room key. 'Your husband has already gone up, madam.'

She blinked, taken aback.

'Sorry,' the receptionist said. 'Have I made a mistake?'

'No, no. It's fine,' Katie replied, touching her collarbone. 'Thank you.'

A thick oak door opened into their room. It was airy and bright and a wrought-iron bed stood proudly in the centre. Her backpack was propped against it, the buckles open and a peach blouse hanging out. She wondered why Ed had started unpacking it. He stood with his back to her, his shoulders hunched as if he were grasping something.

She stepped into the room, closing the door behind her.

'Katie!' he said, spinning round.

Now that he was angled towards her she could see he was trying to conceal whatever was in his hands. She glimpsed a flash of something sea-blue and immediately she knew: Mia's journal.

The scene came into focus; he clasped the journal in one hand, and a fistful of cream pages in the other.

'What the hell are you doing?'

A loud rap at the door startled her. She snatched it open as if the two events were connected, and found a maid holding two plump white pillows.

'Extra pillows for you, madam.'

Katie didn't move to take them, nor step aside from the doorway to allow the maid in.

After a moment she heard Ed's voice. 'Yes, thank you. Could you leave them outside?'

The maid looked affronted by the request and Katie heard the soft flop of the pillows on the landing before the door clicked shut.

She turned to Ed. His hands were now behind his back, like a playground thief. 'I asked you a question.'

His mouth opened and closed, but he said nothing.

She put down the paper bag of art supplies, then crossed the room. She stood in front of him and held out her hand.

He shook his head. 'I won't give it to you.'

'Won't?'

'Sorry. I know that sounds—'

'Give me the fucking journal, Ed.'

He swallowed. 'Do you trust me, Katie?'

She remembered discovering Ed flicking through Mia's travel journal in London. At the time she'd thought he'd been checking there was nothing in it that would upset her – but now she began to question what his motives really were. 'Before I walked into this room, yes, I trusted you. But right now? No. No, I don't.'

'You've already been through enough.'

'You're right, I have. So I'll ask you one more time: give me the journal and whatever you've torn from it. '

He hesitated.

'Now!'

Reluctantly, Ed passed it to her.

Her heart cracked at the sight of Mia's careful script ripped from the journal. It was as if Ed had yanked the hairs from Mia's head. 'What have you done?' she asked, her voice stretched thin.

When he didn't answer, she lowered herself onto the bed and brought the pages into her lap. Very carefully, she smoothed them out.

'Please,' he begged. 'You don't want to read that.'

14

MIA

Western Australia, December Last Year

'Merry Christmas!' Mia said, tucking the phone between her ear and shoulder.

'Mia! Thank God, I didn't miss you! I was literally walking out the door. Hold on a sec,' she said, and then called out, 'Ed! It's my sister. Come back in – I'll be a few minutes.' There was the tread of feet and the click of the door closing, followed by Katie's whisper, 'Will you let your mother know we'll be late? I don't want her to think we're being rude.'

Katie: considerate, organized, punctual.

Mia heard Ed's footsteps move along the hallway and into the lounge. Another door closed. She imagined him wearing a dark overcoat over a V-necked sweater by a quality label, Ralph Lauren or John Smedley perhaps, dressed ready for Christmas lunch with his parents. She hadn't been to Ed's family home, but from Katie's accounts she imagined a holly-and-ivy wreath hung on a solid oak door, a table already laid with a silver dinner service and three sets of cutlery, and bottles of red wine warming on a hearth.

'Where are you?' Katie asked.

'Margaret River. It's on the west coast of Australia.'

'And right now, this second? I want to picture it.'

'In a phone box outside a hostel. You'll laugh – it's actually a red English phone box. The colonial thumbprint still holds strong.'

'What can you see?'

She glanced through the weathered glass panels. 'Blue sky. Eucalyptus trees.' She stretched away from the phone to stick her head out, looking towards the branches of the trees. 'And two kookaburras.'

'The birds that laugh?'

'Yep.'

'I can't even imagine. Are you having a wonderful time?'

Mia pushed her hair away from her face. She thought of Maui and the cold truth that'd sunk to the pit of her stomach, and the brooding month that followed when she was listless and swollen with inertia. But she also thought of skydiving, of swimming in the Pacific, of making love to Noah beside a beach fire. 'It's more than I could have imagined.'

'Good. That's really good.' Then, 'Oh, Mia, it doesn't feel right being apart at Christmas. I miss you so much!'

She smiled, warmed by the way Katie's thoughts always tumbled out so openly. When Mia was younger she had been embarrassed by her sister's earnestness; now she admired it. 'I miss you, too,' she managed.

'Where are these stacks of postcards I was promised?'

'I've bought them. Well, two. One in California and another last week in Perth. I just haven't written them.'

'Well, hurry up. I love getting post from you.'

Each time she'd sat down to write them, she'd found her pen hovering over the blank space, unsure where to begin. There were a thousand things she could tell Katie about her trip so far, but it was the things she couldn't say that filled her head.

'What time is it in Australia? Have you had Christmas lunch?'

'It's six. And lunch was a burnt sausage in a bap.'

'No? Mia! It can't feel like Christmas at all.'

'It doesn't.' Which was exactly what she wanted. Christmas had always been a huge occasion in their family. Last year had been the first without their mother. Katie had foregone Christmas with Ed's family to spend it in the flat with Mia. She put on an apron and an air of determined optimism, and did her best to conjure a festive atmosphere. Despite her efforts, grief clung to them both, exacerbated by the wine they washed back to fill the silences. After lunch an argument erupted, and they spent the rest of the day in separate rooms.

'Finn still insisted on swapping stockings,' Mia offered.

'Tell me it was a clean sock this year?'

'He claimed so, but he only packed two pairs and he hasn't done any laundry for a fortnight. The jury's out.'

Katie laughed. 'What was in it?'

'He couldn't find any satsumas, so he wedged a banana at the bottom, which meant I got a banana-flavoured pack of cards, a banana-flavoured travel book about Samoa, and a banana-flavoured bangle.' She lifted her hand and admired the chunky sea-green bracelet circling her wrist.

'How is he?'

Katie rarely asked about Finn, but perhaps the distance made it easier. 'He's good. Making friends wherever we go. On Wednesday he had everyone at the hostel drinking homemade punch and limboing beneath a belt he'd tied to two poles.' She'd arrived as everyone was dispersing and was sorry to have missed the fun. When Finn asked where she'd been, a flush crept up her neck as she answered, 'With Noah.'

'I can't be too much longer as Ed's waiting,' Katie said, 'but I've got news!'

'Okay . . .'

'On Friday, Ed and I went for dinner at the Oxo Tower. Do you remember it? We took Mum there for her fiftieth.'

'With the waiter who thought the three of us were sisters.'

'So Mum left a 20 percent tip.'

'He's probably tried that every night since.'

Katie laughed. 'It was a different waiter this time – but he got an even bigger tip.'

'Why? Did he say you look like Scarlett Johansson?'

'Even better: when he brought out dessert my plate was decorated with these beautiful swirls of melted chocolate – and in the centre was a ring box. Mia, Ed proposed! He got down on one knee and asked me to marry him!'

Sunlight fell through the glass panels of the phone box, illuminating Mia's fingers as she pressed them to her mouth. Katie and Ed were engaged. Heat prickled across her skin. She wedged her foot in the door to get air.

Her response was important – every moment she hesitated would be counted. Her silence stretched out. A taut wordless void opened up between them.

It was Katie who spoke first. 'Mia?'

'Yes.'

'I'm engaged.'

'Yes.'

A pause. 'That's all you're going to say?'

'No . . . sorry . . . I was just thinking of what to say.'

'"Congratulations" is common.'

'Of course! Congratulations!'

'I wanted you to be a bridesmaid.'

She swallowed. 'Great . . .'

'You're not happy for me?'

'I am – yes. I am.'

'That's odd, because it sounds like you're disappointed.'

'Sorry. It just took me by surprise. I didn't realize things were so serious.'

'You wouldn't since you haven't called in seven weeks.' Her retorts were whip-like in their speed and sharpness.

Mia forced the door wider, jamming her knee through the gap.

Katie's voice became a low whisper as if her mouth was pressed close to the receiver. 'You've never liked him, have you?'

'It doesn't matter what I think.'

'It seemed to when it came to my last boyfriend.'

The lash of the remark struck hard. 'That was completely different!'

'How?'

'You were deliberately trying to hurt me.'

Katie sighed. 'Everything will always be about *you*.'

'No—'

'I just want you to be happy for me. Can you be?'

She wanted to share her sister's happiness and tell her that she loved her, but the memory of what she'd done caught in her throat, blocking her words.

'Merry Christmas,' Katie said, and then the line went dead.

*

Mia remained in the phone box. She felt a familiar tightening in her gut, a cold twist of guilt. Katie had always dreamt of getting married – and now she was engaged. For most sisters that would be cause for celebration and breathless questions about the engagement ring, the wedding date, plans for a venue. But Mia did not think to ask any of those things; she thought only of what had happened in a darkened corridor with the bitter taste of vodka lining her throat.

A group of travellers, ebullient and tanned, passed the phone box. Finn was in the centre of them, the white pompom of his Santa's hat bobbing as he laughed.

'Finn!' she called, pushing through the door.

He stopped immediately. 'What is it? Are you okay?'

The crowd paused, turning to look. She suddenly felt foolish, the urgency of a moment ago shrinking beneath their curious gazes. 'I've just spoken to Katie.'

'Is she okay?'

'Yes, fine. She and Ed are engaged.'

His eyebrows rose. 'Right. That's great news. Isn't it?'

She nodded.

'So, when's the wedding?'

'Oh. I didn't ask.'

He studied her for a moment. 'Are you sure you're okay?'

'Yes.'

'We're going to the pub for dinner. Come? We can have a celebratory drink.'

She'd love to lose herself amongst the easy smiles of the travellers, drink schooners of beer, shoot pool, dance to eighties rock on the jukebox – but she knew her heart wouldn't be in it. 'I don't think . . .'

'Come on, it's Christmas! We haven't had a drink together in ages.'

The criticism was implicit. Her time had been absorbed by Noah. She rubbed her arm; sunlight caught the curve of her new bangle and it glittered like the sea. 'I'd love to have a drink together – but I'm not in a pub mood.' She hoped he'd infer that she wanted to spend time with him. Just the two of them.

'Fair enough.' He shrugged. 'See you later.'

*

Mia returned to her room, slipped her journal and a slim package into her bag, and left again in search of Noah. She passed Zani, one of the group he and Jez travelled with, sitting cross-legged outside the hostel, smoking. She had a bleached-blonde crop and wore wide rainbow-coloured trousers that were trodden down at the heels.

'Do you know if Noah's at the beach?'

'They're all surfing Reds.' She proffered her joint.

'I'm good, thanks,' Mia said, and then moved on.

Crickets and cicadas hummed in the scrub-lined track that led to Reds. The beach took its name from the plateau of red rocks that lay like huge beached whales, now baking under a lowering sun. She slipped off her flip-flops and picked her way across them. The air was moist with a briny vapour lifting from the sea. Great lines of swell were breaking, the white-water re-forming into smaller waves that crashed against the rocks.

Her conversation with Katie drifted from her thoughts the moment she saw Noah. He was standing a few paces away from the edge of the rocks, his surfboard underarm. The sun was sinking to the west and golden streams of light gilded his silhouette. Years of surfing had honed his physique to a lean structure of muscle. Unable to see his expression, she imagined him looking serious, his gaze fixed on the water. She'd come to understand that for Noah surfing was a need, as basic as hunger or thirst.

She wondered if it was his passion for the sea that drew her to him with such unnerving force. There'd been other boyfriends

– mostly brief and unremarkable relationships that passed with the seasons – but she'd experienced nothing like this.

'Hey,' she said, announcing herself.

He turned. Smiled.

'I was just looking for you to say Merry Christmas.'

He loosened his grip on his surfboard, but didn't put it down. 'Merry Christmas, Mia.'

She hadn't seen him all day and wanted to place her lips against his bare chest and feel the heat of his skin. 'I've something for you,' she said, feeling her bag at her side, which contained his present. Realizing that he'd have nowhere to put it, she said, 'I'll give it to you later.'

'Sorry. I haven't got you anything. I didn't think . . .'

'This isn't a Christmas present, just something I found.' It was a Hemingway book, her favourite: *The Old Man and the Sea*. It had been on the swap shelf at the last hostel they'd stayed in, so she'd traded it for her Lonely Planet, and had inscribed on the inside cover: '*To Noah, the freshest words about the sea . . . with love, Mia xx.*' She'd wrapped it in pages torn from a magazine and tied it with string.

'Let's catch up later, then.' He leant forward and kissed her. When he pulled away, his gaze darted back to the surf where the breakers rolled in, smooth and powerful.

'You should get out there.'

He moved back to the edge of the rocks, waiting for a lull between sets. When one came he launched the board into the water and then dived after it, cutting through the back of a wave. It took several powerful strokes to reach the board and then he slid onto it and paddled determinedly through the seething wash.

Mia gathered her hair from her face and tied it into a low knot at the base of her head, then sat, hooking her arms over her knees. She enjoyed watching him surf; she'd spent enough hours on Cornish beaches to recognize his talent. He had an easy, fluid style and she noticed how he hung back from the other surfers who bobbed like seals in the line-up. He'd wait on an outside section, hitting a wave where it broke at its steepest or picking off the set wave that the other surfers chose to leave. She knew the risks he took, but he trained hard for the hold downs. He'd told her that spear fishing helped his agility, and he did other exercises, like carrying rocks underwater to build up lung capacity and strength. She held an image of him gliding along the seabed, his hands wrapped round a boulder, a stream of silver air bubbles floating from his lips.

As he paddled, she recalled how his body had been raised above hers last night, his fists pressed into the white sheet of her bed, the veins in his forearms standing proud. She had turned her head and licked the delicate skin at his inner elbow. At her touch his arms had bent and he lowered himself onto her, covering every inch of her body with his.

A shadow fell over her and she looked up to see Jez staring at her with one eyebrow raised quizzically. 'All right?'

She flushed a deep crimson as if her thoughts had been transparent.

He lowered himself onto the rock she sat on, positioning

himself a couple of inches behind her. She felt it put her at a disadvantage somehow, having to turn more fully to face him.

Jez's skin was weather-beaten; grooves deeper than his years cut into his forehead, and there were sun lesions on his nose. He was wirier than Noah, but they were a similar height. Since the evening she'd met Jez, they'd only passed one another a couple of times in the hostel; she'd smile but would feel relieved when he didn't stop. She found something disconcerting in the way his gaze followed her, as if he was always watching.

'Santa bring you everything you wanted?' he said.

'He doesn't know my address. How about you?'

'What I want doesn't come gift wrapped.' He pulled a pack of tobacco from his pocket and began to roll a cigarette. There was dirt beneath his nails and his knuckles were flecked with pink scars. 'Where are you headin' next?'

'New Zealand. In a fortnight. Have you been?' Mia asked.

'I'm as well travelled as a paper aeroplane. Noah's the jet-setter.' He lit his roll-up and the sweet smoke drifted towards her.

For a minute, maybe two, neither of them said anything more and they both watched the surf. Noah took off on a wave that reared well over head high, cutting back and forth in a whoosh of spray.

'Pretty incredible, eh?'

'Yes, he is,' she said, keeping her eyes on the water. 'Does he ever compete?'

Jez stared at her. 'He was on the pro tour for five years, paid to surf the best breaks in the world.'

'He never said . . .'

'There's a lot he never says.'

'So he was sponsored?'

'Yeah. Had a sweet little thing going with Quiksilver. Until he quit the tour.'

'Why?'

'You'd have to ask Noah that.'

She glanced at him sideways, unsure what he meant. Noah had told her that he and Jez surfed a lot together as boys, spending every second they weren't in school chasing waves. 'You weren't interested in doing it professionally?'

He laughed, smoke bubbling from his mouth. 'Let's just say the opportunity never came my way.'

'It must be good taking time out now to travel together.'

'It's good having no commitments. We can move on whenever we want. That's what Noah's always loved,' he said, looking directly at her. 'No ties.'

He let those words hang in the air, and then he stood. 'See you, Mia.' He dropped the butt of the roll-up in a gap between the rocks. A thin drift of smoke wafted after him.

Christmas on the beach hadn't been all she'd imagined and she felt a surge of loneliness wash over her. She closed her eyes and wondered what Katie would be doing now. Was she sharing Christmas lunch with Ed's family while carols played discreetly in the background? Or were they still having drinks, Katie holding a flute of champagne, her engagement ring sparkling in the light of a chandelier? She would have bought a new outfit for the occasion and Mia imagined her hair swept back, a delicate silver chain at her throat. Then, Mia pictured Ed, his hand on Katie's, and she felt her skin grow cool. Could she really let her sister marry him?

From her bag she took out her journal and set it on her knees. She turned to a fresh page and began to write, the pen moving hesitantly at first, then gaining momentum, words filling the page like liquid flowing into a cup. The truth spilt out of her, raw and ugly, as she confided in the journal what she had been too weak to say to Katie: *'You can't marry a man who's cheated on you. Not when it was with your sister.'*

15

KATIE

Western Australia, June

Katie held the torn pages of the journal between trembling fingers. When she finished reading, she looked up.

Ed had anchored himself to the cherry-wood dressing table, spreading his palms flat against its polished surface. His head hung down and in the mirror above him she could see the patch at his crown where his hair was beginning to thin. He was conscious of it and used his fingers to ruffle the spot each morning when he woke, a gesture that Katie had found endearing, pleased by the vulnerable chink in his armour of confidence.

'You slept with my sister?'

Ed turned. His face had paled and his lips looked dark in contrast. 'I am so sorry.' He ran a hand across his jaw. 'It was a huge mistake.'

'How was it?' She was a poker player with nothing left to lose.

'What? I . . .' he floundered.

In six torn pages, Mia's entry had excavated a buried piece of Ed's history, one that threw into question all Katie had thought she knew. She had read that in a bar in Camden, her fiancé and her sister had had sex in a blackened corridor, knocking a painting off the wall that had cracked, sending a shard of glass splintering into Mia's ankle.

'It was a mistake. And you must understand that we were both terribly drunk.'

'You didn't tell me.'

'No,' he replied. 'I didn't. I regretted what happened so vehemently that I never told anyone. I didn't want to hurt you, Katie.'

'Yet you turned up at the bar where my sister worked, bought her drink after drink, and then had sex with her in a corridor.'

'What you read,' Ed said, 'is her version.'

'Then I'd better hear yours.' She folded her arms to hide the trembling in her hands.

He took a deep breath. 'Do you remember on Freddie's birthday I told you I was meeting the boys straight from work? We started drinking on the Embankment and then ended up – God knows how – in a cellar bar in Camden. I had no idea it was where Mia worked; she had so many jobs I could never keep up.' He waved his fingers through the air in his gesture for Mia: flighty, restless. 'I only noticed her because she was wearing a dress of yours. I quite literally did a double take.'

She was careful not to let her face fall into an expression that she wasn't ready to give away. She continued listening, saying nothing.

'When Mia finished her shift, I invited her to have a drink

with us. It must sound ludicrous now, but I specifically recall thinking, *Katie will be pleased when I tell her*. I knew it bothered you that we hadn't hit it off.'

He was right. Ed and Mia were from different worlds and she'd felt as though her arms could never quite stretch wide enough to reach them both. Whenever Ed talked about business, Mia would catch Katie's eye and begin an elaborate mime of nodding off, her head jerking her awake often enough to smile encouragingly at Ed. He'd caught her mid-performance once, and said, 'Shall I make my conversation more inclusive next time by talking about barmaiding and student debt?' Mia had flicked him the finger and sauntered out.

Ed continued. 'By the time she joined us, the boys and I were steaming. She was determined to catch up and Freddie, as you can imagine, was encouraging her. We all drank far too much. When the bar closed, I offered to put Mia in a cab because I knew how much it worried you when she insisted on walking everywhere. I can't say with much clarity what happened after that, but before we reached the cab we somehow ended up . . .' He cleared his throat. 'It was ridiculous, utterly without forethought or conviction. And I am deeply ashamed of myself.'

At a business seminar, Katie had once learnt about the power of the pause. She let silence fall around Ed's explanation and watched as he shifted, uncrossing his legs, straightening, and then shoving both hands in his pockets.

'It's interesting,' she began, 'because Mia's journal entry was a little different. In your hurry to tear it out, I imagine you didn't have a chance to read it all, so I'll refresh you with a few details.'

Colour rose on Ed's neck and spread up into his lower cheeks.

'She noted that you were flirtatious from the moment she joined you, and insisted on buying her drink after drink. When you left to put her in a taxi,' she flicked through the loose pages to find the extract she was looking for, 'Mia wrote, *Ed put his hand on my lower back and whispered, "You look so sexy in that dress. But what I want to know is: What are you wearing beneath it?" I shrugged and said, "Take a look." So he did.*'

She stopped reading and looked at Ed. He had clasped both hands behind his neck so his elbows angled into the room.

'I have to say, that is a really wonderful image for me. Such a keepsake.'

'What matters are the facts: I betrayed your trust. Being drunk is no excuse. It happened and I am going to do everything in my power to make this right.'

She looked down at her hands, which still held the limp, torn pages. She could feel her poker face beginning to slip. He was her fiancé. She loved him. He was all she had left now that Mia and her mother were gone. Tears slid down her cheeks.

'Darling,' Ed said, moving towards her. 'Please, don't cry.'

Out in the corridor she could hear footsteps and the roll of a suitcase on wheels, then a key turning in a lock: she wished she were that guest, slipping into a different room, a different life.

He sat beside her, his weight lowering her fractionally on the bed so her body tilted towards him. He was careful not to touch her, but in a low voice, said, 'I love you more than anything. We've had so many wonderful times together, and I am not prepared to throw away our future over one dreadful mistake. My whole family adores you. If I screw this up I am fairly certain they will disown me. You know how much I love you – I've flown across the world to be with you – so I am asking you, Katie, to forgive me.'

Tears ran down her cheeks. Could she forgive him? It was such a lot to ask of anyone. He was right to say that they'd shared many wonderful times, but a relationship wasn't a score chart of good experiences versus bad. It was about trust and honesty. But perhaps it was also about forgiveness and understanding.

'I'll get you some tissues,' Ed said.

Watching him move into the en suite, she was jolted by an image of Mia lying on the black-and-white-tiled floor of their bathroom in London, like an unseated pawn on a chess board. She had been wearing a jade dress – Katie's dress – that was twisted at her waist. When Mia had lifted her head and seen Katie standing in the doorway, she'd looked away, unable to meet her eye. That had been the night.

Ed returned with a box of tissues. 'The night you slept with Mia,' she said, her voice deadly calm, 'she passed out on our bathroom floor. I found her the next morning.'

Ed didn't move.

'How drunk must she have been?'

'We were both drunk.'

She glanced out of the window. She didn't marvel at the view of the lake bathed in the late-afternoon sun or the pristine vineyards stretching beyond; she was remembering something else from that day. Katie had been making risotto in the kitchen when Mia had come in wearing her jogging gear. She remembered asking how Mia's head was and whether she needed a plaster for the cut on her ankle. That's when Mia had announced she was going travelling.

She turned back to Ed. 'After screwing you, Mia booked a round-the-world ticket to get the fuck away!'

He didn't baulk at her language; perhaps he'd grown used to this new Katie, the one who flicked from tears to anger as quick as a switch.

'When I found out she was going travelling, I came round to see you.' She'd left a pan of burnt onions cooling on the side and the smell had lingered in the flat for days. 'I was upset that she was leaving me, and do you remember what you said? "A change of scenery will be good for her." I thought you were being understanding – but the truth was, you were pleased she was going.'

'Katie—'

She had found her stride and wouldn't be deterred. 'If it hadn't been for you,' she said, her voice growing louder, 'she'd have never left like that. I knew there must be a reason. I even tried talking to you about it after her funeral, but you told me Mia was just *impulsive, young, bored*.' Her anger burnt in her throat and made her jaw tight. 'If you hadn't screwed her, she'd never have gone travelling. Never have ended up in Bali. Never have been on that cliff top. It was your fault, Ed. Yours!'

'Come on! I didn't make her have sex with me. Just like I didn't make her go travelling, and I didn't make her throw herself from a cliff.'

Her eyes widened. 'What did you say?'

'I said what the police, coroner and witnesses all believe. That's good enough for me.'

'I'm her sister! What about what *I* believe? I knew her better than anyone!'

'You didn't even know she was in Bali.'

The remark smacked her like a punch.

'Christ, don't you see how unhealthy this obsession of yours has become? You've run off to the other side of the world, clinging to that journal like it's some kind of lifeline. Mia is dead. She committed suicide. I am genuinely sorry about that, I really am, but you need to accept the facts.'

She reached for the nearest thing she could find: his laptop.

'What on earth are you doing?'

She lifted it above her head.

'Good God, Katie! You need to calm down.'

She felt the weight of it in her fingers and wrists.

'That's got all my contacts in it. It's very important to me.'

She glanced at the ripped cream pages discarded on the bed. 'Just like my sister's journal is important to me.' She remembered Ed's look of surprise when he found out Mia kept a journal. The next morning she'd discovered him leafing through it, *Checking there is nothing to upset you,* he'd told her. 'This whole time you've been lying to me, trying to cover your tracks—'

'I was protecting you.'

'Protecting me?' Katie realised how desperate Ed must have been to get his hands on the journal to check Mia hadn't implicated him. But Katie had been careful not to let it out of her sight. Until today. 'You manipulated me into going for a walk so you could take my bags up to the room—'

'I mean it, Katie! Put it down before you do something you regret.'

Perhaps it was his tone or the implication that she wasn't in control that spurred her on, but she found her arms drawing back. Then with all her strength she launched the laptop across the room.

She heard Ed's sharp intake of breath and then a loud, satisfying crunch as it hit the wall. Glass and silver plastic shards rained down on the carpet, the screen splitting from the keyboard. An angular dent was left behind in the paintwork.

'Jesus Christ!'

Calmly, she picked up the journal and hooked on her backpack.

Ed was staring at her. 'You are not the woman I fell in love with.'

She caught sight of herself in the mirror. Her hair was loose around her face and her make-up had worn off with the day. Her eyes danced with anger. The faded backpack with its fraying straps and promise of adventure no longer looked so incongruous on her back.

'You're right, Ed. I'm not.'

*

She followed signs to the tourist information office. There she found herself standing before a volunteer who circled a hostel on a map with an orange highlighter and said, 'It'll take you fifteen minutes on foot.'

Katie strode there in ten. She was shown to a dorm where three young women were getting changed. Hiking boots and sweat-hardened socks were discarded on the floor, and the room was thick with the smell of deodorant. Desperate not to pause, not to think, she struck up conversation and discovered that the girls, two from New Zealand, the third from Quebec, were on a ten-day outdoor experience and had just hiked a section of the cape-to-cape trail. They told her about the wide ocean bluffs and the crickets that sprang like firecrackers from the undergrowth, bouncing off their shins.

Half an hour later she found herself joining them in a bar that served pizzas the size of hubcaps. The hikers ate ravenously but Katie's stomach was too knotted for food, so she drank wine and felt the liquid working through her like sunshine. In the next bar they ordered more drinks and played poker and Katie was declared a natural when she beat them following their own tricks.

Now they were in a packed bar where they had to shout to be heard over the rock band playing on a makeshift stage. They'd managed to shoehorn themselves around a table stained by ring marks. She set down her empty glass; her head felt light as if only distantly attached to her body.

'I checked,' Jenny, one of the hikers, who had muscular thighs and a wicked smile, was saying.

'No way he's single,' the girl from Quebec countered, leaning forward so they could hear. 'He does at least, what – ten, twenty expeditions each year? He must have bagged a hot girlfriend on one of them.'

'He's gonna bag another on this trip,' Jenny said with a wink, and they all laughed.

Katie's engagement ring cast a shoal of light across the table and she moved her fingers so the light swam. She had been thrilled when Ed presented her with it, glinting within a black leather ring box. It was a princess-cut diamond, set in a platinum band. She had fallen in love with the simple elegance of the ring and the idea of what wearing it symbolized.

'You gonna keep it?' Jenny asked.

'Ditch it,' the Canadian girl said. 'Do something ceremonial – chuck it under a land train – a final *fuck you* gesture.'

'No! Sell it!' Jenny cried. 'Spend the money on something he'd hate. Drugs, drink, male strippers.'

Katie laughed. Her lips felt numb. She yanked off the ring and pushed it to the bottom of her bag. 'My round.'

The band continued to thrash at their guitars as she jostled at the bar, which was four deep with customers. A barmaid leant forward, a hand cupped to her ear to catch a drinker's order who, after the second attempt at shouting, simply pointed to the draught and held up four fingers.

Was it this loud, Mia, in your dingy cellar bar? Did you have to lean close to Ed to be heard? Did he smell jasmine on your skin and spirits on your breath? Or did you flick him one of your hard looks that always infuriated him, only this time you turned up your lips in a hint of a smile, provocative: 'Well, then?'

You were wearing my dress. You never asked. It was too short on you. I never said, but I thought it looked tarty. Perhaps that's what Ed liked. His friends must have been impressed, a group of suits watching the barmaid who could neck shots like a landlord, and who danced like a tease.

You might have been drunk – more than I am now? – but you knew what you were doing when you felt my fiancé against you. I can see his fingers peeling the thin straps of my dress from your shoulders. Did he kiss you first, or was that too intimate for you? Did you think of me, even once? Your sister! His fiancée! Did you take a second to imagine how I'd feel?

The crowd pushed from behind and she was squeezed tight between thick, sweating bodies. She imagined Ed and Mia this close, his mouth on her neck, her pierced navel, the insides of her thighs. Did he prefer her long legs and her taut stomach? Had he thought Mia more beautiful? Or was it that he wanted to taste her wildness – just to sample a different dish?

How must it have felt to be like you growing up, Mia? With no boundaries, or limits, or expectations heaped on you. You once said I was the sunny-haired and sunny-natured sister who made daisy chains with her friends. You cast yourself as the dark-haired, dark-spirited one, who prowled the beaches alone. But I never once saw us like that. I saw you as freedom, as the open sea. And I longed for it.

Clumsily, she undid the top buttons of her dress and rearranged her bra so her breasts looked fuller. She smoothed her hair behind her ears and licked her lips.

The man beside Katie, whose tanned arms bulged out of a cut-off shirt, winked at her. She smiled, glancing up at him through her eyelashes. When the person in front of him moved away from the bar, he gestured for her to take their place. She slipped into the gap and as the crowd closed around them she felt the heat of his body against her back.

'What's ya name?' he asked, his breath hot in her ear.

'Mia,' Katie told him, feeling something inside her pulling loose.

'You are fuckin' hot, Mia.'

'Then maybe you should come and find me later.'

She ordered double shots for the table and carried them back on a silver tray sticky with spilt drinks. They drank them in one, slamming the glasses down on the table. Then they found a space on the cramped dance floor that smelt of sweat and beer. Alcohol and music pulsed through her as she swayed her hips to the band's rhythm. The other girls laughed and joked as they danced, but Katie felt far away now. Voices cut across one another, glistening bodies spun and wove around her. She coiled herself into sensual shapes and even when the others had gone to sit down, she danced on.

People were turning to watch as she writhed, her eyes closed, her hands running through the air. *Is this how you danced that night? Is this what Ed wanted?* She danced harder, not caring what people thought, not caring that she was drunk.

The man in the cut-off shirt moved in front of her and put his thick hands around her waist. 'Hello, Mia.'

She laughed at the sound of that name, throwing her head back. Above, a mirror ball spun, reflecting her image in a thousand broken fragments.

The man slipped his knee between hers. Their hips pressed together and she wrapped her hands around his waist to steady herself. Then his mouth was covering hers, wet and hungry. She could taste salt and whisky.

They danced on, him spinning her until the lights on the dance floor blurred. She was sweating beneath her dress and her head was beginning to ache.

She broke away saying, 'Toilet.'

'I'll come,' he said, and she let him take her hand and lead her there. He waited outside.

The cubicle smelt of urine and vomit. She had trouble locking the door, and stumbled as she took down her knickers, clinging to the toilet roll dispenser to right herself.

'Okay in there, hon?' a woman shouted from the next cubicle.

'Fine,' she managed, her head spinning.

As she washed her hands in a sink blocked with paper towels, she knew the man would be waiting. She would have sex with this stranger with his thick arms and greedy kisses. She would do it because she was too drunk not to. She would do it because she wasn't the woman Ed fell in love with. She would do it because she didn't care enough to say no.

She wove from the toilets, her hands still damp. A firm grip encircled her wrist and she was pulled away.

*

There were voices somewhere beyond where Katie lay. She opened her eyes a fraction, shifting as the world came into focus. She raised a hand in front of her face to shade the sun streaming into the room. Where was she?

She swallowed and her mouth felt swollen and dry. She'd been drinking. She paused on an image of Ed grasping a fistful of pages. They had fought, broken off their engagement. She felt for her ring: gone.

She pushed herself upright, saw the empty bunks beside hers and realized she was in a hostel. The hikers. She'd gone out drinking with the hikers. Then she remembered a man's mouth covering hers. Nausea overwhelmed her and she lurched from the bed. She took several deep breaths, her head pounding.

What the hell had happened? Had she had sex with him? They had been at the bar together, she was certain of that. She'd told him her name was Mia. Then later they were dancing. She remembered going to the toilets . . . with him?

She glanced down and realized that she was still wearing last night's dress. It was twisted around her stomach, a beer stain spread over the skirt. Her heart was racing. She wanted to crawl into the ground. *So this is how it feels to be you?*

She began tugging at the dress, ripping the buttons open and yanking it over her head. She flung it to the ground and stood panting in her underwear. *What have I done?* She slumped against a table, knocking a plastic water bottle over. It rolled to a stop beside a note. It had her name on it and she picked it up.

Katie,

Thought you might be needing these. [Two hand-drawn arrows pointed from the page, indicating the water and a pack of headache tablets.] *Hope you didn't mind being chaperoned back. He didn't seem like your type!*

Love, Jenny

P.S. Remember, sell the ring! Buy yourself a flight to New Zealand and come stay!

It had been Jenny who had grabbed her arm and led her from the pub toilets. Now she remembered the man, an angry vein pulsing in the neck like a threat, protesting that he would take Katie home, but losing.

Relief swam through her. She swallowed two tablets and then wrapped herself in a towel and left for the showers. Finding an empty cubicle, she turned the shower dial to hot and stepped in. Scalding water pummelled her scalp and turned the skin on her chest mottled red. Steam rose around her and she filled her lungs with it. She washed her hair and smoothed soap over her body, letting the water rinse her skin clean.

Without warning, tears began flooding her face. Deep sobs rattled through her body, drenched by the noise of the shower. She pressed the heels of her hands against her eyes, her head throbbing with the enormity of what had happened. Their wedding would have to be cancelled; there would be guests to tell, arrangements to unravel. But it was bigger than that. She wasn't just losing her fiancé, but the life they'd planned together

– the home they'd imagined building, the children who'd have one day played there.

Look at what you've done to me, Mia! I'm alone in Australia, sobbing in a hostel shower. My engagement is over. And now I've got nobody. You've ruined everything! And for what? A quick fuck in a corridor?

In a burst of movement, she yanked the dial to cold. Icy water poured over her head and down her spine. She gasped, her eyes wide. Instantly she was alert, her skin tingling. She cut the shower and caught her breath, her anger fizzling out.

As cold water dripped from her body, Katie thought back to Mia's entry. *You filled six pages with details of that night. At the end of it you asked yourself, 'Why did I screw him?'*

Your answer was a single line at the bottom of a page: 'Because I'm a bitch.'

But I'm starting to understand more about you, Mia. I don't believe you were the dark-haired, dark-spirited girl you'd have had us think. I know why you slept with Ed. You wanted to take the most important person in my life from me.

Just like I took Finn from you.

16

MIA

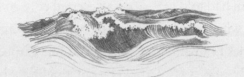

Western Australia, February

She dived down again, her body a slick underwater arrow, toes pointed, fingers together, hair in a smooth dark trail. She cut through the sea like a fish, her eyes open to the blurry blue sting of salt water, her ears filled with its fizz and echoes. Then she pulled her arms to her sides, arched her back and kicked upwards, breaking the surface and feeling the sun on her face.

There was no breeze and the sea settled around her. The shore was empty and the karri forest beyond, still. She floated on her back with her eyes closed. The air was thick and she could feel the weight of heat in it. She wished Katie was floating beside her, the sea making them weightless. The thought caught her off guard. It had been years since they'd swum together and she wondered why she still missed it with such a sharp ache.

She flipped onto her front and swam back in. Water streamed off her skin as she waded in to shore. She wrung out her hair and then shook the sand from her sun-crisped towel and wrapped herself in it.

She padded back to the hostel and dustings of sand trailed her along the corridor as she headed towards Noah's room. There was no swell forecast so she was hoping to spend the day with him. Zani had told her about a deserted cove 20 kilometres up the coast, which a pod of dolphins regularly visited. She had emailed a link of how to reach it and Mia was planning to take Noah there.

She knocked on his door. She imagined stepping from her towel, and slipping into bed beside him, Noah's body still warm. When there was no answer, she turned the handle and went in.

The room was empty: the bed had been stripped and his belongings were gone. Blood began to pulse in her neck.

She hurried along the corridor to Jez's dorm. She knocked twice, then let herself in. A row of stripped bunks framed the room. She swallowed, telling herself there must be some explanation.

Clutching her towel to her chest, she moved outside and followed the perimeter of the hostel, which led her to the garage. She stepped into the musty dimness and waited a moment for her eyes to adjust. Save for the hostel's shared surfboard, huge and dented with a missing fin, the rack was empty.

Then she checked the patch of gravel beneath the eucalyptus trees for his van.

Gone.

She jogged back inside towards the reception desk. Karin, one half of a Dutch husband-and-wife team who ran the place, asked, 'Hey, what's up?'

'Where's Noah? He was staying in room 4.'

Karin closed one eye and squinted towards the ceiling through the other. 'Checked out,' she said, opening both eyes again. 'And the guys from dorm 7, too.'

'What? When?'

'First thing.'

'Where did they go?'

'No idea,' Karin said, picking up a mug of coffee and blowing it cool. 'They were talking about a good forecast. Aren't they always?'

'Are they coming back?'

'If they are, they haven't booked.' With one hand she drew a blue folder towards her and flicked casually through its plastic sheets. 'Nah, we've got nothing for a month.'

He couldn't have left. Two days ago they'd lain on the grass and he'd talked about places he'd travelled to, of islands with no roads, waves that broke over kelp forests, fishes with wings and whales that sang. And she had pictured it all, imagining new adventures on shores fringed with two sets of footprints. 'Was there a message for me?'

Karin opened her palms. 'Sorry, darl. Not that I've been given.'

'Mia!'

She swung round, expectant. But it was Finn. He was strolling towards her holding a piece of toast, jam dripping onto his

210

thumb. 'Good swim?' he asked, then licked the side of his thumb clean.

'He's checked out,' she said. 'Noah's gone.'

*

Finn looked at her closely. Her wet hair was slicked back from her face, and her eyelashes were stuck together in dark triangles. She grasped the top of the towel against her chest and he could see the tracks of dried salt water flecking her collarbone and wrist.

She looked so young: like the Mia of his teenage years who had waited outside his maths class to tell him her BMX had been stolen. He remembered that day. She'd been so distraught that after school he'd gone to the tip, found an old shopper bike with a bent wheel arch, and spent the weekend fixing it up. He'd shaved off rust, replaced the brake clamps and repainted it sky blue – her favourite colour. When he wheeled it round to hers on Sunday evening, she had grinned so hard that her eyes watered. He had loved being able to fix the problem, but he had no idea how to fix this.

'Did you see him? Did he say anything to you?'

It was the small note of hope in her voice that scratched at his heart. But what should he tell her? That Noah had happened to come into the kitchen when he was making coffee, and mentioned they were flying out to Bali? Should he tell her that it was he who'd asked, 'Does Mia know?' and Noah who'd replied, 'I couldn't find her. Let her know for me?'

The guy's offhandedness was an insult. Finn couldn't relay that. So instead he answered, 'Sorry, I haven't seen him either.'

Her gaze fell to the floor.

He saw the faint freckles across the bridge of her nose brought out by the sun. He ached to wrap her in his arms, but he knew it wasn't him she wanted.

'He left for the surf.'

He saw her biting down on her bottom lip. He couldn't bear it if she cried.

'He should've told me. I can't believe he'd do this.'

Neither can I, Finn thought.

They'd been travelling the same route as Noah for weeks and Finn had watched from the sidelines as their romance played out. At night he'd lie awake in their dorm listening to the other travellers moving about as he waited for Mia. He'd hear the door click open, see a triangle of light spill into the room, then hear the soft pad of her feet across the linoleum. He'd watch the silhouette of her shape climb up the ladder into her bunk and hear her shifting above him, moving the pillows and sheet until she was settled. Each night she returned to their dorm he wondered, *How could Noah let her go?*

He'd distracted himself by picking up with a group of Europeans who were spending a season in Margaret River. He joined them for a fortnight of grape-picking at a local vineyard and doubled his cash playing poker with them in the evenings. It wasn't hard to avoid Noah – he spent all day on the water and didn't leave the beach much before dusk.

One afternoon, Finn had been hiking and paused on a

headland to watch the huge breakers peeling off the point break. A van had pulled up and Noah got out. He acknowledged Finn with a nod, then took his board and scrambled down the headland and into the surf. Finn watched for a few minutes. Noah's talent on the waves was clear, but what marked him out as exceptional was his fearlessness. Finn admired him for that but, as he watched Noah catch wave after wave, he knew he could never like him. It wasn't simply that Noah was Mia's lover, it was because he didn't cherish her. When he paddled in and found Mia waiting on the shore, her arms hooked over her tanned knees, grinning at him, he didn't see he was the luckiest man on earth. When he entered a room and she looked up, he didn't kiss her or slip his hand around hers. When he packed up his board and flew out to Bali, Noah didn't even realize what he was leaving behind.

*

Lying on her stomach on the top bunk, Mia wrote:

Six days. Still no word. We're flying to New Zealand tomorrow. Part of me is desperate to leave – but the other part wants to stay because the pathetic truth is, I want to be here in case he comes back.

Another couple have moved into room 4. The man hangs his tasteless shorts over the balcony rail where Noah's rash vest used to dry, and I want to rip them down and grind them into the dust. I resent his girlfriend more: she gets to

213

lie in the double bed now and feel the creak and stretch of the springs beneath her as she's made love to. I want to throw her out, seal up the room, stop them from trampling my memories.

Perhaps it is time for New Zealand.

She closed the journal and pushed it under her pillow, then lay back, staring at the cracked paint on the ceiling. When she was 7, Mia had lain on Katie's bottom bunk with its shimmering canopy, trying to imagine that she was a princess. But it never felt real to her. She couldn't picture the graceful steps, or the prim curtseys, or the pretty gowns, so she had clambered back up the ladder to her lair, content to be an explorer with a ceiling of stars to navigate.

The door clicked open. She heard the cheerful slap of flip-flops, then the creak of the bed frame as Finn climbed two rungs of the ladder. His head poked over the side of the bunk. His eyes were bright and he was grinning. 'I've got a plan.'

She blinked, taking only a moment to remember the expected response: 'What do I need?'

'Just your sleeping bag.'

She took a deep breath and then sat up.

'You want to do this?'

'Yes,' she said, shaking herself into action. She climbed down and pulled her sleeping bag with her.

They left the hostel and struck out in the direction of Reds, Finn leading. She felt the breeze on her skin and the relief of being outdoors. Crickets sang in the bushes and the air smelt of eucalyptus. By the time they reached the rocks, night had fallen and they picked their path by torchlight, her bare feet clinging to the chalky curves of the rocks.

The wind blew onshore and her sundress curled around her thighs. She untied a jumper from her waist and pulled it on. They continued until Finn chose a rock wide enough to lay both sleeping bags on. 'We haven't stargazed yet in Australia. As it's our last night, I thought we should rectify that.'

'Good plan,' she said, settling herself on top of the sleeping bag.

From his backpack, Finn pulled out a bottle of rum and set it down with a clink.

'Very good plan.'

They listened to the boom of waves breaking at sea as they drank, occasionally gazing up at a wide sky filled with stars. She was grateful for the way the sweet, dark liquid ran down her throat, washing away the edges of her sadness.

Later, she lay back on the rocks, her ribcage expanding as she made a pillow of her arms. Above, the stars winked and glittered. 'How many do you think there are?'

Finn took another swig of rum and then lay beside her. 'I read somewhere that there are more stars in the universe than grains of sand on earth.'

'I never noticed them in London.' They were faded by street lights, car headlamps, over-illuminated office buildings, and the glow of millions of homes. She thought of her sister somewhere in the city. It would be morning and Mia imagined her at her desk, leaning close to a computer screen, her face serious. 'I wish Katie could see this.'

Finn raised himself onto his elbows. 'You miss her?'

'Sometimes,' she said, surprised by the tug to her heart.

'Are you going to talk to her about Harley?'

She shook her head, realizing how dizzy the rum had made her. 'I don't want her to know we're half-sisters.'

'Why?'

'It dilutes us.'

'What do you mean?'

Alcohol had always found a way of working into the closed channel of her emotions, allowing her feelings to flow more easily into words. 'Mum had an affair. Do you think Katie would want to hear that? It means we've got different fathers. It stretches apart what's left of our family.' She sighed. 'And she'd want to know all about Harley.'

'So?'

'So I'd have to tell her everything – that he drank and took drugs, that he could be insular sometimes and wildly out of control at others, that his friends and family eventually lost faith in him. And the whole time, she'd be matching parts of him to me.'

'You need to let this go, Mia. You're nothing like Harley.'

'Aren't I?' she said, thinking of the other dark similarity they shared. 'Harley had an affair with his brother's wife.'

'Exactly! You—'

'I had sex with Ed.'

'What?' he said, sitting up. 'When?'

'A month or so before we left.'

'Did you . . . do you care about each—'

'No!'

'Does Katie know?'

She shook her head.

'Will you tell her?'

Mia sat up too and her head spun. She pressed a hand to her forehead as if to hold her thoughts still. 'She loves him.'

A pause. 'So why did you do it?'

'I was angry.'

'Angry?'

'At Katie. At you.'

'Mia?'

She could feel the anger simmering inside her, bubbling into her throat. 'Do you know what it is like having Katie as an older sister? It's like you're always standing in the shade. Every guy in school was in love with her. She was the popular one, the smart one, the one who made the right choices.'

'Come on, that's not—'

'Do you remember Mark Hayes from school? He was two years above us and got the sports scholarship to Ranford Manor?'

'Yes.'

'He went out with me for four weeks just so he could come round to our house to gawp at Katie. And I let him.'

Finn said nothing.

'You were the only one who looked at me first when you entered a room.' The wind snaked in from the sea and lifted the ends of her hair. 'And then suddenly you were with Katie.'

He looked down at his hands.

'You are my best friend. She's my sister. But neither of you told me. Not for a month.'

'I'm sorry, we didn't—'

'I hated her for it. That's the truth.'

She remembered sitting on the plaid sofa in their family home after learning their mother had cancer. Katie was crying heavy tears that soaked through the packet of tissues she carried in her handbag. Mia's eyes remained dry. When Finn arrived, he stood by the wood burner, the third corner of their awkward triangle, his foot jigging up and down as he listened to the prognosis. There was a moment when everything fell silent and his eyes flicked between them, not knowing who to comfort first: Katie, with her tear-stained face, or Mia with her flint-hard stare.

In the end he didn't have to choose: Mia had left the house, slamming the door so hard that the paintings rattled in their frames.

Now, Finn turned towards her. 'Mia, when I walk into a room, it's always you I see first.'

She could tell from the seriousness of his tone that he meant it. Meant something far more than she'd let herself see.

It wasn't Katie he saw first. It was her. Finn had always seen her, she realized.

Looking into his eyes she felt a dizzying rush of nostalgia, as if she were standing on the edge of their childhood and she could reach out and touch it – run her fingers through years of shared memories, feel that easy happiness.

She could hear the waves breaking, see the glitter of the stars. The world was spinning and sliding away and she reached her hand to his arm, holding onto what was solid and firm. Then she leant towards him and placed her lips to his.

'Mia . . .'

She heard it in his voice – he wanted this, had imagined it before. She kissed him again, deeply this time, as if she'd know herself better by sinking into him.

They lowered themselves onto his sleeping bag, the stars on her back. Her hair fell over her shoulders, brushing his face. She ran a hand towards the waist of his shorts and Finn caught it, lacing his fingers with hers. 'No, Mia. Not if you're unsure.'

There was rum warm in her stomach – she knew that – but there was something between them too. She didn't know what it was, she just knew she wanted it.

17

KATIE

Western Australia, June

Katie read with her head bent over the journal, her right hand pressed to her mouth and her left hand gripping the table. She read what happened between Mia and Finn on a smooth, red rock where the waves growled through the night and the stars hung like golden orbs overhead. She read of an intimacy shared on a single sleeping bag that changed the shape of a friendship.

When she glanced up, she saw that the café was empty save for a waitress checking her phone with a private smile. Katie reached for her cappuccino: cold. A coffee machine with gleaming silver knobs had stopped whirring and beyond the café window the rush of traffic had slowed, and everything seemed changed. She looked back at the journal and understood now the depth of Mia's anger at her. But she couldn't regret what had happened between her and Finn. Not when those few months with him were among the happiest of her life.

Katie leant back in her chair, wondering, *Was I that happy with Ed?* He had returned to England three weeks ago, calling her several times a day to leave apologetic voicemails. Twice she had found herself dialling his number, lonely enough to want him back, but both times she had made herself ring Jess instead, who didn't hesitate in reminding her why the engagement was off.

Katie thought she'd been in love with Ed, but now she wondered whether what she had loved was actually the idea of their relationship. Ed was intelligent, charming and successful, but he had never surprised or challenged her. He'd never stayed up talking with her through the night. He'd never made her laugh so hard that her stomach ached.

She realized there was only one person who had.

Reading Mia's intimate journal entry about Finn had prised open Katie's own memories, which she wore pressed to her heart like a locket. Now she found herself slipping back in time as she let herself remember . . .

*

Katie opened the lid of the cooling barbecue, then juggled the charred tinfoil packages onto a spare plate. Peeling back an edge she saw that the glossy kernels of corn had turned a rich gold. She offered one to her mother.

'I couldn't,' her mother said, placing the flat of her hand to her stomach.

'Mia?'

Mia shook her head as she sat cross-legged, dark glasses

shading her eyes from the sun, hands wrapped around a mug of tea. The tea bothered Katie. Their garden table was still filled with home-made chilli burgers, chicken and cherry-tomato kebabs, crisped rosemary potatoes and half a jug of Pimm's. Their mother had spent the morning cooking to celebrate having both her daughters home for the weekend. If she was disappointed that Mia hadn't changed out of her pyjamas, she didn't show it.

Katie spread a knob of butter over one of the corncobs and bit into it, her mouth filling with the sweet, nutty taste.

'How is your head?' their mother asked Mia.

'Still there.'

'Where were you and Finn?'

'At the old quarry. Cliff party.'

'Ah,' their mother said, nodding, for cliff parties were known to involve a few hundred people, generators and decks, beer by the crate and a beach stroll home at dawn. 'I wish my headache was because of a cliff party, but I think I must be fighting off a bug. I'm going to lie down.'

Katie only managed half the corncob and then wiped the butter from her lips with a napkin.

Mia reached across the table and took Katie's left hand, pulling it towards her to inspect her nails. 'Have you had a manicure?'

'I was given a voucher.'

'It suits you,' she said, and Katie couldn't see her expression beneath her sunglasses.

Mia uncrossed her legs, rolled up her pyjama bottoms, and

stretched her long legs across the picnic bench. 'God, it's good to feel the sun at last.'

Katie had a sudden desire to strip down to her underwear and lie in the spring sunshine with her sister, getting giddy on cocktails. It felt as though it had been months since they'd found the time to talk.

She fetched a picnic rug from the porch and put it down on the grass. 'Why don't I make us mojitos? Mum's got a bottle of white rum and there's fresh mint in the fridge.'

'I've got to drive back to uni soon.'

'You're going? You only arrived last night. It's a bank holiday tomorrow. I thought you were staying for the whole weekend.'

'I've got finals.'

'You're going back to revise? On a Sunday night?'

'I'm going back for a gig.'

Disappointed, Katie began clearing the plates, scraping the leftovers into a bowl and piling the cutlery on top.

The noise and activity seemed to aggravate Mia, who slipped from the table onto the freshly laid rug. She rolled up her T-shirt and flung her arms out at her sides.

'It'd be nice if you helped clear up.'

'I'll dry later.'

'You'll be gone later.'

'Before I go.'

'No, Mia. Now.'

She sat up. 'What is your problem?'

'Mum's been cooking all morning when she's not feeling—'

'I didn't ask her to.'

'It would be nice if you offered to help occasionally.'

'I can get you a badge that says PERFECT DAUGHTER. Will that help?'

'Maybe you'll get a discount if you order yourself SHIT SISTER.'

They glared at each other. Then Katie noticed Mia's lips turn up at the corners. 'You've got corn in your teeth,' Mia said, and they both laughed.

Katie put down the plates and moved over to the rug. Mia budged up and they lay together. Katie could smell wool and damp earth. Rolling onto her side, she bared her teeth: 'Gone?'

'Gone.'

Clouds were starting to break up the wide expanse of blue and she imagined that in another hour the sun would be swallowed. 'Are you coming home for the summer, after finals?'

'My housemates are doing MAs. I may stay on, too.'

'To do what?'

'Drugs. Prostitution. Theft.' She sighed. 'I don't know, Katie. There is no grand master plan.' She ran her fingers through her hair and Katie caught the smell of woodsmoke in it.

'If you want me to look for vacancies on our system, I can do. They'd be in the city, though.'

'Christ, the thought of London in the summer – suits, office blocks and clammy Tubes – I'd go mad.'

'Seven million Londoners manage.'

'Maybe I'll spend the summer in Europe.'

Katie laughed.

'What?'

'How are you planning to pay for it? You're at your overdraft limit and you still owe me £500.'

'Thanks for the financial advice.'

'Really though, Mia, I would like my money back soon.'

'What, that big salary of yours just isn't enough to keep you in calendars and highlighters?'

A cloud passed overhead, blocking out the sun. 'You can be so sharp sometimes.'

'And you can be so predictable.'

Katie stood, smoothed down her dress and crossed the lawn. She gathered the stack of plates in one arm and picked up the tray of potatoes in the other.

'And now you're going to do all the clearing up, so I look like the arsehole.'

With a hangover, Mia was most often sullen, but occasionally vicious. Katie wouldn't rise to it. She moved indoors, her eyes adjusting to the gloom. The kitchen smelt of garlic and rosemary and a play was in full swing on the radio. She scraped the leftovers into the composter and then searched beneath the sink for the washing-up liquid.

Mia stalked in, setting down a serving dish with a clang. She snatched off her sunglasses and then yanked open the dishwasher and began forcing the plates into the rack.

'That's clean. It needs unloading.'

With a sigh, she dragged the plates back out and banged them down on the side.

'Mum's asleep.'

'There I go, fucking up again.'

Katie ran hot water into the sink and added a squeeze of washing-up liquid. 'We're getting too old for this, Mia.'

'For what?'

'For this – fights over nothing. We're only together a handful of times a year – I just don't need it.'

'And I don't need you telling me what I should be doing with my money, and how I should be living my life.'

Katie laughed, shaking her head, and the gesture only enraged Mia further.

'You think you're so fucking superior, don't you?'

There was a knock at the back door and Finn walked in with a cheery, 'Hello!' His arrival did not deter Mia, who blazed on: 'You must love hearing about my spanked overdraft and my "aimless" future. But fuck, Katie, you know what? I don't want your corporate bullshit job, your swish pay packet or your pretentious London dinner parties. I don't want to be anything like you, because I look at you and think one thing: *Safe*.'

The word wounded her with its connotations of cautiousness, predictability and conservatism.

'Aren't you going to say something?' Mia goaded, eyes dancing. 'Tell me what a bitch I am?'

Katie turned off the tap and faced her sister. 'You don't need me to tell you that.'

Mia glared at her, then pushed through the back door, letting it slam behind her.

Katie could feel tears beginning to prick her eyelids and she turned back to the sink, slipping her hands into the soapy water.

'I'm sorry,' Finn said behind her. 'She doesn't mean it.'

'No?' At the edge of the kitchen, Katie heard the washing machine click into its spin cycle, a button or zip striking the drum with each rotation. 'I love her,' she said quietly, 'but sometimes I don't think I know her. That's a terrible thing to admit, but it's true. I honestly don't know my own sister.' She looked up at the ceiling but couldn't stop the tears spilling onto her cheeks.

She felt Finn's hand on her shoulder as he gently turned her towards him and wrapped his arms around her.

She had known Finn since he was 11; they'd hidden in the boiler cupboard together, crouching on a mound of warm towels waiting for Mia to find them; he had given her a piggyback home when she'd sprained her ankle chasing Mia's runaway kite; they'd kissed cheeks when she'd arrived at Mia's 21st birthday; but Finn had never held her in his arms like this. She had always thought of him as a boy, her little sister's friend, but as she let her head rest against his chest and her soapy hands lock over the hard muscles at his back, her perception began to shift.

She felt his heart beating against hers and wondered if he was attracted to her. She imagined Mia walking into the kitchen and witnessing this moment – and the thought thrilled her. She breathed in the warm smell of his skin and then, very slowly, she lifted her face towards his.

The kiss was gentle, an exploration of the idea, their lips lightly brushing before sinking more deeply into the softness of one another's mouths.

On the train back to London the following day she leant her

head against the carriage window, watching Cornwall disappear in flashes of greens and blues, but the memory of the kiss travelled with her. That week she called Finn and they met after work for a drink. It was a scorching day and they sat at a pavement table in Covent Garden, Katie drinking white wine and eating olives with her fingers, and Finn sinking cold beers. They watched workers loaf by with rolled-up shirtsleeves and loosened ties; the glow of summer's arrival spread in Katie's chest, and her laughter felt honest and real. They ordered grilled chicken and roasted sweet potato, and moved inside when the sun dipped behind the buildings.

Over the next month they saw one another regularly. With Finn, she discovered parts of London she'd never experienced: picnicking beneath a monkey puzzle tree in Battersea Park; joining a free walking tour of haunted buildings; eating sushi in a basement restaurant in Bank. They made love in his rented flat, Katie amazed at the way her body arched and hungered for his touch.

And then there was Mia. She had not made contact with Katie or Finn since their fight. It was no surprise; she'd always struggled to frame an apology but this time Katie was grateful for her sister's silence, as it meant she didn't need to confront what was happening between herself and Finn.

One Sunday afternoon, Katie was walking with Finn in Hyde Park, their fingers threaded together. They were musing on what to do for dinner when Mia called him.

'Hey,' he answered casually, letting go of Katie's hand. 'It's good to hear from you . . . fine, thanks . . . sorry, I've just been busy . . . No, of course not! . . . In Hyde Park, taking a stroll . . . Yeah, it's hot. I'm in shorts . . . No one's fainted, yet . . . No, I'm with Katie.'

When Finn glanced round, she saw his neck was beginning to redden.

'No, we arranged it,' he said, placing a hand to his ear to block out the noise from a group of passing students. 'We've been seeing a bit of each other . . . Kind of . . . I am being serious . . . About a month or so . . . Well, yes . . . I guess we are.'

Mia must have been talking then for a long time as Finn just seemed to shake his head and say, 'It's not like that . . . Come on, Mia . . . That's not fair . . .' Eventually he held out the phone to Katie. 'Your turn.'

She pressed it to her ear and heard Mia's voice, low, deadly, distilled by outrage. 'Is this a joke?'

'No,' Katie said levelly. 'It isn't.'

'You and Finn are what . . . a couple?'

'Yes.' She felt a flutter of excitement at the word.

'I don't believe this!'

Katie glanced over her shoulder and saw that Finn was hanging back, giving her space. 'We just – I don't know – get on.'

'He's my best friend.'

'So be happy for him.'

'We both know you're doing this to get back at me.'

It was true that at first she'd felt a private triumph over Mia, but there was no satisfaction in it now. 'I care about him,' she said, trying out the words.

'Bullshit. You spent our teens telling me what a fuckwit he is.'

229

That was also true. He had been the scapegoat for everything that was wrong in her and Mia's relationship. 'We were kids. Everything's different now.'

'Isn't it just?'

Six weeks passed and she didn't hear from Mia. It was bad news that finally brought them together. Their mother had called them both home to tell them that the dizziness and headaches she'd put down to exhaustion were, in fact, cancer.

Mia struggled to cope with their mother's illness. She visited home even less, drank and partied with renewed energy, and was fuelled with enough anger to refuse all of Katie's calls. Finn couldn't get through to her either; Katie knew he emailed her every week, but never got any reply. Without him, Mia was like a compass that had lost its magnetic field and was spinning, directionless.

In the end, Katie felt there was no choice. Mia was her sister: she had to come first. Katie finished her relationship with Finn four months and eight days after it had begun. She did it in a bar in Clapham so he couldn't hear her voice waver when she lied, telling him, 'It's been a lot of fun, but I think it's run its course.'

Finn had risen from their table and drifted out of the bar, hurt. Immediately she knew that she'd made a dreadful mistake. She loved Finn. He made her happy. It was too big a sacrifice to make. She had grabbed her coat and raced through the bar after him. But by the time she reached the street, he had gone.

Mia and Finn's friendship quickly returned to its former shape and, eventually, she and Mia came to their own kind of truce

– although it took their mother's funeral to thaw their anger. When the hearse arrived, Katie found Mia hovering on the upstairs landing, her fingers resting at the edge of a framed photo. In the picture, their mother was wearing a salmon-pink sundress, the hem lifted around her knees by a breeze. She was glancing over one shoulder, smiling with a hand shading the sun from her face. Two soft laughter lines bracketed her smile like dimples.

'She was beautiful,' Katie had said.

Mia turned. Her face looked so drawn against her dark hair and flowing black dress that she seemed haunted. 'I should have asked her where this was taken. What she was smiling at. I should have asked.'

That was when Katie had stretched out her arms and Mia had fallen into them. They remained like that until they heard the hearse driver clearing his throat downstairs.

*

'Just to let y'know,' the waitress said, startling Katie out of her reminiscences, 'I'm closing up in a few minutes.'

'Yes. Of course. Sorry,' she said, shutting the journal and getting to her feet. She rummaged in her purse and found a $5 note, leaving it as a tip to apologize for holding up the waitress.

Outside, the evening was thick and warm, a small surprise after the air-conditioned coolness of the café. She drifted along the street, the journal tucked at her side, her thoughts still circling around Finn.

When she had dropped Mia off at Heathrow, it was the first time she'd seen Finn in months. She had worked hard to avoid him, and anything that reminded her of him. She no longer listened to Capital Radio, the station where she'd helped him get placed as a junior producer, or walked the North Carriage Drive in Battersea Park that took her beneath the monkey puzzle tree where they'd once sat.

She congratulated herself quietly on the success of her efforts, but the moment she saw him strolling into the airport to meet Mia, his backpack slung off one shoulder, Katie knew she was undone. It was the smallest details that did it: the fine lines at the corners of his eyes that spread like sun rays as he smiled; the lightness of his tone as he asked, 'Coming with us?'; the smell of soap on his skin as he kissed her goodbye.

As she drove away from the airport, the passenger seat empty, her mobile rang. For an absurd moment she imagined it was Mia or Finn telling her to turn the car around and come away with them. But it was Ed. She shoved the phone into the glove compartment and turned up her music. Instead of returning to the flat, she found herself peeling off the M25 and following signs to THE WEST.

She drove for five hours straight and arrived in Cornwall with stiff arms and the beginning of a tension headache. She parked outside her family home and was pleased the new owners weren't in so no one could see her wandering across their driveway, trailing her fingers through the lavender bushes their mother had planted.

Afterwards, she'd driven to Porthcray and walked the cliff path, her heeled shoes feeling cumbersome on the rutted, wind-swept track, and that's where she cried. Thick, gasping sobs escaped into the breeze and were blown out to sea.

Sometime later she had dried her eyes, filled the car with petrol and then driven straight back to London.

Now she paused on the street, lowering herself on a squat brick wall to rest. She wondered where Finn would be right now. London? Cornwall? Another country, even? Had he found a new job? Did he think about Mia every day, the way she did? Did he think about her?

She regretted her behaviour at the funeral. It was inexcusable. She had lashed out and slapped him: not because he had returned home without Mia, but because he had left with her in the first place.

18

MIA

Western Australia, February

Mia felt the warmth of the sun on her cheek, heard a pleasing watery glug in the distance, smelt salt carried to her on the breeze. She opened her eyes a fraction and a spectrum of colour danced at the edges of her lashes. She raised a hand to shade the sunlight from her eyes, blinking as the world came into focus. Blue sky. Sea. An empty horizon. Red slabs of rock.

She had slept on the rocks.

With Finn.

She inched her head to the side, feeling a new stiffness in the muscles of her neck. Finn lay next to her folded into his sleeping bag, one arm flung out to the side. His lips were parted and his breathing was slow and shallow. The low sun illuminated the clear pores across his nose and the stubble grazing his jaw, which was light brown with a hint of amber nearest his lips.

She was jolted by a sudden memory: his lips on the inside

of her arm. Then came other images: her mouth covering his; the length of Finn's back beneath her hands; a glimpse of his tongue as he ran it over her nipples; her teeth against the soft flesh of his shoulder.

She slithered from the sleeping bag, naked. The air was cool. Swiftly but quietly she slipped on her underwear and pulled her dress over her head, not minding that it was inside out. As she bent to grab her flip-flops, her foot clipped the empty bottle of rum. She froze. It bounced and clattered over the rocks, eventually coming to rest in a crevice, unbroken.

Finn shifted. He rolled onto his back and hooked an arm in front of his face but didn't wake. She studied him for a moment and then she turned and picked a pathway over the rocks with her flip-flops held out at her side. She jumped down onto the hard-packed sand and began to jog. Her head pounded but she pushed herself on, trying to shake off the deep uneasiness spreading through her stomach.

She veered into the shallows, water spraying her bare legs and soaking the back of her dress. She was running hard and it felt as though her head might explode from the pain. She curved away from the shore, picking a sandy path that wove over the heath towards the town.

The scrub was sharp against her feet, forcing her to put on her flip-flops. As she straightened, she glanced back to the rocks and saw that Finn's sleeping form was only a speck against the empty landscape. It was wrong to have left him; he would worry when he woke and found her missing, but how could she stay?

She recalled their night, the firm contours of rock pressing into her back, her words loosening and pouring out. Finn listened so closely that all she could hear was her own voice and the waves. Then he had told her, 'Mia, when I walk into a room, it's always you I see first.'

Not Katie. But her.

The urge to kiss him and be loved was irresistible. She thought of how his hands moved lightly over her body, committing every part of her to memory as if she was a mirage that might disappear. There was such tenderness in his kisses that it made Mia realize she was what Finn had always wanted.

But was he what she wanted?

She stalked through the heath until the sun rose above the tops of the trees; a red blister formed between her toes. The path eventually brought her towards the edge of town and she followed the road into the centre where people were opening shop fronts and putting out chairs. She wanted to go back to the hostel and sleep, but knew Finn would be back soon. They were flying to New Zealand later and she needed time to think.

A sign for an Internet café caught her attention and she went in, desperate only to sit and rest out of the sun. It was an odd place filled with pellucid light, flickering screens and the dull smell of warm electrical appliances. Grey noticeboards stretched around the rectangular room with price lists and Internet instructions typed on yellowing sheets of paper. Even though it was early, she counted a dozen people with their faces focused on screens, fingers swimming over keyboards.

She fished in her pocket and found enough coins to buy her ten minutes of Internet time and an espresso from a coffee machine. She sat at an empty booth, logged on and opened up her email account. Fifty-two new messages swamped her inbox. She scanned them disinterestedly, most of them forwards or group emails. She'd half hoped there might be a message from Katie and was disappointed to see nothing from her. She clicked 'All' and then hit 'Delete'. In the fraction of a second before the emails disappeared, she caught sight of a name: '*Noah*'.

Had he emailed her? How could he when she hadn't given him her address? Her heart began to race. There must be a way to retrieve it. She tried to remember the command for undoing an action – something to do with pressing 'Control' and another key. She stabbed at the keyboard, trying various combinations, but the screen didn't change.

'Excuse me,' she said, interrupting a teenage boy in the booth next to her. He leant back in his chair and lifted one side of his headphones. 'I just deleted an email that I really need. Is there a way to retrieve it?'

'Maybe the "Deleted" folder?' he said with an arched eyebrow. Then he let the headphone snap back into place and returned to his task.

'Arsehole,' she muttered.

She glanced at the screen again and noticed a series of folders: 'Inbox', 'Sent', 'Drafts', 'Deleted'.

'Deleted'! She clicked the folder and all 52 messages spilt across her screen in bold type. She scrolled down until she found the one from Noah. The subject header was empty and she held her breath as the email opened.

Mia, I got your email address from Zani. Sorry I never got a chance to let you know we were heading on to Bali. I feel bad about that. It was a last-minute decision, as I guess Finn said. The hostel we're staying at is a hole, but it's only a couple of minutes from the Nyang break. The forecast is looking good – swell arrives in two days. If Bali's on your route, let me know. I think you'd love the island. Noah.

He was in Bali.

She scanned the message again and then her gaze locked on one sentence: *'It was a last-minute decision, as I guess Finn said.'*

She read it twice more to be sure.

Finn had known where Noah was.

She swallowed the espresso, then rose from her chair and left the Internet café, the message still flickering on the screen.

*

Mia pushed the door open with the palm of her hand. The dorm was hot and airless, empty of people. Her sleeping bag had been rolled up neatly and propped beside her backpack. She gathered up her towel and the bikini that she'd left drying on the back of the door, and stuffed everything in her backpack, buckling it shut.

She found Finn in the communal kitchen. He juggled a toasted sandwich between his fingers before dropping it onto a plate, then took a knife and cut it down the middle, melted cheese dripping from the divide.

His whole face brightened the moment he saw her. 'Where've you been?'

'Walking.'

'Want half?' he said, lifting the plate.

She shook her head. 'We need to talk.'

'Sure.'

They returned to the dorm and Mia closed the door behind them. Finn sat on the edge of his bunk bed, his head bent forwards. He bit into the toastie with a satisfying crunch. A piece of tomato fell onto the plate, the red skin peeling away from the flesh. He picked it up between his fingers and dropped it into his mouth. 'You know your dress is inside out?' He grinned, but there was a nervous energy about him.

Mia stood opposite, pressed flat to the wall. 'Did Noah tell you he was going to Bali?'

Finn stopped chewing. His foot began to jig, causing his flip-flop to lightly slap against his heel. He swallowed his mouthful, then said, 'I saw him the morning he left. You were swimming.'

'What did he say?'

'That he was flying to Bali with the others. There was a good forecast. He said to let you know.'

Her pitch rose to a slap: 'Then why the fuck didn't you?'

Finn pushed his plate aside. 'Because I knew how much it'd hurt you.' He shook his head and said gently, 'Mia, he didn't come looking for you. I happened to be in the kitchen just as he was leaving. I asked where he was going, so he told me.'

'But you never told me.'

'No.'

'I've been going out of my mind, Finn.'

'I'm sorry.'

Her hands were trembling. 'I can't believe you lied to me.'

He stood up and moved towards her. 'Mia, it was too easy for him to leave.'

'And too easy for you to step into his place.'

He looked aghast.

'What a perfect opportunity – Mia gets wasted as usual, and Finn offers a shoulder to cry on.'

'How can you even suggest—'

The door to their dorm opened and a young European couple entered. They said hello and unhooked their bags, somehow oblivious to the tension that filled the dorm.

'Let's go outside,' Finn said.

They moved past a group of girls sunbathing on the scorched grass, and walked to the fence line, which was partially shaded by karri trees. Finn placed his hands behind his neck, locking his fingers. 'What you just said, Mia, is wrong. Totally wrong. I would never take advantage of you.'

One of the sunbathers raised her head and peered over the top of her sunglasses. Finn lowered his voice. 'Shit, Mia, you're treating me like I'm some arsehole who's used you. What happened last night wasn't premeditated, you know that.'

She didn't answer. She felt the sun beating down on the crown of her head, her scalp prickling beneath its dry heat. She hadn't drunk any water and now her hangover was taking full hold.

'I'm sorry for not passing on Noah's message. We've always

been honest with each other, so I regret that, I really do. But last night had nothing to do with Noah.' He dropped his hands to his sides. 'Last night was about how I feel about you. Travelling together has made me realize exactly how much I care about you, Mia.'

'Don't do this, Finn.'

'You wanted honesty, so here it is – I'm in love with you.'

'No,' she said, shaking her head, wanting to put her hands over her ears to block out the words. Her heart was hammering against her chest and she felt the espresso acrid in her stomach.

'I'm in love with you,' he said again, his face open and earnest. 'I have been for a long time.'

She looked away. It was the truth, but she couldn't bear to hear it because it changed everything.

'I know this is a lot for you, Mia. It scares the shit out of me, too. I hate that it could put our friendship at risk, but it's how I feel and I can't do anything about it. Last night—'

'—was a mistake!'

His eyes widened.

'You lied about Noah. How can I trust you?'

'You know me.'

'I need to go,' she said, turning.

'Come on, don't walk away from this.'

'I have to.'

'Mia!' he called after her.

She stopped.

'Remember, it's two o'clock.'

She turned, looking at him blankly.

'Our flight. New Zealand.'

Could she sit beside him for several hours as if none of this had happened? Could they arrive in a new country and travel together after all of this?

'You'll be there?'

'I don't know,' she said honestly.

'I've messed up, I know that. But you can't bail on me. We've got to work things through. You wanted to see New Zealand, so let's see it together. We have to go together.'

Her head was pounding. She needed water. Shade. Space to think.

'I'll be at the airport with our tickets. Two o'clock,' he called, but Mia didn't answer.

She returned to the dorm, collected her backpack and left the hostel, unsure where she was going.

*

Finn waited, hands slung in his pockets, his backpack propped against his legs. People streamed around him pushing luggage trolleys, pulling children by their hands and scanning departure boards with raised chins. He'd positioned himself near the central set of revolving doors, providing a sweeping view of the airport. He resisted checking his watch again. He knew it was only five minutes since the final call for their flight had been made.

He wiped the film of sweat from his forehead. 'Come on,' he said under his breath.

Last night was a mistake, Mia had told him earlier. But he already knew that. He knew the moment he woke alone on the rocks. He'd heard the clatter of the rum bottle as it rolled, but he'd kept his eyes closed, feigning sleep, giving Mia the option to run. He knew her better than anyone and understood that when life loomed up too close, she'd rear away. He shouldn't have let things go so far. He'd allowed himself to believe that she'd wanted it as much as he did, but he had been wrong. Just as he'd been wrong to lie about Noah. And now she was angry and afraid, and all he could do was wait.

Just then, Mia walked through the far right entrance doors, her backpack on her shoulders, her hair scooped up high.

She glanced round, searching for him. She looked lost in the vast space of the airport. He picked up his backpack and began weaving through the crowd towards her. If they were quick, there was still time to make their flight.

She hadn't seen him yet and began moving in the opposite direction towards a check-in desk. 'Mia!' he called, but she was too far away to hear.

He glanced at his watch. Four minutes. They still had four minutes.

He jogged across the airport, saying, 'Excuse me,' as he ducked around other travellers. Squeezing through the centre of a tour party, he saw Mia placing her backpack on the conveyor belt at the check-in desk. It didn't make any sense: he had her ticket and she wasn't in the correct zone for New Zealand.

As he drew nearer, he glanced up and read the screen: FLIGHT JQ110. PERTH TO DENPASAR.

In that moment he understood. Mia was flying to Bali to find Noah.

She was leaving him.

He watched as she took her ticket and moved towards the security-check area. The volume seemed turned up; he heard the rattle of suitcase wheels, the squeak of trainers, the crackle and boom of an announcement, the far-off beeping of an airport vehicle passing. He watched, stunned, as she handed her passport to an official, who looked at it, nodded and then directed her through.

'Mia!' he shouted, waving.

She turned.

A strand of her hair had come loose and fallen over her cheek. She wore the same green sundress she'd made love to him in hours before. He wondered if it still smelt like jasmine.

When she saw him her fingers fluttered close to her heart, then settled on the bangle on her other wrist.

She smiled. It was a poignant, sad smile that didn't reach her eyes but told him that she understood the magnitude of her decision. Then he watched Mia turn away from him and leave.

He would replay that moment for years to come, blaming himself for letting her go. But on that day, he stood in the crowded airport believing it was the most painful moment of his life – with no idea that far worse was to come.

19

KATIE

Bali, July

The air smelt of clove cigarettes, fried fish and motorbike fumes. Westerners filled the pavements and were courted by the Balinese with their winning smiles. Katie wove through the crowd beneath the solid weight of her backpack as the traffic flowed past, taxis shunting and beeping with beads and flowers jiggling from rear-view mirrors.

She paused for a moment in the shade of a doorway while she checked the map: the hostel looked near, two streets away now. She had asked the taxi driver to drop her short of the hostel – the stop-start traffic had made her queasy and the back windows hadn't opened – but now she regretted the decision as weariness spread through her body like the heat.

She tucked the map away and lifted the base of the backpack with her hands to allow her shoulders a moment's respite from the pinch of the straps. Then she pushed on, squeezing through a group of noisy tourists haggling over silver jewellery. She turned right and then immediately left, which carried her down a narrow road flanked by bloated rubbish bags.

The Nyang Palace was announced in faded yellow letters painted across a piece of hardboard. The sign was propped on a plastic chair beside a doorway. She moved into the dim entrance, stepping over a woven basket filled with wilting orange flowers and grains of rice.

Inside, the smell of cooking oil hung thickly in the air. A group of travellers lingered around a tired settee, speaking in a language Katie couldn't place. Behind the reception desk a heavy woman sat on a stool eating rice with her fingers. Beyond her, a man wearing a pair of dark glasses was stretched out on a mattress, watching television.

'Hello,' the woman said, sucking her fingers clean. 'You want room?'

'Yes, please.' Katie kept her backpack on, hoping the transaction would be swift: she wasn't sure she'd find the energy to pick it up again.

'Dorm room? Single room? Double room?'

'Single, please.'

'Fifteen dollar.'

Katie had changed half her money into rupiah at the airport, having been advised to pay in Balinese as the deals were better. 'In rupiah, please?'

'No. No. Dollar only. Dollar.'

She handed over $15, too tired to haggle.

The woman shuffled out from behind her desk; she was wearing bejewelled sandals, her toenails polished a deep, glossy violet. Katie glanced at her thick hands and bitten, ridged finger-nails and wondered what small pleasure she must take in dressing her feet so particularly.

She was led up a set of stairs and along a corridor where paint peeled from cracked walls. The woman unlocked a door and then handed the key to Katie on a knotted piece of greying string.

The orientation of the hostel was brief: 'Toilet,' she said, pointing to a green door with no visible handle. Then she indicated towards the ceiling, saying, 'Terrace for smoking up there. No smoking in room.' The heels of her sandals made sharp clicks along the corridor as she left.

The room was dingy, cast into shade by lank brown curtains that were fraying at the base. She tugged them open, disturbing a mosquito that buzzed groggily to the ceiling. The view through the streaked glass was of the dilapidated building opposite, a slice of early-evening sun visible above it. She shrugged off her backpack and sank onto the bed, trying not to think of how many other people had slept on the thinning mattress.

In the quiet heat of the room, she realized that each of the places she had visited over these past few months had been leading her here: Mia's final stop.

She unbuckled the backpack and pulled out the journal. Flicking her thumb through the leaves, she guessed there could be no more than sixty pages remaining: few enough to read in one sitting. She could do it right now, tear through them in a matter of hours. It was all here beneath her fingertips, waiting for her to begin turning the pages.

But she knew she couldn't read it like that, not all in one go.

Not yet. For months she had been making this journey alongside Mia, coming to understand her sister through her own words. If she read these final pages now, then it would be over. She'd have to leave Mia, for good.

She put the journal away, deciding that she wouldn't read any more until morning. Tonight there was only one thing that she needed to do, something she'd already put off for far too long.

She smoothed her hair behind her ears, picked up her bag and left the room.

*

Her mobile had no reception, so she found a payphone two streets away. It was near a lively bar where travellers laughed and drank in groups like packs of animals drawn to a watering hole. Music drifted down the street, catching a young couple in its rhythm. The girl's hips began to sway beneath her sarong and the boy made a jazzy shuffle step in his flip-flops, causing the girl to laugh. They clasped hands, interlocking their fingers so the hearts of their palms were touching.

As she turned back to the payphone, Katie hesitated. *Is this the phone you used, Mia, when you called me the day before you died? Were you nervous about ringing to ask for money? Or didn't you give it a second thought, knowing how readily I always said yes to you? I can still hear every word of that conversation – the last one we'll ever have – and it haunts me. What I said to you will always haunt me.*

She took a deep breath, then dialled Finn's parents to ask

them for his current number. She hoped his father would answer; if it were his mother there would be too many questions. She cleared her throat and held the phone to her ear.

'Yes, hello?'

His voice was a shock and sent heat flooding to her cheeks. 'Finn?'

A pause, then, 'Who is this?'

She heard the unmistakable note of hope in his voice. The foreign dialling tone, the slight delay on the line, her voice sounding so similar to her sister's. Had he allowed a small part of himself to imagine it could be Mia?

'It's Katie.'

She caught the disappointment lodged in his sigh. 'Katie.'

Would it always be this way, reading into his sighs and tones and pauses, wondering if the man she loved had loved her sister more? She pressed her lips together, allowing herself a moment to compose herself.

'Katie,' he said again, brighter this time. 'I'm pleased you've called.'

'I didn't expect you to answer. I was ringing your parents to ask for your number.'

'I'm staying in Cornwall for a while.'

'Oh. I see,' she said, surprised he wasn't back in London. 'What are you doing there?'

'Working at the Smugglers' Inn again. I've been promoted to pulling pints.'

She smiled. It was the village pub near the harbour where Finn had collected glasses and wiped tables during his A levels. 'Pulling pints? It's a big jump. Are you sure you're ready for it?'

'The empty tips jar suggests not.'

'Is it still the same regulars?'

'Mostly. They all ask after you. Spinney Jackson wanted your address so he could write.'

'That's kind.'

'I didn't know what to tell him.' There was a pause. 'Where are you, Katie?'

She fiddled with the zip on her bag, tugging it backwards and forwards with one hand. 'Bali.'

'Bali? You're actually there? I've heard about what you're doing – following Mia's travel journal.'

'Have you?'

'I was in London a couple of months ago and tried to get in touch. You've changed numbers?'

'Yes, a while back.'

'I was worried. I went to your office.'

He was worried about me? She felt absurdly pleased by the image of Finn asking for her at the office. He'd been there once before to meet her for lunch, and he'd chatted to the security guard by the front desk while she reapplied her lipstick in the reflection of her computer screen before going out to meet him.

'A colleague said you'd quit and gave me Jess's number. She told me the rest.'

Katie had forgotten how well Finn and Jess used to get on. She liked the image of them talking together. 'I'm sorry. I should have told you myself. I left in such a rush, I don't think I even believed I was going until I found myself on a plane.'

'I didn't know Katie Greene did planes.'

'Neither did she.'

'Ed been out to meet you?'

'He came to Australia.' She hesitated, pressing her lips together. 'Actually, we've split up. I found out about him and Mia.'

'Oh . . .'

'Mia talked to you about it, didn't she?'

'Yes, just once.' He sighed. 'I'm so sorry. You've been through hell.'

'Hasn't been my best year.'

'How are you feeling? Really?'

She considered the question. At first, she'd been crushed by her break-up with Ed. But now, she no longer felt the sharp ache in her chest when she thought of him. In fact, as the weeks passed, she had begun to feel a strange sense of relief. 'I think I'm okay. Perhaps Mia did me a favour.'

'What do you mean?'

'Ed and I, we weren't right for each other,' she told him openly. 'What happened forced me to see that.'

'So it was a sort of shock-therapy-type favour?'

She smiled. 'Exactly.'

'Now you're out in Bali alone?'

A moped fired down the street and she breathed in the tang of its fumes. 'Yes.'

'You're being careful? Looking after yourself?'

'Yes.'

'How are you finding travelling?'

'Tough. Lonely. Exhilarating.' She had an urge to tell him how much she missed him, but she stopped herself. Instead, she said, 'It's been interesting going to the same places as you and Mia.'

'What did you think of Western Australia?'

'Beautiful. Barren, of course, but still incredibly beautiful. The space is overwhelming. On the bus we'd drive for hours without passing another vehicle. It was eerie, almost.'

'And what about Bali?'

She looked up. The night was closing in and she felt a low stir of anxiety. Perhaps for her, Bali would always be a map of Mia's last few weeks. 'I'm not sure yet,' she told him. She smoothed her hair with her free hand. 'Anyway, tell me about you. How have you been?'

'Truthfully? Not great. Some days I still can't believe she's gone. I walk down to Porthcray and imagine that any moment she's gonna come running up behind me.'

She thought of the surreal March day they'd buried Mia, remembering the biting wind twisting beneath her coat as she'd stood outside the church. She pictured Finn in his navy suit, his face tanned, but drawn.

The phone line began to crackle. 'Listen, Finn, my connection is going bad. I rang because I wanted to explain something . . .'

'Go on.'

There was so much she needed to say but she wasn't sure where to begin. 'Mia's journal – it's helped me understand some things.'

'What?'

'I know why she went to Bali now.' She paused. 'You didn't leave her.'

'No. She left me.'

'I never gave you the chance to explain. I'm so sorry for what happened at the funeral—'

'There's nothing to apologize for,' he said firmly, the lightness in his tone vanishing. 'Mia was my responsibility. I should have told you that she was in Bali.'

'No, Finn—'

'She should never have gone there alone.'

'It wasn't your fault.'

His voice was flat, toneless. 'Wasn't it?'

The line buzzed with static and cut out.

*

Katie searched out a quiet restaurant where she ordered noodles and sat with her elbows propped on the table, watching them grow cold. Occasionally, she tossed them with her fork and they squirmed, shiny and bloated.

Finn filled her thoughts, warm memories from their past planted like kisses: the light popping of soap bubbles on her fingers as they kissed for the first time; the sound of his humming as he cooked; the touch of his lips against her forehead when he left her sleeping in his bed. But then other images barged forwards: Mia's body poised above Finn's as they made love on the rocks; the grins on their faces as they hugged in the red dust while parachutes bloomed above them in the sky; the swing of Mia's hair as she turned and saw Finn at Perth Airport, waiting for her.

A waiter approached her table in tired black shoes that had been polished thin. Glancing at her plate, he asked, 'Everything okay for you, madam?'

Not wanting to cause offence, she swallowed several mouthfuls, the strong spices sticking in her throat, then paid and left.

She walked with confident, purposeful strides as she always reminded herself to do in London after dark. As she reached the entrance to the hostel, she passed an old man with milky blue eyes dragging a cart by a rope tied around his waist. His shoulders were hunched and he shuffled forwards with short, wheezy steps. The cart, lit by two lanterns, was stacked with treasures made from shells: polished clam bowls, shell-fringed mirrors, pearlescent candle holders, wind chimes dripping with conch and tusk shells.

A necklace caught her eye and she paused. Hundreds of tiny white shells had been pierced and threaded together on a loop of string. In the centre of it was a single pearl. Hairs rose on the back of her neck: it was almost identical to the necklace Mia had been wearing when she died. *Did you stand here, like me? Did the necklace remind you of the hours we spent together searching Cornish beaches for shells? Was Noah with you? Were you happy then?*

She paid for the necklace and fastened it at her throat. The shells were cool against her skin and she pressed her fingers gently to the pearl, warming it.

Entering the hostel she skirted the noisy crowd in the reception area and drifted up the stairway. Through the thin walls of the corridor she heard swearing, followed by a sharp thud, as if a table had been kicked. She would lock her door from the inside tonight, she decided, pleased she had her own room and wasn't sharing a dorm.

She stopped suddenly. A door off the corridor was wide open and there was a dark gouge in the wood below the lock. She spun round, checking she hadn't taken a wrong turn, but there was no mistake: it was her room.

Her heart began to pound. Tentatively, she stepped forward. 'Hello?'

There was no answer. She reached a hand just inside the door frame, fumbling along the wall for the light. It flicked on. The curtain flapped in the breeze and a cockroach scuttled into a corner.

She scanned the floor, the bed, the table. Empty.

Her backpack had gone.

A single thought sliced through everything: Mia's journal.

Behind her a door slammed and she jumped round. A boy with a shaven head glared at her. 'You too?' he said in a gruff Northern accent. 'The fuckers!'

The corridor trembled as he stormed along it.

She turned back to her room, rubbing a hand across her eyes as if she could wipe away what she was seeing. But the picture was the same: she'd been robbed.

She backed out of the doorway, then turned and bolted down the stairs, her necklace bouncing against her breastbone.

'My backpack! It's gone!' she cried.

The woman behind the reception desk tutted deep into her

cheeks. 'Yes. Yes. Police come. Six rooms they break open,' she said, gesturing to the people standing around in reception. Two girls with puffy eyes stood with their arms wrapped around their middles, a man was gesturing wildly as he spoke into a mobile, and an older woman with gaunt cheeks was writing a list on the inside of a book jacket. 'We are sorry. Very, very sorry. But not hostel fault.'

'Who did this? Have the police found them?'

'Many people come here. We not see every face. Police will find.' She tapped a piece of paper resting on the desk. 'Number for police, yes?'

Katie looked at the slip of paper on which seven digits were written. 'This is all? This is all I have?'

The woman shrugged, then turned away.

No, she thought. *No! I cannot lose the journal. It would be like losing you all over again.*

The air in the room seemed to thicken. She struggled to catch her breath, her throat closing. Her vision began to narrow – and suddenly she was fighting her way through the crowd, staggering from the hostel. Her foot caught against something and she stumbled, falling forwards onto the dark street. Her knees burnt as they smacked the pavement.

There was a light tinkling noise, like rain falling. She looked at the ground; her necklace had snapped and the tiny shells and pearl had scattered, every piece spinning away from her.

20

MIA

Bali, February

The taxi roared along the dark street and then ground to a stop. 'Here it is,' the driver said, yanking the handbrake. 'Only hostel in Nyang. Two minute walking to waves.'

The sign announcing the Nyang Palace was propped on a plastic chair. Paint peeled from the cracked exterior wall and a fluorescent light flickered above the doorway, attracting a cloud of mosquitoes. Mia hoped it was the place Noah had ended up at. She paid the fare and then stepped onto the pavement, pulling her backpack over one shoulder.

The air felt heavy and close, the day's heat trapped by the high walls of the surrounding buildings. She smelt spices and something sweet, like burnt honey. Footsteps sounded behind her and she turned to see an elderly man pulling a cart filled with shell decorations and jewellery. Sensing her interest, he paused.

She moved to the cart and was drawn to a necklace strung with white shells and a single pearl. She picked it up. It felt light and delicate in her hands. 'Did you make this?'

'Yes.'

'It's beautiful.'

His face bloomed into a toothy smile. 'Yes, very beautiful. Thank you. Shells from Bali beaches.'

She remembered beachcombing with Katie when they were girls, searching for shells and sea glass. Autumn was the best season, when the big storms would stir up the seabed and wash in limbs of driftwood, bleached rope and stones polished smooth by the waves. On cold evenings when the light had been swallowed by four o'clock, they'd sit cross-legged in front of the wood burner, making necklaces from their loot of shells. Whenever she had worn one of those necklaces – even if it were tucked beneath a scarf and coat – it would feel as though she was carrying the sea with her.

'How much is it?'

'Fifteen thousand rupiah.' He smiled again and nodded.

It was the equivalent to £1. 'I'd love it.' She pressed double the amount of notes into his lined palm, then said, 'Have a good evening.' She walked into the hostel with the necklace swinging from her hand.

The reception was a scratched wooden desk in front of the entrance to the owner's lounge. 'Hello?' she called out.

A side door opened and a woman in a worn nightdress sloped out.

'Sorry it's late. Do you have a room?'

She was shown to a poky room furnished only with a bed, mosquito net and frail bamboo desk. Before the woman left, Mia asked, 'Is there anyone staying here called Noah?'

'Terrace,' she said, pointing her finger to the ceiling. 'People party on terrace. Or beach. Lots of beach fires for travellers.'

Mia dumped her backpack down. There was no mirror, but she ran her fingers through her hair, working out the tangles. She hadn't any make-up on, so licked her lips and blinked several times to moisten her eyes, which felt paper dry from the flight.

She left her room and followed the windowless corridor to its end, where a heavy fire door led to an outside staircase. The metal steps clanked as she climbed and she held on tightly to the railing.

Music and laughter rose from the terrace and she paused, listening. It was difficult to tune in to the wash of voices, but she was certain Australian accents were among them. Her pulse quickened at the thought of seeing Noah. Despite her hurt at the way he left – *Mia, it was too easy for him to leave* – she hoped he'd be pleased that she'd come.

She'd been careful not to let Finn enter her thoughts, but now the image of him waiting for her at the airport rushed forward. She had heard him call out her name and she'd turned, seen him standing with a hand half lifted in a wave. She knew she should have said something, at least tried to explain, but everything she felt was knotted so tightly that the words became lodged in her throat. Instead, she had smiled with her lips pressed together, her eyes stinging with tears. Thousands of smiles must have passed between them over the years – smiles of joy, of collusion, of encouragement, of relief – and she knew Finn understood the meaning of this one: it was an apology for what she was about to do.

All the muscles in his face had loosened, fallen slack with disbelief. She had made herself turn and walk on. If she had glanced back, even for a second, she could never have left him.

Now she took a deep breath and climbed the final steps, which delivered her to the edge of a cramped roof terrace. She could smell coconut oil and marijuana. An old stereo was balanced on an upturned crate, blaring Bob Marley into the night. A group of people were crowded round a low table covered with beer bottles, a splayed deck of cards, tea lights and an overflowing ashtray. Surfboards were propped against metal railings, beyond which Mia could see the headlights of cars several streets away. She imagined that if she turned, the sea would be behind her, dark and watchful.

A man with thinning dreadlocks was saying, 'They're clamping down. That Kiwi did three months, no shit, for weed.'

Opposite, a girl with a bare midriff was arching backwards, laughing at something the person beside her was saying. When the girl straightened, Mia saw that it was Zani.

A voice snapped her attention to the edge of the terrace. 'Look who it is.' Jez was leaning against the railings, one ankle crossed in front of the other. He was holding a bottle of beer loosely at its neck. 'Come to find lover boy?' he said, stepping forward and drawing everyone's attention to Mia.

A flush crept up her neck. She forced herself to look him in the eye as she asked, 'Is Noah here?'

He glanced around the terrace. 'I don't see him.'

The flush spread into her cheeks, turning them deep red,

which she hoped would be masked by the darkness. 'Is he *staying* here?'

'How about I take you to his room?' Jez said, crossing the terrace towards her. As he passed, they stared at each other for a moment and she was disarmed by how similar his dark eyes were to Noah's. She tried to read his expression – resentment? anger? – but he moved past her.

She hovered for a moment, reluctant to go with him, but the thought of seeing Noah pushed her to follow.

Jez ran his beer bottle along the handrail as he clunked down the steps. At the bottom of the stairway he stopped and turned to face Mia. It was dark away from the lit terrace and there was no space to pass him.

'Tell me, Mia,' he stretched both syllables of her name, as if the word were a kiss. 'Why are you here?'

'To see Noah.'

He took a slug of his beer. 'You're what, in love with him?'

'That's none of your business.' The track that had been playing on the terrace must have ended. Silence expanded between them.

'I'm going to offer you some advice because I like you.' He leant close to her ear and she could smell beer on his breath. 'Walk away.'

'I'd like to, except you're in my way.'

He laughed.

A new song drifted down the stairway, pulsing into the night.

'If you don't, Noah will. Maybe not now, maybe not for months, but eventually he will. He's good at leaving.'

Yes, she thought. *I know.*

Jez opened the door into the corridor and they were flooded with light again, the conversation finished. She tried to imagine Noah and Jez as young boys kicking a football on a beach, or skimming stones over the backs of waves. She wondered, had a football ever been angled at a face or a pebble raised in anger? She didn't understand their relationship. It seemed as if neither of them wanted to travel with the other, yet something was binding them together.

Over his shoulder, Jez said, 'I'm guessing he doesn't know you're coming.'

'No.'

'It's a helluva long way back if he doesn't like the surprise.'

'He will,' she said with more certainty than she felt.

'You're about to find out.' He stopped outside a door and rapped hard with his knuckles. 'Special delivery.'

As he left, he whispered, 'I warned you, Mia.'

*

She had forgotten the impact his physical presence had on her. He was taller than she remembered, his broad frame filling the doorway. His face looked deeply tanned against a white T-shirt that was threadbare at the collar. She wanted to place her mouth on his neck, taste his skin.

'Mia?' He brought his hand to his jaw, the dark tattoo stretching over the veins on the underside of his forearm. 'What are you doing here?'

'I was in Bali. Thought I'd look you up.' She smiled casually, but her stomach was dancing with nerves.

'Where's Finn?'

She shifted in the corridor. 'I came on my own.'

She saw his Adam's apple move as he realized the enormity of her action: she was here for him.

He stepped aside to let her enter, careful not to touch her. She felt the heat of his body as she passed.

A small lamp lit the room and a ceiling fan whirled, circulating warm air. She recognized his belongings: a tired green bag at the foot of the bed, a pair of dark board shorts drying on a curtain rail, a surfboard leaning in the corner with a leash wrapped around its fins. She saw the imprint of his body in the creases of the bed, and a book face down on the pillow. She tilted her head to see the cover: *The Old Man and the Sea*. He was reading it.

There was nowhere to sit except the bed so she moved to the window and looked through her reflection to the dark alley below. She heard the click of the door shutting and then the low thud of his back leaning against it.

When he spoke his voice was low. 'This is a mistake.'

She turned. 'Don't say that.'

'Finn knows it. That's why he's not with you, isn't it?'

Tears stung the back of her throat. She couldn't bear to think about what she'd left behind; she could only focus on what she'd come here for. She lifted her chin. 'You emailed me, Noah.'

'I shouldn't have.'

'Then you think it is okay to just disappear one morning without even saying goodbye to the girl you've been making love to for the past ten weeks?'

'We hung out. We slept together. We weren't a couple.'

'It was more than that.'

'Not to me.'

'Don't sling around words so casually. You're better than that.'

His gaze was dark. 'Am I?'

'Yes.' She took a step towards him. 'Why did you send that email?'

He shook his head. 'I shouldn't have.'

'But you did.' She took another few steps until she was standing in front of him, close enough to reach out and place her fingers against his cheek. The fan stirred wisps of her hair against her shoulders. 'Why did you send it?'

'Please,' he said faintly, 'you should leave.'

There were only inches between them. 'Why did you send it?'

He fixed his gaze on her. His words were clear: 'Because I hoped you'd come.'

She had known this the moment she read his email. There was something between them, a connection she'd felt that first night in Maui, and she knew Noah felt it, too.

Slowly, she brought her hand to his cheek, his stubble rough against her palm. She felt the flicker of her pulse in the tips of her fingers where their skin touched. She sensed a sadness in him that she didn't yet understand. Then she placed her lips to his and kissed him. The rush of longing was so intense that she gasped.

He reached for her, folding her into his arms as if he never wanted to let her go.

*

Desire, which began somewhere deep inside of her, rippled outwards. Sweat glistened on their backs; slid between their thighs. His breathing quickened. Her teeth pressed into his shoulder. She shuddered.

He expelled a long, low groan and then sank down onto her, his face buried in her hair.

She lay listening to his breathing and the fan whirring above. She could feel his heartbeat in her chest. *It was worth everything,* she thought, *if only for this.*

Noah pushed himself up onto an elbow and looked at her. The intensity of his gaze made her feel as if he were searching her face for something lost. With his thumb he smoothed a damp strand of hair away from her temple. 'I'm sorry, Mia, for the way I left.'

He said nothing more for a time but she waited, sensing he wanted to continue.

'The forecast looked good, Jez found us some flights and we just left. I should've looked for you. Told you myself. But I didn't know what to say.' His gaze left hers. 'Or what I wanted.'

She swallowed. 'Do you now?'

He rolled onto his back, stretching so that his stomach flattened. He made a pillow with his arms and said, 'This, what we've got . . . it's a lot for me.'

She understood. On the flight to Bali she had flicked back in the journal to reread some of her father's song lyrics. Many of his later songs were about the powerlessness of being in love and she'd found herself rapt by the lyrics, as if he'd opened a door into her own mind and shown her exactly what it was she was feeling. The songs weren't maudlin romantic ballads, they were filled with imagery of both tender ecstasy and emotional imprisonment. They'd become etched in her mind and she felt the symmetry of their lives running like parallel railway tracks.

'It's a lot for me, too,' she said. Yet here they were. In quiet moments, she tentatively pictured a future with Noah: travelling through Indonesia together, walking on empty beaches with their fingers interlaced and, later, a trip to England, to Cornwall, to show him her sea.

'All I know,' he said, 'is that I'm pleased you're here.'

She smiled and tucked the comment away, knowing it would have to be enough for now.

She turned on the bed and lay with the back of her head resting on his stomach. She watched the blades of the fan rotate. Beyond the swirl of air she heard the hum of a generator and the low bass of a song pulsing from the terrace. 'So tell me about Bali,' she said.

He drew a breath and her head rose with his stomach. 'The water is incredible – clear and glassy – waves peeling right in from the Indian Ocean. It's busy, now. The surf is overcrowded and there's a load of attitude at the main breaks.'

'You've been before?'

'I lived here for a year.'

'When?'

'At 16.'

'With your family?'

'No. On my own.'

She tried picturing herself at 16 living in a foreign country, alone. 'Why?'

'I wanted space. I wanted to surf,' Noah said.

'That was brave.'

'It didn't feel that way.'

'How did it feel?'

'It was a long time ago,' he said. That was all.

'Has Bali changed a lot?' She was eager to keep the conversation going.

'When I first came here the surf scene hadn't fully taken off. The beaches were still quiet. There's a break called Seven Point that's really well known – it's in all the surf movies so everyone wants to ride it. A decade ago the only way to reach it was by paying this local guy to take you on the back of his scooter across a dirt track on his land. You had to climb down a sketchy rope ladder and he'd wait with any gear you'd brought until you paddled in. Now a tarmac road runs right up to the point and there's a café on the top selling surf DVDs and ice cream.'

'The locals must hate it.'

'Some were pleased. Tourism made them a quick buck. But yeah, a lot of them resent the changes. It's such a beautiful island but it's been disfigured by developers.'

'How long do you think you'll stay this time?'

'I'm not sure. It depends on a lot of things.' He didn't elaborate on what those things were and instead asked, 'How about you? You got plans?'

'I'm meant to be in New Zealand right now,' she said, wondering if Finn had managed to make their flight. 'Finn and I were planning on working out there for a couple of months to get some money together. But everything is a little up in the air between us right now.'

She felt Noah draw in a deep breath as if he was going to say something. Then the air left his lungs and no words followed.

He placed a hand over hers. She brought it towards her lips and kissed the underside of his wrist where his tattoo began. She studied the wave, intrigued by the numbers inked beneath the broken lip. It was a date, she realized, tracing her finger over it. 'What does this mean?'

'It's an anniversary,' he said, withdrawing his hand and pushing himself up so that Mia had to move her head from his stomach and sit up. 'It's the date that my brother died.'

'You had another brother?' She kept her voice level, hiding her surprise.

'Johnny.'

'How old was he when he died?'

'Twenty-two.'

According to the date on the tattoo, he died eleven months ago.

Noah swung his legs from the bed and pulled on a pair of sun-bleached shorts.

When he turned back, she noticed that his features had

tightened and a muscle clenched at his jaw. 'Noah? Are you okay?'

He pulled his lips into a smile. 'Sure.'

But his reassurance only troubled her because it was a gesture that reminded Mia of herself.

'You got a room here?' he asked.

'Yes.'

'Maybe you should head back now. It's pretty late.'

She had expected this: she had never stayed overnight with him and sensed that now wasn't the time to again ask why.

She threw her clothes back on and moved towards the door. He followed, picking up his room key. 'You're going out?' she asked, turning.

'For some fresh air.'

The light had disappeared from his eyes and she guessed it had been the mention of his brother. She hesitated in the corridor, searching for the right thing to say.

He locked the door and dropped the key into his pocket.

Nothing came to her.

'Night,' he said.

She watched him leave, glimpsing flashes of the black wave on his swinging arm, Jez's words ringing in her ears. *He's good at leaving.*

21

KATIE

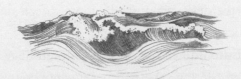

Bali, August

'Have there been any messages?' Katie asked, spreading her palms flat against the cool polished wood of the Khama Heights Hotel front desk.

'Yes,' Ketut replied. 'One message for you.'

Please, she thought as he lifted a slip of paper, *tell me my backpack's been found.*

'It is from Passport Services. A replacement passport will be sent to you by the end of the week.'

'Oh. Were there no others?'

'That is all today, Miss Katie. I am sorry. Perhaps tomorrow they will find your luggage?'

Her hands slid from the desk, a faint trail of condensation left behind. 'How long have I been here, Ketut?'

'Twelve days,' he answered, without needing to check.

Which meant it was twelve nights ago that she discovered her backpack had been stolen. Thankfully, she'd had her bag on her and could pay a taxi driver to take her to a 'safe hotel'.

She remembered drifting, luggageless, into the grand lobby of the Khama Heights Hotel. It was Ketut, standing behind the front desk in a pressed burgundy blazer with neatly oiled hair, who smiled warmly and asked how he could help. On her behalf he made calls to the police and the British Embassy, while she stood next to the desk, picking at a loose thread on her dress until the hem came undone.

She had visited the police station three times since then, waiting in the sweltering entrance that smelt of metal and disinfectant, listening to the bounce and clicks of men speaking Balinese behind a high wooden counter. Each time she was told the same thing: they would be in touch if there was any news.

She had lost everything – clothes, underwear, a bag of Chanel make-up, her new set of acrylic paints, two dresses of Mia's, her engagement ring, her passport – but it was only the loss of Mia's journal that she cared about. She found herself fantasizing about meeting the person who'd stolen it, grabbing them by the shoulders and screaming into their pitiful face until they understood the damage they'd done.

'Miss Katie?' Ketut said. 'Miss Katie, are you feeling not well?'

She placed a hand to her forehead and could feel the damp heat of her skin against her palm. She hadn't been sleeping or eating properly. 'I'm fine. I just need a little fresh air.'

She concentrated on breathing steadily as she moved through the lobby towards the gardens. As she took the tiled steps, she caught her reflection in an ornate wooden mirror hanging from the wall and paused. Her hair had grown out of its style and was lank, darker blonde at the roots where it hadn't been highlighted. She'd lost weight, too, which showed in her hollowed cheeks and the new prominence of her breast-bone. She wore no make-up, not bothering to replace anything that had been lost in the backpack except for a few cheap cotton dresses she'd picked up from a market stall.

She ducked her head and continued on, moving through the manicured hotel gardens where a light breeze carried the sweet fragrance of frangipani to her. Ahead, she noticed an older woman bending to grasp her sun hat, which had been lifted by the breeze. It rolled casually out of reach and the woman flounced after it, her heavy bosoms only just remaining concealed beneath a flame-orange sarong. The hat pin-wheeled into Katie's path and she bent down and plucked it from the lawn.

'Thank you!' the woman said, as Katie handed it to her. 'I keep meaning to grip it in place.'

Katie smiled and moved to walk on.

'Another beautiful afternoon. Aren't we spoilt? I hear it's been solid rain for a week at home. You *are* English?'

Katie nodded. She hadn't yet interacted with the other guests, avoiding the bar and restaurant, and preferring to take her meals in her room where there was no one to watch her pick at the food.

'Thought so!' The woman's cheeks were pink from the heat and a web of broken capillaries deepened the colour. 'I don't recall seeing you with anyone. Here alone?'

'Yes.'

She leant close, placing a warm hand on Katie's arm. 'It's a man, isn't it?'

'Excuse me?'

'That's why you're here. Mending a broken heart. Am I right?'

Katie shook her head.

'Oh. Usually I've got an instinct for these sorts of things. Must be losing my touch!' The woman laughed, pressing her hat to her chest. 'What brings you to Bali, then?'

Katie swallowed. 'My sister died here recently.'

'Oh, goodness! How awful. I'm so sorry. It wasn't that poor girl in the papers? Came off her moped?'

'No,' Katie said, impatient to move on.

'Such a beautiful girl, but no helmet! Could have saved her life! Tragic. But any young person's death is, isn't it, when there's still so much life to live? How did you lose your sister?'

'She committed suicide,' Katie said matter-of-factly, surprised at herself for wanting to shock the woman, but more surprised for wanting to say those words aloud to see if the idea had become any more possible.

The woman's mouth opened but no words came out.

An awful silence stretched between them. Katie could hear the faint trickle of water and the breeze stirring palm fronds.

'I'm sorry,' the woman said eventually, her eyes not meeting Katie's.

Katie left the hotel gardens, her heart pounding. She moved along the beach, passing pairs of sunloungers placed at discreet intervals along the shore, where couples in swimwear lay reading or dozing. She averted her gaze from them and walked for some time, her sandals filling with warm, golden sand.

The sun was hot against the back of her neck and she thought vaguely that she should have applied suncream. When she was well beyond the resort, she sank down in the shade of a palm tree and hugged her knees. Her throat felt dry and she couldn't remember when she'd last drunk anything. She was weary with exhaustion and now wished she'd not left the cool of her room.

Katie rested her chin on her knees. *Am I losing it, Mia? I don't seem to know myself any more. Does that surprise you? Me, of whom you once wrote: 'Katie knows who she is and strides confidently through the world.' Well, here's the thing: now I feel like I'm only tiptoeing.*

I can't afford to stay here much longer, but I don't know what to do next. The thought of going back to England terrifies me. I honestly don't think I have the strength. Your journal was the only thing giving direction to my days, and without it I feel . . . adrift. Hours seem to stretch out endlessly and, God, Mia, it's so lonely. I am desperately lonely.

Nights are the worst. I keep dreaming about you. You're on the cliff top and I'm beside you. We're arguing. You've just discovered that I've been reading your journal and you're furious with me. The wind is pushing your hair away from your face and I can see that your eyes are bright with anger. You demand the journal, but I don't answer you and we both listen to the waves crashing somewhere below. When you ask a second time, I tell you that I've lost it – I carelessly left it in a hostel and went out for dinner, not giving it a second thought. You picture those beautiful cream pages and heart-worn words, lost, completely lost, and become so furious that you start shifting, not watching where you're putting your feet. You're pacing close to the cliff edge and I'm terrified that you're going to fall so I reach out, but instead of pulling you back to safety, I push you.

That's what I dream, Mia. Every night.

Her cheeks were wet with tears. They fell onto her knees and soaked into the loose hem of her dress.

'Katie?'

His voice was an electric jolt and her head snapped up.

He stood in front of her, a hand shading the sun from his eyes. His skin was pale and his hair had been cut short.

'Finn?'

*

He tried to conceal his shock at her appearance. Her grief was something physical; it was the dark shadows under her eyes and the thinness of her arms that hugged her knees against her chest. Her hair had grown darker and it seemed, for an absurd moment, as if he were looking at Mia.

'Finn?' She rose to her feet. 'Oh, God! It's really you!' She lurched forwards, throwing her arms around him.

He breathed in a scent caught in her hair and closed his eyes, folding himself into a memory.

Eventually, Katie pulled away, wiping her face and smoothing her hair behind her ears. She looked small and fragile, like a wilting flower starved of water.

She stared at him, shaking her head. 'What are you doing here?'

'Thought you could use a little company,' he said lightly. He wouldn't tell her that her voice had sounded so flat and lifeless when she phoned, it had scared him. He'd already let one Greene sister come here on her own; he would be damned if he'd make the same mistake twice.

'How did you know where I was staying?'

'I spoke to Jess.'

'She didn't say you were coming.'

'Apparently you're not so efficient at checking your emails these days,' he said with a smile. 'The two of us have been plotting. We didn't like the thought of you here alone.'

Her eyes turned glassy and it was a moment before she asked, 'When did you arrive?'

'Couple of hours ago. I got a taxi straight here. The guy on reception told me you'd be on the beach.'

She smiled at him for the first time. 'I can't believe you're here.'

'Shall we walk?'

They moved along the shoreline. A light breeze stirred the surface of the sea and small waves broke inshore. He could smell the sea in the humid air, but also something citrus that he couldn't place. 'Jess told me about your backpack,' he said eventually.

'Mia's journal was in it.'

'I know.' He glanced at her and saw she was biting her bottom lip.

'It feels like I've lost her again.'

'Hey,' Finn said, nudging her with his shoulder. 'What are a few pages of Mia's ramblings when you've got me here to recount all those travelling tales?'

Katie smiled.

'Anyway, it sounds like you're the intrepid traveller these days.'

'Not really.'

'Manage to do any camping?'

'No. I've stayed in a few hostels, though.'

'Katie Greene in a hostel? That's not something I would have believed.'

'I skydived, too.'

'No! In Australia? At the Slade Plains?'

'Yes.'

'And that from the girl who wouldn't jump a rock pool without doing a risk analysis first. I'm impressed.'

'Don't be. I hated it.'

He laughed.

'Mia loved it though, didn't she?'

'I swear I could see her grinning a thousand feet up!' He remembered her running over to him in her jumpsuit, her goggles pushed up on her head, her smile stretching into her eyes.

'You both had a lot of fun.'

'Yes,' he agreed.

'What did you do after Mia left for Bali?'

'I missed my flight to New Zealand, so I stayed in Aus. I hired a car and headed for the east coast.'

'Long drive.'

'Yes,' Finn said, thinking of the hot, dusty stretches of road, and the cool nights sleeping on the back seat of his car. 'I never made it.'

'Where were you,' she said seriously, 'when you found out about Mia?'

'At a gas station. It was in the middle of nowhere. They had an old computer hooked up to the Internet, so I logged on to check my mail. There were seven messages from my brother telling me to call home urgently. I lost my mobile a few weeks before, so no one had been able to get in touch with me. I paid the till girl $20 to let me use the office phone.' He remembered that she wouldn't allow him behind the desk, so he'd made the call leaning over the kiosk, a rack of mints pressing into his hip bone.

'My dad answered. I knew something had happened as he wouldn't speak to me, kept telling me to hold on while he found Mum. She was in the bloody bath. Took ages for her to get to the phone. I was sweating by the time she came on the line. She just said it outright: "Mia Greene has died. They found her body at the bottom of a cliff in Bali thirteen days ago." She had been dead for thirteen days and I didn't know,' he said, shaking his head.

'Afterwards, I hung up, got back in my car and drove off. I don't know what I was thinking. In fact, I wasn't thinking, it was like my mind went totally blank. Maybe the logic was that if I drove far enough away from that phone, then it wouldn't have happened.'

'Oh, Finn.'

He glanced out to sea where a speedboat raced across the water, the hull bouncing off the waves. 'I pulled in later at a beach and just sat on the shore watching the waves break until it was dark.' He'd cried and raged, and punched a tree so hard he dislocated a knuckle. 'Then I drove straight through the night to reach Adelaide Airport and took the first flight out of Australia.'

'Oh, Finn,' she said again.

'Anyway, that's enough of the happy talk for one afternoon,' he said, stopping and turning to face the sea. 'Eighteen hours on a plane – I'm ready for a salt water bath.' He pulled off his T-shirt and tightened the cord on his board shorts. Then he ran into the clear water, wondering if every ocean would always remind him of Mia.

*

Katie watched him dive under the water. He surfaced, shaking his head, sending silver droplets flying through the air. Then he flipped onto his back and floated beneath the cloudless blue sky.

Finn is here. He is really here.

The sea glittered and the breeze seemed to skate off its surface, sliding over her skin. Two young girls with their hair in braids padded through the shallows, snorkel masks swinging from their hands. She smiled, thinking of Mia. Then she removed her sandals and stepped forward, sinking her bare feet into the wet sand at the edge of the sea. She concentrated on the feeling of salt water shifting beneath her toes, and then she took another step and let the sea spill around her ankles. It was warm and clear, inviting, not the cold sea of Cornwall.

She gathered the bottom of her dress with a hand and took another few steps until water reached her knees. She glanced up, checking Finn was still near. He waved and she managed to lift her hand and wave too.

He had asked her once, 'Why don't you swim in the sea?' They had been sharing a bath in his flat in North London, and the water had turned tepid, foam bubbles melting into a milky scum. She was leaning against his chest, her knees poking through the surface like two white hills, as she said, 'I almost drowned at Porthcray when I was 14. The tide turned while I was swimming.' She had run her fingers over the metal bath handle, wiping off flecks of water as she added, 'I'll never trust it again.'

He had leant forward and kissed her damp shoulder. It was the only response she'd needed.

Strange that she'd never told Ed about her fear of the sea, she thought now as she waded back out of the shallows, only Finn. She sat on the shore, pleased by the swirls of salt that dried on her shins. She turned her face to the sun and closed her eyes, feeling the tension in her neck loosening.

A few minutes later, Finn sank down beside her. The sun illuminated his face and she saw flecks of green in his irises. 'Finn,' she said slowly, sitting forward. 'Why are you really here?'

He picked up a stone and turned it through his fingers as he said, 'It's been hard back in Cornwall. I've felt sort of . . . dislocated from everything. It was like I needed to be in Bali, to be there, where it happened, for it to seem real.'

She nodded. 'I felt the same.'

'Did you?'

'When the police told me, it was so surreal. I don't think I really believed it. Seeing her body helped, though. I needed to be certain.'

'That must've been hard.'

She nodded.

'When you rang a couple of weeks ago and said you were out here, I realized how much I needed to come to Bali too. What you're doing – this trip, going to the places Mia did – that makes total sense to me.'

'Does it? Sometimes I'm not sure it even makes sense to me.'

'You're searching for answers. I get that.'

'Am I? Or am I just running away?' She looked down at her hands.

'Katie?'

'Maybe this trip was never about Mia. Maybe I just used it as an excuse to escape my own life.' She thought of Ed, of her job, of her flat. She missed none of it. What did that say about the life she'd left behind?

'It's okay to be here for yourself too. It doesn't always have to be about Mia.'

For some time they sat on the shoreline listening to waves lapping against the sand. She could feel the skin on her chest prickling pink in the heat. 'I think I should find some shade,' she said eventually.

She gathered her sandals and as they started to walk, Finn said, 'So you went to Maui?'

'Yes. I visited Mick.'

He waited for her to continue, perhaps unsure how much Mia had committed to her journal.

'I know about Harley,' she said.

'Were you shocked?'

Katie nodded. 'I wish Mia had told me herself.'

'She wanted to.'

'But instead she told you.' She glanced away, surprised by the speed with which old jealousies could surface. 'Sorry. I didn't mean that. I'm grateful that you were there for her.'

A cloud passed over his face, something she couldn't understand. But just as quickly as it arrived, it vanished. 'I think Mia didn't tell you about Harley because she was afraid that being half-sisters would change things between you.'

'Maybe it would have. It was awful finding out. It felt . . . I don't know . . . as if it diluted us.'

Finn smiled. 'That's exactly what Mia said.'

'Is it?' Katie smiled too. 'But I don't feel like that any more. *Half* – it's just a word, isn't it? We still grew up together, shared our childhood. Having different fathers makes no difference to me. We're sisters.'

'Exactly.'

'Sometimes it feels like I know more about Mia from her journal than from her. It's driving me mad that it's gone. I've had it in my hands this whole time but didn't read it all. I just keep thinking, what if she'd written something that would've explained things?'

'The police here must have examined it closely.'

'I've been told they would have. And I flicked through the last pages myself as soon as I found it.'

'And there was no note . . . no clue as to what happened?'

Katie shook her head.

'What do the police say about the backpack? Is there any chance it'll turn up?'

'They said if there's no news after a week it's unlikely they'll recover it.'

'How long has it been?'

'Almost two.'

He nodded. 'Have you thought about visiting the British Consulate out here?'

'It's an idea. Aside from the backpack, I want to know where Mia died. I know it was the Umanuk cliffs, but I'd like to know where, exactly.'

'Why don't I arrange for us to visit?'

'Thank you, Finn.'

He found her hand and squeezed it between his.

The spark was immediate. Her stomach fell away and her cheeks flushed red and hot. She withdrew her hand, surprised that even in the bottomless depths of grief, the heart could still want. She marvelled at the feeling, as if she'd just glimpsed the first green shoot of spring rising from the frozen ground.

22

MIA

Bali, February

The wind whipped Mia's hair across her face and pinned Noah's T-shirt flat to his chest. They stood on the shoreline, bare legs smarting from flung sand, watching the ocean writhe beneath the brewing storm.

When Noah spoke he had to raise his voice above the wind. 'Rain's coming.'

She glanced towards the sky. A flotilla of dark clouds, swollen with rain, were bowling in from the east. She guessed they had three or four minutes until the clouds reached them.

A wind shadow quivered across the surface of the sea, like the twitching scales of a fish. Noah took her hand in his and she felt grains of sand pressed between their fingers. 'Here's a big set,' he said, dark eyes shining.

Great mounds of swell the size of buses were building at sea. 'Could they be surfed?'

His gaze swept across the water as if he were mapping out a route. 'It's possible, but you'd be paddling into wind and the waves are breaking over reef. Tomorrow the wind will drop off, but the swell should stick. It'll be perfect.'

He'd been watching the forecast all week, checking the maps as the low pressure travelled in from the Indian Ocean, following a course from Antarctica. She'd been surprised by the technicality of forecasting, listening as Noah talked knowledgeably about weather systems, swell periods and local effects.

The lead wave of the set reared from the sea. It sucked up the water in its path, exposing the reef, jagged and brittle like the bones of a body from which the flesh has been sucked clean. The wave broke with a thunderous boom that reverberated in her chest. Water splintered across the serrated reef.

'My God!' Mia said, gripping his fingers. 'The power in that wave . . .'

'It's humbling.'

She nodded, amazed.

'You must get some big Atlantic storms rolling into Cornwall?'

'We do. When we were kids, our mum would drive us to the quay and we'd eat fish and chips in the car, watching the waves smash against the sea wall.' As soon as they'd finished, she and Katie would bundle up the greasy papers and race to the bin with the wind at their backs. They'd linger for a while, edging close enough to the sea wall to feel the briny vapour kissing their faces. When they climbed back in the car, their hair matted and tangled with salt, it always smelt of chip fat and vinegar, and their mother would be singing along to the radio. 'I miss it.'

Noah turned. 'Cornwall?'

'Cornwall. The storms. My mum. My sister. All of it.' She fingered the shells on her necklace. 'We grew up on the beach. It was our backyard. And now Katie's in London and I'm here.' She sighed. 'Katie avoids spending time on the coast. I know it sounds stupid, but I think of it as our place. Our link.'

'What changed?'

Mia thought for a moment. 'She's afraid.' She remembered that day at Porthcray when the current turned the water dark and rough. She could almost feel the hard surface of the wind-surfing board pressing into her hips as she'd spread herself across it, digging her arms into the sea. She shook her head, freeing the memory. 'You and Jez are lucky – you both surf together still. It must be nice to share that.'

'Maybe.'

She caught the change in his expression. 'Did Jez find it hard when you started surfing professionally?'

He shrugged. 'I don't know. We didn't talk about it.'

'But when you went home, you must have sensed whether or not he was happy for you.'

'I never went home.'

'What do you mean?'

'I came out to Bali for a year. After that I travelled for a while, then joined the tour.'

'You never went back?'

He shook his head.

'You saw your family though?'

'I'd meet my brothers whenever I was in Australia.'

'And your parents?'

A gust of wind blasted across the beach and they turned as the palm fronds clattered behind them. When they faced the ocean again, Noah was silent.

She squeezed his fingers between hers. 'What about your parents?'

'Let's just enjoy the waves.'

They watched wordlessly as the waves continued to thunder in and sand blew across the beach in sheets.

'How about you stay over with me tonight?' she said later, trying to regain some of their lost intimacy.

He shifted. 'I sleep better alone.'

'Who said anything about sleeping?'

He didn't respond and kept his eyes levelled at the water.

'You *are* pleased I came to Bali?'

He released her fingers to wipe salt from his brow. 'I thought we were watching the storm coming in.'

'Not in silence. Sometimes I feel like . . .' How did she begin to explain the cool stack of pebbles building in her stomach each time he pushed her away? 'Like you're not letting me in. Like you're not always *there*.'

'I'm standing right next to you.'

'Yes, but you're not talking to me.'

'You were talking about your sister. I was listening.'

'So let me listen to you.'

He swung round. 'I talk when I want to. Not because it's being demanded of me.'

'Demanded?'

'You've been here, what, two weeks? But you've not mentioned

287

what went on between you and Finn. And that's cool with me. I just figure people tell you things when they want.'

'I only want to feel closer to you—'

'And this is the way you go about it?' He turned from her, his T-shirt billowing in the breeze.

'Don't go,' she called, but already he was striding towards the car.

She wouldn't follow him. She wrapped her arms around herself as his reproach settled around her like clouds.

When the first raindrop fell, it landed on her wrist before sliding downwards, leaving a glistening trail. Then the clouds burst and rain fell in a heavy procession, leaving fine dimples in the sand. The noise filled her ears and within seconds she was sodden, her thin T-shirt turning skin pink. She wouldn't go back to the car. Her eyes were stinging with tears so she turned her face to the sky and opened her mouth wide, letting rain bounce across her lips and tongue. An earthy taste filled her mouth.

When she began to feel cold she rubbed her arms, her fingers sliding over her water-slick skin. Something in the distance caught her attention. A figure emerged from the rain, moving towards the shoreline. Every muscle in her body tightened as she realized it was Noah, board underarm, jogging determinedly into the surf.

*

Mia stood ankle deep in the sea, a hand held to her brow. She squinted through the driving rain trying to keep Noah in focus, while the seascape shifted and swam all around her.

It had taken Noah thirty minutes, maybe forty, to paddle through the hulking broken waves, duck-diving beneath solid walls of white-water. Now he was only a blur sitting astride his board, being lifted and dropped by the swell rolling beneath him. She pictured the concentration on his face as he absorbed the rhythm of the waves, searching for the right one. A wrong choice out here could be fatal.

Mia caught the roar of an engine and turned. The battered truck Jez was renting swung into view, windscreen wipers cutting back and forth. He jumped out with a jacket pulled above his head and jogged towards her.

'He's out there!' she yelled.

'What the fuck's he playin' at?' His tanned skin looked leathery and his lower lip had split from the sun.

A wave stormed in, sucking the reef raw and exposing new patches of jagged coral. Had Noah mapped out where the reef was hidden? Or was he hoping luck was on his side?

'How long's he been out?' Jez shouted.

'Half an hour or so.'

They both watched as he paddled furiously for a wave. As it rose beneath him, he looked no larger than a barnacle on the back of a whale.

'Not that one,' Jez murmured at her side. 'Too fast. Drop back, drop back.'

But he didn't. The wave suddenly took him, carrying him upwards to its crest. The world seemed to slow. Mia felt needles of rain against her scalp, heard the howl of the wind, felt the sea sucking at her feet. Noah pushed himself up from the board and began gliding down the face of the wave and, for a moment, she was mesmerized by the sheer beauty of that image, the muscular power at the throat of the wave, the agility with which Noah danced across the water under a pouring sky.

In a split second, everything changed. Noah's legs skidded from under him as if he'd hit ice. The board shot into the air and he bounced across the wave like a skimmed pebble. The wave smashed into the jagged reef in an explosion of white-water and Noah disappeared.

As the rain lashed down, she began to count silently. *One, two, three* . . . He could have missed the shallowest section of the reef, landed in a deeper channel . . . *eleven, twelve, thirteen* . . . He was experienced, used to being held under by waves . . . *twenty-four, twenty-five, twenty-six* . . . He was fit and his lungs must be strong . . . *thirty-one, thirty-two, thirty-three* . . .

There was a flash of white against the charcoal horizon. His board. It had been snapped in two and spat out further down.

'There!' Jez shouted.

Noah's head broke the surface. He bobbed in the seething water, a man amongst giants.

Behind him another wave loomed. He turned too late; the lip was already crumbling and it crashed down with a snarl that filled Mia's ears. The sea turned white. She imagined him being rolled and dragged with the storm of water, his lungs burning.

She hugged her arms to her middle and waited. Beside her, Jez shifted from foot to foot.

'Thank God!' Mia cried when Noah surfaced.

This time, Noah began to swim. His movements looked awkward, as if he was using one arm. 'He's injured!' she said, turning to Jez.

But he didn't answer. He simply stood on the shore watching, rain pouring from the hood he'd made of his jacket, his gaze never leaving Noah.

For several minutes they watched him making slow strokes towards the beach, diving beneath the waves as they passed, then clawing back to the surface. Wave after wave came, like an army with endless troops, and each time he surfaced he seemed to have been dragged further offshore.

'He's stopped! He's not swimming!'

'Come on, you bastard!' Jez said. 'Kick your fuckin' legs!'

But he didn't. He floated like a piece of driftwood, washing in and out of view.

Suddenly Jez threw his jacket to the ground and stripped off his T-shirt. His chest was paler than his forearms and Mia could see his ribs beneath the skin. He ran into the sea, launching into front crawl; his strokes were hard and nippy but he gasped breaths by lifting his head straight out of the water every few feet.

Mia rubbed her arms to keep warm as the gap between Jez and Noah closed. *He's coming. Just hold on.*

The sky continued to throw down more rain, which slid from her skin in chilled streams. Her fingers moved over the wet shells at her neck, pressing each like a rosary.

Finally, Jez reached him. She paced the shore, her footprints filling like puddles as she waited for them to swim back together. It looked as though Jez's arm was hooked around Noah's neck. When they were closer in, she saw Noah twist free of his brother's grip.

He staggered out of the shallows and she could see at once the torn rash vest, the sleeve of blood. He was panting. His forehead was cut and rain washed the blood down his face, like red tears.

She moved towards him. 'Noah—'

'You crazy fuck!' Jez yelled, cutting across her. His eyes were bright, livid. 'What the fuck were you doin'? You want to drown out there?'

The snapped leash was still attached to Noah's ankle and he looked like a shackled prisoner who'd attempted to escape. 'I didn't need rescuing!'

'Bullshit. You'd quit!'

They glared at each other.

'You want to see how Johnny felt? Is that what this is about?'

'Fuck you.'

'No, Noah. Fuck you!'

Noah turned and stalked up the beach.

'Wait!' Mia called, running after him. 'Let me drive you to the hospital.'

He didn't answer her. Didn't even see her. She stopped halfway up the beach and watched as he opened the car door, pulled himself in and gunned the engine.

*

'There's a spare towel in the truck,' Jez said, moving past Mia. She was standing in her sodden clothes, watching Noah's car disappear through the swaying trees.

The rain began to thin to a steady patter as she followed Jez up the beach, clods of wet sand clinging to the soles of her feet. He opened the driver's door and pulled out a thin blue towel that flapped in the wind. She took it and wrapped it around her shoulders. 'Well, get in then,' he said, and she did, sweeping aside wrappers and an empty can.

She dried her face and hair with the towel, which smelt of motor oil and cigarettes, while Jez put on a dry T-shirt. Then he leant across her, took a polythene bag from the dash and began rolling a joint. He worked silently with nimble, practised fingers, and then lit the joint. Thick pungent smoke filled the truck and she watched his eyes flutter closed each time he inhaled.

'Here,' he said, offering it to her.

Mia placed it between her lips and drew in the warm smoke, feeling it reaching deep into her lungs. She exhaled slowly. 'We had a fight. That's why he was out there.'

'Noah has a private battle with the ocean. It wasn't your fight.'

She thought for a moment. 'What did you mean down on the shore when you asked Noah if he wanted to see how Johnny felt? He was your youngest brother, wasn't he?'

Jez turned in his seat to face her. Rain had flattened the thin tufts of blond hair to his scalp. 'He drowned.'

'Oh. I'm sorry.'

He shrugged, but his eyes had turned glassy.

'Here,' she said, passing the joint back.

'Take this,' he said, swapping it for a small bag of weed he dropped into her lap. 'I've plenty.'

'Really?'

'I wouldn't tell Noah about your stash. He wouldn't *approve*.'

'Thank you,' she said, tucking it into the damp pocket of her shorts, somehow feeling a small victory.

Jez moved his head slowly from side to side, loosening his neck.

'Hurt your neck?'

'Old injury.'

'Surfing?'

He laughed. 'No.'

'What's wrong with it?'

'Fractured it years ago.'

She thought of the way he turned his whole body towards her when he spoke. She'd found the gesture odd, invasive almost, but now realized he didn't have full mobility in his neck. 'How did you do it?'

'*I* didn't. I was punched in the back of the head.'

'That's awful.'

He took a drag on the joint. 'Yeah, it is when it's your old man who's done it. He's pretty handy with his fists.'

Her eyes widened. 'I had no idea.'

'Why would you?'

She thought for a moment. 'Is that why Noah left home? He said he moved to Bali at 16.'

'Couldn't hack it. He just shot through.' His eyes narrowed. 'No fucking word to anyone.'

'Why didn't you leave?'

He glared at her. 'Johnny was a fuckin' 13-year-old. Would you leave a lamb in a lion's cage?'

They sat in silence. Outside, the wind howled through the gleaming trees.

Glancing in the rear-view mirror, Jez hissed, 'Get your window down!' He wound down his window with one hand and ground the joint into the dash with the other.

She hesitated, confused by the sudden command. Too late she saw the policemen standing either side of the truck. The passenger door clanked open and a coke can fell onto the wet dirt with a clink. A policeman with heavy-lidded eyes and an oiled moustache wrinkled his nose at the smoke that curled from the truck.

Mia and Jez were instructed to get out and place their hands on the bonnet. The rain had stopped but left deep puddles on the ground. Mia's bare feet sank into the murky brown water as she splayed her hands over the wet metal. The policeman searched her, pausing at the pockets of her shorts.

He clicked his tongue against the roof of his mouth as he pulled out the bag of weed.

Her blood ran cool.

'We don't like drugs in Bali. No good.'

She felt light headed; her lips tingled. She glanced across at Jez, whose search turned up nothing, but he wouldn't meet her eye.

She was asked for her passport and the policeman flicked to the back. 'English?'

'Yes.'

'You do drugs in England?'

She shook her head.

'Why in Bali?'

'I'm sorry. It was a mistake.'

He clicked his fingers, signalling the second policeman. They spoke in Balinese, the musical lilt of the language now sounding stern and threatening. 'Come,' he said eventually, and she felt a hand pressing down on her shoulder as she was led towards a police car.

'What are you doing? Please! This is ridiculous!'

He opened the rear door and she was ushered inside. She smelt incense and polish, and heard the click of an automatic lock as the door closed behind her.

Panic felt like tiny electrodes prickling at her skin. Was she being arrested? Where would they take her now? The police station? She tried the door, but it was locked. She looked down. Her feet were bare, her shins mud flecked. Everything she wore was wet and water gathered at the ends of her hair.

She pressed her face to the rain-smeared window and saw the blurred forms of the policemen talking to Jez. One of them raised an upturned palm and shook his head. She couldn't hear anything. She twisted her necklace until it tightened around her throat, pressing against her voice box.

The window began to steam up and she cleared a circle with the heel of her hand. Through it she saw Jez handing the policeman something. The policeman nodded. A moment later he was walking towards the car. The door opened and she was instructed to get out.

'Very lucky,' he said, wagging his finger. 'We have your passport information if this happen again.'

Dazed, she moved towards the truck where Jez was waiting, his hands slung in the pockets of his wet shorts.

'Get in,' he said, in a low voice.

She obeyed and pulled herself into the seat, slamming the door. The smell of marijuana and wet towels lingered in the truck. 'What just happened?'

'A Balinese bonus.'

She was trembling. 'You bribed them?'

'Yes.'

'Thank God!' she said with relief. 'How much?'

'Ten million rupiah.'

Her eyes widened. It was a huge sum, near enough £800. 'What about my passport?'

'Got it,' he said, tapping his pocket. 'I'll keep hold of it till you can repay me.'

She was about to protest that it was his weed that had caused the trouble, gift or not, but then he smiled. 'Rough day, eh?' He squeezed her shoulder lightly as he turned the key in the ignition. She wasn't sure if she imagined it, but it felt as if he trailed the pad of his thumb along her shoulder blade before finally removing his hand.

23

KATIE

Bali, August

Katie gazed from the taxi window as they sped inland. Lush rice terraces staggered down the hillsides and were dissected by strings of irrigation streams glittering silver in the sunlight. Tropical flowers flanked the verges and she imagined that if she wound down the window, the air would smell perfumed.

'I could only get us fifteen minutes at the British Consulate,' Finn said, turning to her. He was wearing a short-sleeved shirt and his forearms looked lightly tanned. He'd been in Bali for a week now and his company had been like a beacon shining through the gloom.

'That's all we'll need,' she said.

The taxi pulled up outside a whitewashed building that dripped with bougainvillea. She stepped out into the thick heat and smoothed her skirt against her thighs.

They were greeted by a Balinese woman in a long crimson dress that matched the shade of the hibiscus she wore behind her ear. 'Welcome. Mr Hastings suggested the gardens for your meeting. Please, come this way.' They were led through sun-drenched gardens filled with colourful plants. Butterflies dipped and fluttered near their heads. They were seated at a table positioned in the shade of a gnarled banyan tree and were brought glasses of iced water that sweated on a bamboo tray.

A few minutes later a slight man arrived, dressed elegantly in a light beige suit and polished tan shoes. 'Good afternoon. I'm Richard Hastings.' He placed a notebook and green file on the table, then shook Katie's hand, saying, 'I would like to offer my sincerest condolences for the circumstances that bring you to Bali.'

'Thank you.'

He shook Finn's hand, then hitched up his suit trousers before lowering himself into a seat. 'I know you've spoken to my colleague, Mr Spire, from the Foreign Office in London. I'm pleased to have the opportunity to meet with you also.' He touched the thin gold frame of his glasses and she saw warmth in his eyes that his formal manner belied. 'Now, I believe you came with some questions?'

'Yes.' She cleared her throat. 'I'm not sure whether you'll be able to help me with the first one. When I arrived in Bali three weeks ago I had my belongings stolen from a hostel I was staying in. The Nyang Palace.'

'I am so sorry,' he said, shaking his head slowly as if he were personally responsible.

'I reported it to the police, but they haven't told me anything.

I wondered whether you may be able to find out if there's been any progress.'

'I would be pleased to make some inquiries on your behalf.' He took a fountain pen from his breast pocket and wrote something inside his notebook. Beneath it he drew the pen along the page, underlining it twice. 'We are aware of a gang of Malaysians operating over here, posing as tourists. They have been targeting hostels because the footfall is high and the security weak. The police are alert to their organization and, rest assured, if there is progress, I will personally let you know.'

She wondered how much the contents of her backpack would fetch. The only things of monetary value were her engagement ring and phone. Would they be sold on the black market here or shipped somewhere else? The image of Mia's unread entries snagged at her thoughts again.

She sat forward with a sudden idea. 'My sister's travel journal – I was told the police looked through it as part of their investigation.'

'Yes, that's right.'

'Did they make a copy of it?'

'I am afraid not. I believe it was felt that it did not contain anything that could be used as evidence, which is why they were able to return it to you.'

Hope was extinguished as quickly as a burning match. She tucked her hands in her lap.

'Are there any other questions I may help you with?'

When Katie didn't answer, Finn took the lead. 'We'd like to find out exactly where Mia died.'

'Of course.' Mr Hastings drew the green file towards him and opened it, flipping through a series of papers. Locating a map, he placed it on the table between Katie and Finn. 'This shows a series of sea cliffs in the Umanuk region. This is the route that the police believe Mia took to reach the cliff top,' he said, trailing his finger along a hyphenated line. 'The beginning part of the track is well marked and leads to a lookout point, here. This is where Mia passed the witnesses. The cliff top is another two hundred feet up. The path to it has been disused for years and runs through dense foliage. And this,' he said, tapping the map where a circle had been drawn in pencil, 'is the spot from which Mia is believed to have jumped.'

Katie bit down on her lip.

'I am afraid to say that she was not the first to be found at that location. There have been six suicides recorded there in the last eight years.'

'Why?' Finn asked.

'We imagine people go there because it is . . . certain.'

Her stomach tightened: Mia hadn't wanted to survive.

'If it would be of help, I can arrange transport to have you taken to Umanuk.'

'No!' she said, abruptly.

'Thank you for the offer,' Finn added, 'but we probably won't visit immediately.'

'Of course. Please, keep this map in that case.'

She asked, 'Has anything else about Mia's case come to light? Anything at all?'

'I believe that you've already received the details from the witnesses' statements and autopsy?'

Her fingers were tapping against her thighs. 'Yes, but I'm just struggling to believe it still. Suicide?' she said, shaking her head. 'Are the police absolutely certain?'

'I have paid particularly close attention to this case because the death of a young person is incredibly troubling. But yes, the police are confident it was suicide.'

'But she didn't leave a note!'

He nodded. 'I understand how extremely difficult it is to live with someone's death when they've left no explanation for it, but it is not uncommon.' He placed his hands on the table, leaning in, as if what he was about to say broke some form of protocol. 'Perhaps it will help you to know that in suicide cases, only one in six people leave a note.'

'Why?'

'Often the decision is made on impulse; suicide has perhaps been something the individual has been considering, but when they decide to act upon it, it is with a sense of immediacy. Explanations are forgotten, which, of course, is terribly upsetting for those left behind.'

Something in the earnestness of his expression made her wonder if his experience of this was personal.

'All I can say to you is that while Mia did not leave a note, we do have several important pieces of information. Firstly, we have an account from two witnesses who saw her minutes before her death. We also have the reassurance of the autopsy, which made it clear there was no sign of anything more sinister at hand. You will also recall, Katie, that Mia had alcohol in her system?'

'Yes.'

'It is possible that your sister was not, therefore, fully aware of the consequences of her decision on the cliff. Alcohol is known to inhibit feelings of danger.'

'Yes,' she said again, not trusting herself with any more words.

'What I would finally draw your attention to is that Mia was carrying nothing on her person except one thing: her passport.' He paused, encouraging them to finish his thought.

'As identification,' Finn said.

'Precisely.'

'That is the information that led the local police to their conclusions. I am afraid it is up to you to draw your own.'

Katie swallowed, knowing how difficult that would be.

*

The bar of the Khama Heights Hotel was an elegant space, uplit by discreet amber lights. Beyond the tall stone pillars, floodlit gardens stretched down to the sea.

Finn slapped his cards onto the table, then leant back with arms folded, grinning. 'I'm available for lessons.'

'That's useful to know,' Katie said, spreading her cards neatly beside his.

He snapped forward in his seat. 'A flush? You have a flush?'

'Oh. Do I?' she said with a smile.

He stared at her, open mouthed. 'You hustled me?'

She slid the large pile of money across the table and into her wallet. 'Yes, I believe I did.'

He laughed, a loud, throaty sound that pleased her. 'Where the hell did you learn to play poker like that?'

'On my travels.'

'I can't believe it. You've been letting me win for –' he glanced at his watch – 'an hour and a half, and then you pull out the big guns in the final play. Katie Greene, you've changed.'

She smiled.

'Now I've only got four nights to reclaim my dignity.'

She wished he wouldn't remind her of how little time he had left. She gathered up their cards.

'I suppose the loser should get the next round.' He gestured to her empty glass. 'Vodka orange?'

'Please.'

She watched his easy strides, his shorts hanging low over his hips like a schoolboy's. The other guests wore shirts and light trousers, but she liked his casualness; anything else on Finn would be wrong. He said something to the barman, who laughed and clapped a hand on Finn's shoulder. She remembered how he used to arrive at the house she shared in London with Jess and two other girls and, before he'd even got as far as her room, she'd hear her housemates laughing at some quip he'd made. His ability to make people laugh, to make *her* laugh, was one of many things she'd loved about him.

When he returned with their drinks, he set them down and said, 'Right. I've been very courteous and avoided bringing this up since visiting Richard Hastings, but that was a week ago now. So, I'd really like to know: when are you planning on going to the Umanuk cliffs?'

She took a long swig of her drink. 'Soon.'

'Not good enough. I'm looking for a date. A time. A mode of transport.'

'I'm not ready. Honestly. I can't go there yet.'

'It's a huge thing,' he said more gently, 'I realize that. But you need to do this, Katie.'

She placed her drink down and pressed her lips together. They felt cool from the ice. 'Once I go there, this whole thing . . . following Mia's journal . . . it ends. I always imagined I'd go to the cliff with answers. But I don't have any.'

'Maybe there will never be answers.'

'There have to be. Because what am I supposed to do afterwards? Just fly home? Get on with my life?'

'Does that scare you?'

The couple at the next table stood and carried their drinks through to the restaurant to be seated for dinner. 'There's nothing in London for me any more. No family. No fiancé. No job.'

'It's going to be hard but you *will* manage. You're strong, Katie. Resilient. You've got your friends. You've got me.'

Was he setting himself apart from the category of a friend? She glanced at his face but his expression seemed impassive, difficult to read.

'Why don't we go back together?' he said. 'If you're not ready for London, you can crash at Mum and Dad's for a while. Teach me your poker moves.'

She smiled.

'You've got to go back at some point. I'd rather it were with me.'

'What will you do when you're home?' she said, shifting the focus. 'Are you staying in Cornwall?'

'Depends on work – whether I get back into radio.'

'Will the station take you back?'

'I doubt it. They weren't hugely impressed when I quit.'

'You worked so hard to get that job. I thought you loved it there?'

'I did.'

'Why did you leave?'

He lifted his shoulders. 'I was never able to say no to her.'

The thought of what happened between Finn and Mia reared up in her mind. It was one of the few things they'd not talked about and it hung between them now. She fixed her gaze on him. 'Were you in love with Mia?'

He drew in a breath. 'Yes.'

She felt the stab in her gut, a sharp pain that spread outwards and made her want to hug her arms to her middle. Instead, she picked up her drink to give her hands something to do. 'Since when?'

Finn scratched a knuckle back and forth beneath his chin. 'When we were 16 we were at a gig and she kissed me. Just a peck on the lips, that was all. She didn't mean anything by it. But for me it was the first time I'd thought of her as more than a friend.'

Her eyes widened. 'All this time you've . . .'

'No. No, I don't think so. It's hard to untangle because Mia always meant so much to me.'

'But when you travelled together . . .'

'I realized that I was in love with her.'

Her throat felt tight. She took another drink and finished it. 'It must have been hard seeing her with Noah.'

'It was hell.'

'What was he like?'

'He was an incredible surfer. Completely focused on it. I think Mia was drawn to that intensity in him.'

Katie nodded.

'But he was also distant, a bit of a loner, really. He hung back from the crowd. He always struck me as troubled. I'm not claiming that's an objective opinion. It's just mine.'

'Mia wrote the same thing. She said there was a sadness about him that reminded her of herself.'

Finn swallowed. 'You know, if I'd thought he'd loved her, then maybe my opinion of him would have been different.'

'Why?'

'It would've been easier to let her go.'

They were both silent for a time.

Finn shifted and when she looked up, she saw his foot was jigging nervously. 'I've got questions, Katie. About her journal . . . About some other things Mia may have written.'

Of course he would have, she realized. 'Ask me whatever you need.'

'Did Mia write anything,' he began, his gaze slipping to the floor, 'about why she slept with me?'

She thought back to the entry, the description of the stars dripping from the sky and the rum warm in Mia's throat. 'She wanted to feel what you did.'

Lucy Clarke

'Only she didn't.'

'You'd always been her best friend. She wrote that it was too big a jump for her to think of you as anything else.'

'She regretted it?'

'She regretted how it changed things.'

'Sorry, I know it must be odd talking about this. After us.'

She looked at him closely. 'When we were together, were you . . . in love with her?'

He took a deep breath. 'I found it hard that Mia and I weren't speaking. Really hard. But when I was with you, I was never wishing I was with Mia.'

It was a relief, at least, to hear that. 'I'm sorry for how things ended between us,' she said suddenly.

'It's in the past.'

No, it's not. It's here in the present, she thought. 'Do you remember what I said to you at the end? We went to that bar in Clapham.'

'Course. You told me it had been fun, but you didn't see a future.'

Her heart began to drum. 'That wasn't the truth.'

'What do you mean?'

'I was worried about Mia. It was tearing her apart that we were—'

'Miss Katie!' Ketut was rushing towards their table. 'I have a message for you!'

She blinked. 'A message?'

'Yes, a fax. It is here for you.' He passed her a white sheet of paper.

She angled it towards the light and read:

Katie,

Following your visit, I was pleased to make some inquiries regarding your stolen backpack. It seems that you are in luck: yesterday the police arrested part of the Malaysian gang we spoke of. I am told your backpack has been recovered, although I'm not sure if anything of value remains.

I do not claim any part in having the backpack returned to you. The police were scheduled to do so later in the week; my inquiry simply prompted a marginally swifter delivery. I do hope its return gives you a little pleasure; no doubt you deserve it.

Yours,

Richard Hastings

She looked up at Ketut.

He beamed. 'Your backpack has been taken to your room.'

*

She ran from the bar, her sandals clacking against the tiled floor. Ducking past a family dressed for dinner, she raced along the wide corridor towards her room, Finn behind her. She slipped the key in the lock and burst in.

Propped against the foot of her bed was Mia's backpack. It looked more worn than she'd remembered. There was a rip along the front pocket and a dark stain spread from the bottom upwards, as if it'd been sitting in oil. She crossed the room and lifted it onto the bed, not wanting to think about why it felt lighter. She groped with the buckle and drawstring and then dug her hand into the belly of the bag.

Please, she said to herself, *please be in here.* She began yanking items free – clothes, shoes and toiletries were bundled up together and she tossed them onto the bed. A shampoo bottle had leaked over her belongings, turning her fingers damp and sticky. She pulled out item after item: a green dress, a paperback, a pair of earphones, a torch. Then her hand met with the bottom of the bag. There was nothing more in it.

'No!' She flipped it upside down and shook fiercely. 'Come on!'

She shoved the bag aside and pawed through the belongings littering the bed: flip-flops, a hairbrush, a cardigan, suncream, a pair of shorts. She must have missed it. She turned everything over, shaking out clothing, tossing aside shoes. She sieved through the pile again, twice. 'It's not here! Her journal's not here!'

She turned and saw Finn crouched beside the backpack. He was running his hands along it and then he unzipped a side pocket, which she must have missed in her hurry. She saw a flash of sea-blue as he pulled out the journal, a magician performing his best trick.

'Thank God!' she cried. She took it, her fingers moving over the cover. The spine was worn and cracked and the fabric seemed thinner. She flicked her thumb through the pages: it was all there!

'Finn—' she said, spinning round.

She froze.

His expression was serious and in his hands he held a dress.

It was the colour of wet grass and belonged to Mia, one of the few items of her clothing that Katie had kept in the backpack. She watched as he fingered the light cotton straps that would once have rested on Mia's shoulders. She wondered what memory it stirred to make his eyes close for a moment. He lifted the dress, as if trying to find weight or substance in the empty material, and then he drew it to his face and breathed in the smell of her sister.

Even though you're gone, it will always be you and Finn, won't it?

Finn opened his eyes and his gaze met Katie's. Neither of them spoke. It felt as if Mia's presence suddenly loomed so large that the air in the room constricted with it. They both held part of her in their hands.

Suddenly Finn loosened the dress from his grip and cleared his throat. 'You've got the journal back.'

'Yes.'

'You must be desperate to read it,' he said, getting to his feet. 'I'll give you some space.'

She nodded. Even before the door closed behind him, she was pulling herself onto the bed, drawing the journal into her lap and opening the intimate cream pages.

24

MIA

Bali, March

Mia reached the cliff top and planted her hands on her hips while she caught her breath. Sweat beaded between her breasts and at the waist of her shorts and she was grateful for the breeze funnelling up from the sea.

Noah was sitting in the shade cast by a granite boulder, his knees drawn towards his chest. She knew he'd be here. The lonely ocean view drew him daily to the cliff's crown to watch the waves peeling below. He did not turn at the sound of her footsteps, nor as she lowered herself beside him, pressing her back against the cool boulder.

From a canvas shoulder bag she took out a bottle of water and a sandwich. 'Thought you might be hungry.'

'Thanks,' he said, taking them. His eyes briefly met hers and she saw the hollow rings beneath them. Week-old stubble grazed his jaw and the cut on his forehead had healed over with a brown scab.

After his surfing accident three weeks ago, Noah had driven

himself to hospital, leaving a ragged bloodstain on the driver's seat. The doctor, who wouldn't examine him until he'd returned with proof that he could pay the final bill, told Noah he had an acute tear to the rotator cuff muscles in his shoulder and a 3-inch laceration on his upper back that would need stitches.

'I waited for you back at the hostel. How did the check-up go?'

His gaze was on the sea where lines of swell, smooth and glassy, rippled beneath its surface.

'The cut on my back's infected.'

Yesterday she'd seen the wound as she'd helped him change the dressing. The jagged mouth of it was raw and pink, but in the centre she'd noticed a paler tinge to the flesh and had worried then about infection. 'Have they given you antibiotics?'

He nodded. 'Anyway, they reckon the muscle damage will keep me off the water for at least three months. Maybe six.'

'It'll be sooner,' she promised, placing her hand over his and squeezing it.

The morning following Noah's accident, she'd found him at Nyang beach, using his good arm to launch sticks into the rolling surf.

'I need to know,' Mia had said, coming to stand at his side, 'why you put yourself in such danger?' All night she'd replayed the image of him staggering from the surf. 'You could have been killed.'

Noah had stared at her, the flatness of his expression unreadable. 'I know I could have.'

Since then he'd taken to spending most days alone on the cliff top, watching the peeling waves and listening to the far-off hoots and cries of the surfers who rode them. In the evenings he'd come to her room and he'd make love to her with a desperate urgency. Afterwards they'd lie together beneath the whirling fan, before Noah returned to his room to sleep alone.

'I was thinking,' she began, forcing her voice to sound bright, 'that we could do something different tomorrow. You said Ubud is beautiful. I'd love to visit the temples and water gardens. We could spend a few days up there – stay in one of the lodges where it's cooler.' She imagined a small place set in the foothills, embraced by brilliant tropical plants that perfumed the air. Away from the dusty heat of town she'd draw Noah out of himself. They'd take early-morning walks through dewy grass, spend the afternoons in bed making love, and talk late into the night.

'I'm thinking of leaving Bali.'

'What?' She felt a pressure expanding in her chest. 'Why?'

'I came here for the surf.'

'I came here for you.' The words were out before she could stop them. She thought for a moment of Finn and all she'd sacrificed. The image of him was like a fist squeezing tight around her heart. 'What about us?'

Noah withdrew his hand from beneath hers and she felt the gesture was something larger than that. 'I don't know,' he said eventually. 'I'm sorry. I just don't know.'

Her happiness had become measured with a ruler notched by her interactions with Noah. She'd read books in which characters described themselves as being '*imprisoned*' by love, and had dismissed the term as melodramatic. But now she could think of no better way to describe what it was she felt: she was trapped by the intensity of her feelings for Noah.

'I love you.' The words slipped out unbidden and immediately her cheeks flamed. She looked at her hands, shaken by the enormity of what she had declared. It was the first time she'd said those words to a man.

Silence swelled around them. She waited, willing him to speak.

When he said nothing, she felt her eyes pricking with tears. She glanced up, setting her gaze on two gulls wheeling on the air currents, the undersides of their wings sharp white.

Mia stood and began moving towards the cliff edge, breaking away from his silence. The breeze was stiff against her cheeks and she squinted into the sun as she tracked the gulls. They glided down the cliff face, dipping low to the sea where waves hummed and rolled. She envied their freedom: she wanted to dive from the cliff, fly through the air and drift above the ocean.

She stepped forward, placing her toes right at the edge. It was a 400-foot drop onto angular slabs of rock, which waited like tombstones. The breeze wound around her fingers and she began to lift her arms like wings, the cool air stroking her skin, soothing her. The lure of the ocean, liquid and glinting, beckoned her and a dizzy rush filled her head.

Suddenly Noah was beside her, grabbing her arm and yanking her away from the edge. 'What the fuck were you doing?'

'I . . . I was just . . .' she stammered, shocked by herself.

'You were right out on the edge!'

'I wanted to feel the breeze.'

He released his grip and his fingers left a red imprint around her wrist. 'Jesus, Mia, I thought you were . . .'

'I'm sorry.' Tears stung the back of her throat and she couldn't meet his eye.

'Hey,' he said more softly now. 'It's okay. I overreacted.'

She felt his hand on her lower back and stepped towards him. He folded her into his arms and she pressed her cheek to his chest. She wrapped her arms tightly around him, her hands clutching his cotton T-shirt.

As she listened to the fierce drumming of his heart, she realized that they were no longer hugging: she was holding on.

*

Mia drifted along the corridor towards her room, her mind heavy. Noah had offered no time frame of when he would leave, or explanation as to what would happen between them, but deep within her she already knew: it was ending.

She unlocked the door and stepped into the stagnant heat. She'd forgotten to leave the window ajar so the sun had been blazing in, cooking the dust motes that hung in the air.

'How's it goin'?'

She turned in the doorway to find Jez approaching. 'Fine,' she replied, ducking inside, desperate to be alone. All she wanted was to stretch out on her bed, close her eyes and sleep.

His trainers squeaked across the lino floor as he followed her in. She hadn't seen him in almost two weeks and knew he was here to collect the money she still owed. Yesterday she'd visited the bank and had been surprised to learn that her overdraft was already at its threshold. She knew things would be tight after splurging on the flight to Bali, but had been blithely unaware how desperate her finances were. When she and Finn had drawn up a budget for the trip, they'd built in three months working in New Zealand; now that that was out of the equation, she had no idea how she'd survive.

She dropped her bag on the desk and pushed open the window to encourage the air to circulate.

'You've caught the sun,' Jez told her. He was leaning against the wall with his hands slung in his pockets, the way a bored teenager might stand. A pair of wrap-around sunglasses were pushed back on his head, the lenses cloudy with salt.

'Have I?'

'On your shoulders.'

Mia angled a shoulder towards her face and prodded the skin with a fingertip. A white imprint was left behind.

'Been on the beach?'

'No, I've just come back from the cliffs.'

He must have known her reason for going there but he didn't ask about his brother. Instead, he said, 'Thought I'd let you know that there's a reggae band playing at Loko's tonight. A few of us will be heading down. Fancy it?'

The simple friendliness of his request threw her. She wasn't in the mood for loud music and Bintang beers, and yet neither did she want to break such a newly built bridge. 'Sounds good. I'll see how I feel later.'

'Just knock if you wanna walk down together. Band's on at eleven.'

Having not expected visitors she glanced around the room and saw she'd left a set of underwear at the foot of the bed and a sleeve of contraceptive pills on top of her washbag. When she looked up, Jez was watching her. He smiled lightly, then looked away. Did she imagine it, or did he seem nervous?

'Noah had his appointment today at hospital.'

'Right,' he said, absently scuffing the heel of his trainer across the floor in a small arc.

'The cut on his back's infected. They think he'll be off the water for at least three months.'

He nodded.

'I'm worried about him. He seems, I don't know, depressed.'

'Right.'

'I thought you'd want to know – have a chat with him or something.'

Jez scoffed. 'Maybe you haven't noticed, but me and Noah aren't exactly the kinda brothers that sit around chewing the fat about our feelings.'

'Why do you do that?'

'What?'

'Act like you don't give a shit about him. I saw you in the water, Jez. You risked your life for him.'

He glared at her, the same penetrating dark look as Noah. 'I shouldn't have bothered.'

'You don't mean that.'

'Don't I?'

'He's your brother.'

'You've got a sister?'

'Yes.'

'Then maybe you'll know a bit about love and a bit about hate, too.'

Mia's mouth opened to say something, but then closed again. Jez was right: sometimes the line between the two was so fine it was difficult to see which side you were standing on.

'He's thinking of leaving Bali,' she said eventually.

'Course he is. That's what Noah does. When he can't handle something, he runs from it.'

'What's he running from?'

'You haven't worked it out yet?'

She held his gaze, waiting.

But he didn't give her an answer. 'I guess you'll want your passport back so you can follow him. Got the rest of that money you owe me?'

'Not yet.'

'It's been two weeks.'

'I'm aware.'

'I'm not a rich man, or a patient one either. I need that money.'

Mia hadn't seen exactly how much money had changed hands between Jez and the police, and a niggling doubt made her ask, 'How much was it again?'

His mouth tightened. 'You know how much. Ten million rupiah.'

'I'll need my passport to withdraw it.'

He pushed away from the wall and crossed the room. He

stopped in front of her and their faces were only inches apart. His eyes were narrower than Noah's, she saw, and his lashes were sun bleached at their tips. 'Don't treat me like an idiot, Mia,' he said slowly, his mouth clenched tight around his words. 'You don't need your passport to get cash out.'

He turned as if to leave, but then paused by the table where her bag was. From it he took her wallet.

'What are you doing?'

He pulled out the strip of notes inside and counted them. 'Two million rupiah.' He tucked the money into his pocket. 'Another eight million to go.'

'That's theft!'

'No. It's debt collection.'

'I said I'd pay you back. You don't just go through people's wallets.'

'Thanks for the moral lesson. Here's one for you – if you treat someone like an asshole, they'll act like an asshole.' He closed the door with a smack.

She stared at the wallet sprawled open on the desk. The reality of her situation suddenly hit her: she had no money and no passport. She was trapped here – and soon Noah would leave.

Pressing the heels of her hands to her temples, she tried to think. She had no way of repaying Jez and it'd take months of working on a Balinese wage to gather enough money. She daren't report her passport lost or stolen since the police still held her details. If she talked to Noah about it, she'd have to explain why she didn't tell him about the bribe in the first place, and she was ashamed by the whole incident. She had no idea what to do.

She took out her journal and sank down onto the bed with it. Turning over the clear space of the blank page soothed her a little. She plucked off the pen lid with her teeth and began to write . . .

Noah is going to leave. The thought of losing him is unbearable, literally unbearable. He's unhappy, I see that, but I've no idea how to help. He doesn't let me in. It's lonely standing on the outside.

When he's gone there will be nothing here for me. But I'm stuck. I've got fifty quid in my backpack, that's it. I've fucked up. I've completely fucked everything up.

25

KATIE

Bali, August

Katie pushed aside the journal and stood. Her knees felt stiff and her neck ached from being hunched over. Glancing towards the balcony, she saw that dusk had crept into night. She slowly rolled her head to loosen the muscles in her neck, thinking over all she'd read about: Mia's arrival at the Nyang Palace; Jez's odd remarks in the darkened stairwell; the feel of rain against Mia's face as she watched Noah staggering injured from the surf; the hot stab of fear as she sat in the back of a police car. Reading about the bribe she'd had to repay to Jez, Katie now understood why Mia had rung, asking for money, and her face grew hot with the shame of their final conversation.

She'd also read about Mia's visits to the sea cliffs. She memorized the details of the lower path that climbed to a lookout point and the tough scramble through dense bushes to reach the very top. From her bag she took the map Richard Hastings had given her and slipped it into her dress pocket. She pressed her fingers against it and heard the crinkle of paper. *I will go there, Mia. Soon. I promise you.*

There was a knock at the door. She moved across the polished wooden floor and opened it to find Finn holding a tray of food and a bottle of red wine. 'Thought you might be hungry.'

The smell of steaming rice and fresh spices filled the room. 'I'm starving.' She made space on the dressing table and he set down the tray.

The wine glugged as he poured it. He handed her a glass. 'So how's the journal going?'

'I've barely stopped reading.'

'What did Mia make of Bali?'

'She thought it was beautiful. Loved the beaches. The people. The food.'

'She'd always wanted to go to Indonesia.'

Had she? There was so much she didn't know about her sister. Would never know.

'Was Noah pleased to see her?'

'Surprised, I think. And maybe concerned at first that she'd come for him. But yes, he was pleased too.'

'Did she seem happy?'

She thought for a moment. There were clear flashes of happiness as intense and bright as the sun, like when she was describing an afternoon spent sitting in the shade of a palm tree with Noah, eating ripe mangoes, the sweet juice dripping down their chins. But there was a distinct shift in the pages following Noah's surfing accident, as if her thoughts had become a mirror to his darkened outlook. Many entries seemed overshadowed by her anxiety about their relationship. Wasn't that the way with love: the intense highs of being adored and adoring someone, followed by the aching lows of self-doubt?

'It's difficult to answer that until I've read it all.'

'How far have you got?' Finn asked.

'I'm only a week or so away . . .'

He nodded and she thought she glimpsed something concerned in his expression, but he turned and began laying out their plates. 'I got us nasi goreng. Hope that's okay?'

'Perfect.'

'They've forgotten cutlery,' he said, lifting up a serviette. 'I'll grab us some.'

After the door shut, Katie moved to the bed and pulled the journal onto her lap once again. She flicked through the pages. Yes, there were only a handful left. She took a sip of wine and began reading, unable to wait.

I've done something terrible. I was desperate; there was no other choice. I couldn't ask Katie for the money as there'd be too many questions – so I emailed Finn. I asked to borrow a grand. I said it was to pay for a flight to come and see him, so we can sort things out. And, Jesus, I really want to sort our shit out. I've hated being apart. It feels like part of me is missing. And there's so much I need to explain.

If he sends through the money, I can get my passport back. And then I hope, HOPE, there's enough left over for a flight to find him.

Katie closed her eyes. *Oh, Mia. How could you? After everything you'd already put him through, you then asked this of him. And what about me? Somehow it manages to sting that you went to him first. What happened: Finn said no and that's when you called me? Your second choice?*

She jumped when Finn returned, holding two sets of cutlery. 'A waiter was coming along the corridor with them.' He moved to the dressing table and picked up a plate. 'I'll serve before it gets cold.'

She wondered why he hadn't told her that Mia had emailed him asking for money. Perhaps he was embarrassed that he'd refused her.

'Here,' he said, passing her a plate.

She took it and felt the give of the bed as he sat beside her, drawing one knee up. She watched him scoop forkfuls of rice and vegetables into his mouth. 'Finn?'

He looked up.

'Did Mia contact you when she was in Bali? About borrowing money?'

He stopped chewing, swallowed. 'Yes, she did.'

'But you didn't lend it to her?'

He put down his fork. His expression grew serious. 'She told me she wanted the money for a flight. She wanted to meet to sort things out. So I booked her a ticket myself.'

'Oh, Finn!' Even after everything Mia had done, he had still extended his generosity, offering her a second chance. 'You were so good to her.'

He rubbed a hand back and forth across his brow. 'That's the thing, Katie,' he said in a flat tone that frightened her. 'I wasn't good to her at all.'

*

The room felt too hot. His T-shirt clung between his shoulder blades. He stood and moved to the balcony doors, flinging them open. The warm evening breeze rushed in, lifting the edges of the curtains. He drew the air deep into his lungs, tasting the sea in it.

'Finn?'

Slowly, he turned. Katie was sitting on the edge of the bed, her feet pressed together. Her plate had been pushed aside and she was staring at him with wide, watchful eyes. He ran the heel of his hand over his forehead again, not knowing how to begin. He needed to be honest with her. The journal was back in her possession; she would find out anyway.

'I got Mia's email,' he began. 'It was obvious things in Bali weren't great and that's why she was coming back. But I didn't care: I just wanted to see her. It's pathetic how much I wanted to see her,' he said, shaking his head. 'I was worried she'd change her mind, so, instead of sending her the money for a flight, I booked the ticket myself.'

'But she never got on the plane,' Katie said.

'I waited at the airport for six hours. There was some hold-up with the flight.' He remembered buying an Australian newspaper and reading it cover to cover, testing himself on facts about cricket and the discovery of a new site of Australian rock art dating back 15,000 years. He had wanted to think about anything except for the niggling doubt that she wouldn't come. When the delayed flight finally arrived, he'd scanned the weary crowd, but she wasn't among them.

'I checked her details with the airport staff. They told me she'd never boarded the flight. I wanted to believe there'd been a mistake with her ticket, so I went to one of the Internet pods in the airport to see if I could get in touch. There was a message from her. Just a sentence. That's all she'd bothered to write. "*Finn, I can't come back just yet. Sorry.*"'

He shook his head. 'She used me, Katie.'

'She couldn't fly. Jez had her passport.'

'Jez? Noah's brother?'

She nodded.

'Why?'

'There was an incident over here with the police. I've just been reading about it. She was caught with marijuana on her. Jez bribed the police so they wouldn't arrest her.'

'Shit.' He ran a knuckle beneath his chin, back and forth.

'It was a lot of money. He kept hold of her passport until she could pay him back.'

'That's why she needed a grand?'

'Yes, but she did want to meet you, too. She wrote that. She hoped there'd be enough money left over for a flight.'

Finn felt the blood drain from his face. 'God, that makes it worse.'

'What worse?'

'When I knew she wasn't coming, I was furious. I emailed

back. I should have waited. Cooled down.' He recalled the way his fingers bashed at the keys like a storm being unleashed.

'What did you say?'

'When Mia found out Harley was her father, she was completely spun out.'

'I know,' Katie said, 'because she was scared she was like him.'

He fixed his gaze on her: 'And scared she would *end up* like him. I tried reassuring Mia that she was her own person, nothing like Harley. But there were all these traits Mick described that she was convinced she shared.'

'Why are you telling me this?'

'In my email, I wrote . . .' He hesitated. His jaw felt tight and there was a hard pulse in his head. The dark, barbed thing that had been buried deep in his chest felt as though it was clawing its way into his throat. 'I wrote, "*If you're not careful, Mia, you could end up alone, wondering what happened to everyone in your life. Just like your father.*"'

His fists hardened, like two stones. 'Then two days later, she's dead! She's fucking dead! Suicide. That's what they said. And all I could think of were those fucking words: "*Just like your father.*"' He pressed his fists hard into the wall, feeling the tension in his forearms. 'I never got to tell her how sorry I was.'

'Was it you?'

He dropped his hands, looked round.

'Was it you,' she repeated, 'who sent the moon orchid to Mia's funeral?'

'What?'

'Somebody sent a flower to her funeral.'

He looked blank.

'There was a note with it. All it said was, "*Sorry*."'

He shook his head. 'No. But I *am* sorry. I am so fucking sorry about it all. I should never have let her go to Bali alone. I should have told you where she was. And that money she needed – I should've given it to her, not bought a fucking plane ticket!' He squeezed his head between his hands. 'What I wrote – God, it was callous – I hate to think that she believed it . . . or that she was thinking about those words when—'

'Don't! Don't you dare say it!'

Finn hung his head. He'd been carrying this guilt for months and it had grown into something larger than him. 'Katie,' he said, his voice quiet now. 'I need to know how Mia felt when she got my email.'

He crossed the room and picked up the journal from the bedside table. The sea-blue fabric glimmered beneath his fingers. He thought of all the times he'd seen Mia writing it: the journal balanced on her knees as they drove through California; spread out on the floor of their tent as she wrote by torchlight; her blowing sand from the spine after writing it, propped on an elbow on the beach.

'It'll be in here,' he said, offering it to her. 'Please, Katie, I need to know what she wrote.'

26

MIA

Bali, March

Mia sat very still. Her back was rigid. Her hair hung in front of her shoulders like a dark scarf, and her bare feet were resting on the low wooden bar that ran beneath the computer desk. Only her eyes flickered across the screen as she scanned Finn's email a second time.

Then she blinked, which seemed to release her from the stillness, and suddenly she was moving, pushing back the chair, grabbing her bag, and bursting from the Internet café.

The night was balmy, the street lined with tourists and Balinese stallholders selling their wares. Mia wove through the crowds with her eyes down. A tight wheel of anxiety was beginning to spin deep within her. With every step, Finn's email rotated in her thoughts, gathering momentum. She did not see the stride of each of her tanned feet, a delicate silver chain dancing on her ankle. All she saw, as if scorched onto the insides of her eyelids, were his words: '*If you're not careful, Mia, you could end up alone, wondering what happened to everyone in your life. Just like your father.'*

Her breath felt short, harder to grasp. Traffic fumes and the heavy sweetness of rotting fruit filled her throat. A man passed, smoking a clove cigarette, and she swerved away from the cloying smell, the pavement seeming to tilt beneath her. She knocked into a thin boy spinning a yo-yo from a finger, who stared at her through large, curious eyes.

She began to run. The road was uneven, a deep rut jarring her pace. A pair of feline eyes watched suspiciously from the bonnet of a parked car as she raced on, skirting broken pot plants and sagging bin bags. She ducked into a side street leading to the hostel. She flew in through the entrance, past the reception desk, and along the darkened corridor.

She reached her room and stopped. Her stomach was knotted tightly, her pulse skittering with anxiety. She realized that she couldn't go in; she couldn't be alone.

She retraced her steps and found herself in front of Noah's door. It was unlocked and she slunk into the warm darkness, trying to steady her breathing.

His voice, sleepy and questioning, asked, 'Mia?'

'Yes,' she told him, gently pressing the door closed with her fingertips. 'It's okay. Go back to sleep,' she whispered, slipping off her clothes and sliding into bed beside him. Her heart was racing. She wanted to press her body into the warm curve of his and let her heartbeat slow into his rhythm.

But she lay still, her arms tucked at her sides like wings, her ankle lightly touching his leg – just enough to connect them. He murmured something – a question perhaps, or a reservation – but she made no response and simply waited until she heard his breathing shallow as he was drawn back towards the comfortable folds of sleep. She sighed, relieved. Above, the ceiling fan cut through the warm air, and she began counting the strokes to stave off thought.

By the time she'd reached thirty-two, Finn's email had clawed its way back into her mind and settled there. She imagined him typing the message, the pale light of his computer screen bleeding the warmth from his eyes. He had chosen his words carefully, stripping her down to her bones to reveal what she feared most: ending up like her father.

Mia could taste the bitter truth in his warning. She felt the symmetry of her and Harley's lives running through her veins like blood. He had been caught in a spiral of self-destruction, driving away the people who loved him – just as she was. She bit down on her lip as she thought of the hurt she'd caused Finn. It was cruel of her to have left him for Noah, but unforgivable to lie that she was coming back. She wanted to put her face next to his, nose to nose, and tell him how sorry she was. But she knew it was too late for that. Through the open window, she could hear traffic and voices, and beyond that she caught the faint rhythm of waves breaking.

She didn't know how long it had been since she'd drifted into sleep, but she woke to a sharp blow across her chest. She lurched from the bed, winded. Noah was flailing, his powerful body thrashing beneath the sheet like a trapped animal.

'Noah!'

A string of mumbled, unintelligible words spilt from his mouth as he writhed, caught in the grip of a nightmare.

She backed towards the wall and groped for the light switch. The fluorescent bulb fizzed into life and she shielded her eyes from the glare, blinking.

He seemed to shake himself awake, yanking the sheet from him and staggering to his feet. His body glistened with sweat and he was breathing hard. He spun round, his eyes wide and startled. 'What did I do?'

She was pressed flat to the wall. 'You had a nightmare.'

'Did I . . . did I hurt you?'

There was a dull ache in her chest where his arm had swung out. 'No. I'm fine.'

'What are you doing here? You shouldn't be here.' He turned away from her and moved towards the window. He placed his palms at the edges of the glass, like a prisoner desperate to leave. She saw that the dressing on his upper back had ripped off and his wound looked pink and tender.

She crossed the room slowly and placed her hands on the base of his back, just below the smooth cleft of his buttocks. His skin was burning.

'Noah?' she said, but he would not turn and face her. Whatever the nightmare was about, it still clung to him. She thought of his protests that she could never stay the night: 'This happens often, doesn't it?'

His jaw tightened and she saw from his reflection in the window that his eyes were screwed shut. There was something

333

desperately vulnerable about the thin trail of blood that was beginning to seep from his wound. Placing her hand on his forearm, she stroked her fingers back and forth, skimming the dark edges of his tattoo. 'It's okay,' she told him softly.

The gesture seemed to undo him. His shoulders started to shake and he hung his head.

'Oh, Noah,' she said, threading her arms around his waist. She held him close, felt his sweat cooling against her skin. It scared her to see him like this. 'What was the nightmare about?'

She felt his body tense.

'Noah?'

He didn't answer.

'It was about Johnny, wasn't it?'

He pulled away.

'You can talk to me.'

He said nothing and she saw how similar they were then, each weighed down by their private grief. They could help each other, she believed that. 'I know you lost your brother. Tell me about him. I want to help.'

'Please go.'

'What?'

'I can't deal with this.'

'Noah, I only want—'

But he had already crossed the room and started picking up her clothes.

'What are you doing?' she asked, anxiety spreading like a dark kiss along her chest. 'Noah, please—'

'You're pushing me, Mia. Trying to get inside my head. I can't do it. I should never have started this. It was a mistake. I'm sorry, Mia, but it was a mistake.'

He passed her clothes back to her and she put them on, leaden. As she turned, she saw his backpack propped against the desk. It was packed. 'You're leaving?'

'Yes.'

'When?'

'Tomorrow.'

'Were you going to tell me?'

He looked at her, the darkness of his gaze concealing so much. Then he opened the door onto the corridor.

She moved through it.

'I'm sorry,' was all he said.

27

KATIE

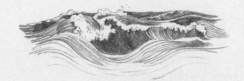

Bali, August

Katie stepped out onto the balcony. A bird nesting in the hotel gardens flew off, startled, its dark wings lapping at the night sky. She wrapped her hands around the wooden railings and inhaled the smells of frangipani and cooling earth.

Finn joined her. Neither of them spoke. She listened to the far-off call of the surf and the breeze stirring the trees. She hadn't yet read on in the journal as he'd asked her to do. Everything was rushing forward, pulling out of her reach. She needed to centre herself, to think.

'I'm sorry,' he said, his voice having lost the intensity of earlier. 'I should have told you about my email sooner. I was ashamed.'

She understood a lot about shame; it lived within her like a second heartbeat. She had told no one about Mia's phone call. Instead, she had lived with the shame of that conversation, feeling its inky guilt sliding through her veins. 'I haven't been completely honest with you either.'

He turned towards her.

She could feel his gaze on her, but she wouldn't look up. She stared into the darkness as she told him, 'Mia called me. It was the day before she died. We hadn't spoken since Christmas when I told her I was engaged. Three months – that's how long it'd been.' She sighed. 'When she finally rang, it was to ask for money.'

'Because I hadn't given it to her.'

'Yes.'

'Did you lend it to her?'

'I didn't even consider it.' Katie closed her eyes and felt the night press against her skin. She thought of their conversation, the one she had been playing back in the bottomless depths of grief ever since.

'What did you say?'

She glanced over her shoulder towards the lit room where the journal lay. 'Do you know why I didn't read her journal when I first found it in her backpack?'

'You said you wanted to keep Mia's memory alive.'

She laughed a single sharp note. 'That's what I told myself. It's funny what you can make yourself believe. But the truth is, Finn, I'm a coward. I've never sat down and read it in one go because I didn't want to know what Mia had written about our last conversation.'

Katie thought of the dark truth she'd so coolly released, and the sound of Mia's breath catching in her throat as it hit her.

'I could not bear to read that it was my words that led her to the edge of that cliff.'

28
MIA

Bali, March

Mia slotted her credit card into the payphone and punched in Katie's number. She waited. Hard bass beats from a nightclub pumped down the street, drumming inside her chest. Opposite, a street light flickered, sending strobes of orange light across the kerb where a scrawny dog nosed an empty food carton.

'Katie Greene speaking.' Her work voice was crisp and professional.

'It's me.'

'Mia?'

'Yes.'

There was a pause. 'I'm at work.'

'Can you talk? Just for five minutes?'

She sighed. 'Wait a moment.'

Mia heard Katie telling a colleague that she'd be back shortly; then there was the sharp click of heels across a hard floor, the sucking sound as a door was pushed open and then the rush of London traffic speeding across the phone waves.

'It's freezing outside,' Katie said. 'I can't be long.'

Mia couldn't imagine the flat cold of a winter's day in London, when here it was night and the air was still so warm her cotton vest clung to her skin. 'How are you?' she asked banally, unsure how to begin.

'Fine.'

'Sorry I haven't called in a while.'

'It's been three months,' Katie said.

'Has it?' Mia wrapped the phone cord around her wrist, twisting it tightly until she felt the blood flow to her fingers restricted. She couldn't think of what she wanted to say. 'How's work?'

'Fine.'

'And Ed?'

'You didn't ring to ask about Ed. Or work. What do you want, Mia?'

Mia pulled the phone cord taut and felt the cool prick of pins and needles in her fingertips. She didn't want to ask Katie for money – she'd rather hear her chat about her life in London or reminisce together about some small detail of their childhood – but there was no one else who could help. She needed her passport back so she could get out of Bali. It was over with Noah. Her friendship with Finn, ruined. There was only Katie . . . she needed Katie to do this for her. 'I need to borrow some money. About a thousand pounds. It'd be a loan.'

'Is this a joke?'

'I'd pay you back within a few weeks, once I've got work.'

There was a long, weighted pause. Up ahead, a group of

young men in rugby shirts stumbled from the nightclub, cheering and jumping onto one another's backs. They were drunk, jubilant. Mia suddenly longed to be surrounded by a group of friends, feeling the warm caress of alcohol flooding through her body.

'Do you know how many engagement cards Ed and I were sent?'

The non sequitur threw Mia and she hesitated.

'Thirty-seven. The flat was filled with them. I had to prop some on top of the fridge as the windowsills were filled. My workmates took me out for dinner to celebrate. Ed's sister came from Weybridge with flowers and a bottle of champagne.' There was a pause. 'But you . . . *you*,' she repeated, a quiet fury contained in the word, 'couldn't even bring yourself to say congratulations.'

'Katie—'

'You haven't been in touch for three months. I thought my *sister* would be the person I shared all this with. I wanted to ask your opinion on wedding dresses and venues and a hundred other details. But you never called – not even to find out if we'd set a date. And now you ring me, *at work*, to ask for money. What do you think I should say?'

Mia's wrist ached. She released the phone cord and the skin beneath was yellowy white. She flexed her fingers slowly, feeling a creaking pain as the blood began to circulate. 'I don't know.'

'You're travelling. You're having fun. Meeting new people. I understand that – but honestly, how hard can it be to make time to pick up a phone? You didn't even call on Mum's birthday. It was three weeks ago. She'd have been 54.'

The numbers on the dial seemed to swim in her vision. How could she have forgotten that? February 14th. Valentine's Day. The postman always said their mother was the most popular woman on his round. The date hadn't registered with Mia this year. Recently, time seemed to have been weaving circles around her and she'd lost track of days and weeks.

'Have you nothing to say?'

Mia could feel perspiration sliding down the backs of her knees. She wanted to explain that she thought about their mother every day; that birthdays had never meant anything to her. She could feel the words rising up and blocking in her throat, like bubbles surging against the lid of a bottle.

'Jesus, Mia, don't you care?'

'Yes, I care!' she cried, slamming her hand on the phone console. 'Just because I forgot her fucking birthday, it doesn't mean I don't care!'

'And what about me?'

'What?'

'It's not just about honouring Mum's birthday – it should be about *us*, being there for each other.'

'I am.'

Katie's voice was quiet. 'You left.'

'I needed to get away.'

'From what?'

From you! she wanted to scream. *Because I fucked your fiancé out of spite and I couldn't look at you, knowing it!*

'What's pathetic is that I wished you'd asked me to go travelling. Did you know that? I actually wanted to come with you.'

'That's crap. You'd never have quit your job. Or got on a plane.'

'I would have, Mia. If you'd asked me. But you didn't.'

'Don't try and push guilt on me.'

'Push guilt on you?'

She could hear Katie's footsteps and the receding sounds of traffic. She imagined her sister walking onto a side street and moving past a row of tall Georgian houses, their front doors black and glossy.

'I'm the one who protects you,' Katie was saying. 'That's what I do. I was handed the role of older sister: sensible, protective, reliable. You were handed younger sister: wild, independent, selfish.'

'That's bullshit.'

'Is it? Who took care of everything after Mum died? I organized the funeral, sold Mum's house, found us a flat, tried helping you find work.'

'You weren't protecting me,' Mia said, anger burning in her throat. 'You were controlling me, shrinking down my life so it could fit into a neat little package beside yours.'

'Is that what you think?'

'I don't see how snatching my best friend was *protecting* me,' she said, and then the words were out there, like a firework launched into the sky. 'Why him? Out of all the men you could pick from, why Finn?'

She heard Katie's footsteps stop. Mia held her breath, waiting for the explosion.

But there were no bright lights or loud bangs. Just three words delivered as quietly as smoke: 'I loved him.'

Love? Mia's head spun. She reached out a hand and held onto the phone console. Her palms were damp. 'No.'

'I never planned to fall in love with him, but I did. I really loved him.'

Mia bit down on the inside of her cheek, pressing her teeth hard into the soft flesh. The metallic taste of blood filled her mouth.

'It was excruciating because I saw what losing Finn did to you,' Katie continued. 'You were a shadow. I hardly recognized you. And then, Christ, Mum got ill. It was terrible for all of us, but I think it was particularly hard on you. And you wouldn't let Finn or me support you. I hated seeing you hurting like that. I felt like there was no choice: I had to let him go. I did it for you, Mia, because I was trying to protect you.' Katie paused. 'And I had to protect you from Mum's death, too.'

'What are you talking about?' Even as Mia said the words, a cool feeling crept over her skin.

'That morning – when she was dying – I left four messages asking you to come to the house to say goodbye.'

'I lost my—'

'Mobile. Yes, you said. Come on, Mia. We're beyond this.'

Mia's ear was burning where the phone pressed against it. She wanted to rip it away, snap the cord with her hands and fling it into the street.

'You weren't at the house with me because you couldn't cope

with Mum dying. I understood that, but I kept calling because I didn't want you to regret not saying goodbye.'

Mia had been walking at Porthcray all morning, her mobile wailing in the pocket of her fleece. A week of southwesterlies had washed in mounds of seaweed that lay rotting on the shoreline, making the air taste sulphuric. She picked her way over them, listening to each of Katie's messages and knowing that 3 miles away in her family home her mother was dying. Her mother who'd told Mia that her eyes were like polished emeralds, who had treasured a story Mia had written about a snow leopard when she was 6, who'd assured Mia she didn't mind what she did with her life as long as she was happy. She couldn't die.

Further up the beach, Mia had picked up a smooth white stone the size of a mussel shell and told herself that if she skimmed it six times, then she'd go to her mother. She pulled back her arm and flicked her wrist; the stone bounced across the water like a jumping fish, sharp and bright, six times. She'd turned and begun to walk back to her car, but halfway there she'd stopped, her legs refusing to take another step. Instead, she found herself bending to the ground, gathering the next pebble. She bargained with herself that it must skim seven times to be sure. Then eight . . . then nine . . .

Finally, when the phone rang again, it was Katie leaving a message in a broken voice to say their mother was dead.

Mia had launched her mobile into the sea. It skimmed once and sank.

Now, Katie said, 'When you finally arrived, I poured us gin

and tonics. Do you remember? We sat at the kitchen table. You asked me how it was at the end. I told you that it was peaceful. I told you that I'd sat on the edge of Mum's bed, holding her hand, and she'd just slipped away, like she was sleeping.' Katie cleared her throat, fighting back tears. 'But I think you know that's not the truth.'

Everything began to recede: the noise of the nearby club, the heat in the air, the feel of the phone pressed against her cheekbone. All she focused on was Katie's voice.

'Mum's death was not peaceful. The morphine dose wasn't strong enough. She was in so much pain at the end that she bit through her bottom lip. She was terrified, pleading, begging whatever God she thought was up there, not to let her die. And do you know what she kept saying, over and over?'

Please, Mia thought. *Don't do this.*

'I'd been at her bedside for weeks and the last thing she said to me was, "Where is Mia?"'

The receiver slipped through her fingers, clattered against the metal base of the phone box, and was left dangling from a dark wire.

*

Mia flicked the light on in her room. The window had been left wide open and the thin curtain billowed in the breeze. She hugged her arms against her middle. Her throat was choked with tears and she closed her eyes. On the backs of her eyelids Finn's email waited. *'If you're not careful, Mia, you could end up*

345

alone, wondering what happened to everyone in your life. Just like your father.'

She wanted to reach through the sky, grab Harley by the throat and ask, *'Was this how you felt?'*

Swiping away her tears, she moved to her backpack and searched roughly for her journal. Pulling it free, she opened it and slipped from the front a photo of her and Katie. They were riding a seahorse merry-go-round on the pier, their hands linked. She stared at the picture, remembering that day vividly when life tasted sweet and easy.

Without hesitating she tore Katie from it.

Then she placed the journal on the desk and sat down in front of it. Her hands were trembling. She flattened out an empty double-page and began to write, ink flowing across the paper like a dark river.

29

KATIE

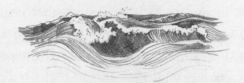

Bali, August

Together they read the remaining pages of the journal. Katie asked this of Finn – she could not face it alone. They sat on the edge of the hotel bed, an inch between their bodies, the white soles of her feet resting on the polished wooden floor, their heads angled towards the journal.

The lamp cast a warm orange glow over the pages, illuminating the precise flicks and measured curves of Mia's handwriting. They swam deep into those final entries, Finn's back stiffening as he read of Mia's reaction to his email: '*What he wrote was true – I just never realized Finn saw it, too.*' They learnt of Noah's violent nightmares and of Mia's decision to ring Katie – but of that final phone call, not a word had been written.

Katie took the corner of the thick cream paper between her finger and thumb, and turned it.

'Is this it?' he asked.

'Yes.' The last entry. It filled only one side of the double page. She'd seen the entry once before in London: it was an outline of a woman's head, and within it were a tangle of intricate sketches. She tilted it towards the lamp to see the minute images more clearly.

'Do you understand what they mean?'

She hadn't, not when she'd first seen them all those months ago. But now, as she studied the images, they began to make sense to her. A sketch of a forearm tattooed with a wave. Two figures pressed together in a corridor. A hangman with six blank dashes, starting with the capital H. The stars falling out of the sky onto a red rock. A hand clamped over a passport. A screaming face with blood dripping from the lips. An empty phone dangling from a wire.

Her gaze moved carefully over each of the drawings, as if making a visual cast to preserve. Just an inch from the bottom she noticed three words written in Mia's minute hand. '*How I am.*'

She swallowed. 'This is how Mia saw herself.'

She trailed her thumb across the entry towards the centre of the journal. The opposite page had been torn out and she touched the remaining rough edge.

'Why is there a page missing?' Finn asked.

'I don't know.' She'd thought about this before, wondering whether it had been another drawing or if Mia had simply made a mistake and removed the page. In darker moments she'd considered that Mia might have written a suicide note on it, which she'd torn out but which had never been found.

There were some questions, she realized, that would never be answered.

'That's it,' he said. 'The end of the journal.'

She nodded.

'How do you feel?'

Her palms were damp and her body felt stiff from the tension she'd been holding. She had read it all, cover to cover, and now she felt empty. A breeze curled through the room, lifting the edge of the page. She stared at the weave of dark images again. 'I wasn't there for her. Not when it counted.'

Her fingers moved to the front of the journal and slipped free the torn photo of Mia riding the seahorse merry-go-round. She looked at Mia: 8 years old, her face flushed with spring sunshine, her expression light hearted, wistful. Her sea sister. 'I was in this picture once,' she told Finn.

Finn took the photo, resting it in the flat of his hand.

'I don't know when she ripped me out. Maybe after our argument. Maybe months before.'

'Katie,' he said softly, 'she knew you loved her.'

But hadn't her love for Mia always been a hair's breadth from hate? 'I was jealous of her. She was bold and fearless and stuck two fingers up at the world, never caring what anyone thought. I always wished I could be more like that.' She looked at Finn squarely. 'And I was jealous of her friendship with you.'

His eyes widened. 'Were you?'

'Mia and I were close as kids. We did everything together. You probably won't know this, but I taught Mia to swim.'

'Really?'

'When the weather was good, we'd cycle down to the beach after school. Mum would read and Mia and I would swim in the bay. She never complained about the cold, or was frightened when the sea was rough. She was fearless in the water.'

'I can believe it.'

'I told you once that I almost drowned at Porthcray.'

'Yes.'

'It was Mia who saved me.'

'What happened?'

'She'd wanted to swim out to a buoy – it marked a lobster pot about 300 feet off shore. Mia was only 11. I said it was too far but she went anyway and she made it look so easy. Later, when she'd gone crabbing on the rocks, I decided to do it, too.'

'Why?'

'I suppose I needed to prove to myself that I could. It's an odd feeling being an older sister and suddenly noticing your younger sister is almost as tall as you, or no longer needs a head start when you race along the beach. I wasn't ready to be caught up.' She smoothed her hair behind her ears and continued. 'So I swam out to the buoy. I was fine reaching it, but when I headed back for shore, I realized that the tide had turned. You know what it's like at Porthcray – when the water rushes out, the current slides with it. Stupidly, I tried swimming against it. But I just got dragged further and further out.' She remembered the muscular grip of the current twisting around her and the cramp that seized her calves. Even now she sometimes woke drenched in sweat, dreaming of it.

'Mia saw me from the rocks. There was this old windsurfing board at the edge of the bay that we used to play on. She managed to haul it into the shallows and paddle out to me. If she hadn't, I honestly think I'd have drowned. I remember lying face down on the board, clinging to it. Mia told me, "It was just a current. You're meant to swim across it." It was one of the first things I'd taught her about the sea.'

Katie sighed. 'I never thanked her. Maybe I felt humiliated, I don't know. But I do know that afterwards I stopped going in the water, stopped spending time with her. I'm not sure how to explain it, but it felt like something between us had shifted. I remember Mia started secondary school the week after that. I wouldn't even sit next to her on the bus on her first day.' She looked directly at Finn. 'It was you who filled that empty seat. Do you remember?'

He nodded.

'The moment you stepped onto that bus the two of you just clicked. I saw it immediately. She no longer needed me.'

'She did. Mia looked up to you.'

Katie laughed at that. 'I was the boring, safe one – remember?'

'That's what you let yourself believe, but that's not what I see. You say Mia was fearless and bold – but what about you? *You* were the one who left home and set up a new life in London. Mia stayed in Cornwall. And now here you are travelling the world. You two weren't as different as you think.'

She could hear the shallow draw of her breath. 'We were awful to each other.'

'You were sisters.'

The past tense of 'were' stalled her thoughts. She would never be a sister again.

Never.

She'd never dance with Mia barefoot in the lounge. She'd never float in the sea beside her, listening for the songs of mermaids. She'd never feel Mia within her arms and breathe in the warm scent of jasmine. In losing Mia, Katie realized she'd lost part of herself.

'I thought we'd have more time . . . I thought things between us would mellow over the years. I had this ridiculous fantasy that one day we'd move back to Cornwall and live close by. I even pictured us bringing up our children together. Mia said she didn't want any but I imagined her with three black-haired, wild-eyed little kids, who would tear through her house barefoot.' She paused, waiting for the hard lump in her throat to subside. 'We wasted so much time.'

Now she had reached the end of Mia's journey and there was nowhere left to go. It was up to Katie to decide the truth of what happened. The word 'suicide' had always fluttered in her thoughts like a moth she kept brushing away. She felt its wings opening wider, the dusty brush of its tips settling over her heart. If she had believed wholeheartedly that Mia hadn't jumped, wouldn't she have pressurized the British Consulate into investigating further? Wouldn't she have used every resource and contact available to her to find out exactly what happened on the night of Mia's death? Perhaps she never made those moves because there was a part of her that always held suicide as a possibility.

'Finn, I need you to answer something for me. I haven't asked you this question before, but now I need to. And I need you to give me an honest answer.' She drew a breath. 'Do you think Mia committed suicide?'

'Neither of us can possibly know for sure—'

'But we both have opinions based on our knowledge. And I need to know yours. You travelled with her. You understood her. You were her best friend. I need to know whether you think Mia killed herself.'

*

Finn stood and moved onto the balcony.

Katie set the journal aside and followed. The moon was high and bright, bathing everything in cool silver light. The wind had picked up and she wrapped her arms around her middle.

Finn sank his hands deep into his pockets and said, 'You really want to know?'

'I have to.'

'When I found out she'd died, I couldn't believe it. Everything I knew about Mia told me there was no way she would've jumped.' He shook his head. 'But then there was Harley. I'd seen how the knowledge of his suicide affected her. It was like his death set her life on a course she couldn't alter. And my email compounded that.'

She heard the soft tap of his foot against the bottom of the balcony railing. 'Since I've been in Bali and we've talked, I understand much more about Mia. I think she felt like she let down everyone she cared about – Grace, Noah, you, me. And seeing that picture in the journal,' he exhaled, the air pushing

353

out through his lips, 'I don't think she even liked herself any more. I want to believe she didn't jump because otherwise it means I failed her.'

Katie gripped the balcony rail, feeling the small bones in her hands pressing hard against it. When she looked at Finn, his features were set, the moonlight casting his eyes into shadow.

'I'm sorry, Katie. But I think Mia did commit suicide.'

*

The ground seemed to sway and tilt, as if she were standing on the bow of a boat. For months she had been searching for answers. And now, all the hope and tension that had been building each day of this trip unravelled at high speed. Her fingers slid from the railing as her legs gave way.

She was aware of Finn's hands guiding her into a seat, felt the give of the cushion beneath her, heard the scrape of a second chair being pulled close to hers. He believed that Mia committed suicide.

And then Katie realized that she did, too.

Choked, grief-stricken sobs escaped her throat. She pictured Mia on the edge of the cliff, on the edge of a decision. She saw her sister standing with her shoulders drawn back, her feet bare, fear flickering in her green eyes. There was no note because perhaps she still hadn't decided if she was going to do it. Perhaps while standing there, listening to the lonely whispers of the wind, she remembered the hiss of Katie's words – and stepped forward.

'It's my fault,' Katie cried, over and over.

'Katie,' he said firmly, taking both of her hands and squeezing hard enough to force her to look up. 'Neither of us will ever fully know Mia's reasons. But it was her choice. It is not your fault. Do you understand me? It is nobody's fault.'

She swallowed back her tears and tried to nod.

'We're going to get through this together.'

She focused on that last word, like an island in an otherwise empty sea. Her mouth was suddenly searching for his, her hands clinging to him. Through the briny taste of tears, she could feel his lips moving with hers, kissing her, soothing her. She needed to hold tight to him, stop herself from drowning.

Then she felt cool air reach her lips as he lowered his chin and rested his forehead against hers. 'I'm sorry,' he said. 'I can't do this.'

She pulled away, covering her face with her hands.

'It's not the right time. There's too much—'

'Please. Don't explain.' She couldn't bear to discuss it. She stood abruptly. 'I'd like to take a shower and go to bed.'

'Don't do this. Don't make things awkward between us. Christ, Katie, we've been through so much. I'm not prepared to kiss you when neither of us really knows what we're feeling.'

'I know,' she said quietly.

'Okay, then. Good. Let's just—'

'No, I mean I know what I'm feeling. I've always known.' There was nothing to stop her from being honest. To mask how she felt seemed pathetic after everything else they'd said. 'I love you.'

His eyes widened: he'd had no idea. 'But you broke up—'

'With you. Yes.'

'Why?'

'Mia.'

He frowned.

'She needed you more than I did.'

'But I thought . . . you said it was just a bit of fun.'

'I had to tell you something.' She smoothed her hair back behind her ears, then looked Finn in the eye. 'I was in love with you. I still am.'

'I don't know what to say.'

She felt the dull blow to her stomach because, didn't that say it all? 'I'd like to be alone now.'

'Let's not—'

'Please.'

Finn was quiet for a moment, considering her request. 'If that's what you need. We can talk more in the morning.'

'Yes.' They both moved through the room towards the door. She opened it and he stepped into the corridor.

'So I'll see you tomorrow for breakfast?'

'Yes,' she said, with a smile designed to reassure him. But she had no intention of being there.

30

MIA

Bali, March

Mia ground the base of the vodka bottle into the sand, then inched closer to the fire. Red and orange tongues of flame licked at the wood, breathing drifts of sweet, charred smoke skyward. Her shins and cheeks burnt from the heat.

Someone was playing the bongos and the slap and bounce of their hands was like an itch in her head. Most of the people gathered around the fire were travellers from the hostel who would be drinking hard until dawn.

She rubbed her eyes with the back of her hand; she hadn't slept in 36 hours. When she'd finished writing in her journal last night, she'd stepped out of the hostel, surprised to find dawn breaking. She'd begun walking, comforted to see other faces emerging into the new day: three men carrying fishing rods, a woman weaving bamboo leaves on her doorstep with the weak dawn light on her lined face. Mia had walked for hours, until the soles of her feet were dirt-black and chafed. When she'd returned to the hostel, Noah's room was bare and his hire car gone.

She imagined him on a plane, hunched forward so the seat didn't aggravate the wound on his upper back. Was he flying home to Australia? Or to a country he'd never visited, one that held no memories? She felt his absence like a hollowness in her chest.

Now evening had swung round once again and she sat with her legs crossed, her hair loose around her shoulders. She grasped the neck of the vodka bottle and swirled the remaining dregs, which sloshed against the glass. She lifted it to her lips, letting the bitter liquid slide down her throat.

She became aware of a shadow by her shoulder and glanced up. Jez was standing beside her, his hands slung deep in his pockets. Firelight danced across his face, illuminating his dark eyes. He said nothing, but she rose, dusted the sand from the back of her shorts and followed him towards the shore.

Away from the fire, darkness swallowed them. She hugged her arms over her chest and waited for her eyes to adjust to the moonlight.

Jez pulled her passport from his pocket. 'I guess you'll be wanting this back, now Noah's gone.' He tapped it absently with his thumb.

'I still can't repay you. I've got nothing.'

She watched his face, waiting for some internal switch to flick from impatience to anger. But Jez looked as though he hadn't heard her. He shifted his weight from foot to foot. 'He left. Today of all fucking days!'

She instantly remembered the date woven into Noah's tattoo. Today was the anniversary of their brother's death. That's why he needed to leave.

'He doesn't give a shit.'

'That's not it. He just isn't coping,' she said, picking her words carefully and wishing the vodka wasn't burning so fiercely in her throat. 'He needs time.'

'Time? Time on his own? He's had that. Noah's like a fucking one-man crew!'

His anger jarred a fragment from her phone argument with her sister. Katie had been talking about the day their mother died, telling Mia how she'd called again and again to ask Mia to come to the house. Mia realized that it wasn't just because Katie thought she should be there, but because Katie needed her.

Just as Jez needed Noah.

She reached out and placed her hand on his forearm. 'I'm sorry, Jez. I'm so sorry,' she told him – for her, and for Noah.

He glared at her hand and for a moment she wondered if he was going to push her away. Then suddenly he was leaning towards her, placing his hands on her waist, his lips pressing clumsily against hers. She baulked. 'What are you doing?' she asked.

'What d'you think I'm fuckin' doing?' he said, his voice raised a notch.

Her cheeks flamed with embarrassment and she turned from him.

There was a sharp pain in her wrist as Jez seized her and swung her round. She cried out, shocked by the sudden force. He pushed his face right up to hers. His eyes were narrowed and when he spoke his words were hard and sharp. 'I'm not good enough – but Noah is? Is that it?'

'This has nothing to do with Noah.'

'Do you remember the first time we met?'

'What?'

'In Lancelin, Australia. You were with Noah.'

She forced herself to think back. He was talking about the day she and Finn stumbled across the beach party where she ran into Noah.

'You were walking on the shore. It must have been real romantic – empty beach, moonlight, waves lapping at your feet, all that crap.' He paused. 'And then you saw me.'

She remembered. She'd thought it was odd the way he stood on the shoreline, staring at them.

He leant towards her. 'You gave me this real fuckin' haughty look, like I was a piece of shit interrupting your night. Do you remember what you thought?' he asked, his face pressed so close to hers that she could feel his breath against her skin. 'You thought, *They're brothers?*'

She said nothing.

'Didn't you?'

'Yes,' she answered, because it was true.

'You judge me when you don't know shit all about me!' His anger seemed disproportionate, something unhinged about him. 'And you don't know shit all about Noah, either!'

'Let go of me, Jez,' she said firmly.

He glanced at her wrist as if he'd forgotten he was holding her by it. He released his grip and she stepped back, rubbing the spot. 'You think he's better than me, but I'm no fuckin' deserter. I stuck by my family.'

Unexpectedly her eyes began to fill with tears. The rage, the bitterness in his voice: was this how Katie felt about her?

'Mia?'

She looked up. Noah was walking towards them, his gaze fixed on her face. 'What's going on?'

She shook her head, stunned to see him.

'What did you do?' he asked Jez.

'What have *I* done?' Jez laughed. 'How about what *you've* done? Where've you been all day, Noah? We thought you'd fucked off. Left. You even know what day it is?'

'What do you think?'

They glared at each other. Jez said, 'Why are you here?'

'I decided not to leave.'

Mia stared at him, trying to read his expression in the moonlight.

'That must be a first. 'Cause that's what you're good at, isn't it? Leaving.'

'Let's not do this.'

'Why? 'Cause you don't want Mia to know what you're really like?' He turned to her. 'He's the reason my neck is fucked. Our old man might have thrown the punch, but it was because he was fuckin' furious at Noah. We all were. He just walked out on us. Left. Went to Bali.'

Noah was standing very still, his arms stiff at his sides.

'And while I was off the water for eighteen months, Noah was travelling and surfing and getting signed up by a big-ass sponsor and suddenly he was some fuckin' hero.' He snorted and shifted to face Noah. 'Johnny had a map on his bedroom wall and he'd put a pin in it wherever you were touring. Stuck on every fuckin' postcard you ever sent. You wouldn't know – you never came home to see us. Pa tore the whole thing down. Three times. But Johnny would always smooth out the creases and tape it back up. He wanted to be just like you. But you know what? It was *me* who stayed when you left. Me who made sure I was the one Pa came across first when he rolled in drunk. Me who told Johnny he shouldn't go out on the water that day we met you on the Gold Coast.'

'I thought he could handle it. He said he wanted to do it,' Noah said quietly.

'He wanted to impress you. It was too big. He wasn't ready.' Jez's fingers curled into fists at his sides. 'You said you'd have his back out there, but you were into your own rides.'

'I didn't know he'd been smoking weed! That's what you'd been teaching him while I'd been gone? If he hadn't been high, maybe he'd have had his wits about him.'

Jez flew at Noah, launching his fist hard at his brother's face. There was a loud smack and Noah staggered backwards, his hand clasped to his jaw.

'It wasn't the weed!' Jez yelled. 'It was nothing to do with me! It was *you*, Noah!' He charged again with his head down.

She heard the forced exhale of air as Noah was shouldered in the chest, the dull thud of two bodies hitting the sand, the rip of a T-shirt, the blunted pounding of fists.

People from the fire began staggering over and a semicircle

quickly formed around Noah and Jez, who were writhing on the ground in a tangle of limbs and fists. Their legs were thrashing, dragging their bodies across the sand like warriors in an awful dance.

Jez grabbed Noah by the neck of his T-shirt and hurled another punch. But Noah blocked it, catching Jez's arm and yanking him off. Despite his injury, Noah was still stronger and managed to pin Jez down with one hand, restraining him.

Jez bucked and struggled beneath him like a crazed animal, his teeth flashing white. He managed to wrench a hand free and swing it at Noah's upper back, precisely where the wound criss-crossed his skin.

Noah let out a guttural cry, arching backwards. Jez used the opportunity to slip from beneath him and stagger to his feet. He brushed himself off and as he passed Noah, who was still down on his knees, he bent to his ear and hissed, 'He drowned because of you!'

In a sudden burst of movement, Noah lunged at Jez, pulling him to the ground in a great spray of sand. He brought his fist hammering down into Jez's face. The crack was sickening. Jez's cry was drowned out by the gasp of the crowd as Noah's fist came down a second time.

Jez curled up on his side, a gurgle of blood seeping from his mouth. Noah raised his fist again.

'Enough!' someone shouted.

Mia could smell sweat, cigarettes, blood. Noah's fist kept pounding down and she realized he wasn't going to stop.

Suddenly she was running forward, grabbing his raised arm and, with all her force, dragging him off.

She saw the whites of his eyes, brilliant against the dark fury on his face, before he pushed her aside, knocking her to the ground.

She lay in the sand, winded.

Noah froze. Then he turned slowly, taking in the crowd of faces watching him. He dropped his gaze and disappeared up the beach.

She crawled over to Jez. 'Are you okay?' she asked as she grabbed her passport off the sand, where it had fallen in the scuffle.

She didn't wait for his reply. People were already crowding in to check he was all right. She stood, dusted herself off, then walked away into the darkness.

31

KATIE

Bali, August

The taxi bounced along the pitted track, sending small stones flying. The driver knocked the car into a lower gear and the engine revved. Katie gripped the door handle, feeling each bump vibrate through her body.

There was a loud clunk as a rock hit the chassis. The driver cursed. 'This is as far as I go.'

She paid him and stepped out. The night was warm, the air tasting faintly of earth.

'I wait for you?'

'No. Thank you.'

The driver shrugged and then reversed along the track, the beam of his headlights flashing up and down over the ruts like warning signals.

She took the map from her pocket and shone the torch on it to get her bearings. It wasn't a long climb, but it would be made harder by the darkness. The cliff loomed above her and her heart thumped against her chest, but she would not give in to fear. At least, she reassured herself as she struck out, it was a clear night and the moon was bright.

She followed the track until it narrowed into a footpath that wove up the base of the cliff. The ground was dry but uneven, and loose stones made her stumble. Her leather sandals pinched the sides of her feet, and she wished the soles had more grip. The foliage was gradually thickening, closing out much of the moonlight. She hoped the torch battery would last.

As she ascended the air grew cooler. Somewhere to the west of her she could hear waves breaking, and she caught the scent of salt blowing in on the breeze. With a few more paces the path delivered her to a lookout point over the ocean. She paused there to catch her breath, laying a hand on the wooden railings. The moon hung over the dark water, laying a stark silver trail.

You always loved the ocean. You told me once that it occupies 70 per cent of the planet's surface. You said you loved the way it constantly changes and shifts, one day mirror calm, the next a churning mess of swell. Perhaps that's what scared me that day at Porthcray: I realized it couldn't be contained. The sea is unpredictable, always moving, always changing – just like you.

Katie realized that she must be standing exactly where the witnesses had paused on the night of Mia's death. She imagined the shells of Mia's necklace jangling together as she ran up the cliff path. *Why were you running? Were you scared that if you stopped, you'd change your mind?* Glancing upwards, she could see part of the cliff top. *This is what the witnesses must have seen. You, standing on the edge, about to make a decision that would change everything.*

Katie's limbs felt heavy with exhaustion but she forced herself to carry on, knowing she wasn't there yet. The upper section of the cliff path was alive with the hum of insects. Bushes choked the way and she used her arms to push aside brittle branches. Moisture breathed from the tangled undergrowth, filling the air with an earth-rich scent.

She cried out as something sharp cut into her shin. Lowering the torch beam, she saw blood. Specks of dirt peppered the bright red cut that ran an inch below her knee. She'd caught it against the jagged edge of an unseen rock. Straightening, she swung the torch beam around her to check for other obstacles, but saw only darkness. She ran the beam westwards again from the path, seeing scrub, then rock, and then nothing – just a sheer drop. The climb was taking her only feet away from the cliff's edge. A few more steps and she would have fallen.

She took a slow, deep breath, then concentrated on placing one foot in front of the other. Twice she slipped, and twice she recovered herself by digging her nails deep into the earth until she found purchase. Whenever her nerve began to waver, she reminded herself that Mia had climbed this path barefoot and torchless.

She was breathing hard and the terrain was steepening. She wrapped a hand around a branch to help pull herself up. Suddenly the wind became fierce and the ground levelled. She had reached the top.

She had imagined this place so many times that she felt as if the cliff had somehow been expecting her. Granite boulders punctuated a small grassy plateau, which fell away to the sea and rocks. Above, the stars were brilliant golden pinpricks blinking in the sky.

She experienced the odd sensation of not being alone. She spun round, air filling her dress, drawing a circle of light with the torch beam. 'Mia?'

But only the wind, curling over the cliff face, answered her. She felt foolish. The cut on her shin throbbed, and a deep weariness spread through her body. It felt as if she'd been climbing this cliff for five lonely months, and now Mia's past and Katie's present seemed to converge, twisting round one another.

The truth of what happened to Mia was one she'd stitched together with the threads of information she'd chosen to use. The journal could never tell the full story. There were gaps, things Mia didn't want to share, perhaps, or emotions she'd rather not admit to. Katie had patched those holes using strands of her imagination. But she realized that it wasn't just Mia's story she had created, it was her own, too.

They had both travelled the same route, trailing the coastlines of three continents in the search for answers about each other – and themselves. The separate threads that made up their lives – no matter how frayed, or faded, or worn – would always be woven together. That's how it was with sisters. And that's why her feet began to carry her closer to the cliff's edge now.

She inched forward until she was standing only a foot from the drop. The breeze stirred her hair and she felt the roar of the waves in her chest.

Here I am, Mia, just like you. Five months too late. How did you feel standing here? Were you so lonely that it felt like a part of you had been carved hollow? Because that's how I feel without you. I'd always thought that if you were in danger, I would know. I believed that some thread in our DNA would scream out so loudly, that I would hear it in my body. But I didn't. The night you were here, I was at the office. I interviewed candidates, responded to emails and got up to date with my admin. I worked as you jumped.

She let the torch slip through her fingers, watching the light turning through the night. It plummeted downwards for several long seconds. And then went out.

She had reached the end of Mia's journey.

And what about hers?

She felt her feet pressing down on the edge of the cliff and she closed her eyes.

*

'Katie?'

The sound of her name cut across the darkness. Something within her tightened as the wind blew cool against her face.

'Katie?'

She couldn't place the voice; it was male and her name sounded deep and fluid on his lips. Very slowly she turned, stepping back.

A man was standing in front of a granite boulder 15 feet from her. In the moonlight the solid shape of his frame was dark against the rock. She regretted the loss of the torch, wanting to trail light across this stranger's face and find something readable in his expression.

'You're Katie, aren't you?'

He spoke with an accent. Australian, she realized. 'Noah?'

'Yes.'

She blinked. Shook her head.

He pushed away from the rock. Stones crunched beneath his feet as he took several paces forward. When they were standing side by side she could see that shadows ringed his eyes and there was a hollowness to his cheeks. His gaze settled on her. 'I thought you would come here eventually.'

'Why?'

'She was your sister.'

Above them the sky glistened with stars, the only witnesses to their conversation. She studied him, trying to match him to Mia's description. In her journal she'd described him as beautiful – an unusual adjective for a man – but she understood it now, because there was a lonely beauty in his face. Moonlight bleached his features of warmth and she reminded herself, *You do not know this man.*

'Did you follow me?' she asked.

'No.'

'What are you doing here?'

'I come here, sometimes, to think.'

She recalled entries about the long hours Noah spent on the cliff, watching waves roll in. 'I've been reading about you. Mia kept a travel journal.'

'Yes, I know.'

'You were the reason she came to Bali,' she said coolly, unable to keep the bitterness from her tone.

His head lowered a fraction. 'Yes.'

'She loved you. But you hurt her.'

He shifted and she thought of how close they both stood to the edge. The wind coiled up from the cliff, pinning the bottom of her dress against her thighs.

Katie said, 'Mia must have stood here.' She stared straight ahead and felt the emptiness stretching in front of her. She remembered skydiving, the terrifying feeling of just leaning forward and there being nothing but air to fall through. 'She must have been so scared.'

She thought about their last conversation. Sometimes it felt as though each word weighed so heavily on her that they had become the paving stones that built Mia's path here. 'I hate knowing she was alone.'

His voice was low: 'She wasn't.'

Every inch of her skin cooled.

'I was here.'

Deep in her chest, her heart began to pound. 'What?'

His gaze locked on the black horizon. 'There are some things about Mia's death I need to tell you.' He took a step towards her and she felt a surge of adrenalin fire through her body. 'It's important that you know how sorry I am.'

'For what?' she asked, feeling the ground beginning to tilt.

32

MIA

Bali, March

Mia moved unsteadily along the shoreline, the vodka still whirling in her system. She wished she'd brought the bottle so she could finish it, drink until she blanked out. A deep sadness that had been hovering close by for weeks settled in her chest.

She dragged her feet through the damp sand, thinking about the night in Maui when Noah pulled her from the water. He'd needed to rescue her because he hadn't been able to save his brother. His guilt was as dark and cavernous as hers.

Jez and Noah had thrown punches.

She and Katie, words.

She could still hear the voice of someone who'd crowded in to watch the fight, saying, 'Aren't they brothers?' as if being siblings could make a difference to the amount you could hate.

She felt exhausted, depleted by all that'd happened. She turned from the beach and made her way back to the hostel.

When she reached her room, she found the door ajar, as if someone had recently been inside. She nudged it wider and quietly stepped in.

A mosquito net hung like a ghostly shadow over the bed and, beside it, a wicker lamp was glowing. Had she left it on? She moved cautiously inside, surveying the room: her backpack was still there, yet she could sense that something was different.

Then it clicked: her travel journal. It rested on the low bamboo desk where she had left it open, except now her pen was lying across it, the lid off. She stepped closer and could see there was writing – not hers – slurred across a previously blank page. The words weren't neat and precise; these were scrawled and slanting forward.

She leant nearer still and saw a dark smudge across the bottom of the page.

Blood.

It took several seconds for the words to come into focus. Then they rushed at her, knocking her off balance so she had to reach a hand towards the edge of the desk to steady herself. Panic rose in her chest, its hot bloom reaching towards her throat. 'Please, God,' she mumbled. 'Please, no.'

With one swipe she tore the page from her journal. Holding it close to her, she fled the room barefoot and vanished into the night.

*

Mia stuffed the torn page into her back pocket to free her hands as she scrambled along the cliff path. The soles of her feet were bruised from unseen stones and tough tree roots, but she raced on, knowing every moment counted.

'Hey! You okay?'

Startled, she spun round.

A couple were standing at the lookout point several feet off the path. They were staring at her.

She was out of breath and her face felt too hot. She imagined how she must look: a lone woman running barefoot at night.

The man stepped forward, asking, 'Do you need help?'

'No,' Mia said. She ducked her head and ran on, disappearing through the dense foliage that shrouded the upper cliff path. She had to push her way through twisted, gnarled branches that scratched her bare arms and legs.

It was minutes before Mia saw moonlight spilling in between a gap in the trees, and then she knew she was almost there. She hauled herself up a final incline and reached the top, drenched in sweat.

Noah was standing near the cliff edge like a sentinel of the ocean, his feet shoulder width apart, his back straight. She had found his note written hurriedly on a page of her open journal, a few sparse words of despair, and beneath a smear of blood – his? Jez's? – staining the page like an omen.

'Noah,' she said, quietly announcing herself.

His head turned only a fraction.

'Don't do this.' She thought of her father, the young man with the intense gaze in the photo of the band. What if someone had found him in time – a neighbour, a landlord collecting rent

– with a kind, carefully placed word that could have changed everything?

How many thousands of people must consider a moment such as this – a cliff edge, a rope from a ceiling, the roof of a tall building, a loaded gun – desperate to stop the rushing sense of despair that fills your ears and your mouth with the bitter taste of hopelessness? Mia had. She'd pictured the exquisite point of blankness when all the rushing, speeding guilt and hurt just stopped dead. Dead. She began moving forward . . .

'Don't!'

She froze. She was 10 feet from him now, close enough to see the flower of blood on his dark T-shirt blooming from his wound.

'Go away,' he commanded without turning. She understood his guilt; she'd always been able to, it was part of what bound them together. She'd walked away from the people she'd loved – from her mother's bedside, from her life with Katie, from Finn – because walking away was easier than sticking right there where the people she cared about could look into her eyes and see her fear. But she wasn't going to walk away from Noah. 'I'm not leaving you.'

'I don't want you here.'

'Why did you come to the beach tonight?' Mia asked him.

'What?'

'You said you were leaving Bali, but you didn't. Why?'

His fingers clenched into fists at his side. 'I . . . I couldn't leave.'

'Because of Jez?'

'Yes,' Noah admitted. 'And because of you.'

'I meant it when I told you I loved you.'

He dropped his head. 'It doesn't make any difference . . .'

Mia began to tell him that it did, but then realized he was still speaking.

'He drowned because of me. I shouldn't have let him go out . . . he wasn't ready.'

Johnny.

'The waves were too big. I didn't even see him get knocked down.'

'You tried to save him.'

'No. Not hard enough.' She could see his shoulders shaking and she thought he might be crying. 'He was face down when I got to him. Already dead. I swam back with his body.'

'It wasn't your fault.'

But he didn't hear her. 'Jez was right. And I hit him for it. I wanted to kill him,' he said, his voice cracking. 'I'm my father . . .'

'You're a good person, Noah,' she told him because she believed it, and she needed him to believe it too. 'You're not your father.' *Just like I'm not mine.* She understood that now. She wasn't defined by Harley's dark legacy, but by her own actions.

'I can't live like this . . .'

The despair in his voice frightened her. She was breathing hard and could feel the vodka still swirling in her system, numbing the edges of her thoughts. It was important that she was lucid – that she said everything right.

'Johnny's death was tragic – a tragic, terrible accident. But do you think he would want this for you?'

She waited, but Noah didn't respond.

'What would he say to you right now, if he could see you?'

Noah grabbed the base of his head. She caught a flash of his tattoo; she'd once thought it beautiful, but now felt as if the black ink was seeping into his bloodstream and poisoning him.

'If he was anything like you, he'd tell you to get away from the edge,' she said.

'What does it matter? He's dead!'

Bile filled her throat. She breathed deeply; she had to concentrate, draw Noah back from the edge. 'What about Jez?' she said, forcing her voice to be level, calm. 'If you do this, he's on his own.'

'He'll be better off.'

'He loves you—'

'No.'

'I saw it, Noah. He came in the surf after you. He was terrified he was going to lose you.' She continued, 'His last memory will be of fighting you, blaming you for Johnny's death. And everything you're feeling right now will be transferred to him. You wouldn't just be taking your life – you'd be taking his, too.'

She watched, horrified, as he inched his feet towards the cliff edge. The movement loosened a stone that rolled forwards, then dropped into darkness. She listened for the sound of it reaching the rocks below, but there was none.

'I'm sorry,' Noah said simply.

Panic flooded her. Her senses sharpened to a point: she could feel the corner of a stone pressing into the arch of her foot, taste salt drawn by the wind from the ocean, hear the tread of her feet as she propelled herself forward.

'Mia, no!'

But already she was at his side. She waited until she felt steady, certain. Then she forced herself to look down. Moonlight glinted off her toe rings and, an inch beyond her feet, the cliff stopped and air began. Darkness stole the depth but she could see the ghostly shadows of the granite boulders below, where waves shattered.

There were no bargaining chips left except one: 'If you do this, Noah, then I will, too.' Slowly she raised her head and turned to look at him. His lip was split and there was blood dried to his cheekbone.

'Don't be stupid!'

She stayed very still, fighting the wave of fear that was rising up in her body.

'Get away from the edge!'

'When you step back, so will I.'

'You're bluffing.'

'You know I'm not.' From her pocket she carefully took out his suicide note. She raised it in the space between their bodies. 'You never wrote this, Noah. You never came here. Take it. Then we step away. Tonight never happened.'

She waited. A cool breeze curled around her hand, making the page flutter. 'Take it, Noah.'

Time seemed to pause. The world was reduced to just the two of them on the cliff edge. She could hear the rapid inhale and exhale of breath, only to realize it was her own. Sweat beaded across her top lip. She willed him to take the page, to end this now.

Then the air shifted and she was aware of Noah's arm, solid and strong, rising. His fingers stretched towards hers where she held the page. She felt the gentle release in her hand as he removed it.

The relief was immediate. The tension that had held her knees rigid now released, and she felt them bend an infinitesimal amount: just enough to tilt her fractionally forward. Time slowed. Her hand stroked the air in front of her body searching for balance, but there was only darkness, emptiness, and her arm swung through it. The momentum caused her to hinge forward from the waist, her other arm beginning to swing, too. Her bangles clinked: she was a breathing windmill whirling on the breeze.

Her weight rolled onto the balls of her feet, her heels peeling from the cliff so she was on tiptoes. She heard the grind of stones as Noah lunged towards her, felt the brush of his fingertips reaching for her.

But she knew it was too late.

She was aware of him calling her name, but already she was far away. She felt the cool rush of wind against her face, saw the brilliant glimmer of the stars, and heard the hypnotic call of the waves as she fell towards them, her body as light as a tear drop.

33

KATIE

Bali, August

Blood pounded in Katie's ears. Everything she had believed had been a lie. 'She fell?'

'Yes,' Noah said.

'But the witnesses—'

'Reported what they *thought* happened. From the lookout point you can only see part of the cliff top. I was in dark clothes, or maybe was just out of view.'

She shook her head. 'What about the police?'

'There have been other suicides here. I suppose it looked straightforward.'

'You never corrected them? You let us all think—'

'A dozen people saw me beat up my brother that night, then shove Mia to the ground. If I'd told the police what'd really happened, they'd never have believed me.'

'I thought she'd killed herself!' Her voice was ragged with disbelief. 'I've been going over and over it, asking myself what I could have done differently. How I could have been a better sister.'

He hung his head. 'I'm sorry. About everything. I am so sorry.'

The word 'sorry' on his lips flashed into the sky like a flare. 'It was you. You sent that flower to Mia's funeral.' She thought of the white moon orchid with the blood-red centre that she'd held, her fingers still trembling after the slap to Finn's cheek.

'Yes.'

'There was a note with it. All it said was, "*Sorry*".'

He opened his palms. 'I didn't know what else to say.'

'My God,' she said quietly as all this new information ricocheted through her thoughts. Her head felt light and she pressed a hand to her chest, feeling her heart beating rapidly. She was no more than a foot away from the cliff edge, Noah beside her. Her dress fluttered in the breeze and goosebumps travelled up her thighs.

'Mia phoned me,' she told him suddenly, 'the day before she died. It was the last chance I'd ever get to speak to my sister. And I said such terrible things.'

She closed her eyes. *If I could have that conversation again, Mia, I'd do it so differently. I would tell you that I'd always admired you. Your determination and strength. Your ability to be yourself. The way rules and expectations never inhibited you.*

I would tell you that most of my happiest times were ones spent with you. Eating fish and chips on the quay. Listening to a radio, the two of us stretched out in the sun. Doing handstands and somersaults in the bay.

I would apologize, too. I loved you more than anyone, but sometimes I felt capable of hating you more, too. And I'm sorry for that. It was jealousy. I wanted to be bold and adventurous like you, but instead I felt stifled by my fears.

If I could have that conversation again I would lend you the money you asked for. I would see beyond myself and sense that you were in trouble and needed help. And then I would tell you that I love you. That I love being your sister.

But I didn't do any of those things. And now it's too late . . .

She began to sob, her face flooding with tears.

'Katie . . .' Noah was saying.

'I can't make it up to her. She must have hated me.'

'No. She didn't,' he said. 'Mia talked about you. Often. She told me about Cornwall. About growing up with you. You spent your summers on the beach. Porthcray, was it?'

She wiped her eyes, nodded.

'When I first met her she was in the sea. She told me she was doing this thing that you two used to do – floating with her face underwater, completely still. "Listening to the sea," she'd said.'

Katie smiled. *You remembered us doing that?*

'There's something you should see.' He reached into his pocket and carefully removed from it a folded piece of cream paper. 'If you've been reading Mia's journal, you'll have seen there's a page missing at the end.'

'Yes,' she said, surprised that he knew.

'When I went to Mia's room to leave her a note – a suicide note, I suppose – I didn't have anything to write on. Then I saw her journal. It was open on her desk on a blank page. So I wrote it there.' He unfolded the paper and handed it to her.

She stared at it. The page was worn and heavily creased. In the moonlight, she could just see Noah's scrawled message.

'I didn't realize, but I'd written it on the back of one of Mia's entries. Look at the other side.'

She recalled the last entry she had seen, the sketch of Mia's side profile filled with disturbing images and the faint words, '*How I am.*' She turned over Noah's note with its jagged edge that would later fit exactly to the journal. The page fluttered in the breeze and she held onto it tightly.

'Here,' he said, pulling a slim torch from his pocket.

It took her eyes a moment to adjust to the light. She blinked rapidly as the page came into focus. At the bottom, Mia had written, '*How I want to be.*' Above was an illustration of a side profile again, but rather than it being filled with images, this time it was clear, light. However, what surprised Katie was the photo beside it.

'It's you, isn't it?'

The torch beam bounced off the gloss of the photo. She lifted the page closer to her face to see. It was a picture of a young girl in a bright red sundress with a white feather tucked into her pocket. With one hand she held onto the reins of a sapphire seahorse, and the other hand was outstretched. It was her, Katie. The missing segment of the photo she had thought she'd been discarded from.

Mia had drawn herself beside Katie.

Together.

Sisters.

'*How I want to be.*'

Her head felt light. She pressed her fingertips to her temples. Below them the sea raged, fists of froth smashing into jagged outcrops of rock. Understanding can arrive in a word, a smile, a glance. It arrived for Katie in that photo, peeling back the years. Years that had been filled with slammed doors and opened arms, with sharp words and heartfelt apologies, with long silences and shared laughter. She understood that despite everything, Mia had loved her and wanted them to be close again.

She pictured Mia coming here to help Noah, running along the cliff path in the dark. She'd have passed the witnesses, but there wouldn't have been time to stop or explain. Katie imagined Mia standing on the cliff edge, her thoughts spinning from alcohol, the night disorientating her and beckoning her forwards. She could see Mia stumbling, her body curving forward, her arms instinctively lifting to become wings.

She would never know what Mia was thinking in those few dreadful seconds of falling, whether time had felt as though it had slowed and she could taste the salt air breezing past her, hear the call of birds roosting in dark nooks of the cliff face – or whether her last moments were filled with memories of life, fanning out like a deck of cards for her to glimpse. But what she did know was that Mia hadn't gone to the cliff to end her life, she'd gone there to help someone she loved.

She felt Noah's fingers firmly encircle her wrist and steer her away from the edge.

Suddenly he stopped.

They heard the sound of footsteps moving across the cliff top and watched as a figure emerged from the shadows. 'Finn?' Katie said.

He was breathing hard. Moonlight fell across his face and she saw that his expression was rigid. Perhaps he noticed the tears in her eyes, and then saw Noah holding her by the wrist, as suddenly he was storming towards them.

'Get off her!'

Noah released her.

'Are you okay?' Finn asked. 'Has he hurt you?'

'No. No. I'm fine.'

Finn's gaze flicked to Noah and tension seemed to pull tight across his body. Finn took a step forwards.

Noah didn't move. His back was to the cliff edge. All Finn would need to do was take a few more steps – Noah would be unbalanced with a single push.

'What the hell are you doing here?' Finn shouted.

'She fell,' Katie told him. 'Mia fell.'

'I was with her,' Noah said. He explained that Mia had come to the cliff top to help him. That her death was an accident.

Finn listened closely, his expression unreadable. Afterwards he said, 'So you've been letting us believe a lie.'

'I'm sorry.'

'You're the reason Mia came out here. We were supposed to be going to New Zealand together. We had plans.'

'I never asked her to come.'

Without warning, Finn grabbed Noah by the scruff of his neck, forcing him backwards.

Katie's hands flew to her mouth. They were only a foot away from the edge. One more step and they'd both go over.

Finn pushed his face up to Noah's, shouting, 'That absolves you?'

There was no fight in Noah as he said, 'I'm not looking for absolution.'

'Finn!' she begged. 'Let him go!'

But he didn't seem to hear her. 'How could you leave her? You fucked off to Bali. Didn't even tell her. She'd already been through hell.'

'I know she had. And I didn't want to hurt her either. I knew I couldn't make her happy because I couldn't even make myself happy. So I left.' He held Finn's gaze as he said, 'But it doesn't mean I didn't care about Mia. I loved her.'

For a moment there were no words between the men, only the sound of wind curling over the cliff top.

Katie felt blood pulsing in her throat.

Finn's hands dropped to his sides and he stepped back. He had once said that if Noah had loved Mia, it would have been easier to let her go.

Katie let out the breath she'd been holding.

Noah ran a hand slowly over his throat. When he looked up, his eyes met hers. 'I wish everything had been different. I'm so sorry.'

She thought of what he'd given her tonight: the truth. More valuable than anything. For that, she said, 'It was an accident, Noah.'

He pressed his lips together, nodded. Then he turned and

moved towards the path, casting a final glance at the sea before disappearing through the trees. As she watched him leave, she hoped that some horizon out there would one day bring him comfort. Mia would have wanted that.

After a moment, Finn stepped close to her, taking her hand. 'Are you okay?'

She nodded. 'How did you know I'd be here?'

'I came back to your room. I wanted to talk to you about what you'd said . . . about us. But you'd left. Ketut told me he'd booked you a taxi to Umanuk. So I came here.'

She looked at him closely and saw the tension melting from his features. She didn't know what Finn had returned to her room to say, but she knew he'd come up here for her. 'Thank you.'

He squeezed her hand. Her fingers felt warm and safe within his – and she allowed herself to hope.

'Are you ready?'

She made a final, sweeping glance of the cliff top – a place that had dominated her darkest thoughts for months. Now she saw that it was just a mound of earth, no more than that. She inhaled deeply, filling her lungs. 'Yes, I am.'

She'd been terrified of this moment: reaching the end of Mia's journey and having to start out on her own. But as they began to move away, their palms touching, the echo of wind and the rumble of waves fading in her wake, she realized that she wasn't leaving Mia behind; she was carrying her sister with her.

When I smell salt air, it is you I'll think of running along the beach with, your hair flying behind you. When I hear laughter, it is ours I'll remember bouncing off the slats of the bunk bed we shared. When I listen to soul music, it is us I'll picture dancing barefoot in the lounge.

I've no idea what happens from here – whether I'll go back to London, or Cornwall, or even fly to a new country – because I'm no longer the same person who once plotted out schedules and itineraries. But I will make one plan. And it is because of you, Mia. Because of us. Tomorrow, I will step onto the beach, drop my towel on the warm sand, wade into the clear Balinese waters and kick my legs and swim.

READ ON FOR a Q&A WITH LUCY CLARKE

Photo ©James Bowden

The book takes place in a number of exotic locations, including Hawaii, Australia and Bali. Are these places you have travelled to, and how does travelling inspire you?

All the settings within the novel are places I've visited. I love to travel and my husband and I spend as much of each winter as we can abroad. He is a professional windsurfer, so we are both able to take our 'offices' with us. Over the past few years, our travels have taken us to Chile, Hawaii, Western Australia, Tasmania, Fiji, New Zealand, Canada and the US.

I keep a travel journal whenever I'm away. There's something delicious about arriving in a country, parking myself on a beach, in a café, or at a hostel, and turning to the first page of a fresh journal. I love to record thoughts and memories of interesting experiences and my travel journals are also a useful research tool when I'm back in the UK and writing about far-flung places.

Mia and Katie have a tumultuous relationship, but ultimately share an unbreakable bond. What does the relationship between sisters mean to you?

I have an older brother who I'm close to, but no sisters. I think this is why I've always found the bond between sisters so fascinating. When researching and writing the book, I spoke to lots of women about their relationships with their sisters and what struck me was the complexity of their feelings towards one another. There seemed to be degrees of competitiveness, admiration, jealousy, and protectiveness – but what always stood out was the love between sisters. This became my driving force in drawing Mia and Katie's relationship. Over the course of the novel I hoped to show that, despite the pain Mia and Katie cause each other, ultimately their love and bond as sisters is what prevails.

The sea is a powerful symbol throughout the book. What drew you towards exploring the sea?

I've grown up on the south coast of England, so the sea has always been part of my life. Cities are wonderful and exciting places to be, but after a few days I feel an almost gravitational pull towards the coast. I love everything about the sea – the pure smell of salt-air, the mirror-calm of a dawn sea, the promise of an empty horizon. My favourite place to write, where I have my clearest thoughts, has always been by the sea.

In the novel, Mia and Katie spend their childhoods by the coast, so it forms an integral part of their early memories. But as they grow older, the sea begins to divide them, both geographically and emotionally. It isn't until Katie begins to understand the reasons behind her fear of the sea that she's able to find peace in her relationship with Mia.

Finn and Ed are very different, but Katie loves them both at certain points in the novel. Why do you think this is?

Some people have a very clear picture in their mind about the type of person they are going to fall in love with – a sort of checklist of attributes or qualities. Katie is one of these people. On paper, Ed is her ideal man, ticking all of the boxes: well-educated, handsome, sophisticated, wealthy. Katie falls in love with him at a time when her mother is seriously ill and perhaps, subconsciously, she is craving the security and safety Ed can provide.

But then there's Finn. He barely ticks any of the requirements on Katie's list, yet she finds a deep connection with him. In Finn's company, she feels more truly like herself – her best self. And this, ultimately, is what comes to matter to her.

The W6 Book Café

Do you want to hear more from your **favourite authors**?

Be the first to know about **competitions** and read **exclusive extracts** before the books are even in the shops?

Keep up with HarperFiction's latest releases at **The W6 Book Café!**

Find us on Facebook
W6BookCafe

Follow us on Twitter
@W6BookCafe